ΗΕΛΙΟΓΡΑΠΗΙ

THE **SKYLIGHT** SERIES

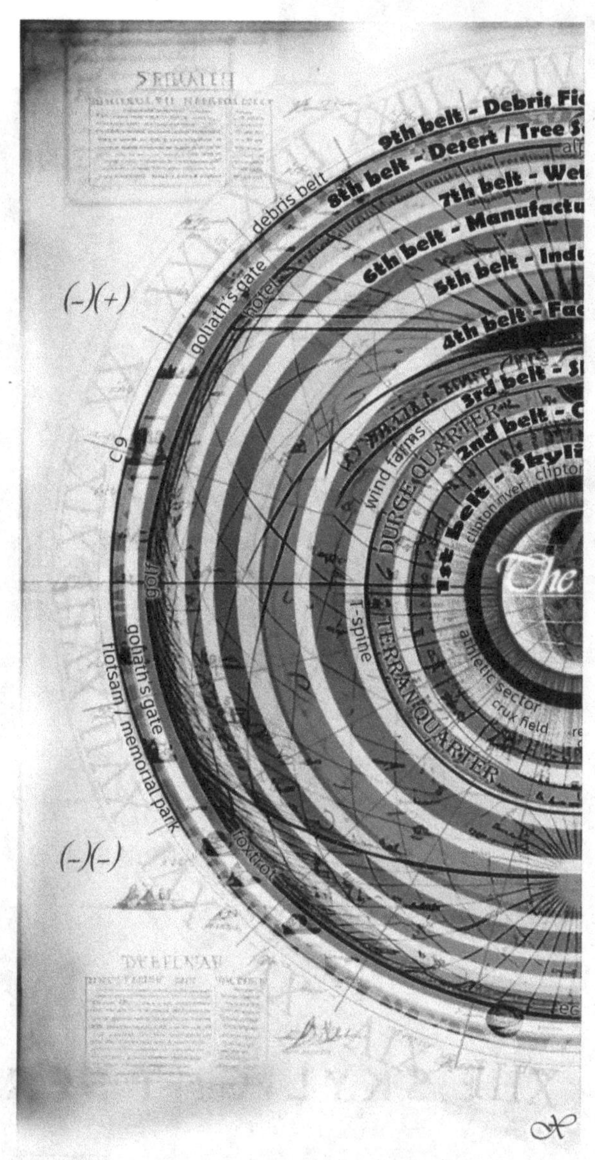

9th belt - Debris Fie
8th belt - Desert / Tree S
7th belt - Wet
6th belt - Manufactu
5th belt - Indu
4th belt - Fac
3rd belt - Sl
2nd belt - C
1st belt - Skyli
debris belt
goliath's gate
hotel
wind farms
DURGE QUARTER
clipton river / clipton
The
T-spine
TERRAN QUARTER
athletic sector
cruk field
re
(-)(+)
c9
flob
goliath's gate
flotsam / memorial park
foxtrot
(-)(-)
Fec

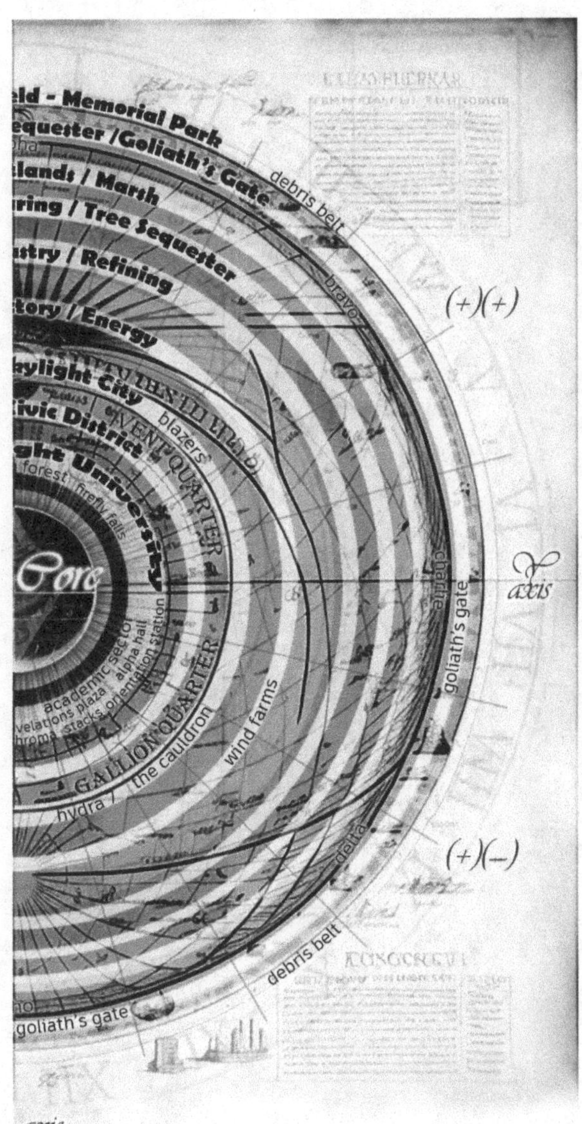
eld - Memorial Park
equester / Goliath's Gate
lands / Marsh
ring / Tree Sequester
stry / Refining
tory / Energy
kylight City
ivic District
ght University
Core
VENT QUARTER
blazers
forest
firefly falls
academic sector
revelations plaza
alpha hall
orientation station
chroma stacks
GALLION QUARTER
hydra
the cauldron
wind farms
debris belt
bravo
charlie
goliath's gate
delta
(+)(+)
(+)(−)
axis
axis
debris belt
goliath's gate

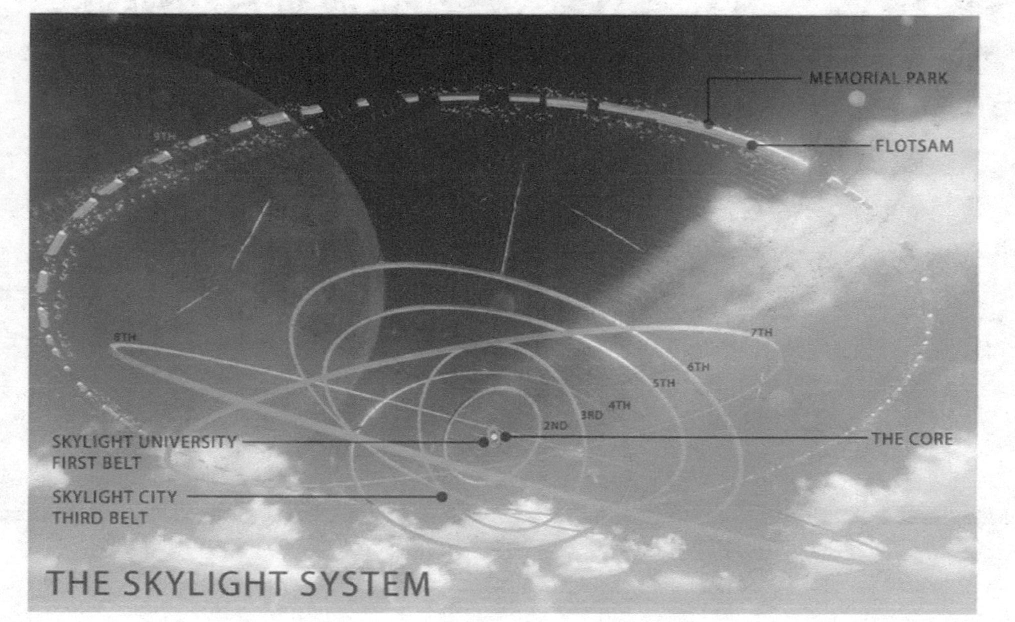

MEMORIAL PARK
FLOTSAM
9TH
8TH
7TH
6TH
5TH
4TH
3RD
2ND
SKYLIGHT UNIVERSITY
FIRST BELT
SKYLIGHT CITY
THIRD BELT
THE CORE
THE SKYLIGHT SYSTEM

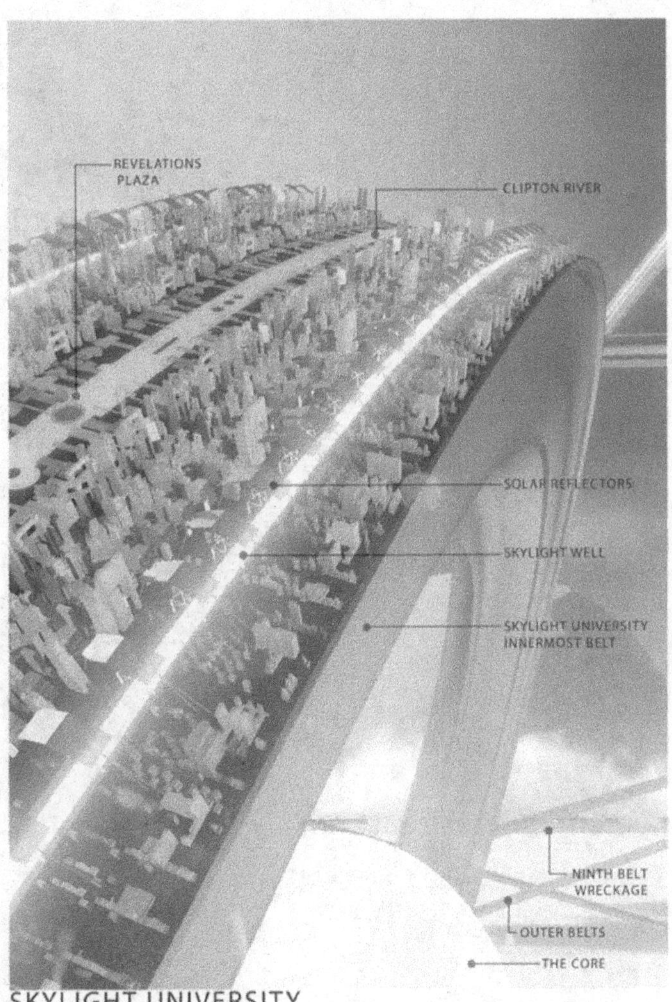

SKYLIGHT UNIVERSITY

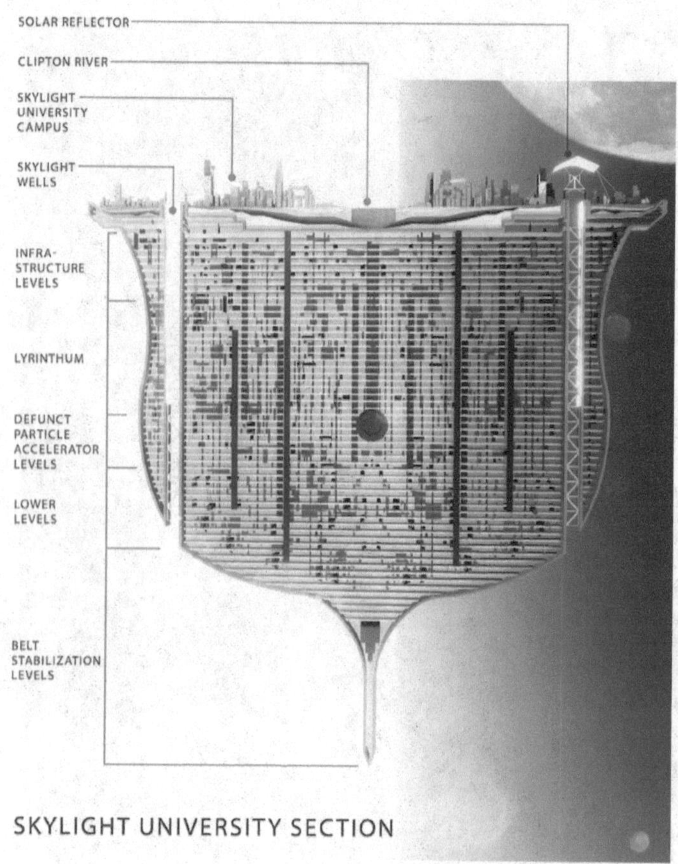

SKYLIGHT UNIVERSITY SECTION

ALBRIGHT
SYBOLD
MOSSTROM
RENZIE
MYRANDA
TETRA
HURSE
BO
SOJAHN
JOSHIA
BOFISTO
BRIT
VAIL
JET
KAMBER
SOLAN
CORD
TI-LEER
DIJINN
HARRIET
BOOKER
TYBERIUS
ANNAKA
SHILOE

THE HELIOGRAPHI MEMOIRS

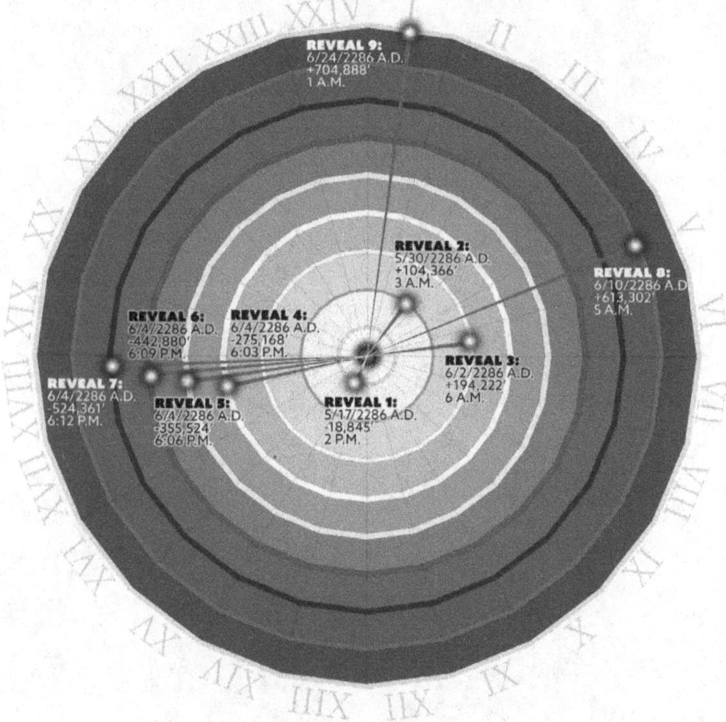

REVEAL SITES & COORDINATES

T H E
HELIOGRAPHI
M E M O I R S

BOOK THREE
OF
THE SKYLIGHT SERIES

www.theskylightseries.com

Copyright © 2023 J. Wint

No part of this book may be reproduced or transmitted in any form or by any means, electronic or mechanical, including photocopying, recording, or by any information storage or retrieval system, without written permission from the author and the publisher, except for the inclusion of a brief quotation in a review. All characters and names are a work of fiction.

ISBN: 978-1-7363029-4-1

Edited by Caroline Barnhill

On the cover: Jinnie Dinn (DiJinn)

* * *

THE SKYLIGHT SERIES

BOOK ONE: *THE PRISM EFFECT*

BOOK TWO: *THE SKYLIGHT FALLOUT*

BOOK THREE: *THE HELIOGRAPHI MEMOIRS*

BOOK FOUR: (FORTHCOMING)

BOOK FIVE: (FORTHCOMING)

THE
HELIOGRAPHI
MEMOIRS

J WINT

"Great moments are born great opportunity."

–Nikola Tesla

For Rebecca

CONTENTS

CHAPTER 1
The Search

JET STROUD AND Kamber Caster raced toward the crash site of Chroma.

It was growing late, and Jet was concerned that the other Lucem would need their help soon. He knew the Atrum would return to search the wreckage, and it was imperative that he and the other Lucem attain Albright's Key first. If it was true that this key would lead to the nine missing Heliographi Memoirs, then it would be a fight to the death.

They entered the Clipton Forest portal that led down into Lyrinthum and ran at full speed through the hidden tunnel system and toward Revelations Plaza. Kamber kept pace behind him with little effort now that she had been converted into a Lucem. He reached out to her with his thoughts.

Keep your eyes open when we get there. The key is a small device, probably about the size of a holopad. It'll be difficult to find in all the wreckage.

Jet slowed as they approached and then came to a full stop.

The entire passageway ahead was gone as if sheared in half by a giant blade. They stood on the precipice looking below. About thirty levels deep, the lower half of Chroma, previously a huge floating clock, had cratered out everything. The upper half of the globe was still intact, though, and it felt like he was standing inside the dome of Crux Field. Everything around them was complete obliteration. Torn steel and structure, ripped conduit and utilities…the inside of the hull's infrastructure was almost entirely unrecognizable.

"Where should we start?" Kamber asked, half-jokingly.

"In the center, as deep as we can get. Keep your thoughts closed for now and follow me." Jet hopped down from the passage and dropped several levels into the wreckage below. With Kamber close behind, Jet found a partially collapsed corridor and followed it. It took them down deeper into the wreckage. At times, they had to kick through collapsed bulkheads and remove debris.

Jet heard a noise and paused. "I think we're getting close," he whispered. "Albright's statue was in the exact center of Revelations Plaza, and Chroma landed right on top of it. If you see the statue, point it out."

"Wonder where the other Lucem are?" Kamber asked.

Jet shook his head. "I assumed we would've bumped into someone by now. Stay close."

Kamber leaned against the tunnel's ruined bulkhead, and it suddenly gave away. Jet grabbed her as the wall tumbled down into a void. They both leaned into the opening and looked down to see that the tunnel they stood in was free-spanning a chasm about twenty meters deep. They watched as the bulkhead cartwheeled downward toward the bottom of the void. A loud bang issued around the space before echoing into silence. They waited, but all remained quiet.

Kamber tapped him on the shoulder. "Over there," she whispered and pointed.

At the bottom of the dark void was the glint of steel. Jet barely noticed the massive, outstretched hand. It was the statue of Christian Albright.

"Let's move," he whispered and crept through the opening and scaled down the side of the tunnel. About ten meters above the ground, he dropped and waited for Kamber. They walked up to the statue's hand and climbed to the top of it. Laying in the center of the palm was the broken body of Hanley Hurse. Less than an hour ago, Jet had been fighting for his life against the Atrum. Now, Hurse was dead, having fulfilled his destiny as the Skylight Fallout by setting the second phase of the Prism Effect into motion. Jet moved closer to examine the body.

Hurse had been at the center of all the calamity, responsible for planting the rare-earth devices that had destroyed Chroma and killed thousands of Skylight Citizens. Hurse had outsmarted Cord in the end with a fourth hidden device. It would take Skylight years to clean up the wreckage.

Jet knelt and slipped Hurse's ring from his left hand, then slid it into his pocket.

"What are you doing?" Kamber whispered.

"This may come in handy later. Come on, we've got to be close now."

Jet hopped from the statue's hand and looked for a passage down. He eventually found one and climbed into it.

It was dark, hot, and humid as they continued downward, thanks to the belt's environmental control system. The smell of charred, burning materials filled the space, and every so often, he heard something snap or crash to the ground. The entire void around them creaked and groaned as if it were about to collapse. Jet grew nervous that they might end up trapped if they weren't careful.

Fifteen minutes later, he was about to give up and turn back when Kamber let out a low whistle and pointed. Shining amongst the debris, something glowed dully. Jet and Kamber moved closer to examine it.

The device was slightly larger than a holopad and glowed brightly as it cycled through multiple colors. Jet picked it up cautiously and held it in his palm, his hands trembling with excitement. He could hardly believe his eyes. *This had to be Albright's Key!*

It was smooth and cool to the touch, with rounded corners. The odd contraption pulsed as if it had a heartbeat, and its color changed to match his glowing eyes if he held it close.

"What now?" Kamber whispered.

Jet took a deep breath and slid the small device into his cloak. "We're not sticking around here. We have to get this back to headquarters." He started climbing up the passage with Kamber close behind.

Once they reached the top, he noticed several blurry shapes in the tunnel above. He held up a hand and moved out of the corridor to a side nook. He and Kamber hunkered down and waited silently.

There were four shadows, which he recognized as Atrum. They dropped down to the hand of the statue and stood over Hurse's body. One of the shapes let out an earth-shattering scream. After several minutes, the

Atrum ventured down the same tunnel Jet and Kamber had just come from. Jet waited a second longer and then motioned to Kamber.

As they scaled back up the free-standing tunnel, more groans could be heard with greater clarity than before. The surrounding void was becoming more unstable, and Jet felt an urgency to vacate the area. Once they reached the passage, he could see the walls of the void begin to separate. It was about to collapse.

Below them, the Atrum emerged.

"Hurry!" Jet urged. "They know we're here."

Jet and Kamber raced through the passage, their footing growing shaky as they ran. Just as they cleared the tunnel, it gave away and tumbled into the void below with a loud bang. Jet looked back to see the Atrum scramble beneath the statue's hand for cover. He pulled Kamber with him just as the rest of the tunnel collapsed, and she landed on top of him as a debris cloud gushed into the passage.

Jet looked into Kamber's wide eyes as she lay on top of him. His heart was racing, but he wasn't sure if it was from nearly being crushed or because Kamber's face was only inches from his.

CHAPTER 2
The Provocation

JET AND KAMBER worked their way out of the ruins.

They could see a group of Lucem in the distance, and Jet recognized them all: Solan, Ti-Leer, DiJinn, and Harriet. The four stood in an open area and didn't see Jet and Kamber. Jet nudged Kamber, and they crept over but stayed cloaked in the background. His instinct whispered to him, that intuitive voice suggesting he stay hidden. He had theorized that it was more than just an inner voice, though; he believed it to be the previous Lucem that had born his symbol of the letter M. But how and why, Jet still wasn't sure.

Jet and Kamber stopped shy of the large open area and watched as the Lucem stood in a line. What Jet hadn't noticed before were the five Atrum across from them. They were cloaked and hidden, no more than a blur to most people. Jet watched as the five Atrum uncloaked, led by Joshia. It was a different group than the one they'd just seen below. That group of Atrum was currently buried beneath tons of rubble from the large floating time dial called Chroma. It had crashed down onto Revelations Plaza just hours prior, and all of Skylight University was still in chaos. Just meters above them, first responders and rescue crews were still searching for survivors, and Jet felt a moment of guilt.

Shouldn't they be up there helping?

Instead, the Lucem had decided to search for Albright's Key or *Easter Egg*. A tough call for Solan, since there had been so many injured citizens needing help. But ultimately, their decision to locate Albright's Key first might prove to save more lives down the line. And now that he *had* the key, he needed to keep it hidden.

Kamber and Jet listened intently from the shadows as the Lucem and Atrum faced off. If things went sideways, he and Kamber were there as backup. But for now, staying hidden felt wiser.

Joshia and Solan stepped forward and stopped just a meter from each other. Jet could read Solan's body language. She was tense, ready to fight. Joshia also seemed on edge, but neither made a move. The two leaders stood facing one another, their stature similar. Joshia was like Solan in appearance—tall, dark skin, and broad shoulders. Her silver hair was shot through the middle with a red streak. They stood silently facing each other. Solan's bright greenish-yellow gaze met Joshia's deep azure glowing eyes.

"Why are you here, Joshia?" Solan said. "Albright's Key would not be safe in the Atrum's possession. I think you know that."

"And you know we can't trust you Lucem with it," Joshia shot back, her lips curling into a sneer. "What makes you think you're any better at looking after Heliographi matters than us? You can't even protect the ones you love."

Solan crossed her arms. "Just like you did with Hurse?"

Joshia tilted her head and waved the comment away. "It's evident we're caught on an island. Our group is isolated, and everyone is closing in on us. The memoirs belong in our hands, Solan."

"Yes, I know. But what are your plans with them?"

"To keep them safe, of course."

Solan smirked. "Yes, I'm sure that's Sybold's plan, Joshia. Speaking of, where is your *fearless leader?* I've seen no sign of her in quite some time."

Joshia glared at Solan. She seemed to be trying to probe Solan's thoughts, or perhaps she was trying to decide how much information to relay. "Sybold is…missing."

Jet watched Solan closely and detected an instant of surprise.

"Well, that's interesting," Solan said. "First Albright, now Sybold."

"And now it's you and me, Solan," Joshia said. "We are tasked with guiding our clans through these difficult times. Much depends on our decisions."

"What are you implying, Joshia?"

"Isn't it evident?"

"You're delusional if you think I'd agree to something like that."

"Still, here we are, having a civilized conversation," Joshia said. "In years past, we would be trying to tear each other apart. Now, others are trying to pit us against each other. Why is that?"

That seemed to get Solan's attention, and she continued to wait, her arms crossed.

"Why would Lybra murder your sister?" Joshia continued, raising her voice. "She tried to murder Stroud multiple times and blamed it on us. Why would she try to frame the Atrum and make those assassinations look like *we* did it?"

Solan held Joshia's gaze for a long second. Jet noticed her grip tighten on her arm, her knuckles white, her face tense as she considered.

"You know what I'm suggesting makes the most sense, Solan. We need each other now more than ever. Our existence may depend on it."

"Is this another ploy to get control of the memoirs?"

"Of course!" Joshia said, a sarcastic edge to her voice. Jet noticed the same sneer on her lips as she leaned in toward Solan and narrowed her eyes. "Listen to me. We *have* to put our differences aside for the moment and do what's best for our race."

"Why do I get the sense that you *really* want the Atrum to find Albright's memoirs first?"

"Wouldn't that be better than Lybra *or* the Agency?" Joshia replied. "Those sacred documents have no place in the hands of mortals. They will twist them and misuse them. They are rightfully ours!"

"I agree. They cannot fall into the wrong hands," Solan said. "But if I've learned anything over the years, it's that I can't trust the Atrum. You never stand by your word. We had a truce that went back millennia, and you broke that trust when you murdered Shiloe Van Saint. The reason we are in this position now is because of the Atrum's treachery."

"We have no choice, Solan!" Joshia barked and stepped forward. "Do you think I enjoy approaching you, making such a proposition? Think about it. I would prefer to die a cold death, but the survival of our race comes first. All future Heliographi may never exist if we don't act now."

"What are you talking about?" Solan gave Joshia a confused look, her brow furrowed. "The memoirs would have nothing to do with ending our existence. They are rumored to hold secrets, our heritage, or a weapon, perhaps. But nothing about ending the Heliographi's existence."

"I have some information that says otherwise," Joshia said. "Hurse…he is no longer here. He will never return."

Solan tilted her head. "What are you trying to tell me?"

Joshia took a deep breath and exhaled slowly. "Never mind—"

"No, Joshia," Solan said and moved forward. Jet heard the waver of concern in Solan's voice. She furrowed her brow and held out a hand. "What do you mean by that? Tell me."

Joshia stared back at Solan, her lips were pursed to one side as she turned to look at the other Atrum beside her. They all stood silent though, and Joshia looked back at Solan. "This isn't the time or place to talk about such things. What we must do now is gather the memoirs. The Lucem and the Atrum need to join forces. It pains me to say as much, but search your inner self…you know I'm right."

"As I said, that will never happen," Solan replied. "You've betrayed our trust too many times. We will *not* fall for your lies again. If it's a fight you want, then we are prepared."

Joshia stared at Solan and shook her head. Her silver hair hung limp in the dead breeze; her glowing eyes lit the darkness around the wreckage. Jet watched her jaw clench and could tell Joshia wanted to fight. Diplomacy was counter to her nature, and she seemed to show tremendous restraint in that moment.

"Look at us…*all of us!* We're in no shape to fight," Joshia said. "There are injuries on both sides, Lucem and Atrum. Neither of our groups are in good shape at the moment. Do you choose death by refusing our offer? For yourself and all the Lucem?"

Solan gave Joshia a wry smile. "Not from my perspective, no."

"Then tell me how you plan to defeat Lybra?" Joshia asked, her voice rising again. "She has us outnumbered a thousand to one, Solan! She has an army of mercenaries at her back. President Harok has teamed with her along with the elite recon troops, some of the deadliest soldiers in the system, not to mention their air force. The Tetrahedron are no longer aligned with us. Lybra has bought them off. Then consider the other factions involved in this…the lone wolves, drug lords, splinter cells. Everyone in the system will be vying for these memoirs. How do you plan to attain them?"

"Whatever my plans are, they are none of your concern and do not include the Atrum," Solan said, her voice raised for the first time. "You've had your shot. The Atrum have no credibility left! How could you expect me to ever trust you? We go our separate ways!"

"I can't believe I'm even offering this, Solan. You know this isn't something I come to lightly. The fact that we are here, not fighting each other…I'm barely able to make myself do this. I don't want it any more than you."

Solan looked to the other Lucem as Jet watched from the shadows, almost forgetting to breathe. He felt Kamber next to him, tense and nervous. He could hardly believe what he was hearing, and apparently, neither did Solan. Joshia, who appeared to be the current leader of the Atrum, now that Sybold was missing, was offering them a truce. How the tables had turned. Joshia seemed to be the voice of reason at the moment, and she made a valid point. If the rumors were true, Lybra intended to hunt down and eliminate *all* of the Heliographi. Then take the memoirs for herself and whatever secrets they held. The citizens of Skylight had no chance if that happened.

"Think, Solan," Joshia pressed, and Jet heard the strain in her voice. There was a genuine plea in her tone. She raised her hands, palms skyward, and stepped in closer. "You're smarter than me. You always were. Why else would I be here? Now is the time."

Solan held Joshia's gaze, letting an uncomfortable moment pass before speaking. "You leave me no option," Solan replied. "The answer is still no."

"I'm not offering peace," Joshia said, gritting her teeth. "I'm offering us a way out of doom. I read Lybra's thoughts, just a few hours ago, when Chroma tore through Revelations Plaza—"

"Which was your doing," Solan interrupted. "Again…how do you expect me to trust you when you continue to murder innocent people?"

"We are paid assassins, Solan. It's what we do, and you know this. Yes, we were paid well for that. But it isn't what I'm talking about right now. I'm talking about what I saw in Lybra's thoughts. She plans to wipe us out. She wants *all* the Heliographi eliminated. We are the only thing standing in her way."

"You mean the Lucem are. I imagine you would run off and hide."

"Wrong. It's only a matter of time before we are found. She only kept the Atrum around for her current plans. She will eliminate us as well. As I said, we are outnumbered. The prototype AI mech units she's helping the Agency develop are nearly complete, and they are a force we will struggle with. Right now, we have a chance to work together and stop her."

"Then tell me how?" Solan asked.

"The Agency's new mech units are designed for one purpose only: to hunt down and kill a Heliographi. They can see into a different light spectrum. They're quick, agile, and deadly, and Lybra is building an army of them. Why do you think she has stockpiled all the rare-earth?"

Jet felt a nervous tension running through his body as he listened. *Joshia wasn't lying*, and Solan knew it too.

"You plan to steal the rare-earth then?" Solan asked.

"We *have* to work together, Solan. We need each other if we are to survive."

"Don't you mean we need each other to keep the memoirs out of mortal's hands? To keep the citizens safe?"

"How can we do that if we're all dead?" Joshia was practically yelling now, and she stood just inches from Solan.

Jet knew Solan didn't like being in a leadership position. Her father, Tyberius, had been the leader of the Lucem, but he had gone missing a while back, forcing Solan to take over. He knew she was still struggling with the difficult decisions she had made recently, ones that she blamed herself for. Now, she was faced with another difficult decision: join the Atrum, or face the hunt for the memoirs alone.

"You ask a lot, Joshia. And had you not betrayed me and the Lucem so many times in the past, I might actually believe this rubbish. You and the Atrum always take the darker path, and right now, I see no difference. I can't and won't accept this!"

Joshia glared at her in the dark. The clouds of steam and dust swirled around her and Solan as they faced each other. Old classmates, former friends. No more. And Jet was reminded of his former friendships with Vail and Bo, lost to the conflict the Lucem and Atrum faced now. In his heart, he believed Joshia. Lybra Howling was dangerous, and she alone was responsible for the death of two of his closest friends: Cutter Jade and Solan's younger sister, Sterllar Sylvant. The thought of those recent losses still tore at him, screaming for revenge. He shoved the thoughts down.

Joshia shook her head, turned, and marched off. "We continue the search for Albright's Key!" she snapped to the Atrum surrounding her. "Search the wreckage below until we find it!"

CHAPTER 3
Albright's Key

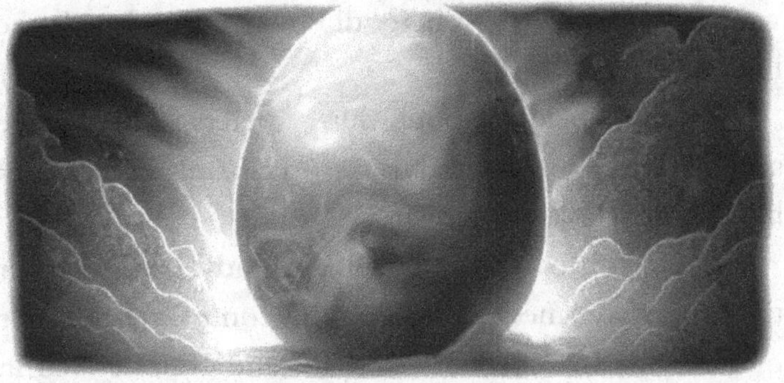

ΑΒΓΔΕΖΗΘΙΚΛ**Μ**
ΝΞΟΠΡΣ ΤΦΧΨΩ

JET AND KAMBER waited for the Atrum to clear out before emerging from the shadows.

Solan continued to stand in the middle of the space, looking after Joshia and lost in thought. Jet didn't have to read her mind to know that she was probably considering if she'd made the right decision. He stepped up next to her and waited. She seemed to be caught in a meditative trance before finally turning to face him.

"Let's get to work," she said to the others. "Join the other Lucem below and search every inch of this place. We need to find—"

"Find what?" Jet cut her off. "*This?*" He opened his cloak just enough to show the glowing device hidden beneath.

Solan immediately covered it and looked around the wrecked chamber. "Where did you find that?" she hissed.

"Buried below, about thirty meters. There were several Atrum just behind us too. We barely made it out before the whole area collapsed."

Solan turned to the Lucem behind them. "Gather the others and meet us back at the control room. Let's move!" She marched off, and Jet and Kamber fell in behind her.

Twenty minutes later, they were sneaking into the lower levels of Lyrinthum and the abandoned control quadrant. Only recently, they'd been evicted from the Agency's headquarters on the ninth belt. Now, this decommissioned particle accelerator inside the first belt had become their temporary home.

The Agency's leery nature toward the Lucem, along with the uneasiness of the recon troops, was the main reason they'd been expelled. In the grand scheme of things, it had been for the best, though. President Harok had secretly joined forces with a wealthy philanthropist named Lybra Howling. She had placed a bounty on Jet, which Harok had agreed to support. Lybra had also bribed Harok to give her access to top-secret information. In return, she was providing mercenary troops and enough money to finish the secret project known as *Goliath's Gate*—the Agency's new particle collider buried in the eighth belt's hull. The project still wasn't complete, though, thanks to all the rare-earth raids. But Jet had recently learned that Lybra, too, had been behind those raids. She was playing both sides, and Harok was too blind to realize it…*or was he?*

President Harok was more slippery than Jet had first realized, and he wondered if there was more than met the eye. Regardless, public enemy number one right now was Lybra. She alone was responsible for the murder of Sterllar Sylvant, Solan's younger sister, *and* Jet's best friend, Cutter Jade. Jet had only just buried his friend, and the emotional effect on him still hit in waves of anguish from time to time.

"Let's have a look," Solan said.

Jet took out the glowing device and set it on Albright's old, splintered table. The rest of the Lucem sat around the table behind their own symbols, peering at the odd-shaped device. Shiloe, Annaka, Booker, Harriet, DiJinn, Ti-Leer, Cord, Solan, Kamber, and Jet watched as it pulsed in slow waves, cycling through the color spectrum in a soothing way. Solan picked it up and held it. There were no markings or any other identifying marks on the small, holopad-like device.

"Cord?" Solan asked. "Any thoughts?"

Cord took the device and held it up to the dim light in the control room. He flipped it over a few times, then shook his head. "I'm just as perplexed. I see no clues or markings, and I have no background knowledge of this. I've seen no instructions about Albright's Key in my studies either."

"We need to figure it out soon," Ti-Leer said, his heavy accent carried around the quiet control room and amplified what they all knew—the first memoir would be revealed in less than a week. "In order to find the memoirs, I assume we'll need this wee device. At least, that's the rumor. Another blasted riddle, eh?"

"Each memoir will only be revealed at the time and date given by Albright," Harriet chimed in. Her appearance was that of a lady in her mid-forties, Jet guessed. Her light blonde hair was cropped close to her neck, and subtle care lines eased around her mouth. She had a gentle disposition, one that was approachable, and Jet had found some comfort being around her in his four years with the Lucem. But he knew she was much older and wiser. In fact, Harriet was probably the oldest Lucem in the room. "Once the memoir reveals itself, we have but one opportunity to attain it," she continued. "If no one reaches it in time, it may be lost forever. Perhaps it is too great a risk bringing this 'key' with us. If it's lost or stolen in the mayhem, we'll be back to square one."

"Are you suggestin' we just sit on this thing and let the memoirs remain hidden?" DiJinn asked. She stared at Harriet with her greenish glowing eyes. Her red ponytails swayed as she placed her elbows on the table and leaned forward. "I don't think we should sit idle on the sidelines."

Harriet sat back in her chair and rubbed her chin thoughtfully. "That's just one strategy. Let the memoirs remain hidden, then their secrets also remain hidden."

"What if we get our hands on just one of the memoirs?" Booker asked. His voice boomed around the control room as he stood, towering over the group. "Maybe we can use this device once, then put it in a safe place? As long as we hold at least one memoir, their full intent won't be realized. All nine are needed to unlock this secret, right?"

"I don't think that's how it works, Booker," Cord replied. "And, if we did choose to hide the memoir, how long would that last? Lybra will stop at nothing to attain *all* of the memoirs. She will rip this system apart to get what she wants. She'll find a way to get them. We should be prepared to go after *all* the memoirs, in my opinion."

Jet held up the glowing device. "We have no idea what this thing does. We're assuming it gives us an advantage, but maybe this isn't a key at all. We have to be prepared for anything, which means we're keeping this thing with us at all times until we know its true purpose."

The room remained silent for a long minute until Cord spoke up. "My apologies for changing the topic, but I feel it wise to reconsider Joshia's offer. I understand the mistrust, but she makes a good point,

Solan, unless you believe she's lying. If Lybra is set on eradicating *all* the Heliographi, then we need to take the best possible course of action."

"Teaming with the Atrum gives us an advantage," Jet agreed. "It makes a lot of sense—"

Solan shook her head and stopped Jet midsentence. "We absolutely cannot trust the Atrum. That option is out of the question. We can't face forward and fight Lybra with the Atrum at our back. I don't trust them now and never will."

"Okay, fine. We don't trust them, and we don't have to. We just have to keep our guard up," Jet said. "It doesn't mean we can't work with them to keep the memoirs out of Lybra's hands. Can we at least take a vote?"

"It's not a bad idea. Lybra has considerably more resources and troops," Booker added. "We can't match her. She'll slaughter us in an open conflict. The sheer numbers are on her side."

Solan crossed her arms and considered again.

Jet knew everyone there had been crossed by an Atrum at some point, and the scars of their encounters over the centuries were evident. They were all more than gun-shy when it came to their darker brothers and sisters, no doubt. But this was different. As much as the other Lucem didn't care to admit it, the memoirs were more important than their grievances with the Atrum. A collaboration between their two groups would certainly face obstacles. But they *would* make a formidable adversary, nonetheless.

Solan looked at the table. "Let's run through the first reveal and see how that goes. Then we can regroup and decide after that. If we can accomplish this on our own, we don't need the Atrum."

One by one, the other Lucem nodded in agreement.

"Before we leave, I think we should discuss our current aliases," Cord said. "Obviously, we're no longer aligned with the Agency. They have our information; we may be in danger now. We need to readjust our identities."

Annaka stood, her silver hair still tangled from the recent battle. Her own dried blood was caked to the side of her weathered face, and it reminded Jet again of how dangerous their situation was now. "It'll take a day for me to reconfigure all our aliases, but you're right. We're no longer safe. The Skylight network is vast, so our appearance won't require much adjustment. I'll make a few minor modifications, and we should be fine after that."

"Just make sure the Agency can't track us," Solan said. "Lybra is running the show now, or she will be very soon. Harok isn't our biggest problem anymore." She turned to Cord. "You need to crack this thing," she said and picked up the glowing device. "We need to know what this is and how it works soon. It may be the one thing that gives us an advantage in the upcoming hunt for the memoirs."

CHAPTER 4
Second in Command

ON JET'S MIND the next morning was something he'd heard Joshia say. *Hurse was no longer here.* But what did she mean by that? Was Hurse truly lost?

Jet knew that a Heliographi's being, or inner light, could never be extinguished. Though the host, that physical representation of the Heliographi, could be killed. When that happened, the light of a Heliographi would simply find another host, one suitable to its liking. Jet could only assume that when Hurse had died during the Century Eclipse—setting off the second phase of the

Prism Effect—his inner light would find another host. That meant Hurse's light, his Heliographi, was out there somewhere, starting over as a child. The Atrum would bring him in and protect him until he could be converted, which had to happen before the age of twenty-four. They should have been scouring the system for him…but they weren't.

So, what if Hurse's Heliographi hadn't returned?

Was Joshia telling the truth? She was mischievous, like all the other Atrum. But Jet didn't think she was playing a game this time.

Regardless, Jet thought he *might* be able to find out exactly what was going on.

Recently, he had learned that their old headquarters had a place called *The Hall of Vital Records*. This secret chamber was buried deep in the Lucem wing. Located in this chamber was the lineage of every Heliographi, both Atrum and Lucem. Though he could not track another Heliographi, he could sense their life force. If Hurse truly was lost, Jet would know it.

But first, he had to get there. Which meant he had to sneak into the heart of the Agency headquarters. The Agency was no longer friendly toward the Lucem, though. It was risky to go anywhere near the ninth belt. If he was caught, he would likely be court-martialed. But his curiosity had been piqued, and he wouldn't stop thinking about it until he knew what was going on.

He had to figure this out.

Plus, it was something the Lucem should understand. If the inner light of the Heliographi was no longer regenerating, that put a whole new spin on their approach moving forward. Had the second phase of the Prism Effect started something more diabolical? Was this all part of Albright's plan?

He would return to the old Lucem wing soon. But right now, he had another matter to attend to.

Over the last few weeks, Solan had been spending time alone in the Clipton Forest. Jet knew why. Her younger sister, a former professor named Sterllar Sylvant, had recently been assassinated by Lybra. Solan had buried her ashes in the Clipton Forest and had been visiting that spot in the evenings. He sensed that Solan needed to talk with him, an intuitive voice that prodded him occasionally. Jet left Lyrinthum under cover of night.

He wound his way through the forest. The chirping of the crickets thrummed as he passed silently along the dirt paths. Past Firefly Falls and close to the rocky shores of the Clipton River. Its churning water filled the air around him with a white noise as he trotted along.

Standing near the edge, facing a stand of evergreens, was Solan. She held her hands behind her back as she stared at the trees, lost in thought. Jet stepped into the clearing and waited silently for her to acknowledge him.

"Thank you for coming. I knew you'd get my message," she finally said and crossed her arms. Jet sensed a split second of hesitation in her movements.

"You…want to talk about the future of the Lucem?" Jet asked.

"Yes, at least that's one of the things I'd like to discuss with you tonight."

"There's more?" Jet tilted his head and furrowed his brow.

"Have a seat." Solan sat down on a log and motioned for him to sit across from her. Jet sat opposite the dancing fire as it popped and hissed. He waited for her to continue. She seemed hesitant, and once again, he sensed how she seemed to struggle with whatever decision was on her mind.

"What's wrong?" Jet asked, breaking the silence. "What's bothering you besides the Atrum and the memoirs?"

Solan simply stared back at him, still considering. "I've…" She paused again and straightened her shoulders. "I've made a decision, and I hope you'll consider it. I want you to be second-in-command of the Lucem."

Jet sat back and narrowed his eyes. "What? You're kidding?"

"You heard me."

"Okay, I heard. But why? I'm probably the least experienced Lucem besides Kamber."

"Experience doesn't factor into my decision."

"Solan. I'm the reason your sister is dead, remember? Cutter's dead because I couldn't protect him either. I'm not even sure I can protect Kamber. What makes you think I can do anything to protect our order?"

"I've been watching you ever since your freshman year at Skylight University. You're a natural leader, Jet. It's an ability you possess, one that's not easy to come by."

"Why are you telling me this now?" Jet asked. "Are you afraid something's going to happen to you?"

"We're entering a dangerous time. I fear that some of us may not survive the war that's coming."

"War, huh?" Jet asked. "We're just seeking the memoirs right now. Maybe a war can be avoided."

"No, I don't think so. A war *is* coming," Solan said and lowered her gaze at him. She clenched her jaw and paused before continuing. "It's something that I refused to accept not long ago, and I need you to understand how serious this is. It's on our doorstep, and when the race for the memoirs begins, every faction in the system will be hunting them. Lybra and the Agency are teamed up with the Tetrahedron Marauder army if we can believe Joshia. The likely scenario is that the memoirs will end up being separated among the factions. The real war will begin after the hunt."

"What about the Recon army?" Jet asked. "You think they'll join with Lybra?"

"They're loyal to the Agency and will most likely follow Harok's lead. The recon troops are a force to be reckoned with. If they team with Lybra and the Tetrahedron, we're in a worse position."

Jet sat back and crossed his arms. He stared into the fire as it snapped and hissed, drowning out the crickets in the background. "Why do I get the sense there's something else on your mind? Am I here tonight because of Sylvant and Cutter?" He posed the question tentatively, knowing it was still a sensitive subject. It was something constantly on his mind and Solan's as well, he assumed. At the moment, it was the common thread connecting them. Things had been so crazy of late that he and Solan hadn't properly talked about his friend and her sister. Apparently, tonight was the night. At Solan's request, Jet had been escorting Sylvant the day she'd been assassinated. Solan had also requested that Cutter be on Chroma the day he'd been murdered. Though both events had been beyond their control, he knew Solan felt the same way he did—responsible for what had happened to their loved ones.

Solan stared at the fire, the sky above dark, lit in the distance by the green sprites of the aurora borealis. "We need to clear the air…you and I." she said, her voice a whisper he barely heard over the crackling fire.

Jet took a deep breath. "I…I think that would be a good idea."

"You know I don't hold you responsible for my sister's death," Solan said and took another long pause before continuing. "I've told you that several times but without any conviction. I apologize for that. I'm not the best when it comes to this. I accept what happened. I feel bad about your friend, Cutter. I thought being atop Chroma would be safe during the Eclipse. I should've seen what the Atrum were up to. That's my fault."

"We all missed the Atrum's plan the day of the Century Eclipse," Jet replied. "We all share in that failure. What happened to Cutter was more my fault than anyone's. I wasn't strong enough to protect him, and I'm going to live with that for the rest of my life."

Solan's stoic façade seemed to soften as she looked at him. He knew what it felt like to lead a team from his days playing blaze—maintaining his composure had been key to his success. But sitting with Solan around the fire and under the trees, he could see she was letting her walls down. Perhaps she was starting to accept that she would never be a perfect leader…and that was just fine. She'd filled in for her father and done her best while leading the Lucem. He was seeing a new side of her for the first time, and she seemed vulnerable at that moment.

"I can't tell you how bad I feel about your sister," Jet said. "She was one of the nicest people I've ever known and a really good friend. She helped me when no one else would." Jet looked away from the fire and trailed off. It had been over a month, but that moment was still crystal clear to him.

The sniper, the voice warning him…just a second too late.

He could still envision Sylvant lying on the forest floor and her final thoughts as she died. It haunted him, kept him awake at night. He never wanted to experience that again. But that voice in his head still whispered to him…

Prepare.

Was it an omen of things to come? Or was it just his own anxious feelings? That voice had only grown stronger since his days as a student. But right now, it felt different. Perhaps even amplified.

Solan shifted and leaned back against a tree to look up at the stars. "I wanted a family. I had Sylvant for a moment, then my father. I was so close to making that a reality. I've never wanted something so much in my life, and it was within reach. And suddenly…it's all gone. Maybe I was trying too hard, trying to force something that was never meant to be? I don't know. I'll never know now."

Jet watched her. She was sharing things he knew she'd never share with anyone else, maybe even DiJinn. "What do you think we should do about Lybra? Should we go after her?"

Solan hesitated for a second. Then shook her head. "No. As much as we both want to, we have more pressing things to worry about. Besides, we must control our emotions."

"You mean…revenge? *Hatred?*" Jet asked.

She sat back and took a breath, then slowly nodded. "You know as well as I do those are dangerous emotions. We can't let it drive us. You've probably felt the warning signs."

Jet remembered the rage he'd felt after burying Cutter. His anger at Lybra and the thought of revenge burned inside, whispering to him to track her down. But that feeling made him uneasy. The intuitive voice had warned him to beware, warned him to purge it from his thoughts.

He grimaced at Solan, "Yes, I know. I understand."

"Good. Maybe we can hold each other accountable on that if the time ever comes."

"What about your father?" Jet asked. Now that Solan was opening up, he wondered how much information he could get from her.

"Actually, that's one of the reasons I wanted to talk to you tonight."

Jet sat forward. "What is it? Have you found him?"

Solan folded her hands into her cloak as she watched him. "I know where Tyberius is."

Jet waited, sensing there was more. "And?"

Solan hesitated again as if weighing how much to share. "He's located Albright."

Jet's brow furrowed, and he looked at her in shock, not sure what to say at first. "Tyberius told you this? You're positive?"

"On the third belt," Solan said. "I'll share the location with you and more, but only if you accept my offer as second-in-command. I need you in case something happens to me. You're the one, Jet, and my father felt the same way about you. Of course, any of the Lucem could step in: Jinn, Booker, Annaka, or Harriet. But you are the one."

"What about Cord?"

"He'd never take the lead," Solan said. "He doesn't care for such things."

"Do you think the other Lucem would even listen to me?"

"Yes, I do."

Jet didn't consider it for very long, though. "I'll do whatever I can to help. You know I will."

"Good…that's good." Solan sighed in relief, then slid him a holopad and some sort of badge. "Here's the location. Keep in mind that I've not told Tyberius I planned to share this with you, though I imagine he will have guessed already. Once you view the holopad, destroy it. If the Atrum find Albright, they will kill him immediately."

"What's this?" Jet asked, holding the badge up to the firelight. The small badge was worn and patinaed. The metal was two-tone, copper and silver, its surface pitted from time, as if it had seen its share of battle. There was some history behind this badge, no doubt.

"It's the Lucem badge, second-in-command. Wear it, and the others will listen to you, if the time comes."

Jet pinned it to his cloak, then looked at her. "Where's yours?"

"In a safe place."

"And…you're not wearing it because?"

Solan smirked and waved her hand, dismissing the question. "I have my reasons."

Jet raised his eyebrows and shrugged but let the matter go. He could tell there was some history behind that topic as well. "Speaking of the Atrum, what do you think about Joshia's offer? I mean, what do you *really* think? I'd like to hear more because I get the sense you're not telling me everything."

Solan sat back again, considering. "Well, as second-in-command now, what do *you* think about her offer?"

"I think she's telling the truth. She makes several good points. But I get the sense that you and Joshia are hiding something. There's something more between you two."

"The Atrum can never be trusted. There will always be an ulterior motive with them. Never turn your back on them."

"I've heard that excuse already," Jet said. "What are you really not telling me?"

"I'm sticking to that for the moment. We've survived this long without them."

"Everything seems to be aligning against us, Solan. Lybra has an army, and it sounds like the Tetrahedron marauders are changing their alliance away from the Atrum. We are more isolated now than we've ever been. Why won't you do this?"

Solan stood and straightened her cloak. "Anything else?" she asked, dismissing his question.

"If I'm really your second-in-command, you need to tell me—"

Solan glared at him and cut him off. "Anything else?" she asked again.

Jet blinked at her, then shook his head. Whatever it was between Solan and Joshia, she wasn't ready to share with him just yet. But if Solan was willing to risk the existence of the Heliographi over this, then it must be something big.

CHAPTER 5
Aggressive Negotiations

ΑΒΓΔΕΖ**Η**ΘΙΚΛΜ
ΝΞΟΠΡΣ ΥΦΧΨΩ

DIJINN SLOWED TO cruising speed and maneuvered her cloaked skiff out of a low-lying cloud bank. The moon lit thousands of tiny god rays of light between all the metallic debris of the ruined belt. There was a bit of steam emanating from the pieces of wrecked hull, having just passed through the system's atmospheric hole into space. The steam was so thick that it inundated the area around each chunk into a soupy mess. She didn't mind the steam. In fact, she preferred it. The cover it provided made it easier for her to break into the Agency's headquarters.

Below her skiff were the leftover remnants of the ninth belt. The pieces of the shattered hull orbited in random directions. Even though the system's Core was hundreds of kilometers away, it still held the ninth belt in orbit and kept the bits from floating off into space. She knew what every other Heliographi knew: Albright had purposely designed a small hole in the system's atmosphere. He knew the ninth belt would move through it unprotected. Shortly after the system's completion, a meteor storm had ravaged the unprotected hull of the ninth belt. Albright's reasoning for this was simple—he had needed a place for the Agency's secret headquarters, which had been codenamed *Flotsam*. What Albright hadn't known back then was how politically charged the climate would eventually become.

The Lucem had been kicked from the Agency just recently and were now labeled an 'outlaw' group. No one from the Agency had dared take the next step, though.

Hunting down the Heliographi.

But she knew that it was just a matter of time now that Lybra was part of the group. Soon there would be bounties on all their heads too large to disregard. Mercenaries would eventually ignore the dangers of hunting a Heliographi and come after them.

And now that Lybra was part of the Agency, it was only a matter of time until she was running the entire organization, DiJinn suspected. Though she knew very little about the old 'hag,' she could judge authoritarianism when she saw it, and this lady was dangerous, as they'd witnessed already. She had assassinated Solan's younger sister just to frame the Atrum. She'd tried to kill Jet multiple times and murdered his friend. The Skylight System was on a dangerous path right now, and President Harok didn't have the backbone to stand up to Lybra. He needed her support, and she was using him as a puppet.

Jinn's console beeped, and she plugged in a coordinate. Her skiff slowed again and dropped into a remote hangar bay on the largest remaining chunk of the ninth belt. Nearby was Memorial Park, and below that was the large hidden headquarters, Flotsam. It housed all the operations for the Agency and had recently been the Lucem's headquarters as well. She knew the area like the back of her hand.

She cloaked as soon as she stepped out of the hangar bay and worked her way through the vast bunker-like dome that was Memorial Park. The museum space had been built and dedicated to the citizens by the Skylight government after the meteor storm a century ago. Normally, the hallways were cluttered with people perusing the art and sculptures, but at this late hour, the galleries were silent.

DiJinn found a hidden passage that led to a back-of-house area. Thanks to her cloak, she was able to bypass several security points. She whispered a silent thanks to Albright. His invention of the Lucem's cloak was a godsend. Its reinforced graphene fibers not only protected her but bent light around her form and kept her hidden. Only the trained eyes of a Heliographi would notice her, and even then, it would be difficult.

About fifteen minutes later, she found the officers' living quarters and stepped up to an apartment and paused. The wide corridors of this wing were dark and silent. She laid her hand on the steel bulkhead, its surface rusted and uneven from the damage long ago. Even from this depth, the impact levied by the historic meteor storm had been catastrophic.

She held her breath and listened, her hand steady on the wall. She let her thoughts reach out to feel for movements in the room beyond. Then she used a special holopad to bypass the lock on the door. It clicked and then slid open. She slipped into the apartment, and the door shut behind her.

Inside, the apartment was spartan-like, with very little décor or furniture. It was clean and tidy—perfect, in her opinion. No clutter or flowery trinkets. General Dane wasn't one for mementos or needless things that took up space.

Off to one side was a row of portal-like windows that looked out over the system. Through brief glimpses in the moonlit clouds, she could see several of the inner belts twinkling in the distance. Far beyond, she saw the bright, glowing core lit up like a distant star. To the opposite side was a galley-style kitchen, then a hallway with a few bedrooms. The open living space had a couch and a fireplace that hadn't been used in ages. The apartment appeared to be almost unoccupied.

DiJinn moved to one of the bedroom doors and nudged it open with her worn tactical boot.

"Glad you could make it, Jinn."

She smiled. Hearing General Dane's gruff voice made her tingle. She'd known him for years, and he hadn't changed during that time. She admired his straightforward approach, his directness, his dedication. But it wasn't until just recently she'd gotten to know him 'better.' DiJinn uncloaked and let it drape to the floor around her ankles.

Lying on his back was Dane. His wide shoulders were covered in scars, his bare chest tattooed with military insignias and tours of duty.

"You doubted me?" she asked, a slight twist to her tone.

"Not a single doubt...*ever*," he murmured and pulled at her.

She dropped onto his bed and curled up next to him. She traced one of the scars along his shoulder. "What's the latest?"

Dane gave her a look and a slight chuckle. "You show up in the middle of the night, then immediately want top-secret information?" He caressed her cheek, letting his hand linger at the nape of her slender neck.

The fingers of his other hand intertwined playfully with her red locks of hair.

She pushed back slightly and stopped his hand. "I know you, Dane. You're loyal to the system, not to any one person or office. Tell me. If Harok is involved in something illegal, are you still willin' to support him?"

"It's not my duty to care what he's involved in. I follow orders."

"If Harok's orderin' you to do things that might risk the safety of Skylights' citizens, does that not change your mind?"

Dane stared at her in the dark. "Do you know something I don't?"

DiJinn sat up on her elbow and fixed Dane with her glowing gaze. "Isn't it obvious that Harok and Lybra are plotting something?"

"How do you know?"

"I have my methods, Dane."

"When did you find this out?"

"I was there in that meeting. You were there too. You know what I'm sayin' is true. Why are you tryin' to deny it?"

"I can't get involved, Jinn. Politics are no place for soldiers like me."

"You're not just *any* soldier. You're a general, with a duty to protect this system and its citizens. Burying your head in the sand does no one any good. You need to decide what side you're on."

"Do I?" he asked. He let his hand stop near her collarbone and stared into her glowing emerald-green eyes.

"Don't you?" she shot back. "Harok's becomin' more authoritarian every day. And you know Lybra is whispering in his ear. It won't be long until that hag is runnin' the show. Add to that all these Tetrahedron Marauders, and we have a recipe for disaster. These mercenaries are on your turf, Dane. That's gotta burn you up. I sense that much. Being forced to team with those untrained hooligans has to be the final nail, or damn close."

"That's not my call."

"But you feel betrayed, don't you?" DiJinn continued. "Everyone knows it was the Tetrahedron who stole the rare-earth minerals from the Agency. Doesn't it seem odd that Harok's so willin' to bring them onboard? Did he even consult you?"

Dane lay there, motionless. She wanted to read his thoughts but resisted the urge. She had too much respect for this man to pry around uninvited inside his head. But she didn't have to read his thoughts to know he wanted to agree with her. Dane was disciplined, maybe *too* disciplined for his own good. But she needed his help. The Lucem needed his help. The fate of the *entire* system may hinge on his decision.

"You've got top-secret clearance, Dane. Don't tell me you've heard nothin'."

"What is it you want me to do, Jinn?"

"Help us," she said and slid closer to him. "Help the Lucem…help the citizens!"

"You're asking me to commit mutiny, you realize this?"

"Your soldiers are loyal to you. They love you and *will* fight for you."

"So, I'm to ask them to commit mutiny as well? How do you propose I make all of this work? I have nowhere to place my troops, vehicles, equipment. There's too much, logistically. I'm not sure I could accomplish such a thing even if I wanted to."

"We have the room where we're at right now," DiJinn said.

"Which is where, exactly?" Dane asked.

"I'd prefer not to say just yet, for your safety."

Dane leaned back, considering. "You talk of a doomsday scenario. Do you really think that's where we're headed?"

DiJinn gave him a serious look as she lay on his bed. Some stray moonlight traced her face and trailed over her bare torso. "I do. And if you're wise, you'll listen to me. If we don't decide soon, we may lose everything dear to us both."

"You realize I could be court-martialed for even having this conversation, Jinn."

"You could be court-martialed for even having me here right now. I don't think that is your real concern, though."

Dane reached out to her again, letting his fingers continue down her collarbone, his other hand trailing down her bare back. He smiled. "Like I said. You want more from me, you're gonna have to be more convincing."

DiJinn returned his smile. Getting intel had never been so intriguing—or dangerous—for them both.

CHAPTER 6
A Friendly Conversation

ΑΒΓΔΕΖΗΘΙΚΛ**Μ**
ΝΞΟΠΡΣ ΥΦΧΨΩ

THE NEXT DAY, Jet met Cord in the stacks at the Skylight University library to talk about his latest findings.

Solan had tasked Cord with analyzing the glowing device Jet had recovered from Chroma's wreckage. Known by many names, including, but not limited to: Albright's Key, Albright's Light, and Albright's Easter Egg. Whatever this mysterious artifact was, they seemed to be getting nowhere quick with it, and there was just one week until the first Heliographi Memoir was to be revealed.

Jet walked into the main library and toward the lower-level basement. His disguise was similar to his previous one—an assistant athletic director named Gunter Kepp. But his name, background, and past history had been completely scrubbed from the system and reworked by Annaka. The same was true for all the other Lucem as well. Jet's new alias was Clint Kregg, an athletic trainer at the university. His short black hair turned to a light gray; his dark scruff became a matching silver. Jet's age of twenty-three—though he was really stuck in a nineteen-year-old body, thanks to the immortality of a Heliographi—changed to a man in his mid-fifties. His normally pale complexion was much darker, though his height and build were essentially the same.

Jet no longer needed to worry about being tracked by the Agency or anyone else. They were essentially 'off the grid' now, and he trusted Annaka's ability to keep them below the Agency's radar.

Down in the library's chilly basement, in an area known as the Stacks, Jet stepped through the false wooden panel and into the bookcase. He walked down the stone stairs and stopped in front of the old claw and ball table. Cord sat there, lost in thought.

Jet bumped the table with his knee, and Cord glanced up. His olive-toned skin was flushed, and his black hair covered his face as if he were somewhat frustrated. He sat slouched in the plush chair, dressed in his signature black attire, which made him nearly invisible in the dark surroundings of the stacks. The thousands of metal racks containing millions of old books stood silently in the background as if holding their breath from the tension in the air.

"You alright?" Jet asked. "You don't look like yourself. What's wrong?"

Cord didn't answer and continued to stare at the holographic equation floating over the old table. A low breeze hummed through the space, threatening to extinguish the candles around them. Refracted light from the old chandelier swayed gently above as Cord blinked a few times but remained quiet.

Jet leaned against the table and crossed his arms. He could tell that Cord had something else on his mind besides his work, which wasn't normal. There was another moment of uncomfortable silence. "Hey, Cord." Jet waved his hands in front of his face and furrowed his brow. "You there?"

Cord looked up and craned his neck slightly as if working out a kink. He rubbed at one shoulder and finally nodded his head. "Jet…I've been meaning to chat with you about the Century Eclipse. We just haven't had much time to talk, I suppose. A lot of things happened that day."

Cord paused, as if struggling with what to say again. Jet sensed that Cord was anxious, something very out of character for him.

"Well, I'm not exactly sure what to say. I'm…not much good at this. Just wanted to mention if you need anything, someone to talk to…you know…about Cutter or Sylvant."

Jet gave Cord a quick smile, then looked at him thoughtfully for a few brief seconds. "Thanks, Cord. It's…going to take some time. Cutter was…a good friend. He accepted me for who I am. He was brave and loyal and protective. He died to save Kamber, and I think he'd do it all over again without question. I just wonder if there was something I missed that day. I feel like I could've done more, maybe *changed* something or done things differently. I don't know. It just doesn't make sense that he had to die. I feel like I'm always in a bad place. Does that make sense? And now I'm afraid that something bad might happen to you or Kamber or to the other Lucem."

Cord started to say something but paused and straightened, then seemed to reset. "I'm sorry, Jet, I wish I knew what to say. This just isn't my strength."

Jet closed his eyes and leaned his head back. The pain from losing his friends was still fresh in his soul. Talking about it was what he needed to do, but it brought back a flood of memories from that day. He could still envision Lybra snatching the curved blade and running it through Cutter's midsection. Jet felt his chest heave and his arms tense. His fists tightened, and he imagined wrapping his hands around Lybra's neck and squeezing the life from her.

Jet let his chin rest on his chest and let out a sigh. He shook his head and looked at Cord. "I want to hate her, Cord. I want revenge on Lybra, but it makes me uneasy, that feeling. I know it's wrong, but it's so hard to make it go away."

"Hate is just another feeling, in my opinion," Cord said in a matter-of-fact tone.

"But it feels wrong, like…like my inner being is rejecting it or something. Don't you ever get that feeling?"

Cord tilted his head, then rubbed his chin. "No. Not really."

Jet took another deep breath. Cord was a good friend, a close friend. Maybe the only close friend he had left. But whatever Cord was, sympathetic he was not. It was an awkward conversation at best. In many ways, Solan was much the same. But he suddenly wondered if Kamber might be someone he could share his feelings with. Perhaps she could help him sort out his concerns about that day.

"Cord. The day of the eclipse, when it was just the two of us on the deck of Chroma, something happened. I don't understand it. I've tried to recreate it but haven't yet been able to."

"Intriguing. You've got my attention."

"When you fell, and I was fighting off all the marauders, there was…well, I don't even know how to explain it. It was like a ghost standing next to me. He was dressed in a Lucem cloak and helped me defend you. I think I know this person."

The look on Cord's face was one familiar to Jet—*fascination*. "Are you sure it was a Lucem?" Cord asked.

"I think so. I mean, I was tired, but I'm not crazy. That Lucem was…what's the right word? *Ethereal,* maybe? I asked Solan, but she said she didn't see anything. There's no way I could have fought off all those troops on my own, not a chance."

Cord thought for a moment. Then shrugged. I believe you, Jet, but I've never heard of such a thing. I've not come across this in any of my studies. That's a tremendous level of power."

"Well, I also managed to use your little trick of moving things too. What did you call it? Telekinesis?"

"That's right. How did you accomplish that?"

"Like you told me. It was like a large pulse of energy or frequency, I guess. I just focused that energy through my palms and pushed the marauders away. It was like an explosion. They just flew off."

Cord chuckled, then cracked a crooked smile. "Well, my friend, you are beyond me. I'm only able to move small objects so far. Sounds like I may be asking for *your* protection soon."

"I don't know if I can do it again, though. I guess I should practice it."

"I would advise you to practice all of this. Something tells me we're going to need all the help we can get, and very soon."

Jet grinned back at Cord. "What can I say? You've taught me well." He held Cord's gaze for a long moment, then asked a question that had been on his mind since the day of the eclipse. "Wanna talk about the rare-earth device now?"

The question seemed to surprise Cord, and he narrowed his eyes at Jet. "No, not exactly."

"Come on, Cord. I know how it feels. It's your turn. Talk to me."

"What do you want me to say? That I made a mistake, and you were right? Yes, I underestimated Hurse. People are dead because of my mistake."

Cord's tone caught Jet off guard. His normally laidback nature had taken a turn. "This isn't all on you," Jet said and held up his hands. "We all failed in one way or another. It wasn't our finest day."

"But I'm the one who missed the last device. Thousands died, and that's on me. I'm looking for revenge." Cord's tone was calm again, but Jet heard the darkness brimming beneath the surface.

"That doesn't sound like the Cord I know. Do you think that's the right approach? I know how you feel. I'm tempted by the same feeling over Cutter and Sylvant."

"My inner light isn't like yours, Jet."

"What's that mean?"

"No doubt you've noticed how different we are amongst the Lucem. Even the Atrum have varying degrees of right and wrong. Where some Heliographi might subscribe to a higher standard, mine doesn't. My inner light allows me to see things by grayer shades of right and wrong."

"You're saying your Heliographi would allow you to harm others without any consequences?"

"That's how I see the world, and I don't apologize for it. If I see something that makes sense, I do it. Right and wrong don't impact me in the same way as you. I sense that my Heliographi is okay with that."

"Sounds kinda chaotic," Jet mused and wondered what he would do if Cord was intent on murder. Would he step in to stop him? Would he stand idly by and let Cord do such a thing? He found himself hoping it would never come to that. But the mood between them had changed slightly. A bit uncomfortable, it seemed. It was the first time he'd felt that way around Cord.

"Maybe we should just move on," Jet said and stood. "What about these reveals coming up?"

"If you say so," Cord said. His emotionless tone was back, as if the conversation had been one of their normal chats.

They'd spent so much time talking that the hologram Cord had been reviewing had shut down. He powered it back up, stood, then motioned to the holographic chart between them. It was the same three-dimensional map of the Skylight System they'd been reviewing for a while now. Cord had highlighted the nine memoirs' locations and dates.

"This map looks familiar," Jet said with a slight grin. "Isn't this the same one you've been working on for the last four years?"

"It is very similar. I've pinpointed all the reveal dates *exactly* as they are recorded in the three paintings. Of course, that's all public knowledge now. The first reveal begins on the first belt, then each reveal moves outward in numerical order." Cord slicked his hair back, stood, and crossed his thin arms over his narrow chest. "The first memoir's reveal will occur next week on this very belt."

"Okay, got it," Jet said.

"We have about one week between the first and second reveal," Cord said. "That's a reasonable amount of time to recover."

"Recover?" Jet asked.

"Remember, this isn't going to be a walk in the park. It'll be a battle for each memoir, and every faction in the system will be there. This will be a fight to the death."

"You think so?"

"I have no doubt. Anyone not prepared will pay the price."

"So, we go in with eyes wide open."

"Correct," Cord said. "Now, follow the rest of the dots and tell me what you see."

Jet looked at the three-dimensional map again. Each reveal occurred in order of the belts, as Cord had stated. But the time of each one occurred closer and closer together as the reveals occurred farther from the core. By the time the fourth reveal occurred, the times were so close together that they were practically stacked on top of each other. There would be no time left for travel to the next several reveals. "Why would Albright do that? The fourth through the seventh reveals are so close together that we won't have time to get to them all!"

"Why indeed," Cord crooned in his smooth drawl. "He must have wanted to split things up. Albright obviously didn't want to make this easy for anyone, including us."

"So, we'll be forced to split up?" Jet asked.

"Either that or pick and choose the reveals we want to go after. Joshia's suggestion to join forces sure sounds like a good idea all of a sudden."

"Does Solan know this yet?"

"No, but she's about to. We're all meeting with her later today to go over the schedule."

"She won't budge, Cord. I just talked to her about it last night. Teaming with the Atrum is out of the question. Something between Joshia and her that I can't figure out yet."

"Well, I'd say it might be out of the question *at the moment*. I'm betting we're gonna get a dose of reality after the first reveal. That might shake things up a bit. At least, that's my prediction."

"I think you're right. Heliographi or not, we just don't have the numbers right now." Jet turned his attention to the glowing device on the table and picked it up. The thing pulsed in his hand, slowly cycling through all the different colors. "Have you made any progress on this thing? Seems like Albright would've left some instructions behind."

"Negative, and I don't know if I'll have anything before the first reveal. Albright doesn't hand out easy advice. Of course, we already know this. He wants us to work for it."

Jet shrugged. "Well, at least we got to it first, and no one else knows about it."

'I'm not so sure about that. Remember, there's still a spy around."

Jet gave him a serious look. "You think someone in the Lucem?"

"How else would the Atrum have known some of the things they did?"

Jet rubbed his neck, his hand brushing across the locket he wore. It was one that Vail had once owned and given to him recently. He rubbed it as he considered. "I can't imagine anyone in our group would do that."

Cord furrowed his brow. "I haven't figured it out yet. We just need to keep our eyes open. Our bigger issue is more evident—we don't know what Albright's Key is meant for, and neither do the Atrum. I can only assume we will need it during the first reveal to get the memoir, though I could be wrong."

Jet stood and looked at Cord. "We're flying blind right now, just like everyone else. Things will unfold as we go. We just have to be ready for anything."

CHAPTER 7
Albright's Coordinates

ΑΒΓΔΕΖΗΘΙΚΛ<u>Μ</u>

ΝΞΟΠΡΣ ΥΦΧΨΩ

JET AND CORD left the stacks and made their way down to Lyrinthum. The hidden tunnel system below Skylight University pretty much occupied the entire first belt. Lyrinthum was dark, dusty, and haunted. Jet had learned recently the voices he sometimes heard in the tunnels—particularly around the old, defunct particle accelerator—were from the violent collisions created decades ago by scientific experiments, according to one of the older Lucem named Ti-Leer. The accelerator's loop was housed in the middle of the belt's hull, and Ti-Leer believed those smashing atoms had created something known as neutrinos.

Otherworldly dimensions, he'd claimed. *That's where the voices come from!*

DiJinn had only shaken her head. "Ti-Leer is crazy. He consumes too much ale. Ignore him!"

All of it was beyond Jet's comprehension. He only knew that the sound of those tortured souls came from a place he never wanted to visit.

The Lucem had holed up in one of the old control sectors of that particle accelerator, down in Lyrinthum. After being kicked out of the Agency, Solan had selected this place as the Lucem's temporary headquarters. But it was looking more and more like a permanent home.

Inside the control room, and dominating the space, was the ancient, splintered table that Albright had built thousands of years ago. Twenty-four chairs surrounded the ancient table, twelve for the Lucem and twelve for the Atrum. In front of each chair was a symbol etched into the wooden surface. The Greek symbols were actually the given names for each of the Heliographi, both Lucem and Atrum. Seated around the table were all the remaining Lucem. Jet's seat was behind the letter 'M,' which happened to be near the bottom of the table. Next to him sat Kamber, his warden. Then Solan, Cord, Ti-Leer, DiJinn, Harriet, Booker, Tyberius, Annaka, Shiloe, and Albright. Though Albright and Tyberius were missing, everyone else was present.

Jet took a seat as Solan stood.

"Cord, you're up," she said and leaned against the old table. "Have you made any progress?"

"Regarding Albright's Key, nothing. I've found no instructions for this device." He laid it on the table. "I have no recommendations at this moment except that we should probably bring it to the first reveal. Perhaps then we will find some answers."

Solan nodded, crossed her arms. "Anyone else have thoughts?"

The room remained silent.

"Let's take a look at the map and the schedule then," she said and walked over to the holopad built into the wall and pressed a few buttons. The projection of a hologram flickered over the table, fizzled, and shut down. Solan hammered the wall about a meter to the left of it, and the hologram reappeared. "Hit the wall here if that happens again," she said to Cord. Jet noticed the metal bulkhead had several fist-sized dents in it now.

Cord kicked the spot hard enough to leave another dent.

"That'll do." Solan patted his shoulder, then sat down.

Cord turned to face them. "We won't be alone at the reveals. Of course, you all know this. The Atrum, the Agency, and Lybra all know what we know. I assume there will be some local gangs, splinter cells, lone wolves, and drug lords there as well. Word has spread throughout the system about the memoirs' reveal. Everyone knows the times, dates, and locations. We need to be prepared for battle."

"What else do we need to know?" DiJinn asked, her boots kicked up on the table.

"You need to know about coordinates and times, especially numbers four through seven." Cord pulled up the times and dates of all nine reveals. The holographic dates hovered over the table for them to read as Cord read the list aloud. "The first reveal on belt one is on May seventeenth at two PM, and the distance is negative 5,744 meters from the Core. The second reveal on belt two is on May thirtieth at 3:00 AM, with a positive distance of 31,810 meters from the Core. The third reveal on belt three will occur on June second at 6:00 AM, and the distance is positive 59,199 meters from the Core.

"Come on, Cord," DiJinn said impatiently.

"Hold on, this is the interesting part," Cord said, raising his hand. "The fourth, fifth, sixth, and seventh reveals all occur on June third. Starting at 6:03 PM, each reveal is only three minutes apart. The distances from the Core, respectively, are as follows: negative 83,871 meters, negative 108,364 meters, negative 134,990 meters, and negative 159,825 meters."

"Why in Skylight are you telling us all of this?" DiJinn asked.

"Allow me to finish, Jinn," Cord said and returned to the list. "The eighth reveal on the eighth belt is on June tenth at five AM, with a distance of positive 186,934 meters from the Core. The final reveal on the ninth belt will occur on June twenty-fourth at one AM, with a distance of positive 214,851 meters from the Core. By the way, all the reveals will occur during a Skylight Eclipse."

Solan looked on with the other Lucem. Then she dropped her gaze. "Why would Albright do that?"

"The fourth through seventh reveals are lined up like boxcars," Ti-Leer bellowed.

"Of course," DiJinn muttered. "Should've known Albright wouldn't make this easy!"

"He's forcing us to make a decision, Solan," Jet said.

"Albright's greatest hope was that the Heliographi work together," Harriet said. "Perhaps this is his way of making us join forces."

"That's insane!" Booker roared. "Albright wouldn't have risked placing our two groups together like that."

"Maybe," Jet said. "But what if he knew that word would get out? Or better yet, maybe that's *why* he chose to project the locations of the memoirs at the Century Eclipse. He knew it would put pressure on us. Alone, we don't have much of a chance. Together, there's a possibility. He's letting the entire system in on this 'easter egg hunt' for a reason. Well, there's your reason."

Solan shook her head. "I don't know if I agree with that theory. That seems like a big gamble, even for Albright. Would he really risk the memoirs to force the Lucem and Atrum back together? If those documents fall into the wrong hands, it could spell disaster for everyone."

"Solan. Are you certain we shouldn't take Joshia's offer?" Annaka asked. "It seems like it's starting to make more sense."

"I'm still not ready to consider that, Annaka," Solan said. "I know what you're all thinking, but right now, I'm going off my instincts. Let's just focus and get through this first reveal, then we can regroup and consider our options. Cord. Let's have a look at the site. Can we get a close-up view?"

Cord pulled up a floorplan and some sections of the reveal site. "The first reveal will occur at this coordinate," Cord said and pointed to an area in the first belt. "Again, this is based on the three-dimensional Cartesian Coordinate System. That puts the memoir *inside* the first belt. Looks like there's a large chamber right here," he pointed at a huge void inside the belt. "Up until a few weeks ago, no one even knew this place existed. There's even a direct route leading to the chamber. A large vent system that has mysteriously opened up a few days ago."

Ti-Leer grunted and nodded at the hologram. "Looks like an arena to me, am I right?"

"More like a death pit," Cord said. "If I were to guess, Albright designed this chamber for this specific event. He's had all of this planned out before the Skylight System was even built."

DiJinn stood and leaned closer to the hologram. "If there's goin' to be the amount of people inside this arena as you claim, then a lot of memoir seekers are gonna die."

"I'm afraid you're probably right," Harriet said. "Which means that we need to pair up."

"One other thing I want to mention," Cord said. "I've noticed that all the reveals occur in only two quadrants, which I find fascinating."

DiJinn sighed. "Cord. Specifics, please."

"The Skylight System is a sphere," Cord continued. "Using the X, Y, and Z axis, we can separate the sphere into eight portions. But all nine of the reveals occur in only two of those eight portions. Let's just call it the *top right*—or the positive portion, and the *bottom left*—or the negative portion. Note how the coordinate in the Z-axis for every reveal is always zero? That makes it a two-dimensional map, just like it is on Albright's table and Van Saint's paintings."

"Any idea why that is?" Solan asked.

"Another riddle. Typical for Albright," DiJinn huffed. "If we haven't learned that yet, then we haven't learned anything."

"Cord, help me understand this," Kamber said. "If we're looking at the Skylight System like it's a round, flat map, you're saying all nine of the memoirs' locations fall in the top right or the lower left area? There is no Z-axis?"

"Correct, that's what Albright's coordinates tell us, anyway. When the specified belt aligns at the proper time and date indicated, a memoir will be revealed. We must be prepared if we want Albright's Memoirs because every person in the system is going to fight to the death to get their hands on them."

CHAPTER 8
Training Day

ΑΒΓΔΕΖΗΘΙΚΛ<u>Μ</u>
ΝΞΟΠΡΣ ΥΦΧΨΩ

JET MET KAMBER in a lower level of the control suite for her first full day of training.

The chamber was large and open, and the Lucem had converted the space into a training room. The ceiling spanned up some twenty meters and disappeared into darkness with hundreds of conduits and defunct control systems barely visible in the dim light. There was a musty smell to the space and creaks and groans could be heard occasionally. To one side were several rugs for meditation, and in the middle were some mats for sparring. Jet had had only one brief training session with

Kamber so far. She'd been converted to a Lucem just a few days ago, but Solan had insisted Jet start her training immediately. He had hoped to give her a breather, considering all that had happened to her during the Century Eclipse. After all, Kamber had nearly died, being thrown over the edge of the observation deck of Chroma. But Solan had saved her, and now Kamber was up to her neck in Lucem business.

Kamber entered the chamber and dropped her bag. She stretched her arm and waved at him.

"Are you ready?" he asked.

"Of course, just excited to get started."

Jet clapped his hands. "Good, join me over here."

He waited for her on a large sparring mat. Kamber wore a light robe over a skin suit. Her build was average height and thin, with powerful legs from years of running track at Skylight University. Her olive-toned skin was smooth. Her long, black hair was tinged with golden highlights, and a few colored beads woven in. Like all the other Heliographi, her eyes glowed, and there was no iris or pupil. Each Heliographi was identified by their own unique color, and since Kamber was next to him on the spectrum, her eyes were similar to his in color: a bright greenish-yellow.

Jet bowed, then started dancing around the mat with his fists up. He gave her a quick smile, and she returned his grin, then matched his movements. "You're not gonna go easy on me this time, are you?" he asked.

Jet dropped and swept Kamber's feet out, bringing her to the mat.

Kamber fell, and Jet tried to roll on top of her. But she was quick and shifted out of the way, then jumped back onto her feet.

Jet flipped onto his feet and circled her.

She winked at him and then lunged forward and kicked out.

Jet was astounded. Here, Kamber had just been converted to a Lucem, but she was already light years ahead of where he'd been at her stage.

He barely blocked her kick. But she'd left herself open and vulnerable. He grabbed her leg and dropped her to the mat again. She landed on her back, and it knocked the wind out of her.

He tried again to pin her arms, but she managed to shove him with her legs and was quickly back on her feet.

Jet let her take the offensive again and waited for her to make another mistake. He'd learned over the last four years that he wasn't the most formidable fighter. But he had learned to be patient, to wait for his opponent to make a mistake, then strike. And though Kamber was already quick, she was still inexperienced.

Once again, she moved in and overreached with a punch. He grasped her arm and brought her down, this time able to straddle her. He pinned her arms to the mat.

"What happened?" he asked. "Too aggressive, maybe?"

"You're the one straddling me," she responded.

Jet felt his skin flush as he stared at her. He grinned and tried to refocus. "You're not making this easy on me, you know that?"

She smiled up at him.

"You're moving in too quickly," he continued. "You need to be patient, especially with your inexperience. You're quick, Kamber, much more than I was at your level. But don't overestimate your ability. Wait for your opponent to make a mistake. It'll give you time to look for their weakness."

As Jet continued to look into her eyes, he felt a stirring. He remembered their conversion just recently at Firefly Falls—at seeing her soul laid bare before him. Her beauty and kindness had been breath-taking. Since that night, he'd fought down thoughts of her...*desires about her.*

"It's a bit difficult to train like this." Jet looked away, stood, and helped her up. "Let's do some meditation."

Kamber followed him over to the rugs. It was quiet, except for the occasional groan from the hull or random beep from some old, barely functioning piece of equipment. Jet lowered the light levels, and they sat across from each other, crossing their legs and placing palms face down on the rug.

"Remember, slow your breathing," Jet said. "Let your mind be at rest. When you feel the Heliographi take over, let it. Don't fight it, and don't panic."

Jet watched as she relaxed and let her breathing slow. Kamber remained steady, and Jet knew she was already in a trancelike state. Then he closed his eyes and joined her.

He felt his inner light, his Heliographi, move in and take over. He let it take control. Soon, he was transported to another plane of existence. He floated in space like he was having an out-of-body experience. As often as he'd done this over the last four years, he still wasn't used to it. The experience didn't feel real. It was difficult to explain or put into words. It felt like some bizarre dream he didn't belong in. *Perhaps this was what living in another dimension felt like?* Regardless, it was the strangest thing he'd ever known.

The Heliographi's light took control. It led him across the universe, zipping past other galaxies and planets. Some of those planets were similar to Earth, with living entities on them. He witnessed the time fabric of the universe being stretched at the edge of the cosmos, ripping and tearing, creating new matter. Things felt warped, suspended…*ethereal.* Voices spoke to him, and he could see other objects too strange to explain. There were some of the other Heliographi nearby as well, streaks of light playing and interacting with each other. This was how his inner light recharged itself, which was something it needed in order to survive. On days when he skipped his meditation, he felt weaker and drained. Now he understood why Cord meditated every chance he got.

After an hour or so, Jet started reeling his inner light back in. It fought him, though, like a petulant child not wanting to come in from recess. His Heliographi would run and play forever, leaving the earthly world behind if he let it.

But why didn't it? he had often wondered. *What kept it tethered to this realm of existence?*

Jet awoke. His eyes fluttered open, and he sat quietly for a moment. He let his breathing catch up and then steady into its normal rhythm. Sometimes, during this transition back to reality, he had thoughts, ideas, or solutions. Once again, as he regained his bearings, another epiphany came to him.

He needed to visit the Hall of Vital Records.

Why he knew this, he wasn't sure. When the intuitive voice spoke, he always listened.

Kamber began to wake, then slumped forward. Jet moved over and caught her and held her.

She looked up at him, slow recognition dawning. "Jet…I must have passed out."

"No, you were in a trance from meditation. Sometimes the transition back to reality can be a bit bumpy."

"I know I've only had a few sessions, but it felt different this time. I felt so…I can't explain it…like I couldn't contain my emotions. Do you feel the same?"

"Yes, always. Our human form and mind are poor vessels for the Heliographi. I know it tries to strengthen us, reinforce our psyche. With time, your body becomes stronger. You'll get used to it the more you practice, but it'll always feel odd. If it's any consolation, you're way beyond where I was at this stage."

She smiled. "You're too kind, Jet. But thank you. You're a good teacher."

Jet continued to hold her, trying to push down the emotions he felt at that moment. He was struck once again by her beauty. Not just her physical beauty but her inner light. The way she made him feel whole…*fulfilled.* They were meant to be together—he knew this beyond a doubt—and it brought a smile to his face. But then he thought about Sylvant and Cutter. And now they were dead because of how close they'd been to him. Was he willing to put Kamber in the same kind of danger? If he allowed her to get too close, would she suffer the same fate?

But it was different, wasn't it? Kamber was a Heliographi now.

He pushed the thought away and turned from her. He didn't want to think about that possibility at the moment.

Kamber noticed his hesitation and sat up, her hand brushing against his arm, and it lingered there. "Jet, is there something wrong?"

He looked at her hand on his arm, then shook his head. "No. It's…it's fine. I just can't stop thinking about my friends."

"You mean Cutter and Sylvant?" she asked. "You shouldn't blame yourself for what happened."

He slowly nodded.

"What does your heart tell you?" she continued.

"That they wouldn't blame me."

"Then listen to that. I'm certain you did all you could." Kamber grabbed his shoulder and shook him gently. Her expression softened as she lowered her gaze at him and smiled.

"I still can't help but feel responsible. Cutter died because he was too close to me and Sylvant too. I wasn't strong enough to protect them. And…I'm still not strong enough to protect you, Kamber."

The look on her face turned sour. "I'm not asking you to protect me. It's not up to you to make that decision. It's up to me, which is why I chose to become a Lucem. This is my battle now, too. You have your own battles to worry about, Jet."

Jet met her gaze and held it for several seconds before nodding. "I understand what you're saying. I just don't want to lose any more friends. If I can prevent it, I will."

Kamber moved closer to him. She brought her other hand up and caressed his brow, tracing his cheekbone and letting her hand linger there. "Jet. You can't worry about *everyone* all the time. Have some faith. I can take care of myself."

Jet fought down mixed emotions as he looked back at her: fear, anxiety, *desire*. His chest tightened as he thought about Cutter and what had happened to him…and what might happen to Kamber if he wasn't vigilant.

CHAPTER 9
The Hall of Vital Records

ΑΒΓΔΕΖΗΘΙΚΛ**Μ**
ΝΞΟΠΡΣ ΥΦΧΨΩ

THE NEXT DAY, Jet boarded his skiff and flew to the ninth belt.

He followed one of the lesser-known lanes to avoid any traffic. Although each belt was spaced a little over twenty-five kilometers apart, they all orbited about the central core and could be seen churning slowly in the distance. Thanks to the humidity emitted from each belt's surface, clouds inundated them as he flew past, partially shrouding them from view. Some of the clouds had even built to thunderheads, and brief flashes of lightning lit the otherwise azure-colored sky.

About fifteen minutes later, Jet docked his skiff in a public hangar near Memorial Park. He used his new alias as Clint Kregg, a low-level Skylight faculty member, to gain some limited access around the facility. Jet's previous alias, Gunter Kepp, had been granted much greater clearance, and he missed that authority. But now that the Agency was no longer friendly toward the Lucem, those old credentials were invalid.

Inside Memorial Park were several events and tours taking place. Most of the space was set up like a vast museum gallery with a clear dome overhead. The panoramic view to Earth was breathtaking, one of the best vistas in the entire system. The noise level decreased as Jet made his way to some of the lesser-known departments.

Their old base was located inside the Agency's headquarters, which meant he would need to infiltrate through some security points. He'd been back to the ninth belt on a few occasions since being banned from the Agency. Still, he needed to be careful. He wasn't as sneaky as DiJinn when it came to breaking and entering.

He'd chosen to keep this particular visit private. In fact, he hadn't even told Cord his plans. If he was caught, there was no telling what the Agency would do to him. He didn't think anyone in the Agency would purposely harm him. But now that Lybra was in the mix, along with the new mech units coming online soon, he preferred not to test his luck and remained extremely cautious.

Once inside the lower departments, he donned his cloak and relied on its ability to scramble the surveillance systems, allowing him unfettered access. The Hall of Vital Records was deep in the complex and near the heart of the old Lucem wing. This was an area that saw no use now that they'd been 'evicted.' That didn't mean he could throw caution to the wind, though.

The abandoned wing was dusty and dim already from lack of use, despite the Lucem's recent departure. Jet heard soft shouts and followed them to an overlook. Below was a large hangar bay where multiple skiffs were being loaded with supplies, weapons, and armor. Across the bay were thousands of troops going through training exercises. But there was something else that caught Jet's eye.

In the corner were a handful of mech units. He could tell they were newer models just by the way they moved. He'd heard rumors of an M-Class mech, which was the next prototype in line. But the program for these prototypes had been scrapped due to cost. All the available finances the Agency had left were being poured into the Goliath's Gate project. It wasn't difficult to see now how President Harok was using Lybra's money— the stalled mech program was back up and running. But it was further along than anyone had realized.

The M-Class mechs stood in line, stationary and unmoving, as several technicians and engineers walked around, checking them. On occasion, one would power up and move around the area. Jet was amazed at how adept the mechs were. They were much faster than their predecessors, which had been somewhat clumsy and predictable. These units, however, were lightning-quick and extremely agile. One mech hovered, then spun and flipped with human dexterity that rivaled any Heliographi. It had one large shoulder-mounted howitzer and a smaller chain gun on its other shoulder. It held a clear shield in one hand that looked to be made of graphene and some sort of energy spear in its other hand.

Jet watched for a few more minutes, then hurried back to the Lucem wing. It appeared the M-Class mechs were progressing quicker than anticipated. Solan wouldn't be pleased. Harok was on a mission, it seemed, and with Lybra's backing, the M-Class would pose a serious threat to the Heliographi and their quest for the memoirs.

He slowed as he returned to the Lucem wing. He meandered through familiar passages and into the heart of their old headquarters, finally stopping in a dimly lit area known as the Hall of Vital Records. The wide chamber had a lofty ceiling and a skylight above that emitted some filtered moonlight. Jet perused the old artifacts lining the walls, many of which hinted at the Heliographi's heritage. The chamber housed a special meditation room for each of the twenty-four Heliographi. Each meditation room encircled a massive central column carved of stone. Jet had always thought it odd—the mix of stone, steel, and the ancient décor. The juxtaposition of materials gave the hall an eclectic vibe. The air inside the chamber seemed to almost vibrate with a mystical ambiance, even though it was abandoned now.

Each of the twenty-four meditation rooms contained charts carved in the stone showing the lineage for a specific Heliographi. Tyberius had once explained that their ancient race dated back millennia, perhaps farther. The Greek symbols surrounding the chambers matched the ones on Albright's table. These symbols were actually the Heliographi's given name and had been created by Christian Albright around 800 B.C. Only later had the symbols been accepted as the first known alphabet.

From the Hall of Vital Records, Jet could feel any Heliographi's life force, though he couldn't use it to track them. This meant he could *sense* if they were alive, one of the reasons he was here tonight. If what Joshia had said was true, then he wouldn't be able to sense Hanley Hurse's life force.

Jet was also there to try and figure out who the ghost Lucem was, and why it had saved his life the day of the Century Eclipse. Not long ago, he'd discovered that the man who'd borne the symbol of the letter M just before him had died in service to the Skylight System. What he was beginning to wonder was shocking.

Was that previous Lucem speaking to him?

He'd heard the intuitive voice throughout his life, thinking it was just his own. But now he was beginning to understand it *wasn't*. It made sense, after all. From what little research he'd done so far, all of the prior Lucem who'd borne the letter M before him were very similar in nature, almost like a long-lost brother. Was it possible that they were guiding him from beyond the grave? Was that a deceased Lucem's duty after death? Were these past Lucem really dead? He intended to try and discover that tonight before he left. He had to because he didn't know when he might return to the Hall of Vital Records.

But first, Jet wanted to check on Hurse. He walked over to the Atrum side of the chamber, which was on the left, and the darker hours, representing the night. The Roman numerals thirteen through twenty-four were etched into the floor, starting near the six o'clock position and ending at the top, representing midnight. Also at the threshold was a carved icon of a serpent, each one slightly different in size and shape. With fangs bared and sharp scales cladding the sinuous body, its eyes seemed to glow in the dark. Jet recalled that night four years ago when he had confronted Sybold during the triclipse. He remembered those glowing red eyes and how they had seared his soul. Jet shuddered and moved on.

When he found the meditation room that was Hurse's, which was near the nine o'clock position, he stopped. It had the Roman numeral nineteen and the Greek symbol of the letter 'T' etched in front of the portal. Jet stepped into the room and sat cross-legged on the old rug, trying to get comfortable.

Sitting there in Hurse's chamber gave him an unsettled feeling. It felt morbid, dark, and unnerving, like he was sitting in the front row of some macabre funeral. Dark mists and eerie voices swirled near his ears, haunting whispers from neglected places he dared not listen to. He felt inside his robe for Hurse's ring, which he'd taken that day at the crash site of Revelation's Plaza. In front of him was a chart, like a graph or family tree of sorts. Near the bottom, where Hurse was represented on the timeline, was an indentation. He placed Hurse's ring in it, then took a deep breath and closed his eyes, letting his thoughts focus on Hurse.

It didn't take long for Jet to sense what he needed to know.

Hurse's Heliographi no longer existed.

It was a feeling he somehow knew. Like the sun rising every morning or the changing of the seasons, there was no doubt in his mind. Whatever spirit had occupied Hurse, and those like him, over the millennia, that essence was no longer around.

Jet stood and shivered as a sudden chill ran through the chamber, and he quickly stepped out. As he stood there, wondering, he felt his own intuitive voice begin to tug at him. He let it take control and walked over to the chamber that belonged to his own class. He found the Roman numeral twelve and the Greek symbol of the letter 'M' at the opening's threshold. On the Lucem side were jewel-like prisms, each one different in shape, color, and texture. Embedded inside the faceted walls of each jewel was an avatar representing each Lucem's essence. If he looked close enough, he could see it, like a tiny heart in the very center. His looked like a skull, and it made him wonder what it meant.

Inside his own meditation chamber was a similar stone wall with a chart and timeline. He traced the family tree with his fingers, its branches stretching up and out of view. The lowest branch, which he assumed was the newest member, was blank.

Because my chapter hasn't been written yet, he thought.

But it was the name above that caught his attention. Though all the names were written in Greek, he could interpret this one. The man's name had been Brindall. Was this the man he'd seen that day of the Century Eclipse? The Lucem who'd saved his life? The *intuitive* voice he'd heard throughout the years?

Jet settled down on the old rug and let his breathing slow. He focused his mind as he looked at the chart of lineage on the stone wall. Jet began to float out of consciousness as he sat there cross-legged. Sitting in his meditation chamber, Jet felt as though his essence were being amplified. It was stronger than he had felt anywhere else. It seemed like the very air within the chamber was charged with energy, bathing him in ancient waves of power.

A presence entered the chamber and stood near him. Like that day on the deck of Chroma, it was the presence of the same ghost Lucem, and he felt goose bumps cover his skin as a chill descended upon the chamber. Even though he was in a trance, he was still able to step outside his physical form and see the ghost Lucem clearly. It stood behind him, looking down over Jet's physical being as he sat there, meditating.

Jet let his own ethereal form move over near the ghost Lucem, and he faced it. The ghost was a man, probably about his age or slightly older. He had dark hair and eyelashes, like Jet, and ashen skin. He was a handsome man, tall with an athletic build and lean, muscular shoulders. His eyes glowed the same color as Jet's, a bright turquoise-green. The ghost Lucem faced Jet, unblinking. The Lucem lifted its arms, motioning outward, as if it held something in its hands, trying to give it to Jet.

Jet stared at the man, not sure how to react. He had no idea what it was trying to tell him. The ghost Lucem mouthed a word and kept repeating it over and over, but Jet couldn't make it out. The ghost left the chamber and moved to another area. Jet followed it, watching as it seemed to glide across the stone and metallic floor. Its

Lucem cloak was torn and shredded, and Jet wondered if perhaps its final battle was the cause.

The ghost eventually stopped in front of a wall and touched it, as if trying to indicate something. Jet waited, not sure how to respond. Then it turned and went back to the chamber. Once there, it knelt and pointed at the base of the stone column at an odd-looking void. Jet bent to look at it, careful not to bump into his own physical form. Jet's hands were cold and shaking as he examined the base of the stone column. It was evident the ghost was trying to tell him something. Jet stood to face the Lucem, hoping to get more clues, but the presence had suddenly disappeared.

Jet roused himself, shaking off the vestiges of the trance. He felt chilled to the bone, like his inner core was frozen. His mind felt rattled, and he had to take a few minutes to clear his thoughts and steady himself. The close encounter with the ghost Lucem had affected him in an unsettling way, it seemed. He couldn't imagine having to battle such an entity.

He took a deep breath and leaned forward to examine the strange rock. Its odd shape seemed familiar. He stared at it for several minutes, wondering what the ghost Lucem had been trying to tell him. Whatever it was, it seemed important enough for the apparition to approach him.

Jet stood and left the meditation room to examine the outer wall the ghost Lucem had indicated. There were no markings or other identifiers on it that he could see. The light of the moon was low on the wall, and it was getting close to dawn. He needed to be back at the first belt soon before the other Lucem noticed him missing. Solan would skewer him if she discovered he'd broken into the Agency's headquarters. But whatever risk he'd taken tonight by breaking in, he knew it was worth it. Whatever the ghost Lucem was trying to tell him, it was important. But the ghost was gone, and Jet had no idea what to do now. His time was running out, and he dared not stick around any longer. He'd have to return but hated to think about it—breaking into the Agency again would be extremely risky.

Even though he hadn't discovered what the ghost was trying to tell him, he had learned one thing: Hurse was gone, and he had to warn the other Lucem that their essence may no longer be respawning. The stakes had just gone up.

CHAPTER 10
A Time for Reflection

ΑΒΓΔΕΖΗΘΙΚΛ**Μ**

ΝΞΟΠΡΣ ΥΦΧΨΩ

AS JET LEFT the ninth belt, he thought back on the events of the last several weeks. All of it had him feeling exhausted. The physical toll from the battles that day of the Century Eclipse, along with his added training with Kamber and his late-night visit by the ghost Lucem, had pushed him to his physical limit. And there was also a mental toll. He was still coping with the loss of his friends, Cutter and Sylvant.

But mostly, his thoughts lingered on the ghost Lucem.

Who was this man?

He knew very little at the moment. Just that he was a former Lucem who had borne the 'M' symbol and had died during a mission about twenty-four years ago. But why was he visiting Jet, and what was he trying to tell him? It was apparent the ghost had attempted to communicate something, a clue perhaps.

When Jet reached the first belt's airspace, it was still dark, but dawn was near. He piloted his skiff around the university, landing near Clipton Point. He needed to think, and he didn't care if the other Heliographi found him missing. Besides, if he went back to his quarters, he wouldn't be able to relax—he'd find no resolve down in the control suite. He needed to be out amongst the stars so he could think, and he knew just the place to go.

Jet took one of the dusty trails and walked casually through the dark forest. The greenish glow of the Aurora Borealis lit his way. The sound of crickets chirped as he strolled, the gravel crunching under his boots. He already felt more at ease as he neared a place called Firefly Falls.

Soon, a low roar greeted his ears, and he saw a glow from a tree-covered glen beyond. He followed the gravel path over a ravine and into the grouping of trees. Several twists and turns led him closer to the low roaring of a waterfall. He finally burst through some underbrush and into the partially hidden glen. The Clipton River cascaded over a cliff some thirty meters above and crashed down on the rocks below. Green and yellow fireflies buzzed overhead and lit the underside of the tree canopy. The spectacular light show reflected into the churning water of the nearby river. Near the bank, blending into the rocky shore and barely visible, was a pyramid-shaped tomb. Jet made his way over and sat down on a large rock in front of the tomb.

He thought back on his time spent with Cutter Jade, losing himself in the memories of his friend and how he missed him already. He had known him for most of his life, going back to their days growing up in the ARC district on Earth. They had both suffered through difficult lives on the streets of the mining town. Jet had met Cutter while playing a sport called Blaze, then ended up attending Skylight University with him, where they'd become close friends. That had been over four years ago.

Cutter's death had come unexpectedly. The horror he'd felt at that moment was still recent, like a fresh wound. Once again, those feelings of inadequacy flooded Jet's thoughts. That fateful day atop Chroma, during the Century Eclipse, Cutter had died defending Kamber. The image of his death was burned into Jet's mind and had been replaying nonstop in his waking thoughts. Though Jet had only been friends with Cutter for a short time, he'd been like a brother. Jet would never be able to repay Cutter for his sacrifice.

Jet pulled his gaze from the grave, closed his eyes, and began to meditate.

Soon his inner light raced off, and Jet clung to it.

He could sense others nearby. It was like a dream, where he could feel the presence of a loved one and knew who they were, even though he could not physically see them. He could hear their thoughts, filling him with emotions. Soon, that intuitive voice he'd heard over the years began whispering to him. It was the same voice that had guided him throughout his life and during his days at Skylight University. He knew now, without a doubt, the deceased Lucem had been that voice.

It was Brindall.

Jet's eyes snapped open like a thunderclap.

…and suddenly, he *knew* what Brindall had been trying to tell him at the Hall of Vital Records.

Someone stepped through the underbrush, and Jet hopped to his feet. He crouched in a defensive position and readied himself.

The dark shape approached him quickly, blurry and cloaked. It was a Heliographi, but he couldn't tell if it was a Lucem or an Atrum.

The Heliographi moved in close, and Jet held his defensive position as they faced off for a few seconds. Then the Heliographi lowered its hood and materialized from thin air.

Jet stared into Kamber's glowing eyes and relaxed, letting out a silent sigh of relief. "Kamber! What are you doing here? It's late."

She smiled. "Did I scare you?"

Jet looked at her and shook his head. "Why are you here?"

"I couldn't sleep, so I checked on you. Your chamber was empty. Then some voice urged me here. It didn't take long to figure out why. I knew you'd be here and thought you could use some company."

Jet crossed his arms. "I was…just getting some fresh air."

"Something's on your mind. Want to talk?" Kamber looked from Jet to Cutter's grave. "You thinking about Cutter?"

Jet sat down on the large rock and stretched out. "Yeah. I mean, I guess. It'll be some time before I get past this, it seems."

Kamber sat down next to him and took his hand. "Anything I can do to help?"

Jet shook his head. "I don't think so. I gotta figure this out on my own."

"Of course…I understand. If you need some time alone, I'll go——"

"No. I mean…it's okay. I'd like you to stay. I could use some company right now."

They sat for a moment, neither saying anything as they looked at Cutter's grave. The sound of the waterfall and nature surrounded them. The sky was beginning to lighten to a soft pink color when Kamber stood and pulled Jet up with her. "Come on. There's something I want to show you."

"Where are we going?" Jet asked as she held his hand and led them out of the glen.

Kamber and Jet jogged out of Firefly Falls, and the sound of the waterfall faded. Kamber released his hand and ran along the dirt trails. Low-lying fog had settled into the lower parts, and the early morning sunrays lit the ground for them. Jet kept pace as they ran. Kamber was fast, having been a track star, but Jet managed to stick with her.

They raced up a switch-back trail that wound up the side of a hill and out of the Clipton Forest. Jet had never noticed this particular trail and wasn't sure where they were heading until they burst into a clearing. They slowed to a stop and stood atop what had to be one of the highest points in the Clipton Forest. They were clear of the tall pine trees now, and he could see the glow of the sunrise.

"I've never been here before," Jet said, trying to catch his breath. "Where are we?"

"I stumbled on this place while running cross-country last year. It's one of the best views around. Plus, it's quiet. I came here a lot to be alone and think."

Jet followed her to the edge of a cliff. They stood by an old tree that clung to the side of the bluff, its roots gnarled and exposed. Kamber jumped to one of the lower branches and climbed out to another limb. Jet joined her, and they sat down, their legs dangling from the thick tree branch.

"Look at it," she whispered. "The sunrise, the sky. It seems like it's on fire. Beautiful, isn't it?"

Jet stared at the panoramic view in awe. He could see the outer system loops crisscrossing in the distance, highlighted in contrast to the earth's dark silhouette. Lightning covered the surface as the edge of its circumference began to glow from the sun's approach behind. It was breathtaking.

"I've never seen it so clearly before," Jet muttered.

Kamber sighed and propped her chin in her hands. "This place reminds me to stop and reflect. To be grateful for what we have. When I was a student, and I thought I was going to die from E.M., I used to come here every day to watch the sunrise. It gave me hope. Just being around nature, the quiet and solitude. I feel a sense of clarity here. Not a bad place to spend your birthday, well, almost birthday, I guess."

Jet turned to face her. "Wait, how did you know?"

She lifted one shoulder. "I did some prying, remember? I know more about you than you think. You're twenty-four. Well, you will be in a few days."

"Yeah, I guess that's right." Jet did some quick math, counting on his fingertips to make her laugh. She smiled back at him. "If I hadn't accepted Solan's offer to join the Lucem, I suppose…I'd be dead in a few days. Strange to think about it that way."

She pursed her lips, and Jet sensed the mood had changed.

"I'm sorry. I hope I haven't ruined the day," Kamber said. "I didn't mean to bring up bad memories."

"No, it's fine. I don't really see it that way. I think joining the Lucem was the best thing that's ever happened to me, honestly. Strange doesn't necessarily mean bad."

"I understand. It's the same for me too. Being a student, my life felt so dark. I had no friends, no real family. Everything was a struggle, especially growing up with my foster parents. The night after the Century Eclipse, when I was converted to a Lucem…well, it might be one of the happiest moments of my life. I was afraid, I still am, but now I have a purpose."

"Growing up with E.M. was difficult for us all, I imagine. You're not alone there. Sometimes I think Albright meant for it to be this way, though I'm not sure why. Cord, Solan, you…even the Atrum have suffered through their childhood because of E.M. I can't believe it's been over four years since I was converted." He paused for a moment and shook his head. "I don't know, it just seems odd that the first reveal is on my birthday, my twenty-fourth birthday, no less. Don't you think?"

Kamber considered, then nodded. "A little, yes. But I'm so new to this that everything seems odd to me, though."

There was a quiet moment, Jet not sure what else to say until she handed him a package from under her cloak.

"I made this for you," she said, a slight waver in her voice. "Forgive the wrapping. It's my first."

Jet took the package and held it, not sure what to do.

"You, uh…you unwrap it," Kamber said, tilting her head to one side. "It's a tradition, I think, in some cultures, anyway."

Jet squinted his eyes at her suspiciously, then chuckled. "What do you mean? I just tear it open?"

"Yes, like this." Kamber reached over and pulled at one corner of the wrapping paper, then gave him a pat on the shoulder and smiled, almost giggling.

With a shrug, Jet tore the corner, then removed the rest of the paper to reveal a box. He opened it and held up a holopad.

"Here," Kamber said and set the holopad on the wide tree branch and turned it on.

The holopad flickered and projected an image of Jet. He was wearing his blaze uniform from his days at Skylight University. Beside him was his old friend, Cutter. They stood next to each other; Cutter's massive arm wrapped around Jet's neck as he ruffled his hair. In the picture, they were both smiling. The three-dimensional image seemed to bring Cutter back to life. It was after Jet's very first game against Ogden University.

Jet smiled and cleared his throat. He felt his eyes begin to well up, and he turned away. "Where'd you find this?"

"Of course, when I did all that research on you during my freshman year. There's more. Look." Kamber inched forward and leaned against him. She swiped the three-dimensional image over and pulled up more pictures. There were several with Sylvant, some with Cord, Vail, and Bo. The slideshow ended with a few images of Kamber.

"I hope that's okay," she said. "Giving you these pictures…of me."

Jet smiled again. "Thank you. It's the first gift I've had in…well…ever, I think. I almost forgot my birthday was coming up, honestly."

"You've never had a birthday gift?"

He thought, then shook his head. "No, never. It doesn't bother me, really. It's something I'm not familiar with because it's never happened, a birthday party or a gift."

"Why don't you tell the other Lucem?"

"I don't really care to. Besides, I don't think they celebrate birthdays anymore."

"That seems odd," Kamber said. "Of course, I'm going to fix that. We need a little cheer around here. I mean, why not?"

That made Jet smile again. He almost laughed aloud, thinking about Ti-Leer or Jinn in a party hat. It's what he would expect from Kamber, which reminded him why he liked her so much. "I think you're exactly what this place needs."

"Things are too serious; we need to have a little fun sometimes."

"I completely agree. Maybe, after all these reveals are over, we can have a proper celebration for everyone's birthday. How does that sound?"

"That sounds like a promise."

"Well, then I guess it is."

She reached over and gave him a hug. "Happy birthday, Jet. You deserve a good one." Then she kissed him.

It was meant to be a quick kiss, but her lips lingered near his as he gazed at her in shock. He wasn't sure how to respond. No one had ever really cared or shown affection toward him like this. It felt foreign, but it also felt…*good.* Just a simple embrace, a gentle kiss, had such surprising power. He hugged her back, and his heart leapt into his throat, his pulse quickened. His lips brushed across the warm, dusky-toned skin of her neck. The fragrance was dry, almost arid, like the smell of a desert flower, he imagined. Her thick hair seemed to shelter that scent, forcing it toward him in a heady rush, like a musky summer breeze. His head began to spin, a sudden buzzing that made him feel awkward and somewhat embarrassed. He was reminded again how difficult it was to focus when Kamber got this close.

Even though it felt good, it also had him confused, nervous, and slightly queasy. He pushed back from her.

"What's wrong?" Kamber asked. "Does this upset you?"

Jet stared into Kamber's glowing eyes, her face still close to his. There was a slight hesitation on her face but the hint of a smile, nonetheless. "No. It's just…I don't know. I've…never been this close before."

"Me neither. What's wrong with that?" she whispered. She was out of breath, too, and that made him want to cave into his feelings even more.

"I suppose…I just wonder if we should be doing this, you know? We have a lot of stuff coming up, a lot we need to stay focused on. If we have something going on, well, we might not make good decisions."

"Good decisions?" Kamber asked and pushed back a bit. "What's that supposed to mean?"

"Just that…I don't know," Jet stammered. "I didn't mean anything bad by that."

"Then what do you mean?" she persisted. She stared at him intently now, her arms crossed.

"Hold on, Kamber. I'm just saying that we need to be careful with the reveals coming up—"

"Careful? Is that how it is? You don't think I can handle more than one thing at a time?"

Jet sat back, wondering what had just happened. "I'm just saying…I'm not questioning…"

"Maybe I should go." Kamber stood to leave, and Jet pulled at her arm.

"Hold on, Kamber. Just…wait a second. Don't leave like this—"

"No, you're right," she interrupted. "I probably shouldn't have come here tonight."

Jet stood, partially blocking her path.

She gave him a meaningful look, then her mood softened. "Of course. You make a good point—we need to remain focused. I understand. But I'm my own person, and I can look after myself; I've been doing that my entire life, just like you. I know you want to protect me. You want to *save* everyone, it seems. But you have your own problems to deal with, Jet. I don't want you to feel responsible for me like you did with Cutter or Sylvant. You don't need that burden."

Jet shook his head. "That's not quite what I was trying to say either."

"Are you certain?" she asked. "You're still afraid someone you know might get hurt. That's why you're pushing me away. It's obvious, isn't it?"

Jet rubbed his head. "Believe me, I want to get to know you better, Kamber. A lot better, really. But I feel all…I don't know, like I can't think when you're around. And with all the stuff coming up, I…*we*…need to be really focused. We're talking about life and death. Had I been more focused on Cutter and Sylvant, maybe they'd still be here. I *can't* lose you like that. I have to be prepared. I have to make sure *you're* prepared and ready for what's to come."

"Jet. I'm not Cutter or Sylvant. I'm a Heliographi."

"I know and…" Jet paused to gather himself. He felt like he was rushing again and took a deep breath. "I'm sorry. I'm not trying to belittle you. I just can't help but feel responsible for you——"

"I am capable. You said it yourself."

"Yes, you are. Maybe you're a little too confident? You still have a lot to learn. I just want you to understand how dangerous all of this is. Why is that so wrong?"

"It's not, I suppose. And maybe I *do* need to be more cautious. I am afraid, but I won't let that fear of what might happen decide how I live my life right now, in the present. Maybe you should too?"

Jet held her gaze as the sun breached the horizon and sunlight flooded through the cloud cover. All was silent around them except the faint murmur of crickets in the background.

"I'll see you tomorrow, Jet. Happy birthday." Kamber gave him a weak smile and brushed past him without another word.

CHAPTER 11
Corridors of an Ancient Mind

ΑΒΓΔΕΖΗΘΙΚΛ**M**

ΝΞΟΠΡΣ ΥΦΧΨΩ

WITH JUST A few days until the first memoir's reveal, Jet and the other Lucem began preparing, each in their own way.

There was an ominous feeling around the abandoned control suite. With so many groups involved in the hunt, the odds were beginning to feel overwhelming. But their primary opposition would come from the Agency and Lybra. They had the troops, the equipment, and the money. Although there were some larger factions that *were* dangerous—like the Dreadnaughts of the ninth belt—most of the splinter cells or gangs seeking the memoirs didn't really pose a threat. Jet wondered again why most of the other groups would even risk being involved in this dangerous hunt. Then again, attaining one of the memoirs would bring a fortune, and the lure of that seemed to drive other seekers into the fray.

But also in the mix were the Atrum. Apparently, they were on their own and without the Tetrahedron Marauders, who, according to Joshia, had now joined Lybra. Between the Tetrahedron and the Agency's elite recon troops, the odds were unfortunately tipped against the Heliographi. True, the Heliographi were powerful. But the opposition starting to stack up against them was unnerving. These anxious feelings in Jet's gut gave him a bad vibe, one he couldn't clear his mind of.

Making sure the memoirs didn't fall into Lybra's hands was their primary goal, not just for the Lucem but the Atrum as well. At least they shared that common goal. To add to the uncertainty, they still had no idea what Albright's Key was meant to do. Did it truly offer them an advantage? No one knew, not even Cord.

Although Jet had several worries over the upcoming reveals, his greatest concern was Kamber's safety and making sure she was prepared, though it was now apparent he'd have to hide those feelings from her. He worried about Kamber more than he cared to admit, but after their talk, he knew she wouldn't allow him to hover over her like a guardian angel. It's the same way he would've reacted; he couldn't blame her for wanting to look after herself. It seemed he and Kamber were more alike than he'd realized, at least in that department.

He desperately wanted to be with her, though. Last night had been exhilarating, if not brief. Her skin, the smell of her fragrance, the intoxication of her touch…

Admitting these feelings to himself was hard. But telling Kamber why they shouldn't be getting so close had been even more difficult.

Have I inadvertently pushed her away?

He needed to clear his thoughts and focus on the dangerous tasks ahead and so did Kamber.

M

The night before the reveal, Jet made his way back to Firefly Falls. He wanted to clear his thoughts and get one last meditative session in, hopefully undisturbed this time.

When he arrived, the familiar setting greeted him— the fireflies, the sound of crashing water, the mysterious stillness in the air.

He sat down at the foot of Cutter's grave and immediately began to wonder why he'd been chosen to be a Lucem. He couldn't protect his loved ones, though he'd had plenty of time to develop his skills. Even Kamber, his warden who had just been converted, seemed to be developing at a much faster pace. She would likely surpass him. At that moment, he felt like the lowest rung in their order. Though he'd made great strides recently, these were powers he couldn't seem to harness—the ghost Lucem…the bizarre telekinetic pulse effect. How had he managed to summon them? He only remembered feeling tired and disoriented afterward, most likely the cost of their usage, he assumed.

Jet closed his eyes in frustration and pushed away his feelings of inadequacy for the moment. After what felt like hours, he was able to fall into a state of meditation. He followed his inner light as it galloped off across the cosmos. Just like he needed sleep, his inner light needed this time to recharge. And, once again, Jet began to hear voices. One stray voice caught his attention, though.

Had he just heard his old friend, Cutter?

He pulled away from his inner light and stopped and tried to turn and look behind him. Above and below was empty space with stars and galaxies beyond. There were random blurs flying all around him, ethereal and wispy, like static noise. But try as he might, he could not see behind him, only forward. He sensed there was someone behind him, though, a lingering presence. But he simply couldn't turn and look.

Then, something bright approached Jet. A glowing, vibrating being—a serpent-like bluish-green streak of light that slithered in his direction. It spoke his name.

STROUD!

Jet awoke instantly, and his eyes snapped open. He was so startled that he fell backward and lay there on the rocky shore trying to gain his bearings. He quickly sat forward and stood.

Someone stepped out from the shadows.

He instantly recognized the glowing bluish-green eyes. It was Vail.

She stopped near the rocky shore and stared at him. Jet stood his ground and stared back at her.

"How did you find this place?" he asked.

She shrugged and held out her hands, wrists skyward as if to say, *'there's nothing up my sleeves!'* Then she smiled at him with a devilish grin. "Does it matter? I know about Albright's Key and that you have it."

Jet lowered his gaze. "Forget it, Vail. You'll never get the key. I'll make sure of that."

"Will you, though? Just like you made sure the Atrum would never find the memoirs' locations? Just like you stopped us from planting the rare-earth devices?" Vail said this with a hint of sarcasm, but Jet noticed her glancing over at Cutter's grave.

"You miss him, don't you? You could have helped me save him. *Why* didn't you?"

Vail's expression seemed to cycle through several emotions: hatred, uncertainty, *anguish*. Her persona had grown darker, and for a moment, he wasn't sure who, or what, he was really talking to. Her blonde hair was still dyed blue and green at the tips but had grown longer and was woven into dreadlocks. Her pixie-like facial features were the same—dainty and petite. But her air of malice was undeniable. She radiated hatred, and Jet sensed that she'd grown powerful in the last four years.

"Are you here to talk about something specific?" he asked when she didn't answer.

Vail nodded and took a seat near Cutter's grave. Jet sensed her mood change slightly as she pulled her knees up and tucked them beneath her cloak. She stared at him, her glowing gaze unblinking. "What do you think about Joshia's proposal?"

"I assume we're talking off the record?"

"Sure."

"I think it's a smart approach. We're obviously outnumbered and outgunned."

"We've lost the Tetrahedron's support, Stroud. I assume you already knew that. The marauder army had a long-standing alliance with us. We were counting on their help to recover the memoirs. But that old hag, Lybra, is throwing so much money at them that they can't say no."

"Lybra's not stupid," Jet said. "She understands what it's going to take to get the memoirs. She has singlehandedly taken the Lucem's support away by offering President Harok enough money to complete Goliath's Gate. Our alliance with the Agency lasted a century. And now it appears she's done the same thing to the Atrum by taking the Tetrahedron Marauder army. Her original goal was to pit the Heliographi against each other. She nearly succeeded during the Century Eclipse."

"Has Solan changed her mind?" Vail asked. "She seemed upset when Joshia asked about an alliance between our groups."

Jet was trying to be cautious. He knew whatever he told Vail, she would most likely share with all the other Atrum. "It's evident that she doesn't trust you all, especially Joshia, for some reason. There's some past history between those two, and it must be something she can't move beyond. She hasn't shared anything about that yet."

"Stroud. As much as I hate to admit it, we're as good as dead if we don't join forces. You know that I'm right."

Jet took a deep breath and gave her a sidelong glance. "I agree. But Solan is our leader right now, and we stand behind her decision. If she says no, then it's no. Not much I can do about that."

"And what do the other Lucem think?"

"The same. But we stand united. If we fail, then we will fail together."

"It doesn't have to be that way, Stroud. There's another way around Solan."

Jet crossed his arms. "What are you getting at?"

"What if something were to happen to Solan? If you assumed control, you could make the right decision. You could save the Heliographi."

Jet glared at her in the dark. The moon shone across her face, highlighting her cheek bones and pale skin. Just then, she resembled a corpse, cold and fearful. "I hope you're not suggesting mutiny."

Vail shrugged. "It's an option, one that makes sense."

"That's not going to happen. If Solan changes her mind, I'll let you know. Until then, we're on our own, you and me."

"We can't win this way, Stroud. You're a fool if you don't do something now."

"It's not my call."

"We've done our own surveillance, just like you. We know about the M-Class mech units. Tomorrow will be our first loss. If any of us die, that's on Solan. Having Albright's Key won't save us."

"What do you know about Albright's Key?"

"Just that you'd better figure out how it works. We don't have much time. We're at war, Stroud. Lybra means to wipe out the Heliographi, and she won't stop until we're all dead."

"I see it the same way as you. Our enemy is Lybra. But while we're talking about our own groups, do you mind telling me where your leader is? I haven't seen Sybold since the night she tried to murder me at Skylight University."

"So what? She thought you were the Skylight Fallout. Guess everyone was wrong about that."

"Answer the question, Vail. Where is Sybold?"

"I can't say I'm the right person to answer that. Speaking of leaders, though, where are Albright and Tyberius?"

Jet shook his head as they both sat there silently, staring at each other. Jet knew he'd get nowhere with Vail. Why was he even trying? But then he knew why.

Because he cared for her. Of all the Atrum, he wanted to save her the most.

"Look, Vail, you and I both know why our groups should team up. But if we can't even be honest with each other, how is this ever going to work?"

"Honesty doesn't have to be a factor in this, Stroud."

"Really? You just expect Solan to 'take your word' that the Atrum won't stab us in the back at their first chance?"

"I could ask you the same question. Why should the Atrum trust the Lucem?"

Jet held up his hands in an 'I give up' gesture. "Fine, you know what? Forget it. But on a personal level, can you *at least* do me one favor? Help me understand who you are now. I get that you're not the same person, but I need to know what's going on in your head. If you ever want my help, and if we ever do team up, I need to know."

"You act like we're a group of deranged entities," Vail clapped back. Jet caught the familiar sarcasm in her voice and couldn't decide if she was really joking, though.

"I think we can agree that you're not the same person you once were. Can't you give me a little more insight? We were once friends. That's got to be worth something."

"I doubt you'd understand, Stroud. None of you Lucem would. Besides, I don't even know if I can explain it—"

"Try," Jet insisted. "For me. Please."

Vail sat on the stone, looking around her, then back to Cutter's grave, as if reminiscing about something. "The only way I could ever convey this is through Vishmu. I only offer this because we were once friends. I'm not sure you're gonna like it, Stroud."

"Any negative effects to be aware of, assuming I agree to this?"

"I'm not the one who makes that determination. If your Heliographi can't take the heat, then it'll let you know. Otherwise, I imagine it will reject the effort before we connect."

"Swear on it. Swear that you won't try anything…swear on Cutter's grave." Jet held out his hand to her.

"Why would I?" she shot back. "I don't care if you can't handle it! I'm not the one asking for this. You are."

"If you ever want my help, then you'll do this."

"Are you saying that you have the authority to accept Joshia's offer?"

"No, not at the moment. But I have some sway with Solan, though. She'll listen to me if I push. I might be able to help. So, what's it gonna be?"

Vail thought for a moment, her legs curled into her cloak and her glowing eyes looking up at the full moon above. She stood, pulling her cloak back and her hands forward. "Fine. Don't say I didn't warn you, Stroud."

Jet walked over to stand in front of her. "Let's do this."

Vail looked a bit nervous for the first time as she stood directly in front of him. She shook both her hands as if in preparation, then reached up slowly and placed her fingers on Jet's forehead. "Do the same," she said, and Jet did. "Let your thoughts go, like you're meditating," Vail continued, her voice drifting off as they stood close together.

Jet felt the world around him fade away. The ground fell, and a menacing sky enveloped him in a darkness so black that it made him feel nauseous. Mist swirled about his feet, and he seemed to float. He sensed Vail's presence near him, guiding him. He felt a sudden touch of fear. *If she let go of him now, he was surely lost! A drifting soul, wandering the cosmos forever.*

They roamed dark corridors of some ancient mind. Perhaps those foreboding chambers were Vail's essence, plagued by supernatural beings, all screaming to be set free. There were thousands, perhaps millions, of ancient souls lingering in the inky darkness beyond. Jet held a small light, one that was allowed only by Vail. He felt cold and weak and helpless, like he'd never see the sun again. The anger of the ever-present beings nearby weighed on Jet, bringing him down into a pit of despair. He hated the feeling, like he couldn't breathe. He was slowly being suffocated.

Just when he was about to lose consciousness, he was back, standing on the rocky shore. The sound of the waterfall crashing over the edge of the cliff filled his ears and grounded him back in reality.

Jet sat down heavily and buried his head in his hands, trying to regain his bearings. His head spun with the gravity of what he'd just witnessed. It was like waking from a horrific nightmare and realizing it had only been a dream. Except it wasn't…not for Vail.

"I'm always in a state of darkness, Stroud. I can control it sometimes, at least long enough to have conversations like this. But it's never long until the darkness claws its way back to the surface. It needs to feed, that darkness. It needs to feel fear and anger and lust…*death*. I'm just a vessel, I think. At times, it takes control, and I'm not even aware. Can you understand now?"

Jet could only nod. He'd had no idea. Had he and the other Lucem wrongly judged the Atrum? Now that he'd had a glimpse, he was starting to reassess how he felt.

And what he felt was pity.

What Vail was dealing with right now wasn't something she had asked for. The hatred and anger being driven into her by whatever being this was seemed inconceivable. Was it in control? It had sure felt that way to him, and Vail was only there as a vessel—it was just as she had claimed. If the Atrum's *essence*, or inner light, had control, then there was probably no way to break free of it. The darkness of the Atrum's light was a counterbalance to the Lucem's light.

"I'm sorry, Vail. I had no idea. I think I understand now."

She looked vulnerable for just an instant, like the Vail of old, who had been fragile, defiant. But it was quickly replaced by a darkness that seemed to descend around her.

"Can you break free?" Jet asked. "I'll help you if I can."

Vail smirked, then chuckled. "No. It would kill me and look for another host. Mention this to no one, Stroud. I warn you." Vail looked around the glen one last time. "I'll see you tomorrow. Prepare yourself."

Vail cloaked and vanished.

CHAPTER 12
Final Preparations

ΑΒΓΔΕΖΗΘΙΚΛ**Μ**

ΝΞΟΠΡΣ ΥΦΧΨΩ

DAWN BROKE THE next day with Cord hammering on Jet's door.

He rose and wrapped his cloak about him. Jet woke Kamber in the room next to his, and the three of them met in the main control suite where the other Lucem had gathered to wait for Solan.

Ti-Leer sat in his chair, feet dangling and tousled hair like a mop covering his eyes. His head lay on the table as he slept. Jet guessed he'd had another long night of drinking, something DiJinn frowned upon but said very little about. He assumed she'd simply given up trying to change him and moved on. The other Lucem sat silently, a nervous tension in the air. They were aware of the dangerous day ahead, just as he was. This was the start of the hunt for Albright's Memoirs. At the end of today, they would know a lot more about where they stood in the hunt. For now, their focus was on keeping the first memoir out of Lybra's hands.

Solan finally entered and pulled up the three-dimensional display and a map of the first reveal site. "Let's go over the plan again," Solan said. "I've had more time to study this 'arena.' I've been over there multiple times in the past few days, and I've seen no clues indicating where the memoir might reveal itself."

"We can only assume it'll appear at the specified time," Cord said.

"By magic? Out of thin air?" DiJinn asked. "C'mon, there's gotta be somethin' more to it."

"Guess we'll have to wait and see what Albright has in store for everyone," Harriet said.

"I want everyone there early," Solan said and gazed at them each in turn. "I know it's right here on the first belt, but it may take a while to get there. Remember, it'll be a packed house, and there are groups already camped out."

Ti-Leer suddenly woke. He ran a hand through his tangled hair and sat up. He slapped himself a few times, trying to sober up. "This is no longer a hunt for a wee bit of parchment. Make no mistake, we're at war. It's exciting, isn't it? I miss this feelin'! Time to strap on your armor, lads."

"Take it easy, Ti," Booker said. "There'll be plenty of time for fightin'. Stay focused."

"Booker's right," Solan said. "We need to remain calm and levelheaded. We have no idea what today will bring, and if we can avoid battle, then we should. I've asked each of you to visit the site. You should all be familiar with it by now."

"Everyone *has* to stay cloaked," Annaka said. "The word is out about us; I assume you all know that. The legend of the Heliographi is over. Someone has revealed our existence, and the Agency has placed a bounty on us. We are classified as an outlaw group of mercenaries now. If caught, you'll be jailed, or worse."

"'Specially with Lybra in Harok's ear," DiJinn added. "Won't be long till she takes over that operation, I imagine."

Jet stood. "There's more to it. I paid a visit to the Hall of Vital Records a few nights ago—"

"You did what?" DiJinn asked. "You can't go back there, Jet. That's too close to the Agency and Lybra!"

"Hold on, Jinn," Solan said. "Jet…what is it?"

"Remember the new M-Class mech units? It was a prototype program, but the Agency halted it because of funding. They were forced to since Goliath's Gate was so expensive. But with Lybra, the M-Class program is back online. I saw several of them already up and functional. What I saw worries me."

Solan looked at Jet with her arms crossed. The room was silent for a few seconds. "Tell us what you saw."

"These aren't the old clunky ones we're used to seeing. These mech units are much quicker. In fact, they practically rival our ability, it seemed. The weapon array was staggering too. If they're planning on mass producing these things, then I don't know who can stand against them. Harok and Lybra won't need an army of mercenaries or recon troops. These mechs will fulfill their needs."

"She's building them the way she wants them, and not by the Agency's standard," Cord said. "That's my guess. She wants to eradicate the Heliographi. I'm afraid she's modified the M-Class specs for one purpose. To hunt down and kill us."

"Are you sure about that?" Solan asked.

"It's an extrapolation on my part—"

"A what?" DiJinn asked. "Speak English, Cord."

"An educated guess," Cord replied. "Anyway, the new mech units use rare-earth. You asked why Lybra was stockpiling all that rare-earth. Well, there's your answer."

"Now it all makes sense…" Jet said. "Sure, the Agency still needs it to finish Goliath's Gate. But I imagine Lybra's still holding Harok hostage over those supplies."

Annaka crossed her arms. "Well, there's not much we can do about it right now—"

"I respectfully disagree, Annaka," Cord interrupted. "We need to focus on taking down those operations where they're making those mech units. In fact, I'd say it may be as important as attaining the memoirs. If we don't, and she builds an army of these mechs, none of us will be around for very long."

"So, now we have two pressing issues?" DiJinn said. "We're already limited. We don't have the numbers!"

Solan looked around the room. "I know what you're all thinking, but the answer is still no. I will not place our hopes in the Atrum. They're as untrustworthy as Lybra and will stab us in the back at the first chance they get."

"Are you letting your distrust in Joshia cloud your decision?" Jet asked.

Solan glared at him, and he could see she was struggling to remain calm. "We've been over this too many times. Let's just focus on the memoirs for now. The reveal is tonight, and we must be ready, no distractions. Got it?"

Jet held her gaze for several seconds as the entire room remained silent. Everyone seemed to be holding their breath. Then he let his momentary frustration ease with a deep sigh and nodded. "Understood."

Solan finally blinked, then looked around the room again, as if to say, 'anyone else?' Then she walked over to the display again. "We'll remain spread out and work in groups of two, as usual. Kamber, you're with me. Jet's with Ti-Leer. Cord, you and Harriet. Jinn's with Booker. Annaka, I want you to stay near the lower entry with Shiloe. You're our safety valve. If someone else gets the memoir, you'll need to stop them."

"Who's going to carry Albright's Key?" Cord asked.

"Ti-Leer," Solan said without hesitation.

"What?" Jinn asked. "Hell, he's drunk half the time!"

"I'm fine!" Ti-Leer said, and rose to his feet, then held out a hand to steady himself. "Just…need a minute…there we go, easy does it!"

"Fine, then!" Jinn said, stood, and shoved her chair in. The sound echoed around the room as she left without a word.

Solan followed her, dismissing everyone. "Get to the site early and be prepared."

Jet followed Cord as they left the meeting.

"Cord, hold on a minute." Jet pulled at his shoulder, and Cord turned to face him as the other Lucem left. Jet waited till they were alone. "I need to tell you something. I didn't want to share it with the others yet."

Cord turned to face him, a quizzical expression on his face. "This about the reveal tonight?"

"No, it's about my visit to the Hall of Vital Records." Jet pondered, trying to formulate his words. He was even beginning to wonder if he should share any of it at this point. Everyone needed to be focused on the reveal tonight, but Cord had been his go-to when he needed advice, and he wanted to hear his thoughts. But how much should he share? Just the part about the ghost Lucem? Hearing Cutter's voice? *The feeling that some dark secret lie hidden within the hall?*

"What is it?" Cord asked, noting Jet's expression.

"There's something odd going on about that place, but I can't quite put a finger on it. I've always felt the Hall of Vital Records seemed out of place like it was scooped up and placed there from some ancient burial site."

"That should go without saying," Cord mused. "Many of Albright's creations are difficult to understand."

Jet nodded. "It does have that feel. It's an odd place. When I meditate there, I feel a stronger connection, like my Vishmu is magnified. I don't get that feeling anywhere else…it's something I can't explain. But that's not what I'm talking about. When I was there, that ghost Lucem showed up again. It's just as I thought. He *was* the previous Lucem who carried my symbol. His name was Brindall, and he died on a mission. Now he's trying to tell me something, I just can't figure out what it is."

"Don't tell me you're going back there again. Jet, it's too dangerous now."

"You know I won't settle until I figure this out. Whatever this ghost is trying to tell me, it has to do with the Hall of Vital Records. I think I *have* to be there to figure this out. Whatever this presence is trying to tell me, it must be important."

Cord thought for a moment. "You know I have great respect for you. Your intuition is one of your strengths. If you feel this is important, then I believe you. My advice is to wait, though."

"I can't wait too long. Something is urging me back. There's something about that place, something special."

Cord gripped Jet by the shoulders and looked him in the eyes. "If you won't wait, then just promise me you won't go alone. If you get caught by the Agency, they will not take it easy on you. Find me and tell me before you go, won't you?"

Jet held Cord's gaze, considering. "Sure," Jet said reluctantly, knowing full well that he wouldn't tell Cord.

He sensed that Cord knew it too.

CHAPTER 13
The First Reveal
May 17, 2286, A.D.

ΑΒΓΔΕΖΗΘΙΚΛ**Μ**
ΝΞΟΠΡΣ ΥΦΧΨΩ

LATER THAT DAY, Jet made his way to the reveal site.

It was on the opposite side of the first belt, and according to the coordinates, the first Heliographi Memoir would be revealed at 2:00 PM somewhere near that location. He felt a bit guilty about not making it to the site earlier. Most of the other Lucem had done their own reconnaissance, where he'd spent his time chasing ghosts at the Hall of Vital Records. He knew he'd have to do better and spend more time researching the sites of future reveals.

Jet took the forest passages under cover of darkness. Each Lucem found their own way there, where they met near the entry into the subterranean chamber. The Clipton Woods were busy that day, with groups of memoir seekers making their way to the reveal site. Jet remained cloaked, watching the groups with some interest as they marched through the forest, making quite a bit of noise. He sensed no real organization amongst the clans. Most of them wore matching armor or insignias, and he assumed many wouldn't make it out alive. He was half tempted to try and persuade them to drop out. *These seekers have no idea what they were stepping into*, he thought. They would only cause congestion. The Lucem's real challenge would be the Atrum and the Agency.

Things were complicated for the Lucem now. They would have to use caution not to injure any of these seekers, if possible, where the Atrum wouldn't be burdened by such things. He also wondered if the Agency would use caution. If Lybra was truly running the show, then more seekers would probably die, Jet assumed.

But in the back of his mind, he wondered how things would really work out. What chance did any one of these groups really have of attaining all nine of the memoirs? More than likely, the memoirs would end up divided between the three major groups: the Atrum, the Lucem, and the Agency. The Agency had the numbers between the Tetrahedron and the elite recon forces. The Heliographi were in for an uphill battle. He just hoped that things wouldn't turn too violent tonight. But the anxious feeling in the pit of his gut whispered otherwise.

He remained cloaked as he paced the raucous groups. The sounds of the forest grew hushed as they approached. As Cord had mentioned, there was a large air vent poking through the belt's surface. The vegetation and underbrush had been cleared away. The large grates had been swung open, and the groups entered the gateway. Jet found a separate portal that led to the underground tunnels of Lyrinthum and disappeared. The hidden passage led to the reveal site, and he snuck forward for a glance inside.

The space Albright had designed for the reveal site was vast.

The chamber was spherical in shape and deep below the Clipton Woods. Jet guessed the chamber was perhaps a kilometer in diameter, with hundreds of levels ringing the side walls. There were also hundreds of catwalks spanning the space. The steel was rusted and gray, the lighting dim. Large pipes for utilities, plumbing, and water ran across the globe, with large building foundations woven into the structure. The chamber was alive with commotion. The shouting and yelling reverberated throughout the space. Cord had been right; this was a death pit.

But it was the Agency's forces that caught his attention. They dominated the middle portion of the globe. Most of the troops were Tetrahedron Marauders, with the elite recon troops around the perimeter. The two maintained their distance. Neither the Recon nor the Tetrahedron liked each other since they were on different sides of the spectrum. Where the recon troops were disciplined and trained, the Tetrahedron were unruly and clumsy. But Jet could see that what the marauders lacked in training, they made up for in quantity. The Tetrahedron were loyal to the money backer, which happened to be Lybra, and they would do her bidding without question.

Jet crept back into the shadows as other groups began to fill the vast chamber.

Jet felt Cord bump him.

"Looks like a friendly gathering of folks, no?" he murmured in his slow drawl.

Behind Cord were the other Lucem, their silhouettes barely visible in the dark.

"I feel bad for a lot of these seekers," Jet whispered back. "Some of these people aren't making it out of here alive."

"Don't be so sure," Booker growled. "Some of these outfits are capable. I see several of the larger, more dangerous clans here. In their mind, they have just as good a shot as any of us. Either way, as soon as the memoir appears, all hell's gonna break loose in here."

"Don't put it past Albright to throw something tricky at us, lads," Ti-Leer chimed in. "Keep your wits about you."

"I just wonder why he did it this way?" Jet whispered. "Surely, he knew a lot of people would die."

"I have no clue," Cord replied. "Once again, expect the unexpected from Albright."

Groups continued to gather inside the chamber until it was packed. The Lucem remained cloaked and hidden in a small corridor looking in as the space filled.

"Look, up there…" DiJinn whispered.

Jet looked overhead to see something shimmer beyond, a barely detectible movement several levels above them. "Atrum," she whispered.

"Looks like all of them, too," Jet hissed.

Solan gathered them a short way down the tunnel. "Remember, stick to pairs. As soon as the memoir reveals itself, get to it and out as quickly as possible. She turned to Ti-Leer. "Do you have the key ready in case we need it?"

Ti-Leer lumbered forward, his lime-green glowing eyes blinking in the dark. "I got it, right here…" He patted his cloak, hesitated, then began searching his other pockets. "Wait, hold on a tick…oh, right. Here's the wee bugger." Ti-Leer brought out Albright's Key, and it lit the tunnel in a dim multicolored light.

"Better not lose it!" DiJinn hissed. "We can't afford any gaffs."

"You worry 'bout yourself, lass!" But Ti-Leer quickly put the key away when DiJinn glared at him in the dark.

Solan checked the time. "Let's move into position. Stay in your group, watch your backs, and keep safe. Kamber, you're with me."

Solan and Kamber moved out, cloaked and silent. Jet stood next to Ti-Leer as Cord and Harriet also moved out of the tunnel. DiJinn and Booker fell in behind and scaled up the catwalks to the opposite side of the arena.

Ti-Leer stifled a silent belch and rubbed his forearm across his lips. "Let's have some fun, lad," he said, and Jet followed him out of the tunnel, leaving Annaka and Shiloe behind as backup.

Jet and Ti-Leer scaled the walls of the arena to get near the top. There was no need to remain silent now with the sounds from all the other groups reverberating around the space. Once Jet and Ti-Leer had reached their spot, they settled in and waited. Jet wrapped himself in his cloak and settled back as Ti-Leer reached into his cloak and pulled out a silver flask. He pressed his thumb to a lock, then he whispered to it, a password, Jet assumed. The lid flipped open, and Ti-Leer held the flask to his nose and breathed deeply.

Jet chuckled. "That's a lot of effort for a drink. Why all the security measures?"

"Everyone's tryin' to get at my stash, 'specially D.J. I tell you, that lass has it in for me drinks. She finds them and empties 'em out!"

Jet smirked and shook his head. "Ti, don't you think you should hold off until the reveal is over?"

"Why wait?" Ti-Leer took a quick swig, trying to hide the flask as he did so. "I may not make it past this reveal. Hopefully, that's the case…hopefully."

Jet gave him a confused look. "What? Why would you say that?"

"No matter, lad. You just stay focused—"

"No," Jet said and faced Ti-Leer. "Tell me what you mean by that."

"Ah…forget it!" Ti-Leer hissed. "Shouldn't have said nothing."

"Why, Ti?" Jet continued.

Ti-Leer held the flask up. "You're persistent, you know that?"

Jet held Ti-Leer's gaze as he waited, then crossed his arms.

Ti-Leer finally grunted and blinked from the stare down and waved at Jet. "Ah, fine!"

"Fine…go on."

"You ever loved anyone, Stroud? I imagine not. You're too young. Youngster!" Ti-Leer laughed, but Jet sensed the hurt underneath it.

"Yeah," Jet said, somewhat uncertainly, though. "As a matter of fact, I have. What about it?"

"Someone who isn't Heliographi? Have you loved a mortal?"

Jet pursed his lips. "Yeah, a good friend of mine."

"Think it through, lad." Ti-Leer seemed to sober up suddenly, and his face turned rigid. "What if Cutter had lived, and you two had been friends till the end. Then, you watched him die, as he grows old, feeble…while you remain young and hale."

Jet considered, and suddenly, he realized what Ti-Leer was getting at. "You've outlived a loved one, haven't you?"

Ti-Leer clenched his jaw, his lip quivered, and a tear brimmed on his lower eyelash. "This ain't a gift, as they tell you, being immortal. It's a curse, *laddie*. The ones we love grow old and die, and we are made to sit an' watch it happen. Age cripples them, and all the power we have…not a thing we can do to help. It's cruel, don't you think?"

It was the first time Jet had thought about it. Of course, he was so new to this, and there were so many other things on his mind that he hadn't had time to consider all the implications of becoming an immortal, a Heliographi. Then again, Ti-Leer had been around much longer. Jet could see now that his happy-go-lucky personality was just a façade. The drinking was there to cover his wounds, like some poor band-aid. A sudden pity hit Jet in the gut.

"Ti. I'm sorry," Jet said. "I hadn't really thought about it like that."

But Ti-Leer looked away. "Ah, go on. No need to say that. We got each other, right! That's what we got. We got our eternal family now. And you got Kamber, I think." Ti-Leer gave him a wink.

Jet nodded and thought about Kamber, thought about the feelings he had for her along with the worries that accompanied those feelings now. She was out there in the masses somewhere, but at least she was with Solan. Jet was placing all his hope in Solan to keep her safe, yet he couldn't help thinking about Cutter and what had happened to him.

He sat back again as Ti-Leer muttered to himself, slapping his own face a few times in the process, then took another swig from his flask. "Don't mention this to D.J., won't you? There's a good lad."

They both remained silent, each wrapped in their own thoughts. Ti-Leer muttered to himself as Jet tried to refocus on the reveal, which was nearly upon them. It appeared that every faction in the system was there now, and the vast arena was filled to capacity. At the upper portion, he could see the Agency, and near the front were the Tetrahedron. In contrast, the recon soldiers stood near the back and a good distance from the marauder army. But he could see no sign of President Harok or Lybra from his vantage. No one knew what to expect, but Jet wondered if this first reveal would set a precedence for the future reveals.

With just a few minutes to go, the Agency made their move. The Tetrahedron Marauders began fighting, most likely to create a distraction. Since they were the largest group in the hunt, it was difficult to ignore them. It was obvious they'd planned this out in advance. The bellowing began, and the sound of rail guns chattered off the hardened walls and steel catwalks.

"The deathmatch is on, lad," Ti-Leer whispered. "Better buckle up."

As the groups on the upper half of the orb began to fight, Jet and Ti-Leer held their position and remained cloaked and hidden.

Then, Jet saw something glimmering in the darkness. At first, he thought it might be the reveal starting. But the shape solidified into a mech unit. In fact, it was an M-Class mech, just like the ones he'd seen at the Agency headquarters. It shot into the middle of the arena, then stopped and hovered there. The mech had the same armament as the others; a large howitzer cannon on one shoulder and a smaller chain gun on the other. It used a laser to pinpoint and target other gangs around the arena and spun like it was on a pivot. The mech moved fluidly and aimed with deadly precision. One of the howitzer rounds hit the section where Jet and Ti-Leer waited, and they were forced to leap over the railing. Jet landed several meters below on another catwalk but didn't see where Ti-Leer had landed.

Then the reveal began.

A loud chiming rang out, as if some grand announcement was about to commence. A black light sprang from the very center of the arena, close to the hovering mech. It glowed in an odd fashion, like dark matter exploding into nothingness. The dark light intensified, and a loud thunderous sound boomed around the arena. It went on for several minutes as the fighting continued to build like a storm crashing around them. In the flood of bodies, Jet lost sight of the other Lucem. He saw several Atrum spring upward toward the top of the arena, leaping great distances. A flood of seekers clambered up the catwalks.

I need to get to higher ground! Jet thought. He gripped the railing, planted his feet, and heaved himself up to the next catwalk, then repeated it. He needed to be at the highest catwalk to achieve the proper angle. The leap would be dangerous, but it was the only way to get to the memoir.

Jet quickly worked his way up the tiered catwalks, hurtling from level to level. He could see the other Heliographi doing the same, and it was a race to the top. Had they known, they could have brought a small skiff or hover packs. Once again, Albright had surprised everyone, except the Agency, it seemed.

Near the top, the fighting was the most intense. Almost everyone was climbing in that direction. Jet managed to reach the top, but soon there were so many people that he was forced to engage the other groups. It was simply too packed to find a clear spot.

Jet fought and hurled people out of his way, trying to find an area to make the leap.

Through the fighting, Jet finally saw President Harok and Lybra. Both sat inside an armored skiff. Harok appeared to be sending orders to the recon troops while Lybra commanded the marauders. But it was the M-Class mech that continued to dominate the battlefield. Its cannon and chain gun mowed down everyone standing in its path. It spun so quickly that anyone caught near it was tossed violently to the side. The large mech hovered toward the black memoir as others jumped and clambered onto its back. But nothing seemed to affect it, as seekers were tossed aside and dropped to the ground far below.

Jet thought about what to do. If he leapt on top of the mech, he'd probably fall, just like the others. He didn't know if he had the ability to slow its whirling arms. Its armor was constructed of reinforced graphene—he wouldn't be able to penetrate the surface.

As he stood there, trying to think what to do, something blurry hurled toward the mech. It was Harriet. She was attempting to do what he had just been considering. Harriet was one of the older, more accomplished Heliographi. Everyone was about to find out how tough these new mechs really were.

Jet fought his way closer, still looking for a clearing to leap from and join Harriet. Several other Heliographi raced in Harriet's direction too. But with all the groups battling for position, no one was able to reach her. The mech slowed its whirring arms, forced to engage Harriet now.

It didn't take long to see she was outmatched by the mech, though. Jet felt a moment of panic as he struggled to fight through the crowd. Harriet grasped the mech's arm and wrenched up on it. But the mech had four arms and used its other two to pry her off. It held her there, suspended in midair as they floated in the center of the arena. Jet watched in horror, his heart racing as he scrambled and flung people out of the way. His goal of getting to the memoir first was forgotten now. Harriet needed help.

But there were just too many obstacles in the way, and the mech was nearly to the center now. The memoir shone like a black star, pulsating in slow bursts. Its dark light bathed the arena, casting a menacing ambiance around the space and lighting up all the fighting with strobing flashes.

Harriet screamed in pain as the mech held her with three of its arms. Jet glanced at Lybra and witnessed the grin on her face. She appeared to be in control of the mech and seemed to be considering her options.

Then, in an unceremonious gesture, the mech reached up and grabbed Harriet by the neck and squeezed. It took only a few seconds, and Harriet went limp.

The mech dropped Harriet, and her lifeless body fell from sight and into the mass of seekers below.

Jet felt a scream rip from his throat as he watched the mech zip toward the black light. It reached into the center of the light and pulled out something that looked like a tube. It glowed in kind, similar to Albright's Key.

The mech unit tucked the tube into a compartment. Its propulsion system roared, and it shot up and out of the arena, leaving the fighting behind. Lybra and Harok's vehicle hovered higher, then followed the mech out of the chamber and into the misty sky above.

The fighting continued around them as the black light in the center of the arena dissipated and extinguished. It grew dark as the noise of battle continued around them. Jet was suddenly backed into a wall and had masses of groups fighting in front of him. He felt himself being crushed by the weight and was struggling to breathe. He focused some energy and felt his fingers begin to tingle. He let a pulse erupt from his palms, and the bodies near him scattered like an explosion. Suddenly, he was free.

"We need to find Harriet's body!" Ti-Leer said. "Get yourself out of here, lad. I'll take care of it!"

Jet sprang over the catwalk and dropped into the lower tiers. He pushed through seekers while sending out thoughts to other Lucem. He heard Cord respond and finally located him.

"We need to get Harriet," Jet said.

"Someone already did," Cord responded. "We need to evacuate. There's too many!"

Jet and Cord eventually found their way back to the lower tunnel and located the rest of the Lucem already there, waiting. Jet looked around, noticing that nearly all of them had sustained some sort of injury except Annaka and Shiloe. Ti-Leer held Harriet's body.

"Let's move!" Solan snapped and hammered the side of the tunnel's metal wall hard enough to crumple it.

The Lucem raced from the tunnel and found their way back to Lyrinthum before finally slowing. Everyone marched silently back to the control suite. Jet wondered if they all felt the same way he did. He'd tried so hard to reach Harriet and wondered why she'd taken on the mech alone.

But then he knew why.

She'd underestimated the new M-Class mech.

There was no way in Skylight they stood a chance against the new mech units. And there had only been one mech there tonight. Lybra had a whole army of them coming, and the skies would soon be filled with them.

CHAPTER 14
Close to Home

EVERYONE ENTERED THE control room and sat quietly at the table.

Ti-Leer continued to hold Harriet's body in his arms as he sat in her chair. No one spoke a word for several minutes. Jet looked to Solan and waited for her, wondering how she'd handle this setback.

"Ti-Leer. Take her to my quarters and return quickly. We need to talk," Solan said.

Ti-Leer stood and left, returning a few minutes later with Harriet's ring and cloak. He set them on the table in front of Solan and sat down.

"What now?" DiJinn asked. Jet heard the hint of emotion in her voice and realized some of the other Lucem had known Harriet for decades, unlike him, Cord, and Kamber. Normally, DiJinn would have been screaming and kicking. But she was unusually reserved, considering the situation. Instead, Ti-Leer was the one raging uncontrollably.

"This hits too close to home, Solan!" Ti-Leer roared and stood, marching around the room. He hammered the walls with his fists, leaving dents in the metal hull. Jet had never seen Ti-Leer worked up like this before.

"Lybra's mechs are stronger than I realized," Solan agreed, her voice light and pensive. Her expression remained stoic, but he sensed that she, too, was rattled. Jet could tell that, once again, Solan was second-guessing herself. Decision-making was something she had struggled with since assuming control of the Lucem. She had been hard on herself, taking some of their bad fortunes personally. *Too personally*, Jet had thought. In his opinion, Solan had done just fine. But she was a perfectionist and didn't like failure. Taking control of the Lucem for her father wasn't something she had wanted or felt comfortable with.

"Just one of those ungodly things could wipe us all out!" Ti-Leer continued ranting. "Suddenly, we've got bigger problems than the Atrum or the memoirs!"

"Solan," Jet said and leaned forward. "This should be the answer we need. I think it's time to reconsider Joshia's offer."

But Solan sat with her head bowed, staring at Harriet's cloak and ring in front of her. Ti-Leer stood and tossed Albright's Key onto the table. It clattered and rolled to a spot near the middle. "I guess this thing is useless after all!" he shouted. "All that effort, and it's worthless!"

"We don't know that yet," Jet said.

"Don't we, though?" Ti-Leer bellowed, still worked up. His face was bright red, and his beard almost seemed to bristle in the dim light. "The bloody robot took the memoir *without* the key and just flew off!"

Jet stood and picked up the glowing key. He gazed at it. "It has a purpose, but apparently not the one we thought it was. Albright didn't do anything unintentionally. We've already learned that lesson several times."

"Where do we go from here?" DiJinn asked. "Our numbers continue to dwindle. Albright, Tyberius, now Harriet. And Shiloe's too young to go through conversion. Now these flying can openers are as big a concern as anything. At this rate, there won't be any of us left to see the ninth reveal." DiJinn stood and leaned against the wall. Jet watched her skin flush red to match her hair, and her fists balled. Finally, her anger was starting to seep through her shock. "That old crone is gonna pay!"

"Take it easy, Jinn," Solan said and took a deep breath. "That's exactly what Lybra wants us to do. We can't take the bait. This is a marathon; we'll take it one reveal at a time. Jet, to answer your question about joining the Atrum, the answer is still no."

Jet stared at her, not believing what he'd just heard. "I don't understand. You saw what the mech did to Harriet. We don't stand a chance against even one mech, and there's an army of them on the way. The new mechs are a game changer. Not acknowledging that right now could spell doom for all of us. We need something to boost our chances—"

Solan glared at Jet, and he paused mid-sentence and crossed his arms. He sat back and looked up at the ceiling. Joining forces with the Atrum was the logical thing to do, especially after what they'd seen tonight. In fact, it might be their only option right now. Something was still bothering Solan about Joshia. *But what could be so bad that she was willing to sacrifice everything!*

"Get some rest, everyone," Solan said, still holding Jet's gaze. "We'll regroup in the morning."

"What about Harriet?" Ti-Leer asked.

Solan glanced down at the cloak and the ring in her hands again. "I'll take care of it. It's my responsibility."

Jet stood and stormed out of the control room, not looking back.

He ran out through Lyrinthum, then up through the Clipton Forest and into the night. He sprinted along the forest pathways, thinking about Harriet, about Solan. Things were only getting worse the longer he stayed in the Lucem, and the death of Harriet was a stark reminder of how bad things might get. Death seemed to follow him everywhere now. *Who was next?*

He ran for what seemed like hours before finally entering the hidden glen of Firefly Falls. He sat at the foot of Cutter's grave and stared at it. He closed his eyes and bowed his head, thinking about his friend.

What would Cutter do?

Jet could almost hear Cutter's voice, speaking his disapproval—*I'd never quit. I'm disappointed in you…*

But Jet just didn't see much hope at the moment. He only wished Cutter was there, just to talk to. He could use some of his encouragement. But Cutter was gone forever.

Jet looked up to see Kamber walking through the glen and stood to greet her.

"Sorry about that," he said. "I didn't mean to storm off. It just seems like Solan isn't seeing the whole picture right now."

Kamber walked over and took his hand, then sat down, pulling him with her.

"I get that sense too. She seems to be holding on to some grudge against Joshia. Whatever it is, it's clouding her thoughts. Even I can see that much. But maybe

Solan is right in being cautious. It's apparent the Atrum are ruthless. Just look at all the people they killed at the Century Eclipse. Even if they were just doing Lybra's bidding, it's hard to put too much trust in someone who can do that."

Jet sat quietly, then nodded. "You're right. I know the Atrum are dangerous. But they are an enemy of Lybra's now, which makes them an ally. As odd as it sounds, I think we can work with them but still be cautious. I don't see another way forward; this may be our only option at the moment. No one else is rushing to join us. We have no army in this fight. After seeing what just happened, marching into the next reveal would be insane. It'll result in the same outcome. Surely Solan knows that."

Kamber continued to hold his hand and stared at the fireflies, the sound of the Clipton River roaring in the background. She closed her glowing eyes and took a deep breath. "Do you remember the first night I met you here when you revealed yourself to me?"

Jet smiled. "How could I forget? You surprised me. I expected you to be shocked. Instead, it was like you'd already known me for years."

"And I felt as if I had. Isn't that odd? I had seen you in my dreams for so long. I knew we were supposed to meet…that we were *destined* to meet." She gripped his hand and looked into his eyes.

"Kamber…" he said, then grimaced and looked away.

"What is it?"

Jet took a deep breath and started over. "What we're facing, this war that's coming…"

She tensed, her jaw clenched as she stared at him. He waited for her frustration to boil over, like it had the last time they'd talked. But she remained calm.

"I don't know," he continued. "I guess maybe…I'm still afraid of losing my friends, losing you. I know how you feel about that. I respect that you *are* capable. I get that. But I can't stop thinking about it. I'm sorry."

Kamber held his hand and looked into his eyes. She nodded, waiting for him to continue.

"That day, on Chroma, when Cutter died, it was the most helpless I've ever felt. I don't want to feel that again."

"Of course you don't. But that *wasn't* your fault," Kamber said. "Look, I believe in destiny. What happened was meant to be. Even if you could go back and change something, destiny would find a way to rectify it. There is nothing you could have done in this universe to prevent those things from happening."

"How can you know that?"

"I just do. It's something that I've always known."

"I'm…just not sure I believe that."

She squeezed his hand. "Jet. I know it's not much, but take some peace in knowing that it was their time, no matter what you think you could have done to save them."

Jet held her gaze for a few seconds, then stared up at the waterfall and the light from the fireflies surrounding them.

"Look at me, Jet." She reached up to touch his face, letting her hand linger on his cheek.

Jet felt something tug at his soul. His heart raced as he returned her gaze. She was beautiful, her face kind and warm. *Innocent.* Not ready for war—not prepared for the harshness they would soon face. They had both grown up in difficult conditions, faced harsh treatment. In a sense, they were both hardened. But Kamber was fresh to this new world. As much as he wanted to protect her, to shelter her from the brutality to come, he wasn't sure he should. Besides, Kamber had already made that decision for him. She didn't want his help because…

…*because she didn't want him to suffer in case she died.*

He could almost hear her whispering the truth to him; *it will be up to destiny to decide what happens to me.*

But he would never stop feeling responsible for her, despite what she might want. After all, his best friend, Cutter, had given his life to save her. Such a sacrifice wasn't easily tossed aside. He owed that much to Cutter.

He hadn't faced such a difficult decision in a long time: Be next to Kamber and enjoy her company or ignore her request and watch over her. He could keep her at arm's length and secretly keep an eye on her. If he let his guard down to spend more time with her—gave in to his desires—could he stay focused? *Could she stay focused?* If she died, he would never forgive himself, regardless.

Kamber drew in a long breath as she noticed his hesitation. "We just can't get a break, can we, Jet? You think that being too close will be a distraction we can't afford."

"Yet, we both want to be together," he finished for her.

"It doesn't have to be that way. I don't have to be a distraction."

"I know that now. This is my problem, not yours."

"You believe it's all or nothing. But we will have breaks. There will be time for us to slip off, visit this place, spend time together. We can live a life away from the Lucem…away from this war if we try."

"For brief moments only."

"Aren't brief moments better than the alternative?"

"It'll always be in the back of my mind," he said. "It's just something I need to figure out."

"Don't let your fear for what may happen decide what your heart truly wants. Remember, I'm not like your friends. I may be the newest member, but don't treat me as one, please. I made a decision to join the Lucem on my own. I know the possible consequences."

"Are you certain, though?" Jet asked. "What happened today is just the beginning."

"Today was scary. I saw more people die. It's made me realize that this is for keeps. There was a moment, a flashback to the day of Chroma and the Century Eclipse. Harriet…she was one of the older Lucem, yet that mech unit killed her with little effort. But I'm not giving in to my fear. I refuse to live like that."

"I'm not saying you should." Jet paused again, then shook his head. "I'm sorry. These are strange times. Everyone is so bent on getting those memoirs. I feel like this is the calm before the storm."

Kamber stood and let go of his hand. Jet stood to follow her.

"We're in the middle of something I barely understand, and I feel there's no way out of it," she said. "I feel trapped. I don't know if life will ever be normal again."

Jet waited next to her as they looked into the river's churning waters. "Things will never be the same for any of us. We have a duty to the system and its citizens now. Protecting them means getting the memoirs. The carefree days before all of this are gone. We *have* to trust in each other. I have faith in Solan, even if she decides against joining the Atrum. Right now, all we can do is wait and hope for the best."

CHAPTER 15
The Unexpected Relative

ΑΒΓΔΕ ΗΘΙΚΛ**Μ**
ΝΞΟΠΡΣ ΥΦΧΨΩ

JET EVENTUALLY LEFT Firefly Falls.
Kamber stayed behind, and Jet let her. She had wanted to do some soul-searching. He felt reluctant to leave her alone in the forest, even after agreeing to respect her space. Kamber was already far enough along in her training to take care of herself. Certainly, there was nothing in the forest at night that could harm her short of an Atrum. But now that Vail knew where Firefly Falls was, that concerned him. Kamber might be moving quickly in Vishmu, but Vail was a powerful Atrum now.

However, Jet didn't think she'd make an attempt on Kamber yet. There seemed to be an unspoken truce between the Lucem and the Atrum for the moment. He sensed they were waiting for the Lucem to make a decision on whether to join together, and perhaps they didn't want to risk a conflict. It seemed their war with each other was temporarily on pause.

But Jet had something else on his mind. It was late, and it had been a long day. But he had business with Solan, and he knew exactly where he'd find her.

After a brief ten-minute jog, Jet stepped into a clearing. Crickets murmured, and the bright blaze of a fire crackled as he stopped next to Solan. She was lost in her thoughts as she stared at the pyre. Harriet's body lay on a stack of branches.

"She was one of our more experienced Lucem," Solan said without turning to face him. "One of my father's favorite pupils. He would be sad to hear the news."

"I wish I'd had more time to know her. I hear she had a special ability with calming others."

Solan continued to stare into the roaring fire. "Yes. She had a knack for comforting others in time of need, one of the reasons my father spent so much time with her."

Jet stood next to Solan, trying to decide how to broach the topic that was bothering him. He hadn't shared it at their last meeting since it had been right before the reveal. But now was the time to tell Solan about what he'd discovered the night he'd met the ghost Lucem. "Solan. I just wanted to apologize for barging out of the meeting."

"Forget it," she said. "A lot of us are frustrated right now. No need to fret over that."

Jet nodded and pursed his lips. "I also need to tell you about the night I visited our old headquarters."

Solan turned to face him. "Go on."

He gave her a long look. "I believe the Heliographi are no longer regenerating."

Her emotionless expression changed to one of confusion, her brow furrowed. "I hope this isn't a joke."

"Why would I joke about something this serious?"

"What evidence do you have?"

"I bumped into Vail. She told me that Hurse was no longer around, that they couldn't locate him. I decided to check when I was at the Hall of Vital Records that night. When I stepped into the meditation chamber with Hurse's symbol, I sensed… *nothing*. It was like darkness or emptiness. I don't get that feeling in the other chambers there. I think Vail is right, and the other Atrum must know something is wrong."

"If what you say is true, that would mean Harriet's essence is gone too." Solan looked at him briefly before turning back to the fire. She placed her hands in the folds of her cloak and straightened her back.

Jet shuffled his feet in the dirt, kicked at a rock. "Maybe the second phase of the Prism Effect set something else in motion? Something more—" He paused, searching for the right word. "I don't know…*Final?*"

Solan crossed her arms and bowed her head. Jet watched as she closed her eyes, and he waited. She seemed to be meditating then, and it was several seconds before she opened her eyes. "We can either wait to tell the others, till all the reveals are over, or tell them now. What do you think?"

Jet scratched his head. "Is this a test?"

Solan shook her head. "I just want to know your thoughts. That's all."

"It would be wrong on our part not to tell the others. They deserve that. I'm sure they can handle it."

"It may affect how they approach the hunt for the memoirs," Solan replied. "But you're right. They should know the truth, if that is indeed the case."

"I wish I knew for certain what it meant," Jet said as he looked up at the night sky. He watched his breath trail off in lazy puffs as he considered. He'd thought about Hurse several times, but still had no answer for what had happened to him, and apparently neither did Solan. "Maybe it's nothing, but it sure doesn't feel that way. I just wonder why?"

"What do you mean?" she asked.

"Just that it appears this was part of the second phase of the Prism Effect, which means that Albright intended for this to happen. Why would he do such a thing? Why would he want to permanently erase a Heliographi?"

"I don't know, but it doesn't change anything. We need to keep the others focused on the memoirs right now. I'll need your help with that. Maybe when this hunt is over, we'll have some better resolution."

"That makes attaining the memoirs all that more important." Jet turned to face Solan and waited until he had her full attention. "Tell me what it is about Joshia that's bothering you, Solan. If I'm your second-in-command, I need to know. More Heliographi will die if we don't do something now. After the ninth reveal, our groups can go separate ways."

Solan returned his gaze and didn't say anything for several seconds, as if trying to determine how serious he was. "And how do you think that will all work out?" she asked, lowering her voice. "When we have a few, and they have a few…it'll be a fight to the death."

"Better them than Lybra," Jet said. "Listen, Solan. You asked me to be your backup for a reason. I know I'm less experienced than just about every other Lucem, but I feel this is the way forward. I mean, what if this was how Albright wanted it? Don't you ever wonder why he decided to broadcast the memoirs' locations? Isn't that kind of odd? Maybe he really *was* trying to force the

Heliographi back together again. That's what he always wanted anyway, right? He must have known we'd need each other. I think he did all of this for a reason."

"That's a bit demented," Solan grunted.

"We've seen some shocking things from Albright. It fits the pattern," Jet replied. "You saw what that mech unit did, and that was just one. Imagine an army of them. That's a battle we can't survive, not without some help. We *need* to find a way to swing things in our favor." Jet sensed he was walking on thin ice again, but he wasn't leaving this time until he knew *why* Solan was so adamantly against the idea. "What are you not telling me, Solan?" he continued, pressing her. "I've known you long enough to see you're not acting like yourself. The Solan I know would never risk the safety of the Lucem over her own feelings. If you want me to stay as your second-in-command, then tell me, or I'm done."

Solan glared at him, gritting her jaw, then looked back at the pyre where Harriet's body had already turned to ash. But Jet waited.

"Joshia…she's…my half-sister."

Jet's jaw dropped. He shook his head, then chuckled in disbelief. "I'm sorry. I'm just a bit…shocked." But shocked was an understatement.

"Now do you understand?" Solan said with a dismissive wave. "Yes, my half-sister is an Atrum. That's the problem."

"I guess…if you say it is. But who cares? It's nothing you did, and I don't think any of the other Lucem would care."

Solan stood, arms crossed, and looked into the fire.

"When did you figure this out?" Jet asked tentatively, hoping Solan didn't explode at the question. He was so used to her stoic nature, but this episode over Joshia seemed to be a topic she couldn't get past.

She paused before speaking. "After I joined the Agency, Tyberius told me. He felt I had the right to know. Sometimes I wish I didn't, though."

Jet considered, then chuckled again. "Sorry, I just didn't realize your father had it in him. Are you embarrassed about having a sister that's an Atrum, or are you worried about what others might think of your father?"

"It's a bit of both, I suppose," Solan said.

"Are you and Joshia close in age? Does she know?"

"She's a few years younger, and of course she knows."

"Well, it seems like she doesn't mind having you for a sister, or does she?"

"I think she's more concerned about saving her own hide than her morals. But to be honest, I have no idea. We've talked very little since we were schoolmates, and when we did, never about that. I can't have an Atrum half-sister hanging around. It'll be unbearable—" Solan stopped abruptly and held up her hands. She took a deep breath. "Alright, Jet. I'm going to consider it. Just promise you'll let me do this on my terms. Do me a favor and keep quiet about this, alright?"

Jet smiled and nodded. "Understood, boss."

"One more thing, Jet. I want Kamber with me."

"What do you mean?" he asked, tilting his head to one side.

"You've seen the schedule. Four of the last reveals are grouped together. We're going to have to split up if we want to have a chance."

Jet finally saw what she was trying to do. "You don't think I can stay focused with her around? That I may place her safety above the memoirs?"

"I know she's your warden. But she is also one of the least experienced Lucem. Having her with me will allow Cord to be with you. That will balance out better, I think."

Jet was reminded of how Solan had placed him atop Chroma during the Century Eclipse. Though she hadn't admitted it, he suspected it was for his own safety. Though that decision had ultimately backfired, he understood why she had done it. Now, Solan was trying to manage him once again. But he didn't try to argue with her. He simply nodded. It made his decision about watching after Kamber that much easier. Kamber's destiny was now out of his hands, at least during the reveals.

Jet continued to look at her, then looked at the fire. It hissed and popped as he considered. He didn't know how Kamber would feel about Solan's decision, but it appeared they had no choice in the matter.

"Alright, Solan…fine," he said. Then turned and left without another word.

CHAPTER 16
Private Conversations

ΑΒΓΔΕ Η̲ΘΙΚΛΜ

ΝΞΟΠΡΣ ΥΦΧΨΩ

DIJINN WIPED SWEAT from her brow. She stood in the dimly lit rec hall that had been converted into a gym. In the middle were several old pieces of office furniture, most of it lay crumpled into a heap of unrecognizable rubbish. She had finally found a use for the god-awful furniture around the control suite. The dated desks, chairs, and sofas were no use and, more often than not, got in the way. She'd spent the last few days dragging the dusty furniture down to the gym and converting it into kindling.

Harriet! she thought. *Sweet Harriet.*

One of her oldest and dearest friends, who she'd known for nearly fifty years, was gone. And once again, because of Lybra Howling. DiJinn kicked at the nearest sofa hard enough to split it in half. Then she lifted it and slammed it into a wall.

Ti-Leer hollered from the room beyond, "Quiet down, lass!"

DiJinn hammered the wall in response.

She sat down on her mat and went right into meditation. She slowed her breathing and relaxed, continuing to think as she closed her eyes. The Lucem were entering a dangerous time, and eventually, Sol would be forced to take Joshia's offer. It would mark the first time in several millennia they had worked together. They had a common foe in Lybra. That old hag had managed to upset just about everyone except Harok.

It made her think about General Dane again. She had seen him at the first reveal, leading the recon forces. By order of Harok, at least she hoped. Surely Lybra wasn't calling all the shots just yet. But it was only a matter of time, and she wondered if perhaps that might be enough to send Dane over the top. Taking orders from a civilian like Lybra would make Dane's blood boil, she knew that much. He was also an honorable man and would follow orders. Dane was loyal to a fault, but even he had his limit, and DiJinn was willing to bet that Lybra would tip him over the edge. Dane was already annoyed with Harok. DiJinn didn't have to read his mind to see that he hated President Harok's style. *And why was that?*

It was because Harok possessed no code of ethics, and she knew that drove Dane crazy.

But would she be able to convince Dane to come over to their side?

It would take more of what had happened today to move Dane. And, perhaps, spending more time in his company. DiJinn knew that wherever Dane went, the recon army would go. If Dane were ever caught, he would be court-martialed and executed.

But, if Dane *did* decide to risk it, the Lucem needed to be prepared. Their biggest issue would be finding an operating base for the recon army to work from. If that ever happened, then it would be a doomsday scenario, as Dane liked to say. Ultimately that would mean only one thing—*the Skylight System was on the verge of collapsing, maybe even civil war.*

It would be total anarchy, and she hated to think about that. But, like it or not, that might be exactly where they were headed anyway. The Lucem needed an army, and Dane was the only hope she could see, especially if Sol was dead set against teaming with the Atrum. DiJinn was doing her part to help their odds. She wasn't content to sit around and wait for Sol or anyone else.

DiJinn stood and cloaked. It was late, but she had Dane's passcode. If she was ever going to convince him, she wouldn't accomplish it by sitting around in her quarters. She had to work to convince him her side was the right path…and she could have some fun along the way.

H

Some twenty minutes later, DiJinn was sneaking around the corridors of their old headquarters, Flotsam. It was one of her favorite things to do, *sneaking*. Hearing others' thoughts, being privy to secretive conversations…it made her almost giddy. However, she was searching for Dane, and she knew where he was at that moment; he was with President Harok. And where Harok went, there Lybra might also be.

It wasn't long until she located Dane and Harok.

DiJinn waited for an assistant to open the door, then snuck into Harok's private office.

Inside, Dane stood at attention, dressed in his dark blue military fatigues. He held his shoulders squared and at attention, as usual. But his jaw was clenched in frustration, his hands balled into fists behind his back. She could sense he was unhappy but remained silent as Harok sat at his desk, looking up at his general and yelling at him.

"You aren't engaged, Dane!" Harok screamed. He was dressed in his typical dark blue suit and tie, his pinstriped shirt impeccably pressed. Harok ran a hand through his dark hair, feathering it to one side, a slight sheen of sweat glistened on his forehead in the dim light. DiJinn noticed the dark circles around his eyes, and his face was pale. She sensed his anxiety.

"Sir, why waste our troops when Lybra can spend her tetrahedron soldiers? They have more troops, not to mention they're less trained and therefore less of an asset."

"Are you sure that's your rationale, Dane? You've held the recon forces back on purpose. Even I can see as much!"

"If there was more on my mind, I would say so. At the moment, I have no issues."

Harok stood and paced around his desk. "I…I just don't know—"

"Sir, you need to calm yourself," Dane said but remained at attention. "The system needs good decisions now. They need you."

"What do you mean by that?" Harok stopped and glowered at Dane. DiJinn could see the panicked look on his face. His eyes were wide, darting around the room as if searching the dark corners for spies.

"Think, sir." Dane lowered his voice, and it almost sounded like a growl. He used his hand with all four fingers to point out of Dane's office window toward the inner belts beyond. "We are on the brink of war. Are you of clear mind?"

Harok marched over and stood in front of Dane. He looked up at him, his short stature trembling with rage. But Dane looked straight ahead and remained calm. "You question my sanity? Is that how it is now? You are under oath to the system, and I am your president. You will *not* question my authority. If I say the Recon forces are to fight, then you must obey my orders!"

DiJinn watched Dane as he stood there, stonelike, his jaw clenching and releasing. She could tell that he wanted to reach out and strangle Harok.

"Sir, yes, sir!" Dane barked and turned on his heels and left the room without another word.

DiJinn moved to follow him but then thought better of it and waited behind.

Harok collapsed into his chair and slumped forward onto his desk as if exhausted from the confrontation with Dane. He sat forward, head in his hands, and muttered under his breath. Then the intercom buzzed, and Harok snapped to and quickly answered the call.

"Are the payments in place?" he asked immediately.

On the other end was Lybra Howling. She sat behind an expensive-looking desk, dressed in a multicolored scarf that shimmered in the light. A pair of solar shades pushed to the top of her head, almost disappearing in her mass of gray, tufted hair. The wrinkles around her face seemed to grow deeper every time DiJinn saw the old 'hag.'

"Well, I can see that you have your priorities straight, my dear," Lybra crooned. "The Skylight System is in a rage over the memoirs. Clans, factions, and citizens fight each other to the death for something they have no right possessing…and their president sits here, worried only about his finances."

"Are the payments in place?" Harok repeated and leaned forward on his desk, staring at the hologram.

"Yes, not to worry," Lybra said with a wave of her hand. "Your pet project will continue."

"Goliath's Gate," Harok corrected her. "You should be more excited—"

"I care nothing of the project," she interrupted him and stood to walk around her lavish study. "All that matters are the memoirs and the destruction of the Heliographi! As long as I get those, you can have all the money and gates you want."

Harok took a deep breath and settled back in his seat. Then nodded and wiped a bit of sweat from his brow. "General Dane doubts us. I know it now. He's holding the recon back."

Lybra dismissed the comment with a wave. "You know Dane better than anyone. He will never falter in his duty. He has served the Skylight System for decades. He is a soldier."

"Are you sure this is the right direction?" Harok asked.

DiJinn watched him, noticing his disjointed movements. Harok wasn't himself, not that he was much of a man to begin with, but something wasn't right.

"Absolutely!" Lybra snapped back at him through the hologram. "Don't you start doubting me now! I will bury you, Harok, if you don't follow through on this. You keep your system's officials in line, and soon we *will* have the memoirs and all their glory."

"It's dangerous to cross the Heliographi," Harok said.

Lybra suddenly stopped pacing, her back to the hologram.

"Especially the Atrum," Harok continued. "They follow no rules, and they have no ethics. I've witnessed what they can do. Besides, why do you wish the Heliographi dead? Wouldn't it be easier to leave them alone?"

DiJinn noticed a slight tremble in Lybra's shoulders. There was a long pause, and Harok ran a nervous hand through his hair.

Lybra finally turned to face the hologram, then sat in her chair. She punched something into a holopad on her desk, and the image of an elderly man came into view. "Do you recognize this man?"

Harok leaned forward, then shook his head.

"Of course you don't. How could you?" Lybra mused, her voice nearly a whisper. But DiJinn heard the slight tremor in her voice and could hardly believe it. Lybra was on the verge of becoming emotional.

Harok watched her but said nothing, apparently not sure how to react. It seemed that he, too, was a bit shocked at Lybra's unexpected emotion.

"This man was my husband." Lybra's face and the deep carelines seemed more prominent then, as if she had suddenly aged by years. For a moment, DiJinn forgot who she was looking at. Lybra had inadvertently let her barriers down, giving away an intimate moment.

Standing there, in the hologram, was just an elderly woman, hunched and withered. A woman who had no one, and nothing of value. The moment caught DiJinn off guard, and Harok, too, it seemed. She was not the cruel, uncaring woman at that instant. Was this really the same lady who was responsible for all the death and destruction during the Century Eclipse? It was a far cry from the murderous 'hag' who had ordered the hit on Solan's younger sister and Stroud's good friend.

"When I was a student at Skylight University… *goodness*, has it been nearly seventy years now? Well, regardless, I majored in the Theoretical Arts. I love *all* the arts, you see, but I wanted to focus on painting. I fell in love with Shiloe Van Saint's work. She had a special talent, and her work spoke to me. Those brushstrokes hold a power I cannot explain. Perhaps I was the only one in my class that saw beyond the fact she was a euph. Then I met Dantier during my sophomore year. He had a love for Van Saint's work as well. It was an instant connection. After graduation, we traveled the system. We were inseparable and eventually married."

Lybra paused and sniffled. Then stood and walked around her study, stopping to gaze at some of her art as she talked. "You see, President Harok, I was fascinated by the clandestine nature of Van Saint's work. The secrets that her work held…I knew it was there, just waiting to be discovered. Danny was skeptical, one of the few things we ever disagreed on. I wished to decipher her secrets, and Danny became concerned. I wanted to know more. *I had to know more!* So, I convinced him to continue purchasing her work. He agreed, though I could tell that he didn't want to. We had the money, of course—an inheritance from his parents. I became a well-known trader in the art community and turned his money into a fortune. Other ventures came and went, but I always returned to Shiloe."

Lybra stopped in front of another large painting and gazed up at it in a loving way, as one might while fawning over their child. "I remember this one, in particular. We bought all of her artwork when it became available. Then, the painting called *The Plan*, her crowning achievement, came up for auction."

Lybra turned to face Harok. Her pupils were dilated as she narrowed her eyes at the hologram. "Danny disagreed with me for just the second time. We argued, and he put his foot down. He yelled at me that night. It was the first time he had ever dared to raise his voice. Well, the audacity of it. Can you believe it? Oh, but Harok…you should have seen how I did it. It was genius, really."

Harok sat back in his chair, an uncertain look on his face. But beneath his bloodshot eyes, DiJinn saw the growing look of horror. "Did what, Lybra?"

"You must understand how much I loved him. I wanted it to be painless." Lybra slid a curved knife from her desk drawer and playfully drew it across her neck in a mocking fashion. It was a blade that DiJinn recognized; there was still dried blood on it. It was the marauder's knife she'd used atop Chroma the day of the Century Eclipse, the same one she had used to murder Stroud's friend.

"He never felt a thing, I promise you, Harok. I'm not that cruel. I simply couldn't have Danny around, not if he wasn't going to help me solve the 'riddle.' That makes sense, doesn't it? Well. I won the auction for Van Saint's painting, of course. And…you know what, President Harok?" Lybra paused and glared at him through the hologram.

Harok waited patiently.

"I can hear her…" Lybra whispered. "She speaks to me through her paintings. Her artwork whispers to me when I sleep. At night, I wander up to my gallery in the moonlight, barefoot, of course. And…she does…she

speaks! Or maybe *they* speak, the paintings…*my darlings.* Do you know what they tell me?"

The look on Harok's face was ashen, vacant. Beads of sweat pooled around his eyebrows. He simply shook his head in response to her question.

Lybra raced quickly toward the hologram, almost gliding like some ghost in her white nightgown. Her face enlarged in the frame to the point where DiJinn could only see her mouth and her stained, yellow teeth. "The voices say to me *kill* the Heliographi… every… last… one!"

The hologram snapped close with a soft, static hiss.

DiJinn stood stonelike in the corner, trying to process what she'd just heard. She had known Lybra was a murderer. What she hadn't known was just how unhinged she was.

Harok sat at his desk and pulled a handkerchief from his suit and wiped the sweat from his forehead. His hand shook uncontrollably.

"What have I gotten myself into?" he whispered.

H

DiJinn waited for Harok to leave his office, which was some fifteen minutes later. He was in a state of hysteria by the look in his eyes, and DiJinn felt a moment of pity for the man. But she quickly pushed it away. *Harok had brought this on himself. He deserved it.*

She snuck down to the lower levels of Flotsam and into the officer's wing. She hacked through Dane's door lock and moved inside, still cloaked.

"Why are you here, Jinn?"

She turned to see Dane leaning against his kitchen island, holding two mugs of tea.

He was still in his military fatigues but had taken off his jacket, and his collared shirt was unbuttoned. His kitchen was sparse, like the rest of his apartment. A bit of stray moonlight snuck in through the side portal window, a dimly lit view of the systems' belts beyond.

She uncloaked, and he handed her one of the steaming mugs.

Dane sat down at the small round table.

DiJinn sat down across from him, staring out the window. "You knew I was there at the meeting, didn't you?"

Dane watched her for a few seconds, then nodded. "Call it a soldier's intuition. What did you hear after I left?"

DiJinn stared at him with her glowing eyes and felt a moment of weakness. She cared for this man more deeply than she wanted to admit to herself. She knew it wasn't wise to get attached to mortals like this, but Dane was so much more to her than those in her past. "You need to be careful, Dane. Harok isn't the problem. Lybra is. That lady is insane."

"I'm aware of that. I can take care of myself."

"I know. But this isn't goin' down pretty. The Skylight System's on a path to self-destruction, and we're lettin' it happen. We could be doin' more…we *should* be doin' more."

"You're not giving up on me, are you, Jinn?" Dane asked.

"I saw your hesitation in the meeting. I witnessed the whole thing." DiJinn sat forward and took his hand. "Have you decided?"

Dane sat back and pulled his hand away. "You really shouldn't be here, Jinn," he repeated.

"Well…I *am* here, and I need to know what you plan to do."

"You never answered my question," Dane replied. "What did you hear after I left Harok's office?"

"Probably nothing you didn't already know—"

"Tell me, Jinn."

DiJinn paused as Dane held her gaze, his arms crossed. She didn't want to bring him into Lucem business—that wasn't why she'd come to him tonight. But now she could see that it was all tangled up together—*of course it was! What had she expected?* If she somehow managed to convince Dane to join them, he'd be front and center of *all* Heliographi affairs…for good. He deserved to know everything. "Lybra plans to kill off all the Heliographi. It's been her plan since the beginning."

There was a split second of concern on his face. "I won't let that happen. I promise you—"

"I can take care of myself too, Dane," DiJinn replied. "I'm just worried about you. I'm worried about the citizens and the system."

"How long have we known each other, Jinn?"

DiJinn furrowed her brow at the question. "I dunno, a few decades?"

"Twenty-three years, five months, and six days," Dane said. "And ever since I met you, I've thought about you. Through all my tours, the early battles at Division, Kleegan's Reach, even the Uprising Wars. You were always there in my thoughts, driving me forward. I need someone to protect, Jinn. You gave me that, and it kept me going through the lonely nights at war. As long as we have each other, we'll both be fine."

DiJinn grasped his hands as she leaned forward. "I wish you would use that same desire for the citizens too. I know that Albright used to count on you, and now the Skylight System needs you. So many lives depend on your decision, and you have to do it soon, or millions may die."

J. Wint

CHAPTER 17
A Tentative Truce

NEARLY A WEEK had passed, and Solan still hadn't made her decision.

Jet was beginning to wonder if she could set aside her concerns with her half-sister, Joshia. But perhaps the bigger question was whether the Atrum and the Lucem would ever join forces.

The second reveal was set for May thirtieth at 12:24 AM on the second belt, and all of the Lucem waited anxiously for Solan's decision. Jet spent that time trying not to think about Kamber and meditating. Kamber had kept her distance, too. After their last conversation that night at Firefly Falls, he sensed her confusion and concern. It reminded him of his first days in the Lucem. He wanted to reach out to her, to console and comfort her. But that would be sending the wrong message. As much as he wanted to be near her, he needed to let her work things out on her own, at least for now.

When Jet approached Cord about the second reveal, he wasn't surprised to see that Cord had already started researching it.

"So, you're saying this is another subterranean site? One that will occur *below* the main government sector on the second belt?"

"The second belt houses nearly all the government and civic buildings for the system," Cord said. "The sublevels of that area are littered with utilities, foundations, and infrastructure. It's much the same as any other belt. I paid a visit there a few days ago. Everything is broken up into compartments. It'll be like an obstacle course this time."

"What, no great arena?"

"Not from what I saw. This one will have a different type of challenge. It'll be like a rat race, unlike the first reveal. That was an all-out deathmatch. And there's no telling where Albright hid this one. We have the general location but trying to find this one may be trickier."

"Well, we have the next few days to think about it," Jet said. "I guess we'd better start game planning then."

"Thankfully, the reveal won't occur during business hours. There should be minimal distraction to the citizens there."

"And what do you think we should do about the first memoir?" Jet asked. "There's been no real discussion about it."

"What can we do?" Cord said matter-of-factly. "Steal it?"

"Well, why not?" Jet replied. "Jinn could probably do it."

Cord crossed his arms and sat back from his work. His desk in the control quarters was littered with holographic images, clouding the air in a static haze. "I don't know. That's a pretty aggressive tactic right now, even for Jinn. Don't get me wrong, you know I like a challenge, but something like that would be an incredibly difficult endeavor, especially with those new mech units. I don't think it's wise to send Jinn into that hornet's nest. Maybe as a last resort."

"I never thought I'd hear you say such a thing," Jet chuckled.

"My suggestion right now is to hang tight and see how the next reveal plays out. Lybra and Harok will have that memoir well-guarded. We're playin' for keeps now. I don't think they would have any mercy if one of us were captured. We don't have the resources available to send out a rescue team either."

Jet considered. Cord was right, of course. Breaking into the Agency headquarters was an insane idea, one that could result in death. He'd been lucky the last time—the new mech units hadn't been fully operational. Yet here he was, considering breaking into the Agency a second time, not because of the memoir, but because that inner voice was urging him back to the Hall of Vital Records. His curiosity would haunt him until he did it, too. It was his weakness, his curiosity, and always had been. But how long would his luck hold out? Yet, there was something there…*something intriguing*. He knew it was a special place now and that Albright had designed it that way for a reason. Maybe it *was* a conduit between planes? How else had he been able to communicate with a ghost?

"Jet," Cord said, "I don't like that look. I told you not to do anything crazy, at least, not until I'm ready. And right now isn't the time."

"You know I'm not going to settle for that for too long," Jet said. "Something is pulling me back to the Hall of Vital Records."

"I understand. Just give me some time to prepare before you go guns blazing into that hornet's nest. Promise me."

"I feel this is important, Cord."

"More important than the memoirs, though? Seems highly unlikely."

"Alright, fine," Jet said and waved it away. "Anything more about this next reveal we should know?"

Cord leaned back and took off his glasses, rubbing his forehead. "Well, Albright didn't leave many clues behind for any of these reveals. We can research each site and prepare. That's about it for now."

"But Lybra and Harok seemed to know something about the first reveal. Was it just a coincidence that they were prepared for it?"

"Unknown. I don't see how they could have any inside information. I've been studying these reveals for nearly four years, and there is no roadmap that I can see except the coordinates. But there *is* something about those coordinates. I just haven't figured it out yet."

"What do you mean?"

"There's another riddle buried in there, just like it was the first time. Remember the number and how the locations were hidden in the three paintings?"

"Right," Jet said. "2,412,631 and 2,412,630. So, there's more to them?"

"Perhaps. Albright isn't done with me just yet."

Jet chuckled. "Done with you? What are you talking about? Are you saying that Albright left these numerical breadcrumbs behind for you to figure out?"

"Remember, I was the other Skylight Fallout," Cord said. "He was gambling that someone on the Lucem side would be able to crack his code. I'm guessing that was me."

Jet sat back and stared at Cord in wonder. "Well, that's a bit of an eye-opener, isn't it? I mean, no pressure, right?"

"Do not concern yourself with me. I can handle it. Just focus on the upcoming reveal."

Jet took a moment, shook his head. "Yeah…well, we have two days until then. I'm going to the second belt for a look around."

"Not alone, you aren't. There'll be all manner of people crawling over that site right now."

"This wouldn't have anything to do with my abilities, or the lack there of, would it?"

"No offense, Jet, but you still have a lot to learn," Cord said and pushed in his chair. "Now, if you can manage to harness those other powers you've mentioned, then you can be my bodyguard."

Jet laughed and gave Cord a playful shove. "No way, I'd charge you too much. But if it makes you feel any better, I think I am stronger than I was at the Century Eclipse. Seriously, I'm not joking. I don't know what it is, but I feel…different."

"Good. That's good. Because you're gonna need every bit of strength you can muster in the days ahead."

Jet gave him a worried look. "What's your biggest concern right now?"

"Obviously, the new mech units will pose the greatest challenge. Lybra holds the ace of spades. I don't see an answer for them. Even if we join forces with the Atrum, I'm not sure it would make a difference against an army of M-Class mechs."

"We're outmatched and outnumbered," Jet said. "Lybra and Harok appear to know more about these reveals than we do. You're not giving up hope, are you?"

Cord gave Jet a disapproving glare. "I'm mildly offended. I think you know me better than that. However, I *am* being realistic. I hope you can appreciate that much. Lybra has her game-changer. The new mechs are beyond any of us. As it stands, our odds of winning a memoir, well…they don't look good."

K

Solan stole quietly through Lyrinthum.

The cold corridors groaned with displeasure; the sound of dripping water echoed in the background. The haunting voices from the old particle accelerator infiltrated her thoughts, whispering to her, calling for her to join them. A parallel dimension, one so disturbing that she shuddered. Solan blocked them off and hurried through the Clipton Woods portal. It was late, and she didn't want the other Lucem to know what she was doing. She should have told Jinn or perhaps Jet.

For backup purposes, she told herself.

But then she knew that they would both insist on coming with her, and she didn't want an entourage tonight. No. What she was doing now *was* risky. And, as much as she hated to admit it, Jet had been right from the very beginning.

They were all running out of time. They needed to make tough decisions now.

She needed to set aside her differences and do the right thing. Though she wondered if it would even matter at this point.

Tonight might be one of the toughest decisions she would make as the leader of the Lucem. Though allowing her sister into the Agency had been difficult— a choice she was still dealing with emotionally—tonight's decision would set something in motion that hadn't happened for thousands of years.

The Atrum and Lucem would rejoin forces.

And maybe Jet had been right, yet again. Had Albright purposely planned it this way over a hundred years ago? Was all of this hunting for his memoirs simply a ploy to force the Heliographi back together? Solan had known that Albright's greatest hope was to recreate their glory days, a golden era in their history. It seemed like too much of a risk to use the memoirs to do this.

But to Solan, this joining would be more of a demented collaboration than a glorious reunion—a fusion of antiquity fraught with misaligned intentions from both sides. How would they cope? Would working together accomplish great things or make the situation worse? And what if they were able to attain at least a few of the memoirs? What would happen after that?

But tonight, her meeting with her half-sister, Joshia Kembler, already had her nerves on edge. They had once attended Skylight University together, ran track together, and confided in each other as fellow students with ephebus mortem. And yet, after all that time spent with her, she'd never known Joshia had been her half-sister.

Solan had kept their secret buried deep. Shame and embarrassment gnawed at her over this. What if the other Lucem found out? What would they think of her? Better yet, what would they think of her father, Tyberius?

Normally, Solan didn't care about what others thought of her. But this was on a different level. Something that ate at the very fabric of her morals.

How could she be related to an Atrum?

Maybe it was just because she sought to uphold her own high values? Or maybe just knowing what Joshia had done—and what she was capable of doing— bothered her the most? Was she projecting Joshia's behavior onto her own character?

Regardless, Jet seemed to be able to cut through the minutia and speak to the core issue, one of the reasons she had chosen him as her second-in-command. Even though she knew Jinn better, Jet possessed qualities that would make him a great leader someday. He was the reason she was here tonight.

Soon she was crawling through the debris of Chroma. The authorities had already begun reconstructing the area at Revelations Plaza, and cranes and barriers were in place at the construction site.

Solan remained cloaked as she worked her way downward through the rubble and to the area where the Lucem and Atrum had met just recently. It wasn't long until she stood in an area where some of the debris had been cleared out. She could see a blurry mirage standing off to one side. Solan uncloaked and watched it do the same.

Joshia stood facing her, arms held behind her back. There was a moment of silence as the two leaders faced each other. Joshia's tall, athletic frame and broad tapered shoulders mirrored Solan. She had always assumed their similar physique was from years of track and field, but the reality was because of their shared lineage.

Joshia brushed her silver hair back and stared with glowing bluish-purple eyes. Her dark voice was husky in the sultry air. In Solan's vision, Joshia seemed to be shrouded in a dark ambiance, almost blurry amongst the wreckage surrounding them.

Solan folded her hands into her cloak. "Here we are, Joshia. Let's hear your proposal."

"I've already said what I needed to say."

"Say it again."

Joshia glared at Solan. "We need each other. Our two groups will not survive the challenges ahead if we don't join forces. You're here because you, too, finally realize this. I imagine that was difficult to get through your thick skull, and if hearing me say it first gives you some satisfaction, then fine. Let's just cut to the chase."

Solan waited to see if there was more, but Joshia remained silent. "We need to be crystal clear on the arrangement, Joshia. I don't trust you. I will never trust you, and this little *collaboration*, or whatever you want to call it, is temporary."

"Then set the terms, Solan."

"Fine. We will operate from our headquarters on the first belt," Solan said.

"Why? Don't you trust our base?"

"No. I don't. Secondly, I call the shots. You and your group will follow our lead. If we team together, then you absolutely *must* keep your group in line. I can't afford to have the Atrum running around unhinged. You must agree to this."

Joshia thought for a moment, then shrugged. "As you wish, *sister*."

"Third. Don't call me that. As far as I'm concerned, we are not related."

Joshia simply shrugged, but Solan noticed her look of defiance.

"Fourth," Solan continued. "I set the groups. You're aware that the pace will increase after the third reveal, and we'll need to divide our forces to keep up."

At that, Joshia raised a hesitant eyebrow. "Why should I agree to that? I know where my group's strengths and weaknesses are a lot better than you. It would be a mistake to let you organize this alone. If we work together, I can assure you the maximum strength."

"I don't trust you. As far as I know, the Atrum could turn on us at any moment."

"Think that through. Why would I want to eliminate our best hope of keeping the memoirs out of Lybra's hands?"

"Maybe not at first, but what happens after we attain the memoirs and the reveals end?"

"You assume we will attain *any* of the memoirs!" Joshia hissed. "That remains to be seen. Maybe we should focus on that first before making assumptions. We might be lucky to collect just one, based on what I've witnessed so far."

Solan crossed her arms, not wanting to admit she agreed with Joshia on that. But still, she had to use caution with the Atrum. "Fine, we can talk about the teams later."

"Anything else?" Joshia asked. "Are those your only terms?"

"One more thing. Tell me what happened to Hanley Hurse."

That question seemed to catch Joshia off guard, and her gaze wavered ever so slightly. She quickly recovered. "We're still searching for him."

"Word is that he's gone. Extinguished. Jet told me himself that he verified it."

"You believe everything Stroud says?"

"I sense that he's telling me the truth," Solan said evenly. "Joshia. This is no small matter. If our Heliographi isn't regenerating, we both need to take that very seriously. We need to find out the cause and fix it if we can. It's in both our interests."

Joshia remained tentatively quiet for a few seconds. "Yes. Hurse is gone, and we have no idea why or how."

"Then it sounds like we both have another issue beyond our temporary truce. Joshia, this may be a bigger threat than anything else we've ever faced before."

CHAPTER 18
An Awkward Accord

ΑΒΓΔΕ ΗΘΙΚΛ**Μ**
ΝΞΟΠΡΣ ΥΦΧΨΩ

ON THE MORNING of the second reveal, Jet met Cord in his quarters.

Together, they left to the second belt without notifying any of the other Lucem. A bit of a risk in case something did happen to them. But this close to the reveal, Solan probably wouldn't like the idea of anyone going out to the site. Though Jet had already been, he wanted a final look around. He wanted to be better prepared than the first reveal.

Cord docked his skiff in a private hangar, then they made their way down through the sublevels of the second belt. Like the other belts, entry below wasn't meant for public access, and Jet had pulled some old maps from the Lucem archives for navigation. Thankfully, they had access to all the plans and schematics. Jet had studied the plans for this site thoroughly, but they were intricate.

They found an access panel hidden in the side of a large bulkhead. Cord was able to discern the rivet pattern, which was the clue they needed, and the proper code sequence allowed them in. The old rusty panel swung open, and they moved in and down.

The interior was hot and steamy, which was typical for most of the belts in the system. Each belt's hull had a support system that provided the heat needed to regulate the surface temperature. Though the Core provided some heat, its main function was gravity and oxygen.

As Jet and Cord made their way deeper, the lighting became dimmer, despite the occasional skylight well. Jet noted the interior was indeed a maze of columns; Cord had been right. Thousands of large foundation piers penetrated down multiple levels and held the surface buildings in place. Large pipes and conduits littered the vast voids of space. Thousands of thin layers of reinforced graphene walkways wrapped around the obstruction to provide passage. The interior of this reveal site wasn't easily defined like the last one. Jet could see no ceiling or walls here, just blackness beyond. If one were to fall over the edge of the walkway, they would surely never be seen again.

"That's the area over there," Cord whispered.

They made their way closer until they stood on a main thoroughfare. It was dark below them for hundreds of meters, it seemed. The coordinates listed on Cord's holopad had the general area of the reveal, but nothing jumped out at them.

They remained cloaked from several other groups of seekers that milled about the space. Jet knew that within a few hours, this area would be teeming with seekers vying for positions. Jet and Cord needed to be quick in their research and head back for a meeting Solan had called.

"I detect nothing out of the ordinary," Cord murmured.

"Me neither. It's a maze of infrastructure, just like you said," Jet whispered back.

Then Cord nudged him, drawing his attention to the opposite side of the vast space. A blurry mirage stood in the middle of another large thoroughfare and appeared to be conducting research as well.

"Let's go have a look," Cord said, and Jet followed close behind.

They stood near the Atrum, and Jet could sense that it knew it wasn't alone. Jet lowered his hood and faced it. Eventually, the Atrum did the same. He recognized the Atrum, one he'd never met but bumped into at the

Century Eclipse named Mosstrom. He was about the same height as Jet, medium in build, with eyes that glowed an indigo so deep they were nearly black. His hair was cropped close to his scalp and shaved on one side with an intricate pattern, his thick black beard jutting down to a point just inches above his waist. Mosstrom's skin was dark, and he nearly disappeared in the dim surroundings.

"Jet Stroud," the Atrum spoke in a languid tone. He tilted his head and took a mocking bow.

"I don't believe we've met," Jet said, ignoring the man's sarcasm.

"Forgive me. My name is Mosstrom. Sybold's warden."

That took Jet by surprise, and the look stole across his face. Mosstrom noticed it and grinned. "I see that name means something to you?"

"Yes, she tried to murder me."

"Oh, that? I'm sure she was just kidding. A little game she likes to play sometimes. Please, do not take it personally."

Jet chuckled at that. This Mosstrom was cynical. His sarcasm seemed to be a common trait in all Atrum. Hanley Hurse, the Atrum who had died at the Century Eclipse, had also been cynical. Jet was getting the same vibes from this Atrum, yet he felt this one was much older, maybe even ancient—and certainly more powerful. Jet doubted he could best this one if things went sideways. He was suddenly thankful he'd brought Cord along.

"Oh, don't worry, Jet. I'm not here to kill you…at least not today. I see that you're not alone."

"Mind telling me where your *warden* is these days?" Jet asked.

"Let's just say she's 'out on assignment.' I think you should focus on your own affairs. I hear you're struggling with Vishmu lately. Doesn't that make you feel a bit insecure?"

The man was prying around in his mind, and Jet could feel it. He had given up too much, even though he'd closed off his thoughts. Yet this Atrum, Mosstrom, had somehow strolled past his defense with ease.

Am I really that vulnerable?

Yes, you are, Mosstrom answered with his thoughts. *Consider your own inability. How could you let your friends down like that? Should Solan really place so much trust in someone like you? Should you really be her second-in-command?*

Jet felt his head begin to swim. Indecision and doubt crept in like a tiny shadow cast on the ground, a door closing and the sliver of light fading with it. What was happening to him? He felt cold, insecure, and upset with himself. Maybe he *should* just give up? He was so inadequate, his ability so weak. It was clear to him now.

Mosstrom smiled. His deep voice seemed to lull Jet into a trance, and he stumbled and nearly fell to the ground. Jet's thoughts grew dark, and he was on the verge of a breakdown. But then the darkness began to fade, the door opened up again, and light began to spill through the crack. Jet knelt, then crawled back toward that light and through the door. Then suddenly, he felt as if he was waking from a dark dream.

When he looked at Mosstrom, Cord had his arm wrapped around his neck and squeezed tight. Mosstrom chuckled and held up his arms. "Relax, Cord. It was just a game."

"I see your games vary from the ones I'm used to, Mosstrom," Cord said in his slow drawl.

Mosstrom relaxed, and Cord released his grip.

"It appears we are to be teammates soon," Mosstrom said in a low, steady voice.

Jet furrowed his brow. "Who told you this?"

"Why, your fearless leader. Solan."

"I don't think so," Jet continued. "She hasn't made up her mind yet."

"I guess we will see. Maybe she can explain more when we all arrive at your control suite inside the first belt."

"How did you know that?" Jet asked.

"We'll talk later, Jet Stroud, he who needs to work on his abilities." Mosstrom vanished without another word, leaving Jet and Cord alone in the dark chamber.

М

Jet and Cord quickly returned to the Lucem headquarters on the first belt. They now knew the reason Solan had called the meeting. Apparently, they were finally joining forces with the Atrum. What they didn't expect was to be greeted by the Atrum in their own control room. When they walked in, nearly all the Atrum were seated at Albright's old table. Only Sybold and Hurse were missing from the Atrum's side. On the opposite side were the Lucem, where only Tyberius, Albright, and now Harriet were missing.

In total, there were nineteen Heliographi seated around the table. It was an extraordinary sight to see. Something that hadn't occurred in millennia was unfolding right in front of him—the Heliographi had finally reunited.

But the tension in the air was thick. All of the Lucem sat anxiously around the table. DiJinn and Ti-Leer glared across the round table at the Atrum, who sat quietly staring back. Vail scowled at Cord when they walked into the room. Cord gave her a crooked smile as he walked by. Jet sat next to Vail and leaned forward to block her gaze, but her eyes didn't leave Cord as he sat down. Kamber sat stiffly in her chair, her hands gripping the edge of her seat. She didn't look at him or say a word, and he could sense that she was nervous.

Jet looked from Vail to Kamber to Cord. He felt that the tension might boil over, and a fight would erupt at any moment. It had been his suggestion they join the Atrum, but now he wondered if that had been a wise decision. He suddenly wondered how in Skylight the two groups would be able to work together and focus on the task at hand.

"What have we gotten ourselves into?" he whispered to Cord.

"This should be interesting," Cord muttered back.

"To say the least," Kamber chimed in.

Solan stood and looked out over them, and Joshia stood to join her. Jet could see that, once again, Solan wasn't comfortable in this position. She gripped the back of her chair tight, her knuckles white. He sensed that she'd rather just fight than talk things out, and clearly, Joshia would be right there with her.

"Well, here we are. Something I never thought I'd see," Solan began. "We all know the situation. We are outmatched and outnumbered. Lybra and Harok have the upper hand with the Recon, Tetrahedron, and the new mechs. They have the first memoir. Tonight, we will find out if our effort to join forces will make a difference or not."

"Let's get to the point. What's the plan?" Bofisto asked, baring his teeth. The tiny metallic daggers attached to them gleamed in the dim light. The large man barely fit in his own chair. He was as large as Booker, perhaps taller and broader of shoulder.

DiJinn lowered her gaze and bent toward the giant, her ponytails falling forward as she leaned in. "Calm down and let her speak."

Bofisto looked to her and grinned. "Tiny Jinn, aren't you a bundle of courage?"

"Relax, Bofisto," Joshia said, then looked at Solan and leaned on her chair. "This isn't what any of us want, Solan. Let's just get to the point."

Solan took another few seconds, then nodded. "Fine. I've spoken to all the Lucem. We see the value in this alliance, but only until the search for the memoirs has ended. I think we can all agree we're officially at war. This merger marks the first time in several millennia that we've all sat around this table. That said, I think it best if we stay separated during this next reveal. We can meet to discuss tactical information regarding the memoirs if needed. Otherwise, we keep to ourselves. If we respect each other, we will get through this. For the Lucem, we have an oath to protect the Skylight citizens. We also have a mutual goal with you all, which is to keep the memoirs out of Lybra Howling's hands. If she gains control of the memoirs, our democracy will fail, and the system will collapse. We cannot allow that to happen."

"Speak for yourself," Bofisto growled. "We care nothing about these petty people you so blindly defend. We only want what's rightfully ours. The memoirs belong to the Heliographi alone."

"There's more I need to say." Solan paused to gather herself and glanced at Joshia. "Some of you may already know this. Joshia and I are actually half-sisters."

A gasp echoed around the room, and a few of the Heliographi stood and gaped at the two.

Solan quickly held up her hands. "Before the rumors begin, let me finish because that's minor compared to the next bit I have to share. So, I'll just say it. We think that the Heliographi are no longer respawning."

At that, all the Heliographi stood, and the room erupted with shouts and yelling.

"How can that be?" Booker roared.

DiJinn shook her head. "That's ridiculous, Sol!"

"It's not possible," Annaka said, raising her voice to be heard. "Our inner light has been around since the very beginning!"

"Please, everyone, sit down!" Solan barked and waited until the room had quieted. "Let us share *why* we think this might be true. Recently, the Atrum noticed something odd just after the Century Eclipse. You all know the second phase of the Prism Effect was set into motion, but it appears there might be more than we realized. Joshia." Solan waved, and Joshia stepped forward.

"Solan is right. We noticed the light that represented Hanley Hurse can no longer be found. Whatever bound his essence to this plane of existence is no longer here.

I'm as stumped as the rest of you. All I can tell you is that he isn't here anymore."

"I'm afraid that it's true," Jet said. "Recently, I snuck into the Hall of Vital Records. I verified what Joshia is saying. Hurse's meditation chamber has gone dark."

"What does this mean for us, moving forward?" Annaka asked, her voice uncertain.

Solan walked over and placed a hand on Annaka's shoulder. "I know this is concerning for all of us, and it changes the way we think now. But we can't let this affect our goal. We still have to go after the memoirs. Nothing changes."

"We are literally fighting for our survival now," Joshia said. "We know that Lybra has vowed to eradicate all of us. She's managed to kill one Lucem already. Maybe we should consider maintaining our alliance until all her mechs are destroyed, especially now that we know about Hurse and Harriet?"

"I never thought I'd say this, but I tend to agree," Cord said, which gathered a few questioning glares from the other Lucem. "We can't ignore Lybra's method. Now that the new prototype mechs are coming online, we are in a precarious position. Never have we faced a challenge like this before. With the mechs, and now this news about the Heliographi not regenerating, I suggest that we stick together to increase our odds."

"What other options do we have available other than joining forces?" Booker asked.

"As of now, that's it," Solan said. "Unless you can magically summon the Tetrahedron army away from Lybra."

"The marauders fight for the highest bidder, which is Lybra," Joshia replied. "We can't match her funds, so they have no reason to leave her."

"What would happen if Lybra betrayed them like she did with us?" Cord said. "Lybra recently framed the Atrum to make it look like you were trying to provoke the Lucem into battle. Might we not try the same approach with her?"

Everyone remained silent, considering.

"Cord Ledbetter, you're so devious," Mosstrom said in a low voice. "I didn't realize you had it in you."

"What you call devious, I call clever," Cord said. "Right now, it's whatever method we can use to our advantage. A bit of clever deception might just swing things back in our favor."

"What about the recon army, Jinn?" Sojahn asked.

DiJinn glared at her. "What about 'em?"

"I hear you have a personal connection with General Dane?"

DiJinn sat forward and leveled a finger at her. "You need to mind your own business, Miss Quark. The Lucem can handle our own affairs."

"Still, here we are, plotting and scheming together," Sojahn replied. "I assume this is just how things used to be, back in the old days, right?"

Solan leaned forward and placed her hands on the table. "Let's just focus on what we can do right now, which is the next reveal. We can discuss our other options after that."

"What do we know about this next reveal site?" Joshia asked. "Did Albright leave any clues?"

Cord spoke up again. "I could sense nothing out of the ordinary at the site today. I don't believe Albright left us any directions. It appears he wanted this hunt for his memoirs to be equal for all parties."

"However, our enemy seemed to know exactly what to do at the first reveal site. Are we to believe that was just luck?" Joshia said.

"Perhaps it was," Cord replied. "The new mech was available, so they used it. They happen to have an onboard propulsion system. I don't think that means they had advanced knowledge, just dumb luck."

"Regardless, maybe it's time to do a little spying," Joshia said.

"We've been thinking the same thing," Jet chimed in. "I propose we do just that after this next reveal."

Solan glanced at Jet, then at Joshia. She shook her head. "That sounds too risky. We are at war, and if the Agency or Lybra capture any Heliographi, they would likely be executed. We can't afford that right now."

"Or they might be used as bait if caught," Cord said. "Knowing Lybra, she'd try to draw others in. Whoever goes does so on their own."

"We need a game changer, right?" Jet continued. "If we want to be on the same footing, we need to know how they're getting information. Otherwise, this all goes down the same path as the first reveal. Maybe some inside information will swing things back in our favor?"

Solan stood with her head bowed and arms crossed in thought. "Let's discuss it after the reveal tonight. Right now, I want to talk about the schedule and then teams. First, Joshia and I have agreed on splitting up into four teams once we hit the fourth through seventh reveals. Those reveals are timed so close together that we have no other option."

"What about just focusing on two of them so that we have greater numbers?" Vail asked. Jet had almost forgotten about her. She sat back in her chair with her arms crossed. "We might have a better shot at getting at least one."

Solan waited for Joshia to speak up, but she didn't.

"I'd rather not give up on *any* of the memoirs," Solan said. "Remember, all the other groups will be forced to divide their focus as well. Going after all four will increase our odds."

"The Agency and Lybra's forces are much bigger," Vail continued. "I don't know that splitting them up will matter much to them."

"I think she just said no," DiJinn snapped, glaring at Vail. "Sol. Tell us about these teams. I'd like to know which one of these *murderers* I'm gonna have to watch my back against."

Bofisto bared his teeth at her, but DiJinn ignored him.

"Here are the teams Joshia and I discussed," Solan said. She kicked the wall, and the mounted holopad sputtered to life. A hologram flickered over the old table with a list of the four groups. "Group one, at the fourth belt reveal is Jet, Cord, Vail, and Bo. Jet will lead that group."

Vail stood. "That's unacceptable! Putting me with Ledbetter is a bad idea. He's an arrogant fool, and I won't have it—"

"That's enough, Vail," Joshia said and held out her hand.

Vail sat back in her chair, but her gaze didn't leave Cord. "Mister brainiac. I can't seem to get away from you."

Jet looked at Bo for his reaction, but he barely moved and sat like a statue in his chair. His hair and beard had grown even longer. Jet had noticed Bo's transformation since his time at the university over four years ago. Then, Bo had been a heralded track star—and a nervous wreck. Now, he seemed to be a zombie and had barely said anything in the few times they'd met.

Cord glanced at Vail. "Why, whatever do you mean, Vail? I could've dispatched you several times. You should thank me."

"You two had better figure out your differences if you want to survive," Solan said and continued. "I'll lead the second group at the fifth belt reveal. With me will be Tetra, Kamber, and Joshia. Group three, at the sixth belt reveal, is Jinn, Ti-Leer, Sojahn, and Bofisto. Jinn will lead this group."

Jet watched DiJinn's reaction. She gave Sojahn and Bofisto a go-to-hell look, who were two of the Atrum she detested the most. Jet remembered her saying they'd been classmates at Skylight University over fifty years ago and had never gotten along. Jet imagined grouping them together would be a tough alliance. But he also wondered if that had been Solan's call or Joshia's.

"Group four, at the seventh belt reveal, is Annaka, Booker, Brit, Mosstrom, and Myranda. Annaka will lead this group."

"Where is Shiloe in all this?" Annaka asked. "I'd prefer she stay close to me."

"Not for this," Solan said. "You need to stay focused. Shiloe will be in a safe place."

"Can we discuss the location?"

"Now isn't the time, Annaka," Solan said and hammered the wall. The hologram snapped closed with a static pop. "We all have some deep mistrust, that goes without saying. This wasn't anything either of our groups wanted, but it's what we're faced with. For tonight's reveal, we've all done some reconnaissance. I don't need to explain the reveal site. I'm sure you've all been there and know the layout. Unlike the last reveal, this one might actually work in our favor." Solan looked at Joshia, giving her an opportunity to speak.

Joshia had a look of indifference on her face as she stepped forward. "Let me say—and I speak for all the Atrum—we do indeed abhor this arrangement. I, for one, hated the idea of having to come to you for this, though we know the outcome if we don't. I don't like you, any of you. I don't agree with your pathetic morals, your ridiculous code of ethics, or your defense of these weaklings who call themselves citizens. These people don't deserve any consideration from either of our groups."

The other Atrum began to nod in agreement, a few hammered on the table in approval.

Joshia waited a moment as the clamor died down. "But that's not why we're here. As Solan mentioned, we only desire to keep our heritage out of mortals' hands, especially Lybra. She is on our hit list, but we have set that aside for the moment to focus on the memoirs. Until such time as we can finish the hunt, you have our word that we will not intentionally harm any of you. I've spoken to every Atrum, and you have that assurance."

Jet looked around at the other Lucem. He could still see the distrust on their faces—narrowed eyes, arms crossed...heads shaking in disapproval.

"However, we will continue our own unique approach to dealing with our adversaries," Joshia continued. "As unsavory as you may find it, I caution you not to interfere with our methods. Likewise, I promise we will not interfere in yours either."

The room remained silent as everyone took in what had been said. Jet wasn't sure what Joshia meant by *methods*, but it sounded like something he wouldn't approve of. Either way, the next several weeks were going to be a challenge for all of them. Not just in their quest for the memoirs but in trying to balance their feelings for each other. In fact, that might prove to be their biggest challenge.

Jinn stood and stormed out of the control suite, not bothering to look back. Vail marched out right after her. One by one, they all left, no one speaking. Jet stayed behind to have a word with Solan, but Kamber pulled at him, urging him into the dark hallway beyond.

"What's wrong?" he asked.

"Seriously?" Kamber asked, sounding miffed. "You seem awfully relaxed, considering what we just heard in there."

"I don't know. Joshia sounded like she meant what she said. Did you not believe her? I mean, why would the Atrum try to cross us now? If they do, that's probably why Solan wanted you near her. She's our top Lucem. She'll take good care of you."

"That's not what concerns me."

"What do you mean then?" Jet asked. "Are you worried about being near Tetra again?"

Kamber gave him a worried look, and Jet knew he'd hit the mark. "Well, yeah. I think maybe that's it. I just don't know what to expect from her. We were never great friends, but I still cared about her. Now, she's all…weird."

Jet thought back about how he'd first felt when he'd seen Vail and Bo. "Look, I know what you're going through. I felt the same way around my friends when I saw them. It was difficult, and it still is. I think there's some hope in me that I can one day change them. I've seen Vail struggle with what she's become. All I can tell you is to focus on the reveal, stay near Solan. I think you're prepared. You're a quick study, much better than me." He grinned at her, but she didn't return his smile. He could sense her fear.

Kamber started to speak but stopped and just looked at the ground.

Jet held her hands in the dark corridor. "Just trust in yourself. Amazing things can happen when you believe, and I already know you can do this. You made it through some of the toughest situations life can throw out. You beat E.M., trained yourself to become one of the greatest runners in Skylight history, you're blazing through your Lucem training. You'll be fine. Just relax, do some meditation, and prepare for tonight. We'll be together for these next two reveals. You're gonna be fine…we'll all be fine."

She looked at him, her glowing greenish-yellow eyes staring up into his. He sensed that she knew what he did, though…

What he'd just told her was a straight-up lie.

He had no idea if they'd be fine. In fact, he had no idea if they'd even survive the night.

CHAPTER 19
The Second Reveal
May 30, 2286, A.D.

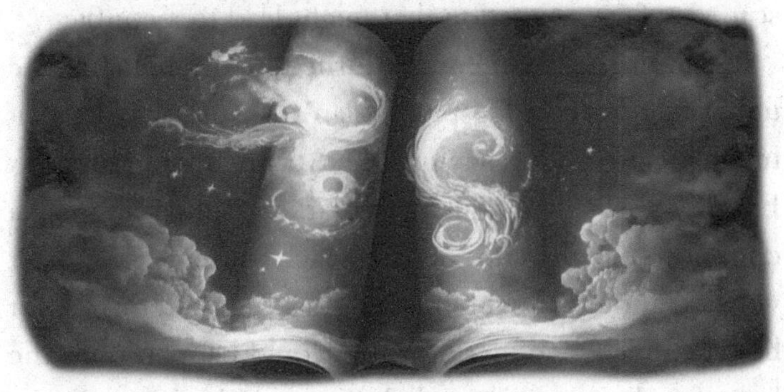

ΑΒΓΔΕ ΗΘΙΚΛ**Μ**
ΝΞΟΠΡΣ ΥΦΧΨΩ

JUST AFTER MIDNIGHT, the entire group of Heliographi met in the control room for one last briefing. Then they split up and silently made their way to the hangars in the lower levels. Everyone took separate skiffs to the second reveal, which was a short flight from Skylight University. In the distance, dark clouds surrounded the second belt, covering their skiffs in rain droplets. Jet piloted his skiff through the misty clouds, a bit of light turbulence bouncing him around.

Since they were all considered part of an 'outlaw organization' now, they had to look for areas to dock their skiffs that were considered to be on the 'shadier' side. Though they all had an alias and were essentially 'unplugged' from the system, Jet still worried they'd someday face a situation that might lead to a conflict.

But at that moment, he turned his thoughts to the upcoming reveal. Despite Solan's suspicions, he felt much better about having the Atrum on board now. Even if they were walking a darker path, they had a common enemy and needed each other. He wasn't worried about watching his back, as Jinn had put it. But he was already wondering what would happen once the hunt for the memoirs ended. How would they split the memoirs up, assuming they even won any? Joshia had agreed to remain until all the M-Class mechs were destroyed. But who knew when that would be.

Their path down to the lower sublevels of the second belt was somewhat tedious. Solan and Joshia led the way as the others remained cloaked and hidden. Once again, hordes of seekers meandered their way into the sublevels through different routes. Most of the local businesses had sectioned off their districts, probably assuming that the fighting would spill over into the streets.

Once into the lower bowels, eddies of steam and raucous chants greeted them. Most of the seekers were beginners and had no business being in the hunt. In fact, many didn't even realize they were standing just meters away from one of the deadliest groups in the system—the Heliographi. Jet noticed the Agency and Lybra were once again in position. Inside the massive chamber, hundreds of levels of walkways spanned across the space, constructed of paper-thin reinforced graphene. The structural foundations thrust down through the levels, creating a kaleidoscope of large metallic columns. Other piping, conduit, and utilities littered the space, and the lighting within was dim and ominous. The obstacle-like course created a maze, and depending on where the memoir materialized, it would be a race to leap down or up to get to it. Solan was right. This layout might favor the Heliographi this time.

At five minutes till, Solan and Joshia ordered everyone to split up and prepare. Most of them would look to the upper levels, while some would station themselves below. Jet and Cord were placed near the mid-levels. Once again, just before the reveal, Agency troops began fighting early. It was the same distraction ploy as last time, but the Heliographi remained focused this time and waited for the memoir to reveal itself.

A loud bang issued from the darkness, and an explosion ripped through the mid-levels. It rattled the walkway, and Jet nearly tumbled over the edge.

"What in Skylight was that?" he asked Cord. Jet felt the large pipe next to him, which he assumed was some type of utility. It vibrated rapidly. "It's coming from the pipe system!" But there were kilometers of piping around them, and there was no telling how far away the explosion had occurred.

Suddenly, five M-Class mech units ripped through the pipes. They just seemed to magically appear about twenty meters in front of them but on the same level.

"Let's move!" Jet yelled, and Cord fell in behind him.

They sprinted along the thoroughfare toward the mechs. But the mechs were fast, and Jet could see they wouldn't reach them in time. The lead mech used a laser to slice through several layers of the pipe. In his peripheral vision, Jet could see the other Heliographi racing up the levels to reach them. Soon, he converged on the mech units just as several other Heliographi arrived. The lowest mech stood on the thoroughfare, mowing down other seekers. Jet hopped onto its back as Cord grappled at its leg. Another Atrum, Bofisto, was there, and he rammed his forehead into the mech's face, which seemed to stun it momentarily. The mech teetered slightly as Solan held onto its neck, trying to twist its head around.

But the mech was enormously powerful and spun quickly, flinging Bofisto off and against a pipe. Soon there were three more mechs that joined it. But the other Heliographi were arriving, and the fight was on. Joshia, Tetra, and Kamber tangled with one as Mosstrom, Jinn, and Ti-Leer tackled another one. A fourth mech unit was brought down by Renzie, Myranda, Sojahn, and Bo. Booker and Annaka joined, and the Heliographi finally managed to disable the first mech unit. It sputtered, took a few wobbly steps, then froze. Jet swung from its head and slammed his legs into it, toppling it over the edge of the thoroughfare and into the abyss below. He quickly turned his attention to the others.

Vail, Brit, and Solan managed to take out another mech. Two had now been disabled, but the other two were handling the rest of the Heliographi. Jet quickly moved to the next mech, wrenching on its arm just as it was about to hammer down on Mosstrom. He slowed it just enough for Mosstrom to roll out of the way, and the blow hit the graphene thoroughfare with so much force that it ripped the walkway in half. The surface began to fracture, and in seconds, it collapsed. Jet hurtled to the surface above and closer to the main pipe where the first mech had cut through.

It finally emerged from the pipe and held a glowing metallic tube in one of its arms, which pulsed in a reddish light. It scanned the area, then looked to the top of the chamber and was about to take flight.

"Cord! Solan!" Jet yelled and pointed to it. They rushed toward it as Jet leapt and managed to grab it by the leg. Its propulsion system roared to life, and it tried to fly off. Jet held on to its leg with one arm and grasped the edge of the pipe with his other. In seconds the pipe's metal casing was tearing, and then it sheared off. Jet still held onto its leg as the mech rocketed up, leaving the others behind. Soon the other Heliographi were so far below that they'd never get to him in time. He was now riding a rocket.

As he and the mech neared an opening in the hull above, Jet saw the pinch-point. He readied himself. Just as the mech passed through the narrow opening, he reached out and grabbed the broken hull with one hand and used his legs to absorb the force. He managed to slow the mech down and bring it to a halt.

The mech turned its head to face him as its propulsion system seemed to kick into overdrive. The strain it was putting on his legs was tremendous. But Jet held, hoping the others could get to him in time.

The mech oriented its main shoulder cannon toward him. It pointed directly at Jet's chest, and at the last second, he released the mech. It shot from the side of the bulkhead and into the night sky, its rocket leaving a vapor trail behind. Jet watched the mech fly off as he hung there looking after it. Following closely behind was a presidential skiff, no doubt with Harok and Lybra on board. Jet waited just a few seconds more, feeling defeated. Then he dropped his way back down to the other Heliographi.

In the middle of the main thoroughfare, there was nothing but carnage. Bodies lay strung about from other groups of seekers as the battle raged on. All around Jet, multiple groups of seekers continued to fight, most of them still unaware that the second memoir had already been taken. Jet located the Heliographi, all of them gathered around the lifeless body of the Atrum named Renzie.

M

Back in the control suite, they laid Renzie's body on the table, wrapped in his cloak. Joshia looked on in silence as Solan stood next to her, head bowed. Only a low thrumming in the background from the old equipment could be heard as everyone stood there. It was like the entire group was holding their breath, waiting for the dam to break.

"I find it odd that you stood there while Renzie was surrounded, Ti-Leer," Bofisto finally muttered. "I hope that wasn't on purpose."

Jet glanced up to look at the large man. His head was still bowed, his arms crossed over his chest. Bofisto balled his fists so tightly that his fingers were white as he looked at Renzie's body. Jet looked over at Ti-Leer, whose face was beat-red now.

"Oi, just like you lot did with Harriet? I don't remember any Atrum running to help her! Maybe we can settle this right now, though?" Ti-Leer gripped the edge of the table and was about to put a leg over the top and hurl himself at Bofisto.

Bofisto grinned at him, his dagger-like teeth glinting in the dim light. He lifted his arms up and curled his fingers a few times in an open invitation. "If it's a fight you want, I'm not going anywhere."

DiJinn tried to move her chair out of the way and shuffle past Cord, who was also trying to move past Jet and Kamber. Jet blocked his path just as Ti-Leer launched himself over the table. Solan moved just in time to grab Ti-Leer by his cloak, also catching a hand full of his beard, and yanked him back. Ti-Leer yelped in pain as Joshia rushed over to stand in front of Bofisto and placed a hand on his chest. She forced him to the back of the room as he continued to stare at Ti-Leer, a malicious grin on his face.

Then the rest of the room erupted with yelling and accusations. Shouts echoed off the walls while Jet stood in front of Kamber as Vail pointed at Cord, her finger pressing into his chest. Though all the Atrum remained on their side of the table, and the Lucem didn't cross over the line either, it was a tense moment. Jet worried that their alliance had just ended before it had even begun.

Solan whistled so loud that everyone stopped talking and looked at her. Joshia stood next to her, her hands on her hips as she shook her head.

"Well, this has gone off as expected," Joshia said, the corner of her lips curling up in amusement. "I knew you all wouldn't let me down. But everyone *must* set aside their differences until this hunt is over! Sojahn, Bofisto. I know you two have history with Ti-Leer and Jinn. There are rivalries among us all, but please stop." She removed Renzie's cloak and ring and slapped them into Bofisto's hand. She curled his fingers around them and stared up into his eyes. "Not right now, got it!" she said, lowering her voice. Then she turned and lifted Renzie's body and walked over to stand in front of Solan. "Can you accompany me?"

Solan nodded and faced the group. "Okay, that's it. Everyone clear out." She pulled at Jet and whispered to him. "Keep an eye on them, won't you?"

Jet watched her and Joshia leave as the rest of the Heliographi stood silently. But Jet sensed there was little desire to fight now; the explosive moment had suddenly faded away. But he knew, just like everyone else, that anger simmered in the back, waiting to boil over again. This tentative truce between the Lucem and the Atrum was going to be a challenge to maintain. Adding fuel to the fire was the that fact they'd now lost the first two memoirs to Lybra, as well as two of their own members. The feeling he sensed around the room was one he never thought he'd see in a group as powerful as the Heliographi.

Fear.

К

Solan and Joshia both made their way up to the Clipton Forest. The sound of crickets greeted them, and the wind whispered through the pine needles. Shimmering and crashing around Skylight's protective atmosphere were the turquoise waves of the Aurora Borealis.

Joshia followed Solan as if she knew where they were headed and soon they stood in a familiar clearing. Joshia set Renzie's body down in a pit circled with stones. They gathered wood and built a pyre. Before long, fire lit the clearing, and they stood back, watching silently.

Joshia held Renzie's ring and stared at it.

"This is where I laid my sister's body to rest," Solan said, her arms crossed. "Harriet as well. We're deep enough into the forest that no one ever comes this way—"

"We've never talked much about our father," Joshia interrupted Solan, surprising her.

"No, we haven't. And how could we? There's never been a good time to do so."

"I know you're ashamed of me, of what I've become. You must know that I had no choice."

"But you seemed to accept it easily enough," Solan replied.

"There's no need to patronize me, Solan. You have no right to stand there and judge me, so high and mighty. Remember, you had a choice."

"And so did you."

"Sure. You mean that I could've just chosen death over joining the Atrum?"

"It's what I would've done."

"How could you know that? You've no idea what any of the Atrum have gone through. I expected a bit more sympathy from you all. You portray yourselves as beings of mercy, of goodness. And all I see are judgmental people, not willing to lend a hand. You're exactly what you profess to despise."

"The things you've done, Joshia, how do you justify it? Lying, cheating…*murder?* We are not so removed from that day of the Century Eclipse to forget all the citizens you killed. Will you blame that on the entity that resides inside of you?"

Joshia turned away from Solan. "I can't explain it to you if you aren't willing to accept the truth about the Atrum."

"I know what it is that possesses you all. I just believe the choice would have been easier for me."

"Forget it, Solan. There's no sense in trying to understand each other, and certainly not tonight. We are not aligned in our beliefs, and I see that will never change. I came here tonight to lay one of ours to rest, not to argue."

Solan sighed, then shook her head. She reached out and laid a hand on Joshia's shoulder. "I'm sorry for your loss. That's really what I meant to say. Our father was never judgmental for his part. I know I am, and for that…again, I apologize."

"Our father," Joshia mused. "I remember the first time I found out that it was Tyberius. You used to talk about him when we were students. You blathered nonstop about how you'd someday find him."

Solan chuckled. "I was a bit obsessed to find him, I'll admit."

"I asked my mother before she died," Joshia continued. "She never knew his real name, just his alias. She did explain how he had E.M., though. I never thought to follow up on who he really was until I became an Atrum. But once I dug into it, things started to align. I did more research and finally figured it out. The great Tyberius Alexander…and he fathered me out of wedlock. Haven't you ever wondered why that was?"

Solan frowned and looked away. "I never asked him; it was none of my business. Besides, I assumed he never wanted to talk about it. I respected his privacy."

"Maybe he's not the *saint* you all portray him to be?"

Solan shot Joshia a steady glare but then shook her head. "I'm not getting into a debate about him tonight, Joshia." Solan turned back to the pyre. It was starting to burn low, and she kicked at a log. The fire sparked and hissed, sending embers into the night sky.

"I was a reject growing up, Solan. Just like you. We share the same father. We are both Heliographi. Maybe we're not so different after all?"

"We are nothing alike," Solan shot back. "We will never be alike."

"Yet we both face the same fate. We are going to lose this battle, Solan." Joshia didn't look at her as she said this. "It burns me inside to know that Lybra will win, that she will hold the memoirs and be the first to research their secrets. Those documents were meant for our eyes."

Solan slowly nodded. The same thought made her inner light flare in anger as well. She hated it as much as Joshia did, especially after what Lybra had done to her family. The assassination of her sister was still fresh on her mind, and at this very location, she had laid two Heliographi to rest. She tried to ignore the possibility that more may follow. Solan was finally accepting what every other Heliographi already knew—they were on a path to destruction unless something changed their fortunes, and quickly. If not, they would all die before the last memoir was unearthed.

CHAPTER 20
The Game Changer

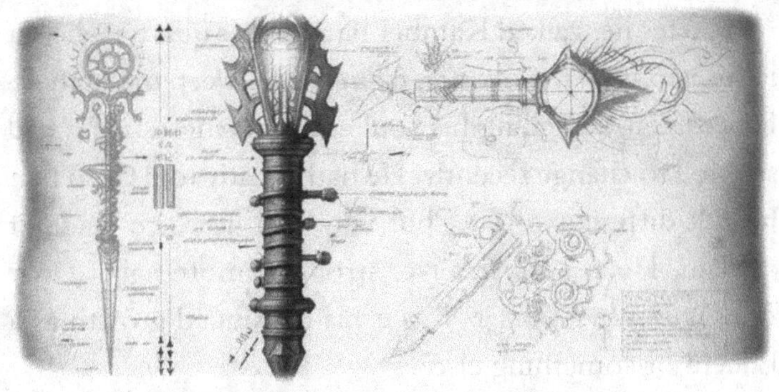

ΑΒΓΔΕ ΗΘΙΚΛ**Μ**
ΝΞΟΠΡΣ ΥΦ ΨΩ

JET SPENT SOME time with Kamber later that night.

They walked and talked under the moonlight. He felt the need to calm her nerves. She was, after all, still his warden. But in truth, he also wanted to calm his own nerves. He cared deeply for Kamber, though he was still afraid to admit his true feelings for her.

Their stroll had once again taken them to Firefly Falls, where they sat and talked near Cutter's grave. Jet was learning more about who Kamber really was, and the more he knew her, the more he wanted to be around her all the time. A dangerous time had arrived for all the Heliographi now, a point of no return, he sensed. Something had to happen…*had to*. They needed a break, some good fortune—*a blessing*.

After he walked Kamber back to her quarters, he sat in his room on the old rug, falling into a deep meditation. He relaxed, searching his soul and noticing how he had seemed to change recently. He had already told Cord that he felt different of late, but why and how, he couldn't explain. He felt more alive, stronger, more agile…*more sensitive to others' feelings*. Was it his continued growth as a Lucem or something else?

He let his inner Heliographi, or light, run and recharge.

And once again, an epiphany came to him as he woke.

Sometimes his transition back to reality brought little moments of clarity, a rare gift, Cord had claimed. This time, he finally knew how to solve the riddle at the Hall of Vital Records. He knew what the ghost Lucem named Brindall had been trying to tell him.

Though it was late, he dressed and stole out to his skiff.

He used one of the lesser-known traffic lanes and guided his skiff out to the ninth belt and the Agency headquarters. He talked down the voice in his head, calling him crazy for going this late. Security would be much tighter now, especially with two of the memoirs at that location. There would be mech units patrolling the area. The thought crossed his mind to wake Cord and tell him. But he dismissed it, knowing Cord would likely try to prevent him from going tonight. But Jet knew his conscience wouldn't let him rest until he did this, and he wouldn't wait any longer. Something was telling him this was important.

Soon he was winding his way through the vacant corridors of the old Lucem wing. Once inside, he found the Hall of Vital Records and stopped just inside. The moonlight washed down over the old wall the ghost Lucem had pointed out during his dream. There were glyphs written in a language he couldn't read, but that wasn't what he was concerned about.

He sat down in front of his symbol, crossed his legs, and fell almost immediately into a state of meditation. Before long, he felt the presence of the old ghost Lucem standing near him. It was Brindall.

Jet stood in his out-of-body self and stopped in front of the tall Lucem. The broad man's long, flowing hair seemed wispy in the moonlight, almost like a gossamer web. The man gave him a grim look, then lowered his gaze. Jet focused his thoughts, letting his mind open up.

He felt as if he stood at the end of a long tunnel. At the opposite end was Brindall. The Lucem beckoned to him, and Jet opened his thoughts. Jet was now conversing with the ghost of a dead Lucem. *Does it get any more bizarre than this?* Jet mused.

The ghost's thoughts began to flood into his mind, images from ages past. Eras of life, love, and misery. He was seeing into Brindall's past now—trials, tribulations, and accomplishments. His youth and growing up in underground caves—the ARC district! Jet's own home. He'd had no idea Brindall had been born there, but well over a century ago.

But that wasn't what he needed to see, and he focused deeper. A shape kept coming to the forefront, something small, about the size of his hand and rounded at the edges. Something very similar to Albright's Key.

A key he'd just recovered at the Century Eclipse…

A key that would unlock something of great power…

A key that the Skylight Fallout had died to reveal…

Jet snapped out of his trance, his skin cold with goosebumps lining his arms and neck as he reached quickly into his pocket. Thankfully he'd had the sense to grab it that day after Ti-Leer had set it on the table. He had Albright's Key and *knew* that it unlocked something special now.

Jet's hand trembled as he held the key and raced over to stand before his symbol in his meditation chamber. Just below it was a slot, the same shape as the key he held. He slid Albright's Key into the slot, and it began to pulse rapidly. The symbol of the letter M glowed in different colors before finally stopping on the same color as his eyes, a vibrant turquoise. He pulled the key back and placed it in his cloak. Then he heard something click.

A stone panel slid open.

Jet peered into the opening, then stepped inside an old dusty corridor. All was silent. He reached tentatively into a crack in the stone wall. Inside, he felt something cold, smooth. It was anchored in place, and he gave it a swift tug and fell on his backside. In his hand was what appeared to be an old, wooden staff. It was perhaps two meters long, with rounded ends. There were jagged edges in the middle of it, which reminded him of a lightning bolt, in a way. The staff was more like a bionic wooden branch, like it had been shattered at some point and reconstructed with gears and gadgets to make it whole again. Shards of the ancient wood appeared to have been scientifically stitched back together by some mad scientist. It was a hybrid of nature and metal, with a twist of magic and mysticism, it seemed—a steampunk miracle. The closer he looked, the more he noticed inner metal rods and gears. There was a faint inner glow that seemed to be dormant. It was an intricate and impressive feat of engineering—*but what did it do?*

Near the middle of the staff was a spike-looking peg. Around the ends was a strange metallic material, like a collar, and etched into the length of the staff's middle portion were Greek symbols. On further inspection, he noticed they were all twelve of the Lucem symbols.

He stood and held the staff up. It was light, as if it were hollow inside. But when he swung it, there was a weight to it that carried some heft. As he held the staff, the natural ergonomics of it placed the long, spiked peg near his right hand. The hole in his hand, which had been burned through during his conversion ritual, seemed to be a perfect match.

His entire body trembled as he placed the spike through the opening in his palm. What happened next nearly caused him to drop the staff. It flickered like an old fluorescent light bulb coming to life. Then the entire room lit up in a turquoise light. The staff began to vibrate in his hands as if it were waking from a long slumber. The Greek symbols pulsed and almost seemed to whisper to him, at least, that's what it sounded like to his ears.

"What in Skylight have I found?" Jet muttered.

Holding the staff, he felt an immense power flooding through his hands and body. He simply stared at it for several minutes in awe.

Then a voice whispered to him. It was Brindall.

Leave!

Jet turned just in time to see the shadow of something glittering in the dark. It was an M-Class mech unit.

Jet knew then he had stepped right into a trap.

The mech unit hunched through the doorway and then stood to its full height of nearly four meters. Two more mechs stepped in right behind it. Jet was trapped. There was only one way out. Jet lifted his hood and disappeared.

But the mechs could see into multiple spectrums, and his cloaking ability was useless.

The mechs circled, and Jet brought the staff up defensively. The first mech fired a round at him from its large shoulder cannon. Jet stood his ground and shifted the staff, placing it in front of his body. He flinched, expecting the wooden staff to shatter. But the round hit it and ricocheted back at the mech, blasting one of its arms off.

The second mech lunged at Jet so quickly that he was barely able to move the staff over. He thrust it up and under the mech's chin. It struck home, wedged in place. Jet hauled backward on the staff, pulling with all his might. He felt his back muscles strain as the head of the mech popped off like a toy and slammed into the wall. Jet watched in shock as the mech powered down and dropped to its knees. He quickly brought the staff down on a wide, sweeping arc, landing it between the void in the mech's shoulders. The staff literally split the mech unit in half. He kicked it away just as the third mech maneuvered in behind him and grabbed his left arm. Jet felt a searing pain as it clamped down on his bicep. He did the only thing he could think of and slammed his staff onto the floor.

An electric pulse, similar to what was known as an EMP, radiated outward, and the current passed through the metal floor. The mech unit convulsed as the electricity sizzled up its legs and through its graphene-reinforced metal body. Jet let the staff stay in contact with the floor for a few seconds, then pulled it away. The mech released him and dropped, smoking in a twisted heap of scrap. The first mech had caught the EMP pulse as well and dropped to the ground.

Jet stood in the center of the space, looking around him at the smoking remains. A look of confusion, surprise, and elation lit across his face. He didn't know what to do until he heard Brindall's voice again.

RUN!

Jet bolted from the chamber and didn't look back. He could sense there were more mechs heading his direction, probably alerted by the ones he'd just fried. He raced through the empty Lucem corridors and to the outskirts of Memorial Park. He tossed the staff into the cockpit of his skiff and fired up the engines. He was airborne and cloaked in seconds, shoving his thrusters into overdrive. He felt a moment of relief until his console blipped. A warning signal lit up his display.

Jammer class skiffs, two of them.

The missile-shaped skiffs were advanced beyond the capabilities of his recon-issued skiff. He already knew he couldn't beat them in a head-to-head battle. He piloted his skiff closer to the terrain of the eighth belt and maneuvered low to the ground, weaving between the lush vegetation and trees. He might be able to evade their tracking system if he stayed close to the surface. But he was also dangerously close to Goliath's Gate, the particle collider hidden in the eighth belt's hull. This was probably the one other place he shouldn't be, considering it was run by the Agency and funded by Lybra.

Behind him, the two jammers were making up ground. He was running out of time, and soon they'd get a lock on him. His recon skiff was capable, one of the top attack skiffs available. But as he had recently learned, Lybra was funding all kinds of advanced prototypes, and the jammers were unmatched in the sky.

His console began to chirp. Jet was faced with trying to outmaneuver the two jammers or bail out and take his chances on the ground. He decided not to risk it and grabbed his staff and ejected. Seconds later, the jammers got a lock, and his skiff erupted in a ball of flame. He used his hover pack to quickly land on the ground and rolled into the heavy underbrush and waited.

The jammers circled back and hovered nearby. Once again, his cloak was of little use, as the jammers could see into different spectrums. They lined up and readied to open fire on him. Jet stepped up, stood, and held the staff in front of him. Like before, it began to vibrate rapidly and glowed a bright turquoise color. The jammers opened fire, using their heavy forward cannons to mow down everything around him. But he felt the staff begin to move in his hands, and it easily deflected the rounds coming in. The railgun rounds sizzled past him, but most of the incoming fire was reflected back at the jammers. It wasn't long until a round hit one with enough force to tear through the cockpit and into the pilot.

The jammer dropped immediately into a tailspin and crashed into the adjacent jammer. They slammed into the ground with enough force to send a shockwave out that blew him over and onto his back. The loud explosion reverberated around the forest trees and into the night sky.

I

Cord sat up in his bed.

He swung his legs over the mattress, grabbed his cloak, and marched into Jet's quarters. He turned the light on only to see his bed empty.

Cord cursed under his breath.

He already knew where Jet was. But he also sensed that Jet might be in trouble.

Ten minutes later, Cord was in his skiff and rocketing toward the eighth belt. He landed it on the outskirts of one of the larger provinces. It was growing close to dawn, and the sky was beginning to glow a fiery pastel pink. The corona of the sun was just about to edge past the dark sphere of the earth. Cord settled his skiff down in the dense forest. He hopped out, cloaked, and let his mind reach out for Jet. He sensed he wasn't too far away. Once he began moving in that direction, he recognized a faint hiccup that was Jet's mental signature. Cord eventually stumbled across the remains of a wrecked skiff. It was a recon-issued skiff, one that matched the same marking as Jet's. Cord knelt low and searched the smoking remains, drawing in a sigh of relief when he found the cockpit empty.

What the hell was Jet up to now? Cord thought.

Jet was always doing these crazy things, but he had promised to let Cord know this time. Although Jet was good at working his way out of tight situations, tonight, his luck seemed to have run out. He'd have to have a talk with him.

Cord could see the guard towers in the distance. Those watch posts were for Goliath's Gate, and he had to take caution not to get too close or risk alerting the Agency. But Jet might have already done that anyway. Cord needed to locate him quickly.

He let his mind reach out again, calling to Jet, and eventually heard another faint hiccup. Cord followed the mental signature down a winding trail and through the trees, where he stumbled upon a clearing. The entire area was smoking and cratered as if a recent battle had occurred there. The trees looked like kindling, and the ground was pitted from heavy rounds of ammo.

Cord continued to work his way through the ruined field until he saw Jet propped against a tree.

CHAPTER 21
Mystical Contraband

ΑΒΓΔΕ ΗΘΙΚΛ**Μ**
ΝΞΟΠΡΣ ΥΦ ΨΩ

MIND IF I enquire what the *hell* is going on?" Cord asked in his slow drawl and helped Jet to his feet.

Jet stood, cradling one arm. The nasty cut from where the mech unit had grabbed his bicep had clotted, but his skin was still black and blue. There were a few cuts on his face, but he felt fine otherwise.

"Why are you here, Cord!" Jet hissed.

"I'm here to bail you out, it seems."

"I can handle it," Jet replied. "You shouldn't be here."

"Well, I'm sorry to say that I am. And by the look of things, you should be glad."

Jet turned and limped a few steps. Perhaps he was angrier at himself than Cord. The last thing he needed was to place another one of his friends in danger. Jet took a deep breath. "Well…thanks for coming after me, I guess. I'm fine, I think, but I could use a lift."

"Mind telling me what this is all about?" Cord asked.

Jet pulled the staff from his cloak and held it out for Cord. "You've noticed all the wreckage, no doubt?"

Cord nodded. "What happened here?"

"Two jammers shot down my skiff. I used this staff to take them out."

Cord took the staff and held it. "How could something like this accomplish that?"

"There's more. I also took out several M-Class mechs with it too. I got ambushed in the Hall of Vital Records. They were patrolling the halls of our old Lucem wing. It was a trap."

Cord looked at the spike in the middle of the staff. He held his own hand over it, but the staff remained silent. Jet took it back, placed the spike over the hole in his hand, and it lit up.

Cord gasped. "We need to get this back to headquarters, Jet. We need to research this thing."

Jet stopped him. "No. Not yet."

"Something else to add?"

"Well, yeah…actually." Jet hobbled a bit as they hurried back toward Cord's skiff. "Apparently, this staff was made specifically for me. With it, I took out those two jammers and multiple mechs by myself. *By myself,* Cord. It took four Heliographi to bring just one M-Class mech down. This is the turning point we've been looking for! Albright designed this staff for a Heliographi. He must have known we'd need this in times of war. We're on the brink of extinction, we're losing Heliographi, and we've all but lost the hunt for the memoirs. This is what we needed, and I'm guessing there are twenty-three more of these back at the Hall of Vital Records. And…I know how to get them." Jet held out Albright's Key.

"Intriguing," Cord said. "Albright's Key was literally a key. It wasn't meant for the memoirs, though, but for these staffs. Yet, that makes little sense. The key was supposed to be used for the memoirs. I don't quite—"

"Later, Cord. We can figure it out later. We have to move now if we want to get back in before word gets out."

"But you just said they ambushed you in the old Lucem wing. That place is probably crawling with mechs now. I predict we are unlikely to succeed."

"This may be our only chance to get the staffs," Jet said. "And remember, Memorial Park will be opening soon."

Cord rubbed his chin. "Using our alias, we might be able to get past the front areas and into the back. I suppose that might work. But this all seems pretty risky, even for my liking. I don't know about this—"

"Cord. If we don't get these staffs now, we're as good as dead. The way I see it, this is our only way forward. Plus, don't you want your own staff?" Jet held the glowing staff in front of Cord's face and watched his eyes twinkle in wonder.

"Very well. And how do you propose to hide that thing? We can't very well just stroll into a public space with a battle staff."

Jet held the staff upright, then he hammered it on the ground a few times. The staff reduced in size by about two thirds. It looked like a small stick now, compact enough to hide inside his cloak.

"Let's roll," Cord said and led the way.

M

Memorial Park was already bustling with field tours and day camps. Tour guides entered the space, and Jet and Cord donned their alias and fell into line with one of the tours. Jet led the way as they eventually broke off and moved into the back-of-house areas. Jet tried not to rush, but he felt a sense of urgency coursing through him. He only hoped that no one would assume they'd be dumb enough to return so soon.

Surprisingly, the hallways of the old Lucem wing were mostly vacant. Jet and Cord drew their cloaks and moved silently through the corridors. They paused just outside the Hall of Vital Records and listened. Cord reached out, scanning the area. He held up two fingers, indicating two mech units inside. Jet nodded.

Jet snuck inside, working his way around the chamber and holding his staff in front of him. He checked the space, making sure it was clear, then he returned to Cord and handed him Albright's Key.

"Look to the individual chambers," Jet whispered. "You'll see the slot at the bottom matching the key's shape. I'll guard the front. As soon as the mechs see us, they'll send a distress signal. We'll have only a few minutes to get out."

Cord nodded and hurried off.

Beyond, Jet could see the shadow of several more mechs patrolling the area. Apparently, the two mechs were now six. Jet lifted his staff and felt the ache in his injured arm. He sensed the mechs were aware of their presence now and began circling around him. The AI in these units was scary compared to the previous models. They were working as a team, and he felt that they'd already learned from their first attack against him. Jet sent a mental thought for Cord to hurry, then prepared himself for the assault.

The mechs moved in, all six approached from the front. Jet inched into the hall, still holding his war staff in front of him. They moved in sequence, using their artificial intelligence to work as one unit. The mech to Jet's right lunged forward, followed by the one to his left, which forced him to parry on two fronts. It stretched his motions to the max and left him open to the frontal attack. The middle four units moved in quickly, and Jet was nearly overwhelmed. His staff moved so quickly that it was a turquoise blur. He managed to disable the mech on his left and then the one on his right. But after several minutes of fighting, he was suddenly struggling to fend off the remaining four.

He was forced to duck and roll, then he backed toward a wall, which placed the mechs in front of him now. In the background, he could see Cord still gathering the staffs. But the mechs also sensed the movement and turned to engage Cord. Jet tried to block their path, but a mech managed to sweep his legs out from beneath him, and he lay on his back now. He raised his staff and blocked the mech's fist as it hammered down. Jet pressed up and thrust his staff through its neck. It stuttered, then powered down. He flung the carcass to the side, then flipped to his feet.

But as soon as he regained his balance, the other three mechs pressed in. His arm screamed at him in pain, and he was growing tired. Jet continued to block and parry between the three mechs, trying to give Cord as much time as possible. He finally saw an opening and drove his staff through one's midsection and ripped backward. Mechanical bits and pieces exploded onto the floor, sounding like wind chimes. Jet finished it off, bringing his staff down on the mech's head. It split in half with a burst of light that lit up the chamber. Jet hobbled backward from the two remaining mechs. They were forcing him deeper into the chamber now, and Jet scanned the dark for Cord, wondering where he'd gone.

"Cord!" Jet hissed. He knew if they didn't finish this up quickly, backup units would soon arrive.

A yellow-greenish light shone from the dark behind the two mechs. The light moved so quickly that Jet could barely follow it. The lightning bolt moved up and through one of the mechs, splitting it in half. The final mech turned just in time to see the bolt of lightning slam through its visor. All four of its arms reached up to grasp Cord's staff just before it powered down and dropped to the steel riveted floor.

Cord stood over it, holding his own staff, then looked up at Jet and smiled his crooked smile. "I think this is gonna be interesting."

Jet shook his head and chuckled. He leaned on his staff. "Yeah, that was my reaction as well. Let's move before backup arrives."

Minutes later, they were moving through the public thoroughfare of the museum, dressed in their guises. They tried to blend in with all the other citizens. Jet imagined how awkward they looked, though; two middle-aged men dressed like professors, each carrying a dozen wooden staffs while dropping them to the floor and cursing as they raced out of Memorial Park Museum.

Jet tossed the staffs into Cord's skiff. Cord jammed the thrusters into overdrive, cloaked it, and maneuvered under the belly of the ruined ninth belt. Then he rocketed over to a nearby, free-floating chunk of debris. He pulled the skiff into a shadowy area where he powered down the thrusters and anchored to the side of it. He shut down all the systems and waited.

"What are you doing?"

"Hiding." Cord nodded to the horizon, and three jammer class skiffs roared by their location. Jet watched as the jammers wove in between the thousands of free-floating chunks of the ninth belt's debris. The jammers searched frantically, zipping from one chunk to another.

"Good thinking," Jet said and settled back, rubbing his arm. "I should have thought to do that."

Cord picked up his staff and examined it. "You mentioned a game changer. I think you may have located it."

"Yeah, I think so too. But have you ever heard of anything like this? I had no idea Albright created these. The wood is light but hard as steel. It must be interlaced with graphene or something. I split that last mech's head open like it was made of tin."

"Something tells me there's all kinds of secrets to discover in these," Cord said. "I've read nothing in my studies about them. Albright kept them a secret. I wonder if each one carries the same abilities or if they vary between staffs?"

"Good question. We'll have to test them out. But…should we trust the Atrum with these?"

"We may not have a choice," Cord replied thoughtfully. "If we want to survive and beat these mechs, we're going to have to share this with the Atrum." Cord set his staff down, then looked at Jet's arm. "We need to get you back to base."

Jet lifted his sleeve and rolled back the fabric of his cloak. The deep cut had healed, but the bruise was still evident. He guessed that his arm had been broken but was already starting to heal amazingly fast.

"Cord…" Jet paused and sat back in his seat, and winced.

Cord looked at him. "Something to say?"

"Yeah, I was just wondering…I've never asked anyone this, but when you meditate, what do you see?"

"Colors, lights. Stars and galaxies. I suppose that's how I would explain it."

"Do…you ever see other people? Do they talk to you?"

Cord narrowed his eyes. "No, not exactly. Dare I ask why?"

Jet rested his head on the back of the seat and closed his eyes. He rubbed his arms as he considered if he should tell Cord what he'd been seeing and hearing during meditation. Something seemed to be holding him back, though.

"Jet. What are you implying?"

"It's nothing, Cord. Never mind. I must be woozy from the day."

Cord held his gaze, then slowly nodded. "Sure. Just let me know when you're ready to talk about that."

CHAPTER 22
A New Power Revealed

ΑΒΓΔΕ ΗΘΙΚΛ<u>Μ</u>
ΝΞΟΠΡΣ ΥΦ ΨΩ

WHEN JET AND Cord arrived back at the first belt, they smuggled the staffs in through the lower levels of Lyrinthum, dropping a few of them as they hurried into the control suite. Jet suggested they stash them in the old furnace room where he and Cord occasionally met for private conversations.

Jet asked that Cord give him time to think about what to do with them. But both agreed that Cord would keep his own staff...*for research purposes*, Cord had argued. He had a genuine fascination with the staffs, and if anyone could dig up more information about them, it was Cord.

With just one day until the third reveal, Jet had to make a big decision, and quickly. If he and some of the other Lucem just showed up at the reveal with their own shiny new toys, the Atrum allegiance would likely crumble from lack of trust. Even though he'd fought off several mechs with his staff, he'd still had a few close calls and a pretty nasty injury as well. Plus, he'd seen with his own eyes the staggering number of the new mechs Lybra had at her disposal. It was just a matter of time until she unleashed them. War staffs or not, the sheer amount of mechs would eventually overwhelm them. He had made up his mind. The Atrum would be given their staffs. It was evident that Albright had meant for it to be that way. After all, he'd purposely designed those staffs for all twenty-four Heliographi, and it wasn't up to Jet to deprive them of that.

Then a thought suddenly hit him, a tactic Lybra had used against the Agency. In fact, she had used it to gain leverage over Harok. She was *depriving* him of the much-needed rare-earth minerals by disrupting his supply lines. The raids had been devastating to the Goliath's Gate project.

So, why couldn't the Heliographi do the same thing to her?

They knew now that Lybra had been hoarding the rare-earth for multiple reasons. Not just using it as leverage, but she needed the minerals to build her army of mechs. But there was a finite amount of rare-earth minerals in her stockpile. If the Heliographi could steal it or disrupt her supply lines, they might be able to limit the number of mechs being produced.

But that might have to wait, at least until they could find a break in the action. The next reveal was their main focus right now. After that, they might be able to quickly turn their attention to it. Jet made a mental note of it as he stepped into his quarters.

He ached all over, his muscles sore from the events of that day. He slid his cloak off, compressed the staff by tapping it on the ground twice, then set it on his nightstand. Anyone who didn't know what it was wouldn't think twice about it.

He crossed his legs and began meditating. He needed the healing, both physically and mentally. But what he really wanted was answers, and he hoped that when he finished his session, he might have an answer for how and when he should distribute the staffs.

M

When Jet awoke in the morning, he rolled on his side to check the time. When he glanced at his nightstand, he noticed his staff was missing.

He sat up and searched his room, trying to remain calm. Had it all been a dream?

"Looking for this, Stroud?"

Jet wheeled to see Vail standing in his doorway. She held his staff, but it was still compressed. In the dim light, Vail resembled a serpent for just a split second—eyes glowing, scales reflecting the light, and fangs bared.

"Hand it over," Jet said and held out his hand.

"Mind explaining what you're up to?" she said in a casual tone, but he could hear the anger and distrust behind it. "This doesn't look like a toy. I get the sense that you and brainiac are holding out on us."

"I don't know what you're talking about, Vail. But I don't appreciate you going through my things."

"Oh, but you do know what this is, I believe," Vail stepped into his room and twirled the compressed staff in her fingers. "We're a team now, Stroud. You, me…*Ledbetter!* We don't hide things from each other. At least, that's what I thought this agreement was supposed to be. And already I see that we can't trust each other."

"Who said I was hiding anything?"

"Oh, I suppose this is just a trinket?" she asked. "Don't lie to me. You're no good at it, you never were."

"Hand it over, Vail. I don't want to hurt you."

"As if you could!" she chuckled. "You're so weak. You need to toughen up, you and the other Lucem, if you want to survive what's ahead! I can teach you how. Let me show you how easy it is." Vail crept closer to him, walking around him and stopping just behind him, her mouth near his ear as she whispered. "You could be the ultimate killer, Stroud. You have the ability. You just have to want it! This is no time to hold back. Won't you let me show you how?" she teased.

"You're losing it, Vail. Or have you already? If you lose your calm, you'll never find your way back. I can show you how to find the light again." Jet circled *her* now, poised and steady. But inside, he could hardly believe they were on the verge of fighting each other. He'd hoped they had left all that behind them by joining forces, but he sensed things were teetering on the edge.

Vail continued to hold the staff with both hands. "If you don't tell me what this is, I'll break it in half. I know it means something to you. Tell me. What are the Lucem hiding?"

"Give it to me, Vail. The staff wasn't meant for you," Jet said, lowering his gaze at her. He shook slightly though as he held his hand out. He was worried she might destroy the staff, and if she did, what then? Back to square one?

"Fine!" she said. "It's your decision." She lifted the staff, then brought it down on her knee in one swift motion.

"NO!" Jet lunged forward, but too late.

Time seemed to move slowly as he watched Vail wrench the staff on top of her knee.

But nothing happened.

The staff didn't even bend, and Vail dropped it in surprise.

Jet lunged to grab it, but Vail snatched it up again and sidestepped him. "What the hell is this thing?"

Jet lunged again and tried to pry it from her grasp. She held on to it, though, and yanked it from him, then swung the compressed staff at his head. Jet ducked, and the staff struck the bulkhead with a resounding thud that echoed around the room, but it did little harm to the wall. Had he been the one swinging it, there would've been a large hole in that wall.

He stood up straight. "You really don't want to be doing that, Vail."

"What, protecting myself from you?"

"Are you really here to fight or to get answers?" he asked. "Hand me the staff if you want answers."

Vail continued to hold the staff, her eyes still wide with shock and wonder.

"The staff doesn't work that way, and it won't work for you or any other Heliographi."

"Where did you get this? Tell me where, and I'll give it back to you."

"You'll give it back to me regardless," he said.

But Vail stood her ground, still uncertain.

"I'm not going to backstab you or the other Atrum. You know me better. That isn't how I work. I have a decision to make, and this isn't helping your cause or any of the other Atrum."

"I know you, but I wouldn't put it past Ledbetter, or some of the other Lucem. DiJinn seems to have it in for us."

"Can you blame her?" Jet shot back. "How many times did you murder Shiloe when you had her captive?"

"That was before me, and you know it."

"But you sat there and let it happen, didn't you?"

"What would you have me do, challenge all the Atrum?" Vail asked. "Stroud, if we're gonna work together, you have to understand something. We aren't like each other. You want to change me, but that's not gonna happen. As much as it might bother you, we are on opposite sides of the spectrum. We're a team, but you have to let us do things our way, and you aren't going to like it much."

"And I sense that you want to change me, too," Jet replied. "That's not possible."

"So, let's do each other a favor and let it go," Vail shot back.

Jet looked at her. "I guess we'll see how that goes. Right now, let's start with a little trust." He held out his hand for the staff.

She looked down at the staff, then reluctantly handed it over.

Jet took it and examined it. There wasn't even a scratch where Vail had brought it to her knee. He held it above his head, then placed the spike into the opening in his palm. The staff immediately lit up with a turquoise light, and the glyphs along the staff began to glow. The ancient wood almost seemed to hum as if it were trying to speak to him. Then he brought the staff down on the floor, and it decompressed to the full length, some two meters. The metal endcap seemed to spark when it connected with the thick steel plate, and the room quivered and vibrated. Jet held the staff there, letting Vail get a good look at it.

"If you behave, and don't mention this to anyone else, you might even get your own," Jet said.

M

Jet had plans to meet Solan out in the Clipton Forest the next evening.

As he stole through the old Lyrinthum passages, he blocked off the voices that seemed to haunt the area. He popped up through the Clipton portal, greeted by the murmuring crickets and the moon that peered through the wispy clouds. The branches of the tall evergreens cast skeletal patterns on the forest floor as he jogged along.

Jet had decided to bring the war staff with him, tucked under his cloak in its compressed form. He had made the decision to tell Solan after his unexpected clash with Vail. She needed to hear this from him, not another Atrum. He knew just where to find her, too, now that she spent nearly every evening at the clearing.

Jet stepped into the firelight and stopped next to Solan. The fire flickered and popped as she stared into the flames, her arms crossed.

Jet glanced over at her. "You sure seem to spend a lot of time out here lately."

Solan turned and gave him a puzzled look. "And you spend a lot of time at Firefly Falls. Yes, I know about that place and that you buried Cutter there. Seems logical that we'd both do as much. Why don't you say what's really on your mind?"

Jet shuffled his feet in the gravel and looked up to the sky. "You've been oddly controlled over this whole thing. The Solan I used to know wouldn't have slept until your sister's killer was brought to justice. Instead, you've hardly said a word."

"Does this have something to do with Cutter?"

"Well, I just…" Jet paused and took a deep breath, trying to rein in his sudden emotions. "When Lybra murdered Cutter, I saw the whole thing, just watched it happen as those marauders held me. I felt hate, rage. I wanted revenge. And yet, if Lybra was standing here in front of me, right now…I don't think I could do it. I've decided she's not worth it. Maybe that makes me weak?"

Solan reached out and grasped his shoulder and gave him a gentle smile. "No. It means *you* have control over your emotions. I felt the same, that day you brought my sister's body. I felt the hate and rage. I was teetering on the edge."

He nodded, took a moment, then asked her the question that was really on his mind. "I sense there's something more you want to tell me, though."

She seemed to hesitate for a second, her head bowed and eyes looking at the fire. "You're right. And now that you're second-in-command, I suppose I shouldn't keep anything from you. Tyberius asked me to refrain from avenging my sister's death."

"And you agreed to that?"

"Well, I never *quite* said that. He seemed to be warning me, though."

"Warning? In what way?"

"Something about my soul's essence and how it depended upon me *not* taking action. He only said justice would come on its own and urged me not to seek it out. Others might follow my lead if I didn't control my anger."

Jet thought back to the night he'd buried Cutter's body. He remembered how he'd nearly lost control for a second time. But then the intuitive voice had calmed him, warned him to be careful with that feeling of hatred. *Avoid it*, it had said.

"You're not alone, Solan. Maybe we can fight this together? Our own little support group," he said with a chuckle.

"I'll consider it," she said with a weak smile. "We've got plenty of other issues to worry about right now. So, why are you here? Surely not to talk about a support group."

Jet slid the staff from his cloak and held the small branchlike object up to her.

Solan took it in one hand, balancing it on her finger. "What in Skylight is this?"

"Honestly, I'm not entirely sure." He took it back, then placed the spike into the opening of his hand. He knelt and hammered it on the ground and the war staff decompressed to its full size. It roared to life, bathing the clearing in an eerie turquoise glow. The shadows seemed to flee the area as if being expelled.

"Well, well," Solan said, her eyes glowing a bit brighter in the fire.

Jet handed it to her, and the glow from the staff faded. "This thing seems to generate its power from me or from my inner light, I guess. Look," he said and took it back. He walked over to a nearby tree and then slammed the butt of the staff into its large trunk. The tree quivered and shattered. It fell to the ground with a loud crash.

Solan narrowed her eyes. "Where did you get this?" she whispered.

"The Hall of Vital Records…by using this." He held up Albright's Key. "It turns out that this thing really *is* a key. It just wasn't meant for the memoirs, I guess."

"What else did you find?"

"There's one for each of us, Solan. Even the Atrum. Albright must have built these for a time of great need. A time like now. And the fact that he built one for each Atrum tells me that he intended for us to fight through this together. He knew we'd need these war staffs."

Solan stared at him, then she kicked the fire with her boot and extinguished it. "Show me."

Jet led Solan back to the control room. Together they snuck through the corridors, watching for any Atrum. They entered the old furnace room, and Jet was surprised to see Cord sitting there, holding his staff. It glowed the same color as his eyes.

"Evening," Cord said and stood. "I assumed it wouldn't take long for you two to arrive. Pardon my intrusion."

Solan considered for a second, then shrugged. "It's fine. This secret won't last long."

Jet walked over to the old furnace, a massive iron grate with a small defunct reactor in the middle. He kicked the grate, and it swung open like a prison cell door with a low groan. He walked into the furnace, and the other two followed. Tucked behind the reactor was a bundled blanket. Jet slid it across the floor toward Solan. She nudged the bundle open with her boot and watched as the other twenty-two staffs spilled onto the cold metal floor.

"So, I guess the question is, how much do you trust the Atrum?" Jet asked.

"You know the answer to that question," she scoffed.

Jet nodded in agreement. "I suppose the bigger question is, what will the Atrum do if we show up to the next reveal with these war staffs and they have none?"

"They'd leave us," Cord chimed in.

"Do we even care?" Solan asked in a half-joking tone.

"Let me just say this," Jet said. "I hear the reluctance, but it's apparent Albright meant for this to happen. Otherwise, he would've only designed staffs for the Lucem. He's even built one for Sybold."

Solan stood, her arms crossed. "I don't like this arrangement for a lot of reasons. I don't trust the Atrum. They'll abandon us as soon as the opportunity presents itself. But you *are* right…I sense this was meant to be, at least for now."

"Grudgingly, I must also agree." Cord leaned on his staff. "We're giving them a tremendous power, and if things go askew between us, we'll probably regret it."

"We just have to think one step ahead of them, then," Jet said. "Right now, we need the Atrum if we want to beat Lybra."

"Let's call a meeting for the morning. We're going to take the risk and hope for the best. But first…" she knelt and searched the pile for her own staff. As soon as she touched the staff, it began to glow. Solan stood and slammed it on the riveted floor, and her staff decompressed to its full height. The shape of Solan's staff was much longer and thinner, almost delicate. It had a jagged angle at both ends, like a splintered branch that had been struck by lightning.

Solan's eyes seemed to light up brighter as she held her staff, and a smile eased across her face. She knelt and kicked through the other staffs, finally lifting three others.

"What are you doing?" Jet asked.

"Cord. If you don't mind, please keep this quiet for the moment. I'll address this in the meeting tomorrow. Right now, I have other business with these three staffs." Solan held the staffs up in the dim light to get a better look at them. Then she slid them into her cloak and stared directly at Jet. "You're coming with me."

CHAPTER 23
Lost Lucem—A Reunion

ΑΒΓΔΕ ΗΘΙΚΛ**Μ**
ΝΞΟΠΡΣ ΥΦ ΨΩ

JET FOLLOWED SOLAN as they snuck into Shiloe's quarters.

Solan stood over Shiloe as she slept. The teenager tossed and turned; her dreams filled with nightmares. Solan placed a hand on Shiloe's forehead, and she calmed. Jet didn't have to read her thoughts to feel her fear, anger, and darkness. The torture she'd endured over the last century was beyond comprehension. No one should have to face such an ordeal, and he feared that the young Shiloe might never be the same. It appeared that Vishmu therapy could only heal so much. Jet suddenly realized that Shiloe didn't belong with them, at least not right now. She was beyond their help. Add to the fact she was too young to go through the conversion ritual—not to mention all the challenges ahead with the upcoming memoir reveals— Shiloe would be better off away from them.

Solan roused Shiloe, then quieted her. "It's alright, Shiloe. It's me."

Shiloe sat up and stared at them, her glowing reddish-orange eyes already brimming with tears. "What are we doing?"

Solan took her hand. "We're going someplace much better for you. Trust me."

M

Some thirty minutes later, Solan's skiff uncloaked in the airspace outside Skylight City and near the Galleon Quarter. Jet sat in the back seat, not asking any questions. He was curious to see where they were headed, but in the back of his mind, he thought he knew.

Solan settled her skiff at a private hangar and led them down the dirty streets of the Galleon Quarter. They hurried past old shops and boarded-up homes, eventually stopping in front of a narrow building with large steel doors. Solan pounded on it three times, paused, and then hammered on it twice more.

The large doors cracked, then swung open. An old lady with gray hair pinned in a bun and a sweater with holes in the sleeves quickly ushered them inside. She shut the doors behind them and secured several digital locks.

Jet, Solan, and Shiloe stood in a musty smelling living room. A couple of disused couches and a rickety table and chairs occupied the space. A galley-style kitchen lined the opposite wall, and there were no windows. Facing them was the old lady, and Solan gave her a quick hug.

"Back so soon?" the lady asked, then turned to face Jet. "It's nice to finally meet you, Jet Stroud."

"Stell," Solan acknowledged. "Sorry to bother you so early. Jet, this is Stell. She heads up one of the top spy syndicates in the Skylight System called Vine. She's helped the Lucem on multiple occasions, and we are grateful for her help over the years." Solan turned to Shiloe, who was trying to hide behind her and peeking under her arm. Solan put her arm around Shiloe and guided the girl to stand in front.

Stell gasped as she looked into the girl's glowing eyes. "Well, this is a surprise!" she said, then held out her hand. "You are welcome here, Shiloe. Do not worry, you're safe with us."

The teenager took the lady's hand and followed her into the kitchen. Stell opened a cabinet and punched in a code on a keypad. The large island slid sideways to reveal a staircase. The four of them walked down the stairs and into the lower portions of a secret complex. The hidden basement was vast and housed a half-way home funded by the Lucem and several other wealthy backers. Recent construction to expand the facility was nearing completion, and the underground complex stretched for multiple levels. Stell guided them through the space as she spoke to Solan.

"I think I know why you're here, but why now?" Stell asked.

Solan walked along behind them, her arms crossed and folded inside her cloak. "We can't afford to lose her, and we can't protect her against what's coming. I think you *know* what's coming."

"Yes, I'm aware of the reveals. Those first two were tough losses," Stell said. "We've heard all the news about the lost Heliographi as well. Lybra is a dangerous person. She has President Harok's ear, and he's vulnerable right now. Her strength is the ability to exploit others. I'm worried about what that might mean for the Skylight System."

"But is Harok really that vulnerable?" Solan asked, and it sounded more like an observation than a question. "I'm not so sure," Solan continued. "He may be ambitious and needy right now, but he's not an idiot. I don't think he's that gullible."

They stopped in front of a large door. A pair of armed guards stood aside as Stell walked in. As soon as the doors opened, a tall man stood in their way, his glowing orange eyes staring back at them. The man's long, silver hair was pushed to one side and his matching beard was braided with colored beads.

Solan gave the dark-skinned man a hug. "It's good to see you, father."

"Solan. I thought we agreed this wouldn't happen," Tyberius said.

"I know. Please, spare the lecture. This is important."

Tyberius crossed his arms and looked at her. Then, Solan guided Shiloe forward, and the young girl looked up at him.

His expression softened as he smiled at the girl, then knelt to her eye level. "Forgive me. I understand now. My name is Tyberius Alexander. We were good friends in a past life. It's nice to see you again, Shiloe."

Shiloe smiled up at him and held out her hand. Tyberius took it, then stood. "I see you've brought something else."

Solan took the three compressed staffs from her cloak and handed them to her father. Tyberius held them up to the light. "Ah, yes. I haven't seen these in a long while."

"Wait, you knew about the staffs?" Jet asked.

"It's good to see you too, Jet," Tyberius said with a wink and a nod. "Indeed. I helped Albright create these staffs…in secret."

"So, they *are* a weapon," Jet said. "That doesn't seem like something Albright would create, though."

"Think of them more as a deterrent to our enemies," Tyberius corrected him. "They are not meant as a weapon of war, but available when the Heliographi are in danger."

"You say as a deterrent?" Solan asked. "I don't understand."

"Well, yes. Let's just say that others may think twice about confronting us. Albright knew a time would come when we'd need these. Now is that time. The Heliographi *are* at war, and our lineage is threatened. I know about Harriet and the other two Atrum. Their deaths are a trigger for these staffs. These artifacts are now alive."

"When did Albright decide to create these?" Jet asked.

"Just after the Prism Effect, when his table splintered. He used the shards from the table to craft these staffs. It was done in secret, and the staffs were hidden until such time as they were needed, which is now. I assume you located these, Jet?"

"Yes, I found them in the Hall of Vital Records."

"As was intended, long ago," Tyberius said. "A Lucem once known as Brindall. Albright charged him with the duty to carry that secret. It was his final act, and he sacrificed his life to do so."

"What more do you know about these?" Solan asked.

"Some, though Albright is the real mastermind behind their design," Tyberius folded the staffs into his cloak. "Come with me. We have an important discussion ahead. I advise you to pay close attention."

The group followed Tyberius deep into the complex. Jet noticed that the rooms were filled with children of all ages, who sat on rugs and listened to instructors. They followed Tyberius into a back area and deeper down into the lower portions of the facility. He finally stopped in front of a small, rusty door.

Tyberius punched in a code to a keypad, and the holographic display went through a series of beeps and tones before the door swung open. Standing in the middle of a room was a teenage boy, his hands stuck in his pockets, and a boyish grin lit his face. His eyes glowed a bright red.

Shiloe stared at him, uncertain. She took a few steps forward, and the teenage boy met her halfway. He reached out and held her hand in his but didn't say anything as the others watched. He smiled at her, a bit sheepishly, then held her other hand.

"I think I know you. Though…I don't think we've ever met before," Shiloe said.

"Haven't we, though?" the young Albright said. He closed his eyes and seemed to go straight into a meditative state. "Think, Shiloe," he whispered, "We've known each other for *eons*."

Shiloe closed her eyes and slowly shook her head. "Maybe…" she whispered back. "I think you're right. You're…Christian Albright?"

"Yes," he said and smiled at her again, his eyes still closed. "You've suffered, but I will help you. Here, you will be safe with me now."

There was a long moment of silence as Stell, Tyberius, Solan, and Jet looked on. Tyberius eventually broke the silence. "Well, I believe we are all happy to witness this reunion. You two have a lot of catching up to do, and I do apologize for interrupting that. But we have an important discussion, Christian."

The young Albright continued to gaze into Shiloe's glowing eyes, apparently not ready to pull away from her yet. He led her over to the others. "I've been waiting for this moment for a very long time," Albright said, his voice cracked with the hint of adolescence, his coming of age near.

Tyberius held out the three staffs. Albright took one, which Jet assumed was his own. He twirled it on his fingertips, moving with the dexterity of someone much older and wiser. Jet watched, taking note of Albright's appearance for the first time. He was tall, for a teenager, almost as tall as Tyberius. Albright had shoulder-length blond hair and fair skin. His eyes glowed the bright red of his position on the color spectrum. He was the Alpha, the all-father, and the leader of the Lucem. This young teenage boy was responsible for the Lucem's ascendance to protector of all people—at least, the essence within his soul was. His creation of the Skylight System was the human race's greatest hope and had saved millions of lives. Albright was unrivaled in Vishmu, and he could see into his past and maybe the future with greater clarity than any other Heliographi, save perhaps Sybold.

"I designed these staffs specifically for the Heliographi," Albright said as he faced Jet. "You already know that much, I presume."

Jet had so many questions to ask. Here he was, standing in front of the great Christian Albright, and he felt tongue-tied. His mind raced as he tried to think of what to ask. He hadn't known this would happen tonight, and he was struggling to think through the haze. Jet felt beyond intimidated as he stared into the glowing eyes of the boy.

"Why…why did you build these staffs for the Atrum too?" Jet asked.

"Because we are all Heliographi. Though some may not want to accept it, we originate from one. True, we have opposing natures, but we are also bound to the Atrum in duality, which makes our essence intertwined. That bond cannot be severed without damage to all of us. We need the Atrum. These staffs were designed for a time when our lineage would be challenged. That time is now. War will be upon us soon, if not already."

Jet nodded, though he was slightly confused by the answer. It sounded as if the fate of the Lucem was tied to the Atrum and vice versa. "Can…can you tell me anything about your memoirs? Do you remember what you wrote in them?"

"It was a long time ago, but I remember everything," Albright said. He looked at Shiloe again, then nodded for Jet to follow him and walked off.

Jet looked at the others, confused, then hurried to catch up to Albright.

Jet and Albright walked side-by-side, deeper into the steel chamber that he assumed was Albright's hidden dwelling. It wasn't a very cheerful place, with its cold steel walls and low ceilings, and Jet wondered how long Albright had been holed up here.

Albright looked at Jet as they walked. "If I tell you about the memoirs' secrets and you are captured, that would not be a good outcome—you have another purpose. That's why I have left clues behind. Follow those clues, and you will find what you're looking for."

"You talk in riddles," Jet said with a chuckle, thinking about Cord, and wondered if he would be just as awe-struck at that moment.

"Not in my mind, but I do apologize."

"No…it's fine. I was just thinking of a friend of mine."

"Cord Ledbetter," Albright said. "We should be thankful he is a Lucem. I predicted him to be one of the Skylight Fallouts."

"Right…he guessed that too. But why all the riddles and secrecy? Why didn't you just hand the memoirs over to us?"

"Had I done that, they would have been in Sybold's hands long ago. We cannot risk the secrets of the memoirs. I've not shared them even with Tyberius, and he does not ask. And now, our list of enemies is growing. If captured, only I could withstand the interrogation. I'll hold the secrets of the memoirs, at least until they are rightfully discovered. I'm sorry that I can't say more."

Jet sighed but nodded, knowing asking about the memoirs further would gain him nothing.

The young Albright stopped walking and turned to Jet. He glanced around and lowered his voice. "There is some advice I *can* share, though. But it is for you and only you. Will you keep it to yourself?"

Jet looked at him, still in a state of shock, trying to remember to breathe. Here he was, talking one-on-one with the great Christian Albright, sharing secrets, no less. Yet, standing there, facing the legend, Jet felt suddenly unsure of himself. "I…sure, Albright. I mean, of course."

"You're aware that every Heliographi possesses a special power, a gift, so to speak. But you may not be aware that each gift is *unique* to our given symbol. Mine is foresight. Tyberius has the wisdom of insight. Your friend Cord has an ability to learn at a greater pace than other Heliographi. These staffs, once modified, can amplify those powers. But be aware that they also draw energy from our light, our Heliographi, draining our strength quicker when used. The previous Lucem who shared your symbol, the *M*, sacrificed himself because it wasn't his time. Your gift is unique, one we have never seen before."

"What do you mean, *once modified*?" Jet asked. "Will the staffs change?"

"A time will come soon, you will see," Albright said, the hint of a devious smile on his face.

"I…I don't quite understand," Jet replied. Christian seemed to be speaking in riddles again. Jet could hear Cord's voice whispering to him.

Remember, Albright is a trickster.

"You've talked to the ghost Lucem, correct?" Albright continued.

Jet stared at Albright for a few seconds, wondering how he could possibly know this. "Yes, a few times. I don't know how, though. It just seemed to happen."

"You need to figure it out. Alone," Albright said. "The answer you want is there. It is crucial that you learn your special power, Jet. The fate of humanity may depend on it."

Jet imagined the stunned look on his face, and he wanted to laugh.

What was he supposed to say to that? The fate of humanity may depend on him!

He had never felt so shocked at hearing something before, not even when he'd found out about having ephebus mortem. When he had awoken that morning, he'd had no idea that the one and only Christian Albright would secretly share the fact that the survival of the human race might depend on him figuring out a riddle. And, apparently, Albright had no intention of sharing what the answer was, either.

"Why can't you just tell me?" Jet asked. "It seems so important. What if I don't figure it out?"

"I can't help you in this," Albright replied. "And neither should the others. Only *you* can endure what has to be done. That is part of your gift. Getting help from another Heliographi would place them in peril. Besides, you *must* learn to stand on your own. A time will come when you can't depend on others. You have to be able to stand alone."

Jet glanced at Christian, then to the others beyond. Everyone stared at them, probably wondering what they were discussing. "I…don't really know what to say except that I'll do my best."

"The next time we meet, it will be under different conditions. Look after yourself and trust in your heart, Jet Stroud. You will find the right path." Christian turned and walked back to the others, and Jet followed behind him. He felt numb all over, his brain racing to process everything he'd just heard. There were so many questions flooding through his mind at that moment, but he couldn't seem to speak or think. And he knew that a golden opportunity was slipping by as he walked stunned next to the young Christian Albright. The only thing he could think to ask was…

"*Why?*" Jet blurted out.

Albright stopped and turned to face him, the others watching from a distance. Jet looked into his glowing red eyes and felt nervous again, as if he was asking a question that shouldn't see the light of day.

"The Serpent and the Prism," Jet continued. "Is that why you set the Prism Effect into motion?"

"I see that you've heard about the legend."

Jet shrugged, not sure what to say. He didn't want to out Solan, though he assumed Albright had already guessed that much. "It's supposed to be a great war. That's about all I know. But what does it mean?"

"Why are you asking me when you already know the answer?" Albright asked. He crossed his arms in a way that gave him the appearance of someone much older, much wiser than a fresh-faced kid.

Jet was caught off guard by the response. But as he stood there, staring into the teenage boy's glowing eyes, he realized Christian was right—Jet knew the answer and had known all along. "I'm to fight Sybold, aren't I?"

"*She* is the Serpent. *You* are the Prism. Sybold is out there, and she will reveal herself when we least expect it.

She is the essence that drives the other Atrum. You *must* be prepared."

Jet shook his head. "I don't see how I'll manage anything against Sybold. I'm probably the least capable Lucem."

"Not everything is as it appears, especially with you. Do not doubt yourself."

Jet pursed his lips to one side, then tilted his head. "So, this prophecy, the one in the Book of Vishmu, involves me? But that book was written centuries ago."

"More like *millennia*," Albright said.

"How could anyone possibly know all that, especially thousands of years ago?"

"The same way you know how to talk to the ghost Lucem."

"Wait. I don't know *how* I did that. It just happened."

"Exactly. It just happened. *Intuitively.* I imagine those who wrote this legend just intuitively knew what they were doing as well."

"But how can you be certain?"

"Because I wrote much of the Book of Vishmu myself."

Jet narrowed one eye and then chuckled. "You wrote the Book of Vishmu—"

"Parts of it," Christian interrupted. "Other parts were written by the rest of the Heliographi, even you, or your former self, at least."

"Okay," Jet replied slowly, still not sure what to believe. "I assume this all has something to do with me finding my gift?"

"You've already found your gift. Now you need to unlock it, then understand and perfect it."

"I've found it?" Jet asked and furrowed his brow. "But I don't think I—"

"Yes, you have. Listen to Brindall. He was meant to guide you. Still, you must unlock your gift first. This can only be done in a special location, a conduit of sorts. You must do this alone."

Jet continued to stand there, hands hanging at his sides while shaking his head. *He'd already found his gift? When and how?* "Why do I have to be alone?" Jet asked.

"As I said earlier, other Heliographi cannot handle what you can. Your essence is designed for this alone."

Jet was even more confused now. What could his gift be that was so dangerous to others, even Heliographi?

He waited to see if there was more before continuing. "Why would you go to all the trouble to set the Prism Effect into motion without knowing more about the outcome?"

"Because it was our only option—"

"I must apologize," Tyberius interrupted as he walked up with the others. "Our time is limited. You two should probably return to your base. We don't want the Atrum asking too many questions. Solan. Do not return under any circumstance. Besides, we will likely have to relocate now."

Solan pursed her lips but nodded and gave her father a hug. She nodded to Albright and knelt to Shiloe. Solan looked into the young girl's eyes, reached up, and brushed a strand of her blonde hair from her brow. A tear welled on Shiloe's cheek. "Take care. Continue to practice your Vishmu, won't you?"

Shiloe hugged Solan and nodded.

Christian stood next to Shiloe and held her hand. "We'll take good care of her." Then he took the three staffs and handed them back to Jet. "These are not meant for us, at least not right now."

"I don't understand," Jet said. "Won't you need them to protect Shiloe?"

"At some point, yes. But for now, you will need them more than me."

"But we can't use them. I mean, they only seem to respond to the Heliographi they're aligned with."

"Take them," Albright insisted.

Jet shrugged. He took the three compressed staffs and placed them in his cloak.

Jet and Solan left the halfway home. She cloaked her skiff and used another route on the way back to the first belt.

Jet turned to face her. "Well, that went as expected," he joked. "Lots of riddles and very few answers."

"At least we know that Shiloe is safe. Out of curiosity, what did Albright say to you?"

Jet paused and didn't look at Solan. "I…I can't tell you that."

Solan started to speak but stopped and turned back to her console. "That serious, huh? Fine, I won't pry, but you had better bury that conversation deep. In fact, so should I. We can't share this, even with the other Lucem, including Cord or Jinn. And not because we can't trust them, you understand? Now that we're around the Atrum, we can't afford any stray thoughts."

"Yes, I understand."

"They'll ask where we took Shiloe. Let me handle that. The third reveal is tomorrow, and I've called a meeting in the control room with all the Heliographi in the morning."

"That should be interesting," Jet muttered.

"We'll just view it as a peace offering, these staffs are a gift, and I want you to hand them out."

"Why me?"

"I have my reasons," Solan replied. "Things are going to move fast now. We need to be prepared, and I want your help keeping the ship steady. Tensions will be high, not just hunting the memoirs but balancing emotions with the Atrum. They will try to push our buttons, and we mustn't take that bait. Spread the word to the others. You have a levelheaded approach. Work to keep everyone calm, alright?"

Jet nodded. "You're stuck with Joshia. You gonna be okay?"

Solan gripped the console tighter. "I hate that I'm in this position, but there's no way around it now. I accept that we have to find a way to coexist with the Atrum, at least for the immediate future. There will be challenges. That goes without saying. I fear the Atrum have plans. After the last reveal, we must be prepared."

Jet glanced over at her. "*IF*—and it's a big if—we do happen to claim one of the memoirs, where should we keep it?"

"This will be a topic of hot debate," Solan said. "The Atrum won't trust us, no matter what. It'll have to be in a place where both sides can keep an eye on it, and I know just the spot."

M

When Solan and Jet returned to the first belt, it was late. Luckily, they didn't meet anyone on the way back to their quarters. Jet was tired but couldn't sleep as he thought about what Albright had said to him.

Figure out how to unlock your gift.

Jet wondered why Albright couldn't just tell him, though. If it was such an important matter, why gamble on the chance he might never crack the code? He wasn't very good at riddles and wanted badly to share it with

Cord. But if he wanted to become a stronger Lucem, he needed to take these challenges on alone. Besides, Albright's warning that his gift might be dangerous to other Heliographi was all Jet needed to know. He didn't want to place any more of his friends in danger. It appeared that Albright was pushing him to be more independent.

So…what *was* his special gift?

Jet thought about his little epiphanies after meditation. But that was always random and never guaranteed. He didn't think that was it. What about the telekinetic pulse? He didn't think that was it either since it wasn't unique to just him.

Talking to ghosts?

He thought that might be it, and if so, it was a tremendous power…maybe even epic.

But how was he to unlock it?

Jet sat down on his meditation rug and crossed his legs. He slowed his breathing and closed his eyes, letting his inner light run free. The turquoise Heliographi charged across the cosmos in a random zigzag path. He thought about the ghost as he followed the light, the former Lucem named Brindall. Jet focused on him and what he knew about him, which wasn't much. Just that he had died in service to the Skylight System, delivering some secret for Albright, in fact. He knew what the man looked like or *had* looked like. He knew they shared the same symbol, the M. He knew that—

He died for you!

Jet snapped out of his meditation so quickly that his head spun. He felt chills run down his body as he sat back, gasping for breath. The voice had yelled at him with such clarity that it still rang out inside his head.

He knew that voice.

It had been Cutter's voice.

CHAPTER 24
The Chow Hall Incident

EARLY THE NEXT morning, Jet dressed and hid the compressed staff in his cloak.

When he walked into the mess hall, he was shocked to see most of the Lucem *and* Atrum sitting there, eating silently. The Lucem sat on one side of the hall, gathered around one table, and the Atrum sat on the opposite side, hunched over their food and looking darkly at him.

Jet grabbed some of the soupy-looking oatmeal, which he'd started growing fond of, and sat down next to Cord and Ti-Leer. Ti-Leer looked pale and seemed to be half awake, his curly hair matted flat to one side. Jet thought he smelled ale or brandy on his breath.

"Where'd you sneak off to last night, lad?" Ti-Leer asked.

"I don't know what you're talking about," Jet said, avoiding his gaze.

"Come on, pony up the goods, son. I know you been sneakin' out. It ain't the first night, neither. Ah…fine then, be like that," Ti-Leer said with a dismissive wave.

"He's right, Jet," DiJinn chimed in. "You've been spending a lot of time out and about in the evenings lately. We aren't that blind."

"What is this?" Jet said with a slight chuckle. "Spy central? Can't I have my own agenda, or are we all babysitters around here?"

"Babysitters, I think, Stroud," Vail said from across the chow hall.

"Mind your manners," DiJinn barked. "You lot are lucky to be here. If it was up to me, I'd have left you all to rot. Why are you even here now?"

"To keep an eye on us, I imagine," Booker grumbled.

Bofisto stood and leaned his massive arms onto the table. "Tiny Jinn. Going to run back to Solan and tattle on us? It's what I'd expect. You're such an embarrassment."

"I may be tiny, Bofisto, but try me on for size. I dare you!"

The Lucem all stood. Booker and Annaka shuffled around the table, and Jet stood to move in front of them. "Hold on, you two." He placed a hand on Booker's shoulder, trying to maneuver him back to his seat. "This isn't what we want. Not now, got it! All of you—Vail, Bo, and the rest of you. We have to stay focused on the reveal. If we can't even eat in peace, how are we supposed to work together?"

But everyone remained standing and glaring at each other. Jet grew concerned that he wouldn't be able to hold all of them back, and his words seemed to be falling on deaf ears. "Just…everyone, please! Sit down and take it easy. We need to save our energy—we can't afford this."

After several seconds, things seemed to be cooling down until Cord winked at Vail. Jet saw it and closed his eyes.

Vail flung her plate across the room. Cord ducked, and it hit a rusty bulkhead and shattered. The porridge exploded into the air and landed in Ti-Leer's beard. He seemed to suddenly wake up. His face turned bright red. "Oi, what's a wee bit of fun in the mornin' then?" He hopped over the table, and the other Lucem followed behind him.

The Atrum met them in the middle of the chow hall. Jet was nearly knocked over by the charge, and he didn't know where to start.

Brit and Bo tackled Annaka, but Booker had them both by their cloaks, trying to wrap his massive arms around them. DiJinn and Sojahn exchanged blows while Bofisto and Mosstrom wrangled with Cord. Myranda and Tetra charged after Kamber while Ti-Leer grabbed Vail by the arms and head-butted her. "Oh, you like that, do you, lass!" he bellowed. Vail spun and kneed him in the groin. Ti-Leer went down, laughing and groaning.

It wasn't long until Jet was pulled into the fighting. It was a frenzy, with food, plates, and tables being shattered and scattered around the hall. Someone grabbed him by the hood of his cloak and flung him to the floor. When he hit the ground, his compressed staff tumbled out and rolled under the remains of a table. He was pinned as he tried to grab for it, but it was just out of reach. Jet focused his thoughts, felt his hand begin to vibrate, and the next thing he knew, he was holding the staff. He slammed it onto the floor, and it decompressed instantly. The staff erupted to life, lighting up the chow hall in a blaze of turquoise lightning that sent everyone near him flying into the air.

As the thunderclap faded to silence, everyone in the hall gawked at him. Ti-Leer and Vail held each other by the cloak as Brit, Bo, Booker, and Annaka all lay on the floor staring up at him. DiJinn held Sojahn in a headlock while Bofisto, Mosstrom, and Cord stood next to each other, bruised and bloodied. Myranda, Tetra, and Kamber looked at Jet, shocked expressions on their faces. Tetra held a raised plate near Kamber's head, but she let it drop. It broke when it hit the ground and shattered the silence.

Jet stood in the center as everyone continued to stare at him in bewilderment. He muttered a silent curse under his breath. This is exactly what he hadn't wanted to happen.

"You all weren't meant to see that, not yet anyway," Jet said, his voice echoing around the room.

Standing in the doorway was Solan, with Joshia just behind her. Both glared at the mess in the hall.

"Everyone! To the control room," Solan roared.

Five minutes later, all the Heliographi sat in the control suite. Near Jet was the pile of war staffs. Solan sat in her own chair, glaring around the room at each of them. Jet gave her a quiet shrug as if to say, *I tried*. Almost every one of them had some cut or bruise from the fight. Ti-Leer had a black eye and grinned at Vail, which revealed a chipped tooth. She blew him a kiss just as Solan stood.

"If you all put as much passion into this hunt as you do fighting each other, then we shouldn't have any problems." She crossed her arms and glowered at them, then shook her head. "I had hoped to hand these war staffs out as a peace offering, to show you all there can be trust amongst us. But I see now that it isn't going to be easy. What do you all have to say for yourselves?"

Ti-Leer pointed at Vail. "Blame it on that lass. She threw the first plate—"

Solan held up her hand. "Let's just move on. We need to stay focused on the reveal. We've already set the teams, and now we have a possible game changer in these staffs. But even with these, we will fail if we can't learn to work as a team and believe in each other. Can I trust each of you?"

Most of them slowly nodded, but everyone remained silent.

"Joshia, I believe you have something to say?" Solan sat down and waited.

Joshia stood. "Solan has offered us a powerful tool, one that I believe will swing the advantage back to us. We are grateful to the Lucem," Joshia said. Jet could sense it was difficult for her to say, though. "We *will* work together as one group on this hunt. Is that clear, all of you?"

Each of the Atrum finally nodded, some more grudgingly than others. But it was the first solidary commitment Jet had seen out of them yet.

Joshia turned back to Solan and nodded, then sat down.

Solan looked at Jet, and he stood. He walked around the table and, one by one, handed each Heliographi their staff.

"Where did you find these?" Sojahn asked as she held her staff and looked at it in wonder.

Mosstrom stood and twirled his staff, a dark smile on his face, a hint of lust in his gaze. "Why have I not heard of this wonderful relic before? Though there are several out there still hidden, this is something new to me. I've been around for a very long time. I'm certain I would remember this."

"Does it matter?" DiJinn snipped. "Just be grateful you have one."

"Easy, Jinn," Solan said. "Where we found them isn't important. What *is* important is that you familiarize yourself with them. These staffs have special powers, but they will drain your energy. They pull from your inner Heliographi, and to recharge, you will need to meditate. I ask that each of you practice, get a feel for it. Tomorrow, you're going to need it. Our teams are set, we'll meet in the forest near the hangars. Cord, the coordinates, please."

Cord stood and kicked the side wall. The holopad sputtered to life, and a three-dimensional map flickered over the table. "Here we are," he said. "The third reveal, which places the memoir on the third belt. Take care to note the general location. Although the first two reveals were in less populated areas, this one will take place near Skylight City. Hopefully, the area will be clear."

"We must be careful not to injure any citizens," Solan said. "I know this may not mean much to you

Atrum, but it is one of our directives. If we agree to let you play by your rules, then you can at least respect ours. We will *all* help protect citizens where we can."

Joshia looked around the room. "Agreed. We will do our best."

M

The rest of that day, Jet spent in the forest with Kamber at Firefly Falls. Kamber's staff was much shorter than his, with a hooked talon on one end and a blunt knob on the other. It had three metal collars at equal points and glowed the greenish-yellow of her eyes. Like the other staffs, it had the Lucem symbols of the Greek alphabet and other strange glyphs. Its size matched her perfectly as if it had been designed specifically for someone of her stature.

Together, they worked on exercises using their staffs while trying to incorporate them into their typical training session. Kamber seemed to be a natural with her staff, and once again, he was reminded of how adept she was at picking things up. After a few hours, they took a break, sitting near Cutter's grave.

"You look tired today," she said.

Jet grinned at her directness. "Just concerned about all of this, I suppose."

"Are you sure? Seems like there's more going on," she replied, then continued, but with some hesitation. "I saw you last night in my dreams. You were walking, as if in a trance. I think you were looking for someone, or something. You're searching for answers. Am I right?"

Jet gave her a look. "I forgot you have that ability. No hiding from you. But you're right. Something happened that…well, it kind of frightened me a bit."

"Can you share what it was?"

Jet leaned back and gazed at Cutter's grave. "I…I don't know. This might sound crazy."

"You can talk to me. I want to help if I can."

Jet considered for a second. "I think Cutter was trying to tell me something, in my meditation, that is."

Kamber stared at him, a look of disbelief lit across her face. She pulled her knees up to her chest and hugged her legs. "What makes you say that?"

"Well, I heard his voice. I'm sure it was him. There was no mistaking it. You know the strange things we experience during meditations. I can't explain half of them—those sessions can sometimes be a bit outlandish, to say the least. Well, last night, I was looking for…I'm not sure how to explain it, actually. I'll just say, 'an answer.' This may sound a bit odd, but I think I've been seeing a ghost since the day of the Century Eclipse. I'm sure of it, in fact."

"How come you haven't told me this already?"

"Because I'm still trying to figure it all out," he continued. "Anyway, that ghost is a Lucem from the past, one who bore my symbol of the letter M. His name was Brindall, and he led me to the staffs. But there's more. I just haven't figured it all out yet."

"How is this connected to Cutter?" Kamber asked.

Jet shrugged and shook his head. "That's a good question. I've tried to summon this ghost Lucem, but I haven't been able to. He just shows up randomly."

"Do you think Cord could help you? He seems to be the most knowledgeable on these things."

"I already asked him. He's uncertain. Said he'd never heard of anything like this before."

Kamber placed her arm around Jet's shoulder and leaned on him. "It sounds pretty spooky, though it doesn't surprise me, considering how strange things have been since I joined the Lucem. Maybe I can focus my dreams on it and get some answers for you?"

Jet leaned back and looked up at the fireflies surrounding them. He wondered if he should even bring Kamber into this. She was new to this, he didn't want to burden her with anything more, especially right now. She needed to focus on her own training and the reveals. "It's okay, Kamber. Don't worry about it. I think this is something I'm meant to figure out on my own. If Cutter's out there somewhere, trying to tell me something, I'll find him eventually."

Kamber leaned her head on his shoulder. He felt his heart skip a beat, thought about shifting over, but took a deep breath instead and settled back.

"What do you think will happen at the reveal?" she asked.

"I'm not sure, but I don't think it can get any worse than the last two reveals." He said this half-jokingly but then changed his tone. "Actually, that's not true. Things could get a lot worse. I hope these staffs will make a difference, and I hope the Atrum use them responsibly. They're a powerful tool."

"If the Atrum are intent on destruction, hopefully, the staffs don't strengthen that."

Jet hadn't thought of it that way. He was still wondering if they'd done the right thing. "I guess we'll just have to wait and see. Things are in motion now that we have no control over. Destiny, as you believe, is moving, and perhaps we're just along for the ride."

CHAPTER 25
The Third Reveal
June 2, 2286, A.D.

EACH OF THE Heliographi flew in separate skiffs.

There were numerous traffic lanes to the third belt, and they split up to avoid detection. The rendezvous point was a few kilometers away from the reveal site on the third belt. The entire assortment of Heliographi regrouped at an old, abandoned factory, not far from the secluded café where Jet and Sylvant had once frequented called *The Hydra 7*.

Outside of the abandoned factory was a pitted field. Beyond that was the factory complex that housed the Agency's secret chambers called *The Cauldron*. A few kilometers above were floating wind farms, something Jet had always noticed but had paid little attention to. These turbines were tethered to the belt's hull by large cables and painted in bright pastel colors. The locals simply referred to the floating turbines as talloons, or sometimes just 'toons,' a clever mix of the word turbine and balloon. The talloons were packed so tightly that it was hard to see the sky at times. Their spinning blades created soft wind currents that caused them to undulate in a whimsical fashion amongst the clouds and mist. In size, they ranged from a few meters to perhaps thirty meters in diameter.

Solan and Joshia gathered the group of Heliographi.

"Let's put this morning's incident behind us and stay focused," Solan said. "For practice, we're splitting into our groups to prepare for the next several reveals. You'll need that chemistry, might as well try it out now. Team One: Jet, Cord, Vail, and Bo. Team Two will be Joshia, Tetra, Kamber, and me. Team Three: Jinn, Ti-Leer, Sojahn, and Bofisto. Team Four: Annaka, Booker, Brit, Myranda, and Mosstrom." Solan looked at Joshia and nodded.

"Each team needs to stay spread out," Joshia said. "When the memoir reveals itself, you'll have a better chance of getting to it quicker. I think the best approach is to anchor our skiffs to these toons. If you manage to get the memoir, just take it and go. Don't wait, not even for your team."

"Don't go directly back to our headquarters either, in case you're being tracked," Solan said. "Our rendezvous point will be in the Clipton Forest. I've sent the coordinates to your rings. Is everyone clear?"

The group remained silent. Jet assumed everyone was already mentally preparing themselves. The last two reveals had cost the Heliographi two of its members, and the realness of the moment was on everyone's mind.

"Watch after yourselves and your team. See you all later this evening." Solan led them back to the skiffs.

Jet and Cord flew in separate skiffs next to Vail and Bo.

"I guess the crew is back together again, huh?" Jet said into his intercom as he and Cord cloaked their skiffs.

"Just don't let your guard down," Cord replied.

"I think we can trust them for the moment," Jet said.

"I suspect you're probably correct. We *can* trust them, for the moment. But you know as well as I do, as we all do, this truce is only temporary. The biggest question is, how long will the truce last?"

Cord maneuvered his skiff next to Jet's toward a particularly large toon. The thrusters cut off, and the skiffs thudded onto the hull of the bright blue pastel surface of the toon. They both anchored their skiff to it to prevent it from floating away. They left their skiffs cloaked, just in case.

Jet stepped onto the riveted surface of the toon. It was slightly rusted and flaking from all the moisture over the years. The wind caused the toon to bump and sway a bit, and the metal hull thrummed from the spinning internal turbine. Its surface was a bit slippery, but the view was breathtaking. In the distance, thousands of colorful toons bobbed in and out of the heavy cloud cover. The morning sun shone through the haze, causing millions of tiny prism effects to inundate the sky.

Jet decompressed his staff and used the pointed end like a stave, puncturing the hull and steadying himself. Vail's and Bo's skiff settled down next to theirs. Both hopped out and stood staring at them. Jet noticed the odd look Bo gave him. He still hadn't talked with Bo since their days as students over four years ago, though they'd sparred on several occasions. Bo's attitude and personality seemed dark, and he showed no emotion.

Jet looked up just as the sunlight started to diminish. Then he remembered Cord telling him that each reveal would occur during a skylight eclipse. He hadn't noticed before since the first two had been subterranean reveals. Miles above, he could see the fourth belt aligning in a way that would blot out the morning sunlight in just a few minutes. The slow-moving belt was swinging around, and already it was entering the sun's corona.

"We'd better move," Jet said and led the way.

All four of them remained cloaked and used their staffs to pole-vault between the toons. It was like playing hopscotch, each toon spaced anywhere from three to fifteen meters apart—close enough for the Heliographi to traverse with little effort. The plan was for each of the four teams to position themselves equally around the general area of the reveal's coordinates. Jet's group was positioned on the port side, lower area. The four of them would remain somewhat separated and hidden but close enough to each other in case someone needed help.

Other seekers were starting to show up now. Littering the thousands of floating toons were the typical assortment of gangs, splinter cells, and lone wolves. While the toons were full of people, there were also thousands of skiffs clogging the skies. Since no one knew where or how the memoir would reveal itself, they didn't know what to expect. But this is where the Heliographi had an advantage at least, Jet assumed they did. They'd be able to leap between the toons quickly, where other groups would be stranded if they weren't in a skiff. And the toons were spaced so closely that piloting between them would require skill and caution.

But the toons were also difficult to navigate due to the large spinning turbines and the wet surface. On the sides, each toon was open to the whirling blade. While some of the newer toons had grates over the blade, most of the older models were missing such safety precautions, probably because of the constant maintenance they underwent. They'd have to be careful not to get caught up in the turbines.

The eclipse was just minutes away when the positioning began. Seekers pushed and shoved, which caused the fighting to start early again. Before long, it was a full-on riot. Seekers began sliding over the edge of the toons, plummeting into the spinning blades or toward the belt's surface below, though some of the smarter ones had brought hover packs.

Jet made contact with his thoughts. Cord was positioned to his left about twenty meters while Vail and Bo leapt to the toon above and waited. When the eclipse hit, the sunlight faltered, then faded. Each of them moved their staffs into the ready position and looked for any sign of the memoir.

Like the first two reveals, a blinding orange light cascaded down from one toon just twenty meters above them. Jet sprang in that direction, using his staff to clear the way. He could see the blur of the other Heliographi racing toward it as well as the mass of other seekers flooding that way. Now he could see dozens of M-Class mech units fire their propulsion systems and rocket toward the toon. Getting to the toon ahead of the mechs wasn't going to happen. He needed a faster way to get there.

He lifted his staff above his head and concentrated all his energy on the blunted end of it. The three metal collars around the shaft began to vibrate with energy, and the symbols glowed. He swung the staff downward with tremendous force, slamming it into the toon's hull. Jet leapt at the same time, and the force shot him upward like a rocket. He reached the toon just ahead of the mechs and grasped the metal hull with his left hand. His trajectory landed him in the toon's turbine intake, but just out of the way of the spinning blades. Immediately, several mechs cruised toward him. He used the end of his staff and punched out a riveted wall panel, forcing his way through the hull of the toon.

Inside were gears and gadgets, mechanical devices that he assumed were used to convert the spinning blade's energy. Enormous battery cells occupied much of the interior. Jet assumed these large walls of batteries stored all the energy before transferring it to the grid down below.

Jet ran between the battery cells as mech units began pouring into the space. He raced toward the bright, pulsing orange light that he knew to be the memoir now. The tall batteries were like a maze, though, and he moved between them, turning into dead ends several times. Finally, he saw it. The third memoir.

It glowed in a golden-orange hue, bathing everything around him. Its light pulsed in slow bursts. Jet stood motionless, gazing in awe before snapping out of his trance. He grabbed the metallic tube and stuffed it into his cloak, then raced between the narrow paths of the batteries. But soon, he was trapped with mechs on both ends.

He had nowhere to go.

The mechs moved forward, pressing in on him. They were lined up in front and behind him now, but the space between the battery walls was so narrow only two mechs could engage him at a time. He turned sideways so he could fight the mechs on both fronts. Jet used his staff like a spear, impaling mechs on one side while using the opposite end as a battering ram. The staff had a tremendous concussive impact when he focused his energy. As soon as the blunt end hit a mech, it flew backward into the mechs beyond. The pointed end cut through their strengthened graphene armor with ease.

However, he was soon struggling to move through all the parts lying on the ground. He even lost his footing a few times. The mechs continued to flood in—he needed to find a way out.

Jet looked above and noticed the battery cells were only about ten meters tall. He squatted, then jumped to the top of the batteries. He raced along them as the mechs reoriented and flew up to block his path. He leapt across the batteries and toward the outer wall of the toon's hull. Once he reached the end of the batteries, he held the pointed end of his staff above his head, squatted, then hurled upward. A portion of the hull split open, his staff puncturing it like a knife through a tin can.

He steadied himself as he landed on top of the toon's surface. The eclipse was just ending, and sunlight spilled through the clouds. Mist and wind surrounded him as he breathed a momentary sigh of relief. But he quickly began searching for the toon where he'd docked his skiff. He spotted the bright blue pastel color of it some thirty meters below him now.

Around him, groups of seekers were still fighting, unable to see his cloaked form. But the mech units *could* see him, and they were pouring through the opening just behind him.

Jet bounded from the toon and dropped to a smaller orange one below. He could see the other Heliographi falling in behind him as he reached out with his thoughts. They knew he had the memoir and formed a protective wall behind him as he raced toward his skiff. He felt like he was holding a blaze ball under his arm and racing for the goal line.

The Heliographi's combined might, outfitted with the new war staffs, were shredding the mechs now. The mechs were focused on the memoir, and ignoring the other Heliographi was a mistake. They were quickly being picked off one at a time as Atrum and Lucem landed on them and disabled them with their staffs. It was a new ballgame, literally. Parts and pieces fell like a waterfall, banging and clanging off the toons. Some of the mech parts landed in the whirling blades and shot out in different directions, taking out some of the nearby skiffs.

Jet finally reached his skiff and settled quickly into the cockpit. He fired up the engines and rocketed away, cloaking as he maneuvered his skiff between the toons. But it wasn't long until Agency skiffs, including some jammer class skiffs, fell in behind him. This was something he hadn't planned out. The jammers were faster and more agile. Though the pilots weren't necessarily better, the jammers' capabilities made up for it. Jet would have to use his piloting skills to lose them now.

He wove his way between the toons, banking and hugging them, trying to throw his pursuers off. Agency skiffs fired rounds and rockets at him, which exploded into the toons. Occasionally, a jammer would get a lock on his skiff, the beeping console blaring at him. But within seconds, it would go quiet, telling him the other Heliographi were behind him in their own skiffs, taking out the jammers.

Jet gambled and flew his skiff through the center of the toons. His timing had to be perfect to avoid the spinning blades. Some of the Agency skiffs made it through, but each time he flew through a toon's intake, he'd lose another pursuer. The number of jammers following him was starting to shrink, and eventually, it was down to just two. Jet tried to maneuver into another toon, but this time, he miscalculated, and his skiff took a hit from a spinning blade.

The massive blade sliced the back half of his skiff off. He immediately went into a tailspin and had no option but to eject. Jet shot from the cockpit with a hover pack strapped to his back, but now he was a sitting target. The last jammer moved in for the kill. Jet held his staff in front of him and braced for the incoming fire.

But suddenly, the jammer burst into a ball of flame.

Jet landed on a large toon and rolled to his feet. He slipped on the slick surface and used his staff to steady himself. A skiff uncloaked and hovered near him. It lowered onto the toon, and the cockpit slid open.

"Get your ass inside!" Vail roared and waved to him.

Jet hopped in, and they rocketed off, cloaking as they left the third belt's air space. Jet eased back in his seat, then turned to face Vail. "Thanks for that."

She didn't look at him, just focused on the console as she piloted the skiff toward the first belt. She set a course for Skylight University. "You owe me, Stroud."

"Right," he said. "I'll make a note of that." He slid the memoir's metal container out of his cloak and held it up to her. "In the meantime, we finally got one. I think seeing what's inside of this should pay that debt."

CHAPTER 26
The Heist—Part One

AB ΔE ΗΘΙΚΛ**M**
ΝΞΟΠΡΣ ΥΦ ΨΩ

JET AND VAIL followed the coordinates Solan had sent. Vail found a clearing and settled her skiff down in the Clipton Forest.

They made their way to the rendezvous point, which was a secluded location several kilometers from their headquarters. Solan was being overly cautious, not wanting to lead anyone back to their base in case any Heliographi had been followed. They waited for the others to show up and were soon surrounded by the remaining Atrum and Lucem. Jet counted them all and noticed there was one Lucem missing.

Everyone sat quietly on large boulders or felled trees in the clearing. The morning sun was partially blotted out by the thick tree canopy, casting purple shadows on the forest floor. Crickets chirped contentedly in the background as the sky began to soak through to a blood-red color. From what Jet could see, only a few of the Heliographi had sustained any injuries. Booker leaned on his tall staff and favored one leg, and the Atrum named Brit looked to have injured his arm.

"Where is Annaka?" Jet asked.

Booker stepped forward and held up her cloak and staff. The look on his face was grim as he held onto her personal effects.

Solan stepped forward, planting her staff in the soft grass. She held out her hand. Booker held onto Annaka's staff, cloak, and ring a few seconds longer, then placed them in her hand. He wiped his sleeve across his cheeks and quickly turned away. DiJinn placed a hand on his arm and rubbed his back, then leaned her head on his shoulder.

Solan stood in the center of the group, holding Annaka's belongings. Everyone remained silent. Jet looked on in shock. He'd assumed the staffs would prevent this, though, in the back of his mind, he'd known the danger was still there. Lybra was continuing to pour more M-Class mechs and jammers into the mix. Soon, there might be so many that it wouldn't matter what new weapon the Heliographi had in their possession.

Solan gave everyone a moment. The look on her face told Jet everything he needed to know; it was déjà vu all over again. Another reveal, another Heliographi lost. With Harriet's demise, there had been anger and outrage—for Annaka, it was silence and subdued shock, not because they had cared any less, but because there was a realization starting to settle in.

They couldn't sustain this pace.

Ti-Leer's eyes were red and puffy. He sniffled and rubbed one of his stubby arms across his nose and blew into the crook of his elbow. "You lot did it again," he muttered.

"Is there something you want to say?" Bofisto growled. "I suppose this is our fault, once again? Or is it because the Lucem are just weaker?"

"I keep tellin' you all to toughen up!" Vail said. "Let us show you a better way—"

Solan held up a hand as she glared at Vail. "That's enough." She tucked Annaka's things into her cloak. "We can't afford any more outbursts. Jet, let's see the memoir."

Jet walked into the center of the clearing and held out the cylindrical tube. It was embossed with delicate scrollwork and odd patterns and motifs. The metal case was gold in color and had a vibrant orange glow about it. But it had no buttons or openings.

Solan took it and looked at it. Then she handed it to Cord.

Cord examined it. "Clearly, another one of Albright's riddles. I assumed this wouldn't be as easy as pressing a button. Albright is gonna make us work for this. I'll need time to look it over."

"Any idea what the symbols mean?" DiJinn asked.

"Negative." Cord held the tube up to the dim sunlight as he looked it over. "I imagine the answer is hidden in these symbols, but there is no telling with Albright. Let me get it back to my lab and analyze it."

"I think it's safe to assume Lybra hasn't been able to open the memoirs either," DiJinn said. "If we don't understand it, how could she?"

"I wouldn't necessarily assume that," Cord replied. "She has enough money to hire the right people. And they've had a head start on cracking the code. Regardless, I'm as anxious as anyone to see what's inside." Cord tucked the scroll into his cloak.

"The next four reveals begin in just a few days," Solan said. "Remember, we'll all be split into our groups again—"

"Hold on, Solan." Joshia stepped into the clearing and stood in front of her. "Did you think we'd let the memoir out of our sight so easily?"

"Back to this again, I see," Solan replied and crossed her arms. "We're not trying to steal the memoir, I assure you."

"Can we assume you'll tell us where you intend to store it then?"

"I was kind of hoping we would make that decision together," Solan said. "It will show our trust in each other. How does that sound?"

Joshia glanced around the group of Atrum, and they all nodded in agreement. "Fine. Let's talk."

"I'm open to suggestions," Solan said, and held out her arms. "It needs to be in a place only we know, of course. A place that is also accessible to both sides."

"I would assume Lyrinthum is the perfect place," Cord said. "My lab is down there anyway, and for the moment, that's where it'll be as I research it. After that, we can move it to an agreed-upon location. I have a safe that's built into the hull of the belt. If anyone can make it through the haunted areas, somehow find my lab through the maze of corridors and manage to crack my code, then they probably deserve the memoir."

Once again, Joshia turned to face the Atrum. "For the moment, that should work. I'll need that code."

Cord closed his eyes and sent a thought to Joshia. She nodded to him. "Right, we're good to go then."

Everyone was about to leave when Jet spoke up. "I have something to add."

The group stopped and looked at him. Jet waited until he had everyone's attention.

"We got the memoir today but still lost another Heliographi. Even with these new staffs, we are facing more M-Class mechs and jammers. Eventually, we'll be overwhelmed by Lybra's forces."

"What are you gettin' at, Stroud?" Vail asked.

"We need to take the fight to Lybra. We need to make her hurt," Jet continued. "We can't just settle for one little victory and hope for more. We have to push our advantage now and set ourselves up for victory by taking something away from her."

"I like the sound of where this is going, lad!" Ti-Leer said, and the others nodded.

"Go on, Jet," Solan said.

"Look, I was barely able to outmaneuver those jammers today, even against lesser pilots. They would have taken me out if it hadn't been for all the toons to use as cover. Out in open-air space, we're sitting targets. Our recon-issued skiffs are outgunned."

"Agreed," DiJinn said. "So, what's the plan?"

Jet continued. "Think. What can we do to slow down Lybra's army? She's cranking out mechs and jammers faster than we can take them down."

"Don't forget about the Recon and Tetrahedron. She has access to the largest army in the system," Joshia said. "Sometimes I wonder if those two are even necessary for Lybra anymore."

"There may be nothing we can do about the Recon and Tetrahedron," Jet said. "But we *can* slow down the mechs and jammers. Here's my plan. We have a few days until the string of reveals, right? Instead of sitting around waiting, why not take out some of Lybra's assets? It'll give us a little more breathing room."

"And how do you propose to do that?" Joshia asked.

"Split up into groups," Jet replied. "We're already doing it, might as well get some more team building in. The first group will steal some jammers. We know where they are, and we need to upgrade our own skiffs anyway."

Joshia looked at Jet, uncertain. "Is that it?"

"No. We need an army, right? Solan, you wanted to free the slaves in the ARC pit. Why not do it now? There's our army. We have plenty of room down in Lyrinthum, and I'm sure we can get Stell and some of her team to come over and help train them up. I was there, and I saw plenty of people I once knew in those prison cells. A lot of them are ex-military."

"It's aggressive, lad," Ti-Leer said, twirling his beard thoughtfully. "I like it!"

"Wait, there's more," Jet interrupted. "Group three. Let's get that stockpile of rare-earth. We know it's Lybra who's been stealing it. She can't manufacture any new mech units without it. At least it'll slow her down. We know where it's at unless she's moved it—"

"She has moved it," Sojahn said. "And I know where it is."

"Good. You're going with that group, Sojahn," Jet said. "Last, we should probably keep a few of us back here in case of an emergency or one of the groups needs backup. We don't want everyone away from base. I think four to a group should do it."

Jet watched everyone's expression. Most of them were nodding in agreement, but a few had doubtful looks on their face. "If all of this works out, there'll be so much chaos for Lybra and Harok to handle they won't be focused on the next four reveals. It may give us an advantage."

A smile eased across Solan's face. "Who am I to argue? When do we start?"

M

Jet slept little that night and was up and around before sunrise. In the chow hall, most everyone was already there, eating quietly. There was no food flinging this time, and Jet noticed that Sojahn and even Bofisto sat next to Ti-Leer, chatting about the upcoming mission.

Everyone met in the hangars and divided up into their groups. For Jet's group, it was a long flight to the ninth belt where the jammers were located. Since there were only four of them, they'd have to use something called a 'ghost pilot.' It was a standard function on most skiffs that allowed the lead pilot to control multiple ships, usually up to six. But it would also slow them down considerably. They would be able to commandeer twenty-eight jammers between the four of them if all went well. Jet had spent the night thinking about it, and they had uploaded Agency uniforms and badges to their disguises.

With the help of their rings, they would hopefully be able to steal the jammers without any issues. He just hoped that Vail and Bo were up to it. Jet had been planning this for a while, trying to work out the kinks in his head. The possible pitfalls were numerous, but if they did succeed, the outcome was worth it. Plus, he felt the teams needed this. Each group would only succeed if they could work together. This team-building exercise was something they needed more than anything else, especially in the days ahead.

When Jet, Cord, Vail, and Bo neared the ninth belt's airspace, they left the common traffic lanes and cloaked. Jet knew the Agency headquarters' layout and where the hangar bays were located. The port was busy, as usual, with transports and frigates coming and going. The four of them landed on the topside bunker, docking their skiffs at a public hangar bay in a location they could get to quickly, just in case their plan fell apart. But, if all went well, they would simply abandon their old skiffs.

Each of them wore a different guise as they entered the busy museum. It was Jet's first time seeing an Atrum in disguise. As was typical for most aliases, the frame and height matched their physical appearance. But their hair, eyes, and skin color were all different. Basically, they were all older versions of themselves. Once they found the back areas, they switched into Agency uniforms.

"This way," Jet whispered and led the group through the lesser-used corridors. He had a specialized holopad to help get through some areas, now that the Lucem's credentials were no longer valid. The four made their way deep into the lower sections and paused before moving further.

"Try not to make eye contact or speak to anyone," Jet said. "Our uniforms are mid-level rank, high enough to get access to the jammers but low enough to avoid attention. It's still early, so hopefully, we can load up and move without notice."

"I'm completely turned around, Stroud," Vail hissed. "Don't you lose me."

"You always were, Vail," Cord whispered.

"Zip it, Brainiac!" Vail snapped as the two faced each other in the dark corridor. Bo stood behind Vail, waiting silently.

Jet held up his hands. "Can we not just get along for an hour?" It was as if nothing had changed between them. Vail and Cord had always been at each other's throats, going back to their days at Skylight University four years ago. Jet had hoped this exercise would help ease tensions between them. Apparently, he'd made a mistake. "We're going to need each other. You two *have* to put your differences aside for the next few days."

Jet turned and looked into the vast hangar bay. There were hundreds of jammers hovering in place. Their sleek hulls represented the latest design in aeronautics. The Agency was battle ready.

He began to rethink their plan as he looked at the jammers.

"What's wrong, Stroud?" Vail asked.

"Just thinking how in Skylight we're going to stand a chance against so many jammers once we're airborne. Even if we manage to steal the handful we need and make it back alive, the Agency has a legion of them—we'll eventually be facing too many jammers."

"Sounds like we need a new plan," Cord said.

Jet gathered them into a huddle. "We're gonna steal what we need, then we're taking this joint out."

"How will we do that?" Vail asked.

"What if we sabotage them while they're just sitting here?" Jet replied.

"Planting that many devices on each jammer would take hours," Cord said. "It'll be dawn soon. We'd need some sort of mass device."

"Could we rig the hangar doors to collapse?" Bo asked.

They all looked at him in shock, even Vail. It was the first time Jet had heard him say a word since their days at Skylight University.

"What? You're suddenly speaking now?" Vail asked.

Bo blinked, then shrugged. "Seemed like a good time to speak up." His voice sounded husky as if it was some unused mechanism.

Was Bo beginning to wake up? Jet wondered.

He faced Bo and grabbed his shoulders. "Focus on me for a moment."

Bo held Jet's gaze as they locked stares, their glowing eyes unblinking in the quiet corridor. Bo shook his head a few times as if trying to clear his thoughts. "Things feel so hazy. It's like I can't think for myself sometimes."

Vail gently moved Jet out of the way. "Bo, listen to me. I know the feeling…I know the anger. You can't rid yourself of it, but you can suspend it from time to time. It's hard and sometimes painful. But it's possible. Try that."

"Are you saying that you have to work at *not* killing people?" Cord asked, sounding intrigued.

"Ledbetter, you wouldn't understand!" Vail shot back.

"I'm curious to know more, though."

Vail heaved a sigh. "We get our energy from the dark side of human nature—"

"No time to discuss it right now," Jet said and snapped his fingers in front of Bo's face. "What's your idea?"

"Those barrier devices on the bay doors, see them?"

Jet looked. Blocking entry into the hangar bays' doors was a horizontal stasis field. "What about them?"

"That stasis field will shred anything coming in or out unless they're deactivated. I think I can modify them in a way that will reverse the energy field. By the time they figure it out, we'll be long gone."

"And it'll take out a lot of jammers before they do," Cord said.

"Alright. It's the best plan we've got," Jet said. "What do you need from us, Bo?"

"Just need a distraction once I get started. Five or ten minutes should do."

Jet looked at Cord and Vail. "You two up for this?"

Vail looked at Cord, and the two of them smiled. "Let's do this," she said.

The four of them cloaked and made their way into the hangar bay. The guards on duty were few, and Bo uncloaked near one of the control consoles. He probed the guards' minds. Jet watched them slump unconscious in their chairs. Then Bo set to work on the stasis field.

Jet, Cord, and Vail walked over to the center of the hangar bay. One by one, they dispatched the guards on duty. Jet and Cord simply tapped their foreheads, causing them to fall into a deep sleep. Vail used a more aggressive tactic by hitting them on the head hard enough to cause permanent damage or worse. Jet made a note to talk to her about it later.

The morning shift was coming in, and it wasn't long before the downed guards were noticed. Soon the entire base had been alerted. Lights flashed, and horns blared. Jet sent a thought to Bo, asking him to hurry as he, Cord, and Vail waited near the front of the jammers. Guards poured into the hangar bay, and they were forced to engage them. With their war staffs decompressed, Tetrahedron bodies began to pile up. Jet sent another thought to Bo, urging him to hurry before the mech units showed up.

Finally, Bo appeared, and they hopped into the leading jammers. Jet settled into the cockpit and quickly engaged the ghost pilot function. A stasis field encompassed the six jammers behind him, and he slammed the thrusters forward. His jammer shot out of the hangar bay, followed by Cord, Vail, and Bo.

Bo triggered the hangar bay stasis field immediately after they cleared it. Jet looped his jammer around in time to see multiple explosions as other jammers tried to fly through the invisible energy field. The pile of wreckage quickly blocked the bay door.

"We'd better move!" Jet said and cloaked his jammer. "Won't be long until they figure it out."

Their four jammers dropped into one of the lesser-used lanes. Jet was amazed at how agile the jammer was, even with six other jammers in tow. The craft seemed to almost read his thoughts as he flew. Its console fit around him in an ergonomic style, with holograms enlarging and diminishing just with his thoughts. The craft was advanced far beyond his recon skiff, explaining why the jammers had been so difficult to defeat.

By the time they neared the fifth belt, Jet noticed several blips on his screen. Soon the Agency jammers would catch up to them.

"I suggest everyone prepare," Cord said. "I predict they'll catch up to us near the third belt."

"We're going to have to split up," Jet said. "Even cloaked, the jammers will see us."

"Maybe," Vail hissed. "But this time, it'll be an even fight!"

"Except we're towing six other jammers," Bo said. "It's slowing us down."

Just as they entered the third belt's air space, the Agency jammers overtook them. Jet only counted eight that had made it through the hangar bay wreckage. *Not too bad*, he thought.

Jet brought his jammer in low, using the air traffic and tall skyscrapers for cover, and the other Heliographi followed him. But they quickly split apart as the Agency jammers began to arrive. He used the cloud cover and looped around behind the first jammer, dispatching it easily. Even with six jammers in tow, he was still flying faster and banking sharper than his old recon skiff.

"We need to get out of the populated areas," Jet said. "Head to the wind farms. Use the toons as cover."

The next jammer pilot was more skilled than the last. Jet managed to leave the city and find the wind farm. He weaved through the clouds and toons, trying to shake the jammer, but it stuck to his tail. It spit out rounds from its powerful rail cannon and eventually had a lock on his jammer. Jet slowed and, at the last second, released the last jammer in tow, which caught the Agency pilot off guard. It clipped the jammer's small wing, sending it into a flat spin. The jammer crashed into a large toon and erupted into a ball of flame. Jet eased back in his seat for just a second, then banked and looked for his next target.

He spotted one of the jammers zeroing in on Vail. She tried to lose it between the toons, but it was stuck to her tail and eventually had a lock on her skiff. Jet dove in from above. It was an aggressive line that caught the Agency pilot completely off guard. He fired rounds from his main cannon, drawing a perforated line along its narrow hull. The jammer ripped in half and disintegrated in midair.

"Cord, Vail, Bo. Everyone okay?" Jet barked.

"I'm fantastic," Cord said.

Bo's jammer showed up on Jet's radar, but he heard only silence through his intercom.

"That means he's okay," Vail said.

The local authorities were starting to show up, and the four of them cloaked and left the area.

Fifteen minutes later, they were circling the first belt's air space and the hidden hangar bay. Jet estimated they'd taken out several hundred jammers while hijacking enough for the Heliographi. Now, if and when there was a dogfight, they would be on equal footing, even if they were still outnumbered. It bought them some time while inflicting a little pain to Lybra and the Agency.

Just as Jet and the others landed their jammers, he received a distress call from DiJinn.

CHAPTER 27
The Heist—Part Two

SOLAN LEFT THE control room feeling anxious that morning.

Jet's plan of conducting a surprise mission had been a good one, great, in fact. But she had several concerns. Her biggest fear was relying too much on the Atrum, which so far had gone smoothly. But how much could she trust the other Atrum with her life?

Would it not be just as easy for the Atrum to avoid aiding them if it came down to it?

She and Joshia had made a connection, at least at some level, being siblings. Both had been leaders in

327

school, on the track field, and now with their own respective clans. It made sense that they would connect. But Solan could see how different Joshia was. Her old personality had been caring and kind. Now she was dark and sinister—even if that was, for the moment, on pause. It still lurked beneath the surface of her being, and Solan had thought about that for a while.

What made an Atrum an Atrum?

She felt it had something to do with a manifesto or perhaps a twisted satisfaction of sorts. Did the internal workings of an Atrum need to feed on bad deeds, fear, and suffering? If it was the opposite of how the Lucem worked, then that was *exactly* what it meant.

But most of the Atrum could exact some semblance of control, as far as she could tell anyway. Just like there were some gray areas in the Lucem's philosophy, there seemed to be some areas of gray with the Atrum as well. In fact, she herself could, at times, be more aggressive, angry, and cause harm, though she would never purposely kill another person when it could be avoided. But often, she wondered about the other Lucem. Cord, for example, didn't mind breaking the rules more than the others. He viewed things through a different lens, it seemed. She had watched him over the years and had developed a theory. Each Heliographi's inner light held morale at different levels of acceptance. Even though Cord was mostly a good person, he did things that one might expect from an Atrum, and his inner light, or

Heliographi, seemed to be fine with that. Whereas Jet's Heliographi would never allow him to interact on such morally gray ground.

All that said, Solan felt she could trust the Atrum, at least for the moment. Once the memoirs were obtained, she knew things would probably change, and the Lucem would once again have to put their guard up.

With Solan that day were Joshia and the two newest Heliographi, Kamber Caster and Tetra Wride. She'd made that arrangement because she and Joshia were two of the stronger Heliographi. They could do more between them than four of the others, and she didn't want to take away any firepower. This meant her group would take on two of the weakest Heliographi in Tetra and Kamber. Plus, she was pretty sure Jet and Kamber were secretly spending time together. She didn't want Jet to be distracted by Kamber and knew Jet felt the same way. He *knew* he couldn't focus on his missions and watch over Kamber at the same time, which is why he'd given her very little pushback. Solan had simply taken the decision out of his hands, which she felt he was thankful for.

She watched Jet and his group gear up and leave. The third group, led by Jinn, had left before sunrise. This left four Heliographi back at base: Mosstrom, Brit, Myranda, and Booker, the lone Lucem. She had pulled Booker aside and asked him for a favor.

Go quietly and find Stell. Ask her to join us here at Lyrinthum. We're going to need her assistance.

Stell had deep resources, which were tied to her group known as Vine. They were friendly to the Lucem, working alongside them over the years. They were a covert operation, and Solan felt that it might be time to bring them in. If things continued down the path they were headed, better to get Stell and her group here now.

Joshia walked into the hangar bay and prepped her skiff, ignoring Solan as she went through her preflight check.

"You're not having second thoughts, are you?" Solan quipped.

"Why would you think that? I'm here, aren't I? At some point, we will have to trust each other, Solan. Like it or not, we are tied together."

"So, we're to confide in each other now? That was never a requirement of this arrangement."

"Confide and trust are two different things. I never said confiding in each other was part of it, either. We have a common enemy. I want to see Lybra dead just as much as you."

Solan finally stopped loading her skiff and faced Joshia. She leaned on the nose of the skiff and glared at her. "That's exactly why trust is so difficult between our groups."

"You mean to tell me that you wouldn't kill Lybra if she stood here in front of you now? Don't forget, Sylvant was also my half-sister."

"Spare me, Joshia. You barely even knew her," Solan said through clenched teeth. "That's another excuse, and you're full of those!"

"So, why not kill Lybra?" Joshia pressed and walked over to stand directly in front of Solan.

"I'm confused. Are you *confiding* in me or trying to gain my *trust*? If you think throwing my sister's name out there will make a difference in how I view you and the other Atrum, you're wrong. If you want my trust, then why don't you tell me what happened to your fearless leader. Where is Sybold, Joshia? Why isn't she here with you and the others?"

"You know full well what happened," Joshia shot back. "She was assassinated by Albright and our father...two years ago. Why are you pretending ignorance?"

"Because something tells me that you're lying."

"She was murdered!"

"Oh, I know that much. But what else are you not telling me? What are you hiding about Sybold?"

Kamber and Tetra entered the hangar bay and walked over to stand next to them. "Are we interrupting something?" Kamber asked.

Solan pulled her gaze from Joshia. "No, nothing. Let's load up. Kamber, you're with me."

K

It took a little over thirty minutes to reach Earth's outer atmosphere. Their two skiffs punctured the troposphere and entered the storm that covered the entire planet. The Unbalance had been given its name over a century ago due to what it had done to the planet's surface and way of life. Thunderheads towered, and lightning crashed around their skiffs as turbulence bumped them around.

Solan had paid several visits recently to the ARC district, otherwise known as the 'Pit.' It was a mining operation located below the great plains of North America. In order to mine all the minerals, the Tetrahedron army used slave labor. It was something that enraged Solan, and she had vowed one day to return and free the imprisoned citizens. That day was today.

A huge stasis dome covered the Pit, preventing rain and wind from entering it while allowing access to thousands of transport frigates and skiffs of all sizes. Hundreds of portal-like doors spiraled open and granted access into the Pit. Solan entered one, followed closely by Joshia.

They docked their skiffs at a private hangar, and the four of them switched over to their disguises. Dressed in the standard garb of the ARC citizens, each wore dusty overalls, ripped and stained, and heavy boots with worn soles and hats to keep dirt off their scalps. Their disguise matched the skin complexion of most citizens, which was pale from lack of sun with dark hair.

They trekked down one of the hundreds of dusty trails leading into the Pit below. Further down was a large, cavernous chamber and thoroughfare that stretched for kilometers. The vast chamber was shaped like a halfpipe, with thousands of earth-colored strata ringing the upper perimeter. The walls and ceiling were smooth, scraped clean by some massive drilling machine. The place was lit by thousands of plants known as shale ferns, bioluminescent plants that grew right through the brittle rock. A dull greenish glow permeated throughout the cave system. The main thoroughfare had hundreds of roadways branching from it, filled with shops and markets. Projecting above from the vaulted ceiling were thousands of half-moon-shaped pods that appeared to be housing. Stacked below were more levels like the one they were on. It was busy, with thousands of people and vehicles moving around. The sounds of all the activity echoed through the district, and a fine film of dust particles shimmered in the air.

Soon they could hear the mining operations taking place. The sound of sonic chisels and explosions filled the air as they moved deeper into the complex. It was a massive operation, and the last time Solan was there, she'd managed to free some of the slaves and cause a riot. That had been quelled, though, and violently. But she was betting that most of the slaves were anxious to give some payback, and she was here to give them that chance.

"We need to move to the lower levels," Solan whispered. "The cell blocks are below the loading docks. Stick close."

"There'll be Tetrahedron down there," Joshia warned.

"Probably," Solan agreed as she guided them across the busy thoroughfare. "But remember, most of the Tetrahedron are stationed on the ninth belt now. Their focus is on the memoirs because that's where Lybra wants them."

"How are we supposed to transport all these people?" Kamber asked.

"We're going to steal some mining frigates," Solan said.

"Are we still comfortable with our approach?" Joshia whispered. "We have a lot of cell blocks to work between the four of us."

"Once we free a few of the prisoners, I'm betting they'll help us. We need to search for the ex-military officers first. They'll be our best bet."

"Then we'll need charts to find them," Joshia said. "If we raid that control tower first, it'll have logs. My guess is they've separated the militia members to prevent future uprisings."

Solan considered. "That's a good idea."

They split into two groups as they entered the loading area. The translucent domelike stasis field covering the vast pit soared up about one hundred meters. Lightning strikes from outside strobed through the cavern, and thunder rolled in low, booming echoes. Multiple crane towers, topped with snipers, surrounded the large mining pit. Solan counted hundreds of mining frigates, which were being loaded with precious metals and minerals.

Tetra and Joshia climbed the long staircase of a crane tower on the opposite side of the pit while Solan took Kamber with her.

Quietly! Solan sent the thought to Kamber.

But Kamber pulled on Solan, and they stopped at the base of the crane tower.

"What's wrong?" Solan asked.

Kamber stared at Solan with wide eyes, then took a knee.

Solan tapped her leg impatiently. *There's no time for this!* she thought to herself. But she could tell that Kamber was frightened. This was her first real mission, and Solan thought back to her early days. She, too, had once been a fresh recruit and remembered feelings of doubt.

Solan knelt in front of Kamber and took her hand. "You got this, Kamber. Remember your training. Stick near me, and you'll be just fine."

Kamber started to say something but paused. She took a slow, steady breath and started over. "I…I don't know. You say training, but I feel like I just started all of this yesterday."

"Jet tells me you're a quick study. He says you're already better than he was, and I trust what he says. You're a Lucem now, which means you need to be brave and protect others. These people are counting on you. Let that thought strengthen your confidence."

Kamber looked at Solan, their glowing gaze locked.

"Come on," Solan said and pulled Kamber to her feet. "You can do this. Just take it bit by bit."

They cloaked and climbed the crane's staircase, waiting for a guard to open the tower door. They slipped inside and saw four guards sitting behind holographic screens, monitoring the mining operations. Above were multiple snipers, scanning the loading bay for any theft, which didn't concern her. As long as they remained cloaked, they'd be fine. Right now, she needed intel on the prisoners.

She probed one of the guards' thoughts, suggesting he open the records file. She scanned through the thousands of files and found two high-ranking officers. She noted the cell blocks and left the tower.

They met Joshia and Tetra back at ground level and hid near some empty storage crates.

"What did you find?" Joshia asked.

"There are four high-ranking officers near the lower cell blocks. There's one named Linon. He was a captain in the local militia, according to the logs. I think we can start with him."

They continued downward onto dusty paths and along a large rock formation that eventually transformed into a tunnel. It grew darker, and the traffic noises faded. Ahead, the tunnel opened up, and Solan saw the outline of iron cages in the distance. She pulled the group to a halt.

"The cell block is ahead. Stay cloaked and watch for guards. Kamber, stick with me for now. Tetra, you're with Joshia."

They split up, communicating through thoughts. Solan eventually found a cell with the label she'd noticed in the guard tower. Inside, wearing a dirty T-shirt and pants that were ripped and stained, was a man of about thirty years of age. He had a narrow face covered by a thick black beard and long curly hair to match. The man was thin with a tall frame and dark skin. Along his arms were tattoos from his military service and tours. He leaned against the cell wall, his arms crossed and his head bowed, apparently sleeping.

Solan sent a thought, and the man sat up, startled.

"Linon," she whispered. "Is your name Linon?"

Solan remained cloaked as she spoke to him, and the man looked around cautiously. He rubbed his eyes as he began to wake. He leaned onto his hands and then knees, tilting his head. Solan whispered again, and the man nodded. He settled in the center of the cell and waited.

Solan looked around, searching for guards before uncloaking. The man took in a sharp breath as he looked into her glowing eyes as if he were staring at a ghost.

"My name is Solan. I need your help."

"What is this about?" he asked. "Who are you?"

Solan held up a hand, trying to calm his voice. She looked around again. "We don't have much time. I can explain later."

"How can I trust you?" he asked. "I have no idea who you are."

"You've heard rumor of the Heliographi?" Solan asked.

He nodded.

"I'm here to save you and these people. But I need your help. There's too many, and we need to move fast. I assume these people will listen to you?"

Linon sat forward. "That's impossible. I thought the Heliographi was just a myth."

"Can you help or not?"

"Yes, I speak for these people. They'll follow me."

Solan reached up and twisted the lock off his cage. The rusted door swung open.

Linon considered for a second longer, as if making a final decision, then crept silently from the cage.

Solan led him to a quiet nook in the massive stone cavern. She sent a thought out to the other Heliographi, and soon, Joshia, Tetra, and Kamber stood next to them.

Linon looked at the four Heliographi. "Can someone please tell me what this is about?"

"This is Joshia, Tetra, and Kamber," Solan whispered. "We are all Heliographi and here to free these people. We can offer safe haven for them, but we need your help. There are too many, and we don't have enough time."

Linon considered. "Why would you risk yourself for us? We can offer little in return."

"We need people with a military background," Joshia said. "Many of these people have experience."

"Is this about the hunt for the memoirs, then?"

Solan glanced at Joshia and then looked at Linon. "Yes."

Linon scratched his chin, then spoke softly. "I can help you free these people, but there are snipers everywhere. Escaping this place won't be easy. Some of these people are weak. They will not survive the trip."

"Better to die fighting than in a prison cell," Joshia said.

"I couldn't agree more," Linon said and held out his hand.

Solan could sense that this man, Linon, was a hardened troop who had probably seen his share of battles. She knew immediately she could trust him without reading his thoughts. She shook his hand. "We'll do our best to protect these people. No one deserves to live like this. It ends today!"

Linon bowed his head in a gesture of thanks. "Before our families were forced into this, we lived here in relative peace. At first, the Tetrahedron came offering good jobs and pay. That quickly changed. Family members turned up missing, and strict laws were soon put in place. Now, the Tetrahedron have run off the other businesses, and they're the only operation left. Families have been ripped apart; lives have been destroyed. If anyone speaks up, they are imprisoned. They have taken everything from us."

"I'm so sorry to hear that, Linon," Solan said. "But I promise, we will get your people out of here."

Linon nodded. "I can lead you to three other generals. Between us, we speak for these people—they trust us. What is your plan?"

"Joshia and I will take out the snipers first. That'll buy us a little time to free the others. We'll start by freeing your generals," Solan said. "Once they're free, we'll just have to split up and spread out. If we are noticed, Joshia and I will provide cover for you."

"I might suggest we raid the weapons' locker first," Linon said. "A lot of these people are trained soldiers. If we can get railguns into their hands, it'll make your job easier."

Solan could see that Linon would be an asset. "Good call. Kamber and Tetra, take Linon and get the weapons." She turned to face Linon in the dark and reached out to grasp his shoulder. "Do you know where the hangar bays are?"

"Yes, I know this place like the back of my hand."

"There are enough frigates here to transport everyone. If you don't hear back from Joshia or me, then lead your people to the frigates, and we'll meet you there. Kamber and Tetra will assist you. Is everyone clear?"

Kamber looked at Tetra, and they both nodded. "We're ready," Kamber said and followed after Linon.

Solan and Joshia split up. Solan cloaked and decompressed her staff. Perched high in the vaulted stone ceiling above were half-moon-shaped pods with snipers camped out. Solan scaled the wall, leaping from pod to pod and dispatching the snipers. Across the chamber, she saw Joshia doing the same. Below, she saw the blurred movements of Kamber and Tetra.

Once the snipers were cleared, Solan sent a psychic message to Kamber and Tetra. Then she moved on to the next cell block with Joshia right behind her. Solan watched as Tetra and Kamber escorted Linon to a few of the cages, freeing the ones he claimed to be generals. They hurried to the weapon vault, which was a small rock alcove off to the side of the cell block. Soon, there was a group of prisoners handing out weapons and freeing people from cages.

Solan and Joshia continued clearing the way of snipers from each cell block. Tetra and Kamber led the way below, following just behind Solan and Joshia. They would wait for Solan's message, then a flood of prisoners would rush into the cleared cell block and free more prisoners.

But after the third cell block, the prison chambers opened up to larger vaulted areas, and more snipers and foot soldiers patrolled the upper thoroughfares. It would be impossible for Solan and Joshia to take them all out.

She gathered with Joshia to discuss the best approach.

"There are too many troops ahead," Joshia said, and Solan nodded in agreement. "We'll need to find another way around."

Solan looked around the chamber. The area below the thoroughfares was dark, and she wondered what lay below. "There's got to be a bottom down there," she said.

Joshia glanced to the dark chasm below them. "Seems like a risk. We don't know what else is down there."

Solan thought for a moment, her brow furrowed. "It may be the only way, unless we try to fight our way through. We'd lose a lot of prisoners if we did that. They're tired and worn. Even with weapons, we can't take out all those Tetrahedron."

"If they hear us, we're on the lower ground. They'll hammer us from above."

Solan could see Joshia's logic. But she wasn't willing to risk prisoners' lives on a frontal assault. "Let's talk to Linon. He may know more."

Solan and Joshia met the others back in the cell block. All the prisoners had been freed now, and there were thousands of them. It wouldn't be long until the commotion was noticed.

"You want to go *beneath* the thoroughfares?" Linon asked. "That's risky. Those are old paths that were used before the graphene highways were developed. They haven't been used in ages. It's rough terrain down there with lots of pitfalls."

"Won't these people make too much noise?" Kamber asked.

"That won't be an issue," Linon said. "With all the noise in the upper chambers, they shouldn't hear anything. I'm just worried about the rough terrain. A lot of us are tired and weak. I'm afraid some of these people won't survive that trek."

"I don't see another way, Linon," Solan replied. "There are too many troops patrolling the highways. Even with us four Heliographi and all the weapons, I'm afraid we'll lose more people in a head-on battle."

Linon thought for a moment, then turned to his other generals. The woman and two middle-aged men remained composed as they whispered. After several seconds, Linon faced Solan and Joshia. "We agree. Though we have enough weapons for the men and some of the women, we'd prefer the path of least resistance for our people. Lead the way, Solan."

CHAPTER 28
The Heist—Part Three

ΑΒ ΔΕ **Η**ΘΙΚΛΜ

ΝΞΟΠΡΣ ΥΦ ΨΩ

DIJINN, **TI-LEER**, **SOJAHN**, and Bofisto left in separate skiffs.

The sun hadn't crested the Earth yet, and the outer loops of the Skylight System's belts could be seen twinkling on the horizon. Mist shrouded their skiffs, and far-off thunderheads clung to a few of the belts, illuminating them with bursts of blues and greens. The ominous view made DiJinn wonder if they were in for a rough ride that day. She wasn't happy about her group's pairings. She detested Sojahn. A close second was

Bofisto. She had no doubt that Joshia had selected that pair just to upset her. And with Ti-Leer along, she hoped this mission wouldn't turn into a circus. At least Ti-Leer had avoided his typical heavy drinking the night before.

"D.J., pay attention, lass," Ti-Leer said through her intercom.

She tore her gaze from the distant storms and refocused. The traffic lanes were getting crowded with citizens heading to work. She maneuvered her cloaked skiff in and out of the busy lanes, with the other three following close behind.

Their mission was simple; steal Lybra's stockpile of refined rare-earth. According to Sojahn, the rare-earth minerals had been relocated to an area of the ninth belt known as *Cranium Nine* or C9. The ninth largest free-floating section of the ninth belt was in a dangerous area. The undeveloped areas of the ninth belt were filled with gangs and drug lords. It was a 'dodgy' area, as she liked to say. One could easily end up in the wrong territory if they weren't careful. DiJinn was familiar with these areas, having conducted numerous undercover raids there over the years. As her alias, Detective Marsh, she knew most of the debris field by heart. But she had only heard rumors of Cranium Nine, and many claimed that it didn't really exist.

About thirty minutes later, they entered the debris field, and DiJinn took manual control of her skiff. Thousands of chunks floated randomly across their path, leftover remnants of the ninth belt from the meteor storm a century ago.

"Ah, look at all this crap!" Ti-Leer hissed. "We'll likely be shredded to bits in this place. I'll never forgive you, D.J., if you get me killed. Better take it nice an' easy, lass."

DiJinn ignored him and focused on her instruments. It was like flying upside down and sideways all at once. Bits and pieces of smaller chunks pelted her skiff's hull like hail stones. DiJinn slowed her speed and let Sojahn take the lead. Their skiffs flew in single file, cloaked in the early morning light. The mist that engulfed the random chunks of the ninth belt made the way forward treacherous. The larger chunks were easy to avoid, but the smaller debris was more difficult. Even the tiniest ones were large enough to rip her skiff's hull in half. Sometimes, a random piece would reveal itself at the last second, leaving her little time to adjust.

Deeper into the debris field they flew, further than DiJinn had ever dared to go before. They eventually slowed and stopped near a particularly large chunk of belt about a kilometer in diameter. Sojahn kept the intercom silent and reached out to them with her thoughts.

They followed her and anchored their skiffs to the wrecked hull of C9. In the early sun, it looked like a grinning skull, rusty with ancient damage—dented and beaten.

They remained in their skiffs, scanning the area for signs of activity. The thunderheads DiJinn had seen on the distant horizon had finally caught up to them. Turbulent wind pushed on their skiffs as rain and lightning hammered down around them. Still, they waited.

A grouping of ships approached. The area of the skull's maw opened up like a grinning giant, and the ships entered and vanished.

Let's go! Sojahn sent the thought, and they leapt from their skiffs.

C9's surface was rough and pitted from the constant space debris banging into it. Since the entire ninth belt was exposed to outer space for a brief period once a day, they had to time things perfectly. DiJinn had no desire to be near C9 when it passed through the hole in the Skylight System's synthetic atmosphere. She estimated they still had plenty of time before that happened, though.

They followed Sojahn across the rough terrain. DiJinn gripped exposed conduit, punctured pieces of hull, and anything else she could grasp. When they reached the area where an eye socket was located, Sojahn stopped and held up a hand. She disappeared into the large crater while the others waited patiently. Dead trees and burnt vegetation clung to the metal remains of the hull. Nothing lived on the exposed hunk of steel, thanks to its constant exposure to outer space. The damage from the meteor storm nearly a century ago was still evident, and the metal hull juxtaposed with the dirt and dead grass felt otherworldly to DiJinn. It looked like a war zone from some twentieth-century battlefield.

Sojahn poked her head through a vent and waved. They followed her down into the orbital socket of C9's left eye. At the bottom was a vent, and she pried it open, then wedged herself inside. DiJinn and the others followed and landed on a steel grate. Below them was a chasm of catwalks from what was left of the ninth belt's infrastructure. It was dark and bottomless, with the sound of low groans echoing up from the depths. It was like some great vessel, rocking and rolling in an angry ocean. The unstable hull seemed to barely hold itself together.

Sojahn led them deep into the inner bowels, across bent catwalks and ruptured bulkheads. A light ahead glowed brighter, and they inched toward it. DiJinn heard noises from the area beyond. The sound of voices filled the air and drew them forward.

They settled into a dark corner of a vast chamber, getting a good view of their surroundings; they'd definitely located the loading bay. DiJinn noted the frigates being loaded with crates of supplies. Pallets of rare-earth sat near one end and were heavily guarded by Tetrahedron marauders. In one of the adjacent loading bays, she could see dozens of patrolling M-Class mech units.

Of course! she thought to herself. *They couldn't seem to get away from these can-cans.*

She tapped Ti-Leer and the other two Atrum, pointing at the mechs.

"Look. They're loading the frigates now," Sojahn whispered.

Some utility mechs were hauling crates of the stolen rare-earth onto three large frigates, which were nearly full and ready to ship out.

"Oi! It's our lucky day," Ti-Leer whispered. "Didn't think they'd already have 'em loaded up an' ready for us."

"I wasn't planning on running into M-Class mechs, though," DiJinn said. "No matter! We stick to the plan. Set your alias to match the Tetrahedron uniform. We position ourselves on those frigates and wait till they're airborne. Once I give the signal, we take control. It appears we'll have some mechs to deal with, but nothin' we can't handle."

"Tiny Jinn, those frigates aren't exactly what I'd call fast," Bofisto growled. "I don't see any jammers now, but you can bet your sassy pigtails they're not far away!"

DiJinn felt her cheeks flush as she stared at the behemoth. "Don't start with me, Bofisto!"

"Once we hijack those frigates, they'll figure it out and send jammers," Bofisto continued with a grin that infuriated DiJinn even more. "We'll be sitting ducks in those lumbering relics. Was that your plan?"

"That's why we need to wait as long as we can," DiJinn shot back. "The further away from the ninth belt, the further the jammers'll have to fly."

"It's a gamble, Jinn," Sojahn said. "You know it is. I don't think we can get back to the first belt before they catch us. The jammers are much faster."

"Big dumb has a point, D.J.," Ti-Leer said, nodding at Bofisto. "We'll be too slow…" He paused and slapped his forehead. "Hold on a tick! Where would Jet's group be right about now?"

M

Jet, Cord, Vail, and Bo had just entered the first belt's air space and landed all the jammers when they got the psychic distress call from DiJinn.

Turn yourself around and find me. Hurry!

In the newer jammers, they were able to reach the debris field of the ninth belt in about fifteen minutes, much faster than his old recon skiff. He managed to follow the breadcrumbs of her signature, and they remained cloaked as they wove between chunks of debris. Soon he was looking at a large floating section of hull that resembled a human skull. Jet's console showed this one to be the ninth largest chunk in the ninth belt's debris field, based on its surface mass. Interestingly though, it didn't appear on his map. This remnant of the belt didn't seem to exist.

Jet settled his jammer next to DiJinn's skiff, then he and the others followed her mental signature through an old vent and down deeper into the bowels of the wrecked hull. Soon they could see the light from a central portion that appeared to be the heart of the facility. The orange light led them closer until he saw several shimmering figures huddled near one end.

"What's the rush?" Jet whispered as he nudged up against DiJinn. Vail, Bo, and Cord waited silently near Ti-Leer, Sojahn, and Bofisto.

"I assume you got the jammers?" DiJinn asked.

"And then some."

"Good, 'cause we're gonna need your help," Ti-Leer chimed in. "Once we commandeer those frigates, we gonna have Tetrahedron all over us."

Jet looked at the others. "We'll keep them off your backside. By the way, we managed to shut down the main hangar bay at the Agency. They're going to be distracted for a while, so this is the perfect opportunity."

"As soon as the last crate is loaded, we're boarding the frigates. We plan to go disguised as Tetrahedron, then hijack the ships. Once we take out the crews, we'll make a line to the first belt. These frigates aren't exactly fast, so stay cloaked and pick off any ships tailin' us," DiJinn said.

Jet, Cord, Bo, and Vail made their way back to the jammers and waited. They watched for the frigates as several marauder ships came and went. It was taking longer than expected, and Jet grew concerned that something had happened. But finally, he received a mental signal from Jinn. The other three heard it as well, and they detached from the hull and moved into position.

DiJinn hadn't gone into much detail about how they planned to hijack the three frigates, but he assumed it involved 'aggressive negotiations.' It didn't take long, and he guessed the crews were mostly pilots or engineers. However, each frigate had a jammer escort, and as soon as the frigates changed course, the jammers fell into attack formation behind them.

Jet, Cord, Bo, and Vail didn't wait. They quickly positioned their jammers behind the escorts and within seconds had destroyed them.

"You're clear, DiJinn," Jet spoke calmly into the intercom, and the three frigate's thrusters roared to life.

The large frigates were slow and cumbersome. Finding a path through the debris field required caution. Jet and his crew remained hidden behind the frigates, though. Occasional jammers would move into attack position behind the frigates but were quickly dispatched. It appeared he'd been correct—there was no flood of jammers rushing to challenge the frigates. Apparently, the Agency was still dealing with the damage to their hangar bay.

All seemed to be moving well. *Maybe too well,* Jet thought.

Then DiJinn hailed him over the intercom. "Looks like we're gonna have to make a pitstop on the way back."

K

Solan was forced to move slower than she cared to. The craggy tunnels below the main thoroughfares were dark, and the footing treacherous. Still, they were far enough down that the weary prisoners—many of them sick and feeble—couldn't be heard by the guards above. But the problem was twofold. One, they were slowed by the rough terrain and the weaker prisoners. Two, it wouldn't be long until the missing prisoners were noticed.

There was an army of people following Solan. And, at the pace they were moving, she could see they'd never make it to the transports before being discovered. Furthermore, even if they did make it, she and the other Heliographi would never be able to take on the platoons of guards up top without loss of life to the prisoners. That was a deal breaker for her. She wanted to take the path that led to the least loss of life.

Solan realized now that she needed backup.

And why couldn't she get it?

Jet, and perhaps Jinn, should be on their way back by now, assuming all went as planned.

Before the Atrum had joined them, Solan had always used care when sending mental signatures, or distress calls, since they could be intercepted by the Atrum. But now, that wasn't an issue.

It was worth a shot. She would try to reach out to Jinn first.

She paused the group and knelt to the ground. Joshia, Kamber, and Tetra were next to her almost immediately.

"What's wrong?" Kamber asked.

"We're moving too slow," Joshia said. "We'll never make the transports on time."

Solan nodded to Joshia in the dark. Her glowing eyes lit the jagged walls of the rocky chasm. "I'm going to send a mental signature for backup. We need help."

"I think you're right," Joshia said. "Better hurry, though. It'll take time for the others to get here."

Solan had no idea where the other Heliographi groups were but focused and sent the signal. A minute later, she stood and urged the prisoners forward, speaking words of encouragement. The line trudged through the dusty cave system, Solan listening to her thoughts for a response. Before long, she heard Jinn's voice speaking to her. It was distant, but she still heard it.

We're coming…

Solan sighed in relief and signaled Jinn her location, then placed her focus back on the prisoners. Minutes passed as they slowly made their way. But before long, she sensed something was out of place and knew that an alarm had been set off. They would encounter resistance soon.

"Hurry!" Solan whispered, and the group passed her words down the line. She sent Joshia and Tetra to the back of the line just in case they were attacked from behind. Solan gripped her war staff tighter, thankful that Jet had found the relic. Even so, she would be hard-pressed to protect all of the prisoners. Linon marched next to her. He had managed to arm a multitude of militia soldiers with rail guns. But they had no armor and would be outmatched by the Tetrahedron.

Several minutes passed as the path began to climb. They were moving up to the main levels now and toward the hangar bays. She could see a light ahead and the opening of the tunnel system. The noise of feet marching on gravel echoed in the rocky tunnels. Some of the prisoners whispered in fearful voices. Solan braced herself for the worst. Once they hit the main thoroughfare, all hell would break loose. But they couldn't wait in the lower passages any longer, or they'd be sitting targets from snipers above.

M

Jet slowed his jammer and circled the frigates. He was able to use one of the stolen access codes Stell had sent. With the thousands of other skiffs and frigates moving in and out of the ARC District's airlocks, they went unnoticed and landed in one of the numerous hangar bays. With the frigates locked up tight, Jet led the other Heliographi into the mining facility, still cloaked. There were eight of them, not an army exactly, but enough to cause some major headaches, especially with the war staffs.

Jet, Cord, Vail, Bo, DiJinn, Ti-Leer, Sojahn, and Bofisto raced down a dusty trail and deeper into a cave system that Jet had no recollection of. He could hear shouts in the distance and the sound of fighting. Jet and the others burst through the opening of a cave and barreled into several platoons of Tetrahedron and freed prisoners, fighting and yelling. In the center of it was Solan. She used her glowing staff in a wide arcing shield that deflected rounds from the marauders, while her cloak protected the prisoners nearby.

Jet, Cord, Bo, and Vail engaged the unprotected flank of Tetrahedron on the left while DiJinn, Ti-Leer, Bofisto, and Sojahn tackled the right flank. The marauders were caught completely off guard, and their ranks folded under the might of the Heliographi. Within minutes, the platoon of Tetrahedron were scattered and fleeing or wounded on the ground.

"Let's move!" Solan yelled.

Jet and the others helped some of the wounded prisoners, and the line of people hurried to the hangar bays.

"Over here," Linon barked. He and the other generals led the prisoners. However, the transports were loaded with minerals and had to be cleared from the cargo hold to make room. Using the heavy mechs to move the crates slowed things down long enough for enemy reinforcements to arrive.

Fighting erupted once again. The Lucem and Atrum moved to the front to engage the marauders while Linon and the others cleared the transports. But the Heliographi were a force and again managed to beat back the scores of Tetrahedron. But more marauders were soon filing into the hangar bay.

"We have to board now!" Solan roared at Linon. "Just sit people on the crates if you have to."

They were able to hold off the marauders long enough to get the prisoners aboard, then the Heliographi dispersed. Jet looked around for Cord, but he was missing.

"We need to get back to the frigates of rare-earth, Solan," Jet said. "They're in the next hangar bay."

"The prisoners are more important," Solan replied as she helped some of the older ones on board. "I need you to stay until we're out. I'll get the last of them on board."

Jet glanced around the large hangar bay. Several Tetrahedron platoons were starting to reorganize. More marauders were pouring in from the opposite tunnel. Jet gathered the other Heliographi. Linon, and hundreds of other prisoners who could fight, stood behind them.

"We'll do what we can," Linon said. He raised his railgun and readied it.

Jet led the Heliographi forward, their staffs glowing like lightning.

Just as the fighting began, marauders went flying in all directions. Jet looked up to see Cord in his jammer. He strafed sideways and leveled the jammer's powerful forward rail cannon. It chattered rounds into the enemy lines and scattered them.

"We have another problem," Linon yelled over the explosions. He pointed up at the airlock in the massive translucent dome overhead. "They've locked it down. No one's leaving now!"

Jet glanced up. The large airlock shimmered from the lightning flashes beyond. He noticed that a second stasis field was now covering the main one.

"That's just great!" Jet said. He waved at Cord's jammer, drawing his attention.

Cord hovered in low. Jet pointed up to the airlock and mouthed the words 'take it out.'

Cord nodded and flew off.

The Tetrahedron were regrouping again. This time, they were maneuvering several mounted howitzer cannons into position, which could take out the transports. Jet could see it wouldn't be long until they had nowhere to go. They were running out of time.

Above them, Cord focused the jammer's firepower on the airlock. He released an assortment of rockets and heavy rail guns on it. The rounds peppered the airlock's metal frame, and it began to heat up. The second stasis field flickered, then faltered.

Solan returned and grabbed Jet by the shoulder. "All the prisoners are loaded up. Keep them off of us until we clear the airlock. Then get yourself out of here!"

Cord dropped his jammer back down and hammered the Tetrahedron platoons again. Jet waved to him, then grabbed the other Heliographi, and they left the hangar bay.

Ten minutes later, Jet, Bo, and Vail guided their jammers out of the ARC District, followed by the three frigates and DiJinn, Ti-Leer, Sojahn, and Bofisto. Cord met them as they followed behind the massive transport ships carrying the prisoners. The turbulent storm shook Jet's jammer as he ascended into the Earth's atmosphere and finally into space. Jet leaned back and relaxed his grip on the controls.

"Not sure how we managed all that," Jet said.

"The odds were unlikely," Cord said. "I predicted we should've been—"

"Oh, shut up, Ledbetter!" Vail barked over the intercom.

Jet smiled at that. "Good job, team."

But he knew what all the others knew. Tomorrow they would be tested by a gauntlet of reveals.

The rest of the flight back, Jet couldn't get Albright's words out of his head, though.

Unlock your gift!

He was starting to get a clearer picture in his mind about the Hall of Vital Records. A theory was forming, one that made sense now…

…it had been designed by Albright for *one* main reason.

The Hall was a conduit between planes of existence.

It explained why he felt stronger when he was there, why his abilities seemed supercharged. Whether by some mystical force or higher power, Jet wasn't sure. But he knew it was what had allowed him to communicate so clearly with the ghost Lucem named Brindall.

But returning would be a dangerous venture, much more than his last few visits. The place was crawling with mech units and Tetrahedron. Lybra was consolidating her forces. What was once the Agency's headquarters was fast becoming Lybra's new lair. Breaking into it yet again was a huge risk. The last time had nearly gotten him killed.

But he knew that Albright wouldn't have asked him to do something so dangerous unless it was extremely important.

The answer to unlocking his gift lay at the Hall of Vital Records, and he knew his curiosity would not leave him in peace until he went back.

CHAPTER 29
Small Comforts

ΑΒ ΔΕ ΗΘΙΚΛ**Μ**

ΝΞΟΠΡΣ ΥΦ ΨΩ

LATER THAT DAY, Jet strolled through the Lyrinthum hangar bay.

The place was packed tight with ships, troops, and freed prisoners. The bay had never been meant to be used in such a capacity. What the Heliographi were trying to do was create a base of operations out of the secret passages below Skylight University. They still didn't have everything they needed, but it was a start.

Their missions that morning had been a success. In one day, some eight thousand prisoners had been freed, which in turn helped them in creating an army—albeit a hungry and weary one. They had also destroyed a few hundred jammers while commandeering enough for themselves, stolen the majority of Lybra's rare-earth supplies, which would certainly hamper her ability to manufacture more M-Class mechs, and hijacked several transports and heavy frigates. Inside each frigate was a large cache of rail guns and armor to boot.

Not bad for a day's work.

But the prisoners, many who were weak and tired, wouldn't be of use for a while. Having an army ready for the next few reveals was pretty much out of the question. It would take time to train them, though the majority had a military background. The good news was that Stell and her team, with all of their resources, had joined them in Lyrinthum. But there were a lot of hungry and sick people to look after. Once the freed prisoners were cared for, then the training could begin. *We'll handle it*, Stell had said, and Solan was grateful.

To Jet, it was pretty obvious that Captain Linon was their unspoken leader. He could sense that the man was honest and trustworthy just in his actions and mannerisms. He cared for his people, and they listened to him. He was tall and slender and walked with conviction. His confidence bolstered the others as he spoke with Solan and his other generals. Solan waved Jet over.

"…you feel there are enough military personnel in your group?" Solan was asking Linon.

"A large portion of them, yes," Linon said, his tall, wiry frame ramrod straight and rigid.

"Captain Linon," Jet said and shook his hand. "I'm also from the ARC District. I'm curious how the Tetrahedron got such a strong foothold there so quickly?"

Linon looked at Jet and gave him a nod. He had trimmed his beard and cut his hair from the tangled mass it had been. Now he looked like a military leader with his cropped hair. "It started peaceful enough, about three years ago," Linon said. "They came in and offered jobs and good pay. But soon, they had a monopoly and ran the other business owners off. Before we knew it, they were running raids on the citizens. A few years back, they took my son and forced him into the mining pits. I joined voluntarily, right behind him. I looked for him in hopes we could escape. After years in the pits, I found no signs and lost hope. Not long after, I was singled out because of my military background and isolated in a separate cage. The Tetrahedron kept most of us in small groups and rarely shifted us around. But I managed to make contact with the other generals, and we developed a communication system. I had word sent out, but no one had seen my son. I fear there are more prisoners back in the ARC district. My guess is they're being used in places other than the mining pits. The district is vast with many offshoots that even I don't know about."

"And we will go after them soon," Solan said. "But right now, we have bigger concerns."

"What is it you really want from me, Solan? You say you wanted to save these people, but I can see there's another reason you've brought us here. No one risks their own neck out of kindness."

Solan gave Linon a thoughtful look, considering. "We are in a difficult spot, me and the other Heliographi. I'm not going to force you or any of these people into a war they aren't ready for. But your captors, the Tetrahedron, work for someone, a dangerous lady, who has managed to corrupt the system's President. They are responsible in part for what you and these people have suffered through. We can accomplish several things if we work together."

"You want me to train these people to become an army for you?"

Solan leaned against the jammer and crossed her arms. "I'm offering you a chance to bring some pain to the ones who have harmed you."

Linon stared at Solan as if trying to read her thoughts. "I'm grateful to you, Solan. You have freed us, given us a new opportunity. There is nothing to go back to in the ARC. Most of these people are all that's left of their family. They have no possessions, no livelihood, no money. The pit is no place to live. But here, even inside the hull of a belt, we have a chance at a better life. There's enough room down here for generations of people. But we need food, beds…a social network. How can we accomplish all of that?"

"We have the capability to create and sustain that. Stell is a friend. She'll supply those necessities. She has the resources to care for your people and set up housing. I'm only asking that you consider joining our cause against the Tetrahedron. Of course, your people can stay here regardless, and we will protect them."

Linon didn't consider long. "Solan, it would be an honor to fight alongside you. I can speak for my people. But many of the elderly and younger are hurting. If you can help me provide for them, I will fight with you. I don't know when we'll be ready, though. My generals and I have a lot to coordinate."

Solan smiled and shook his hand. "Gather your generals. We'll talk more soon. In the meantime, make yourself at home. Right now, we have some very important business to attend to."

Solan introduced Stell and her group of assistants to Linon and his team, then gathered the other Heliographi in the control center. Jet sat next to Kamber, who he hadn't talked to much recently. He wanted to ask how she was holding up but nudged her and smiled instead. She continued to look straight ahead and didn't acknowledge him.

Every remaining Heliographi was there, sitting in their own chair. The mood in the control room was somber, quiet, and tense. There was still an air of mistrust between the two sides. Jet had hoped the missions would help build some camaraderie amongst them but could see that it wouldn't be so easy to wipe away centuries of distrust that quickly.

Solan laid her staff on the table and gazed around the room. "Tomorrow night, we will have to run the gauntlet, just like the other seekers. The next four reveals will occur almost simultaneously. It'll push us all to our limits, but with the staffs and the jammers, we should hopefully be one step ahead of Lybra this time."

"Not to mention the hit on her," DiJinn said, her tactical boots kicked up on the edge of the old table. "She felt that, I'm sure. Is it possible we might finally have an advantage?"

"Let's not get ahead of ourselves, Jinn," Solan said. "Remember, you'll all need to work as a team to pull this off."

Jet looked around the room, noticing how everyone seemed to be upset with the assignment. Of course, pairing Lucem and Atrum was putting fire and ice together. Jet knew that. But apparently, their little impromptu 'team building' mission hadn't helped much, at least it didn't appear so. DiJinn shot Bofisto and Sojahn a go-to-hell look while Vail and Cord glared at each other. Tetra and Kamber sat with arms crossed, looking in opposite directions. The others made no eye contact either and sat quietly, waiting to be dismissed.

Solan glanced around the room, shook her head, and threw her arms up in a hopeless gesture. "I give up. Everyone be prepared and ready to leave at dusk tomorrow."

Jet followed Kamber out of the meeting and grabbed her hand. "Hey, hold up."

Kamber faced him. She held his hand loosely but didn't speak.

"Everything alright?"

Kamber shrugged and seemed reluctant to talk at first. "I…I had another dream last night."

"What was it about?" Jet asked, but he already knew. The last time Kamber had had a dream that worried her like this, his friend Cutter had died at the Century Eclipse. "Is it about another death?"

She nodded. "Should we tell Solan?"

Jet thought for a moment. "Are you sure?"

"Yes. It felt just the same as last time."

Jet thought, then shook his head. "Solan's so busy right now. I don't know. Maybe it was just a bad dream or something—"

"No, Jet," Kamber interrupted him. "I know this feeling."

"Do you know who it was?"

"Unfortunately, no."

Jet stood there, looking at Kamber and trying to think what to do. If they told Solan, it would only cause her to worry as well. And they couldn't just call off the entire mission. Solan would want to know who it might be. Jet tried to guess what the other Heliographi might do if they knew about it. Would it change anything? Would any one of them want to sit this out?

Of course they wouldn't, none of them.

"I feel like we should say something," Kamber said. She held his gaze, her brow furrowed with concern, her voice a bit unsteady.

"I just don't know what good it would do except put everyone on edge, and we don't need that. If we don't know who, then maybe it's better not to say anything—"

"What if it's you, Jet?" Kamber said and gripped his hands tighter. She stared into his eyes, and he could see she was close to tears. She had already been through so much, and there was more to come.

Once again, he felt his heart ache for her. There was a sudden desire to take her away from all of this uncertainty and death. Deep down, he still wanted to protect her, to shield her from harm. But he knew that wasn't the answer. Kamber would only get through this by facing it head-on, just as he had and every other Heliographi before them. Shielding her would only make things worse.

"What if it's me?" she continued, still holding his hands. "What would you think?"

The thought of it being Kamber made him pause, and a sudden anxiety coursed through him.

"It won't be, Kamber. Don't think that—"

"How can you know?" she asked and wiped tears from her cheek.

Jet gently took Kamber by the shoulders. "Answer this question for me, Kamber. If you knew it was you, would you run off and leave the others? Leave the Lucem to fight through this alone?"

Kamber stared at him, her eyes wide. "Of course not. I would never do that. You know I wouldn't."

"And neither would I or any of the others. All we can do is what we *have* to do, what's in front of us. Our friends need us to be brave so that they can be brave. If it's our time, then so be it. Think about how we can help each other and just focus on that. I promise you that all of the other Lucem, even if they knew it was their turn to die, would still face it head-on. You and I are Lucem. We need to stay strong for ourselves and the others, now more than ever."

Kamber nodded and wiped another tear from her cheek. Jet waited as she lingered, though, and sensed there was more she wanted to say.

"On my mission with Solan…I froze up. I just couldn't seem to get a grip."

"There's nothing to be ashamed of, Kamber. I was nervous before my first mission."

She sniffled as she continued to hold his hand. "But I was terrified. I'm *still* terrified. I mean, it's great having the others around for support. I don't know. I just need someone to talk to. Jet, I…don't want to be alone tonight," she stammered. "Can we talk somewhere more private?"

Jet considered. They had a lot going on tomorrow, and he wanted to be prepared. But he could sense that Kamber needed him. He began to wonder if there was more to it, though. Talking was one thing. Comforting, well, that was something else completely. And he still hadn't quite made up his mind on how to approach the whole situation between them. But he knew he couldn't leave Kamber alone in this state; she needed him. It was the eve of the gauntlet, and the next four reveals would happen in quick succession. Everyone was nervous. She needed a little comfort, at whatever level that meant, and maybe he did too.

He lowered his voice. "Why don't we meet at Firefly Falls. Give me an hour."

M

Jet waited in the shadows, the fireflies buzzing around his head, the waterfall roaring. *His heart pounding.*

Soon, a blurry mirage emerged from the opposite side of the hidden glen of Firefly Falls. Jet took a deep breath and muttered to himself. *This is crazy.*

Kamber stood in the middle, surrounded by the fireflies. The green and yellow luminance seemed to highlight her skin in a way that made her look ethereal. She noticed him and smiled, then moved his way. Jet nearly turned around and left. He was still struggling with his own feelings about Kamber. Could they handle this, especially now with so much going on? What if things turned sour?

What if she doesn't like me after all?

"Hi, Jet. I'm…I'm glad you could make it," Kamber said and stepped forward, as though she was moving in for a hug. But she stopped and crossed her arms instead. She stood there, rising up and down on her tiptoes and avoiding his gaze.

Jet could hear the tension in her voice; he wasn't the only one who was nervous.

He gave her a quick smile, feeling like he'd fall apart at any second. He placed his hands awkwardly behind his back, wondering why he felt this way now. He'd had so many conversations with Kamber, but at that moment, he could hardly stand still. "Why is this suddenly so awkward?" he asked with a chuckle.

She shook her head, then laughed. "I think it's what happens on a first date. That's what they call this, you know?"

"A date, huh? Is that what this is?"

"A *first* date," she corrected him and turned and walked toward the rocky shore of the lake.

"We've been here before…alone," he replied and fell in next to her. "Doesn't that count as a date?"

Jet watched how the moonlight seemed to create a halo around her. He felt as if he were in a dream at that moment. His head already felt light, his vision was beginning to swim, and all he was doing was walking next to her.

Kamber took his hand but didn't answer him. She sat on one of the larger boulders and pulled him down next to her.

She stared at the waterfall, lost in thought, and Jet leaned back and enjoyed the moment. Eventually, he sat forward. "You…wanted to talk?"

She pulled her knees up and rested her chin on them. She stared at Jet for a second. "I think I just needed to get out of our dreary headquarters. I was so upset at myself for not being more prepared with Solan. I don't know why I feel like a failure. What was it like for you on your first mission?"

Jet considered. "My first mission was with the Recon army when we were still a part of the Agency. That was four years ago in an area around the ninth belt. The debris field is a haven for illegal activity, lots of drug overlords there. Raids are pretty common along the trade routes to the eighth belt. I remember being terrified on my first mission—you're not alone. But I guess I turned out okay. And you're much sharper than I was at your level. You'll be fine."

She gave him a smile. "You've been so kind. I can't thank you enough for helping me through all this." She caught him off guard when she leaned in and kissed him. He felt the longing in her kiss, but it was reserved, and she pulled back. But it was nothing compared to what she did next.

Kamber quickly stood, unclasped her cloak, and let it drop down around her feet.

Jet was too stunned to react and simply stared at her, not sure what to do.

The smile she gave him was magical—a shy, mischievous grin that left him shocked and breathless. But there was also a confidence in her movements that he found irresistible and attractive. She took several steps and stood knee-deep in the lake, the mist and spray from the waterfall creating an ambiance that surrounded her silhouetted figure in the moonlight. Misty prisms outlined her body, backlighting her in a mysterious way. Kamber turned and dove into the water and disappeared beneath the surface.

Jet stood and took a deep breath, hoping what was about to happen wouldn't come back to haunt him in the morning. He tossed his cloak onto the shore and dove in after her.

He swam to the middle of the lake to meet her. Kamber was treading water, waiting.

When Jet met her, Kamber didn't give him a chance to say a word. She wrapped her arms around his neck and pulled him to her. Jet didn't push away. He folded into her embrace and let her lips meet his.

He felt a lifetime of pain and rejection slip away with that kiss. All his life, his youth growing up in squalor, and rejection and confusion seemed to fall away with the water around him. It was as if the lake was working to cleanse his soul from all the torment. He sensed the same for Kamber. He could almost read her emotions then like the universe was trying to right the pain that mankind had wrought upon them. He wondered if Firefly Falls was simply an extension of heaven, and they were guests for the night.

He didn't know how to feel at that instant. It was beyond description, an earth-shattering moment that would stay with him for the rest of his life. In his mind's eye, it seemed like all the colors of the universe were coming together to create a pure white light, bathing them both and asking for their forgiveness.

They moved over near the far shore and found a moss-covered rock behind the flowing sheets of the Clipton River. The pounding in his head and heart was drowned out by the roar of the waterfall. He felt utter oblivion take him as he lay there with Kamber. He experienced feelings he'd never thought possible, emotions he didn't know existed.

They spent the night at Firefly Falls, forgetting what tomorrow's reveal might bring. Jet didn't care how tired he would feel or how unprepared they might be in the morning. Nothing mattered more at that moment than sharing these small comforts with Kamber.

They talked deep into the night, sitting under the moonlight, laughing, crying, and sharing secrets. When there was nothing left, they would repeat it all over again, neither wanting to say good night or let go until the sun began to rise that next morning.

CHAPTER 30
The Gauntlet—Part One

ΑΒ ΔΕ ΗΘΙΚΛ**Μ**

ΝΞΟΠΡΣ ΥΦ ΨΩ

THE HELIOGRAPHI MET in the Lyrinthum hangar bay at dusk the next day. The vast bay was littered with equipment and people now. Stell had moved all of her operations over, abandoning her old base back on Skylight City. This meant that every single orphan had been moved over, as well as her entire staff, security, and operatives. Her operation, known as Vine, was a large network of undercover spies. Stell had her own assortment of gear as well, which added to the clutter inside the hangar bay. Stell helped organize the new layout along with Linon's team. There were thousands of cots lining the walls of the hangar bay now, at least temporarily, until they could be moved into the control quadrant. It felt like a makeshift city had sprung up overnight. The Lucem's new operation was taking shape, and Solan seemed to be calling in every favor she could.

Jet talked quietly with Kamber. He pulled her into a secluded corridor, hoping to give her some last-minute encouragement for that day's reveal. But their conversation quickly devolved into more of what had happened at Firefly Falls the night before. He had completely given up his resolve and given into Kamber entirely now. He was out of control, and for the first time in his life, he felt he was living his *best* life and enjoying it. The recklessness of it all was intoxicating, like he was breaking the rules. He felt as if he'd simply flung all his cares to the wind and was barreling blindly down this new chapter with Kamber. It was fun, scary, and exhilarating. It was a first for him.

After several minutes, Jet and Kamber emerged, both slightly out of breath. She smoothed her hair as he straightened his cloak, and each went their separate ways. Jet gathered with Cord, Vail, and Bo near the far end as Kamber found Solan, Joshia, and Tetra.

Jet stood next to the others, anxious to be on his way. He inspected his new jammer skiff and once again marveled at its design. The long missile-shaped craft was sleek and carried the latest weaponry. He felt more confident now that the Lucem were on even ground with the Agency and Lybra, at least from a weapons standpoint. And if they could pull together their patchwork army, they might be even closer to competing with her.

Once ready, the four groups of Heliographi boarded their jammers and, without a word, set off in different directions. Solan's group, DiJinn's group, and Booker's group rocketed off just before cloaking. Jet cloaked his skiff as Cord, Vail, and Bo flew behind him toward the fourth belt. It was a quick flight, and soon they were greeted by the industrial clutter that covered the belt's surface. The skies around the belt held a murky glow, a maroon-colored tint that reminded Jet of the factory area of the third belt. The soupy clouds covered everything in a reddish hue like the landscape was covered in blood. The ominous spectacle set him on edge and reminded him of the warning in Kamber's dream. *Someone would die today.* He couldn't bear to think of any of the Lucem, especially Kamber or Cord. But what about the Atrum? Even though he didn't know most of them very well, he still didn't wish them any harm.

Regardless, he needed to focus on getting the memoir. That was their main goal, and they needed to level the field. Lybra had two, and this was their chance to even the score.

Cutting through the red clouds, he could see more wind turbines ahead. These wind farms were connected to the ground by rigid poles, much different than the tethered toons on the third belt. The turbines remained stationary and held their position, which provided a more stable surface. They were also spaced further apart, unlike the other toons. They wouldn't be able to leap between them at these distances.

Massive spinning blades cut through the red cloud cover as if magically appearing, then disappearing. There was a rhythm in the blades as they spun, Jet noticed, and they positioned their skiffs to maneuver between them.

The four of them maintained radio silence as they positioned their cloaked jammers near an area where the reveal was supposed to occur. There were far fewer ships about, since every group had faced the same decision as them—split up, or concentrate their forces. It seemed that most of the seekers had chosen to split up their forces, though. Either way, the odds favored the Heliographi now, especially with the new toys they had.

K

Solan and crew rocketed toward the fifth belt as the other teams of Heliographi cloaked and went their separate ways. In the back of her mind, there was a foreboding she couldn't place. They had everything in order—the jammers, rescuing the prisoners had been a success, Linon and his team were preparing, Stell had agreed to join them and had relocated, and, of course, the war staffs had been a game changer.

So, what was she missing?

She forced the feeling from her mind and focused on the next reveal.

Before long, the outline of the fifth belt punched through the thick fog. The immense loop towered above them for miles, and they could see the steady stream of other crafts building around one area in particular. Seeing all the seekers was intimidating, though there weren't nearly as many ships as she had originally expected.

Through the mist, the heavily forested belt was vibrant with greens and lush vegetation. In the waning sun, Solan, Joshia, Tetra, and Kamber found a secluded area of forest and settled their jammers. Solan led them through the trees and along dirt trails until they stumbled on a small, barely visible vent.

"In we go!" she whispered, and Joshia led the way, with Solan bringing up the rear.

It took nearly half an hour to scale down the metal duct and into the belly of the fifth belt. Much of the vegetation had crept into the internal systems, and the reflected light had a greenish tinge. All manner of plant species clung to the metallic equipment. Much of the area appeared to be defunct or on the verge of being overrun by the organic invasion as if nature disagreed with the manmade intrusion.

In the distance, Solan could see the gathering seekers. They were already making a racket that echoed through the large hull of the belt. Once again, Albright had positioned the reveal site in a vast pit, which would force the groups into close proximity. It was apparent that he intended the reward to be earned. Nothing was free in this hunt. Solan was surprised to see a rather small grouping of Agency and Tetrahedron troops, though. The Heliographi's most challenging opponent was practically non-existent. It made her nervous as she realized something.

Harok and Lybra intended to focus their forces, not split them up.

It meant that at one of the other reveals, there would be a greater challenge for one of their groups.

H

DiJinn and her group of Ti-Leer, Sojahn, and Bofisto flew side by side in a secluded skiff lane while maintaining radio silence. It was growing dark, and she felt anxious. She assumed that the others felt the same. It was something she rarely experienced, and she hated the feeling. It made her angry, and when she grew angry, she made bad decisions—something she couldn't afford today.

The sixth belt was similar to the fifth in appearance, just larger in diameter. The surface was clogged with trees and resplendent with emerald tones and vibrant greens. Occasionally, she could see large factories, which were responsible for the logging operations. The factories were equally dispersed across the belt to prevent too many trees from being felled at once. Like the fifth belt, the sixth belt also shared in carbon sequestering, which kept the Skylight atmosphere balanced.

As DiJinn flew around, she could see the cleared areas where the mills were cut into the lush, green landscape. The group settled down and gathered near a logging mill. She looked at Ti-Leer, Sojahn, and Bofisto and shook her head. *She was stuck with this crew again!* It only added to her frustration, and she had to refocus.

"The reveal site is a kilometer that way," DiJinn said with a nod. "Keep up, or you're on your own."

"Don't get too far ahead, D.J.," Ti-Leer whispered. "I got your back. Just keep pace, lass."

Bofisto seemed to growl behind them, which made DiJinn turn and face him. Her emerald-green eyes met his deep blue glowing gaze, though she had to look up. She felt her skin flush, and her fists balled. "Something to say?"

Sojahn stepped up next to Bofisto and leveled a finger at her. "Jinn, I don't think you're up to this challenge. You were lucky on the last mission. Jet and the others bailed you out."

"Tiny Jinn," Bofisto muttered, the steel daggers embedded in his teeth glinting in the dull light. "If I detect one misstep from you or this runt, we're going our own way."

"Ah, let 'em. D.J.," Ti-Leer muttered. "Good riddance."

"Believe me, it wouldn't hurt my feelings," DiJinn shot back. But she took a deep breath and closed her eyes. She knew Sol would kill her if she didn't hold this group together. Sol had placed a lot of trust in Jinn, and she wasn't going to let her down. She had to set her disdain for Sojahn and Bofisto on the back burner for now. The mission was more important.

The site was so heavily wooded they could barely see through to the other groups. There was a thick fog that clung to the ground as the sun set. The sounds of nature came to life as the sunlight faded behind Earth. Crickets and tree frogs hummed in the background. But as DiJinn and crew approached the reveal site, the sounds of the forest grew silent, replaced by skirmishes and shouts.

DiJinn and the others settled in.

"Might as well get comfortable," Ti-Leer whispered. He leaned back against a large pine, crossed his legs, and almost instantly fell asleep.

DiJinn shook her head and kicked his boots. Ti-Leer grunted but didn't move. "So much for watchin' my back," she muttered under her breath.

Sojahn and Bofisto glared at DiJinn but didn't speak as they sat in the shadows and watched the seekers beyond.

DiJinn couldn't sit still, though. And she had no desire to chat it up with Sojahn or Bofisto. She cloaked without a word and left the area. She hurried through the heavy woods and found a tall evergreen on top of a hill. She scanned the seekers, trying to get a better idea of how many there were. But after several minutes, she could tell that it was a much smaller crowd than any of the other reveals so far. She supposed the other groups of seekers had also decided to split their forces. But the more she looked, she noticed something else was out of place.

There was no sign of the Agency or the Tetrahedron.

CHAPTER 31
The Gauntlet—Part Two

AB ΔE HΘIKΛ**M**
ΝΞΟΠΡΣ ΥΦ ΨΩ

JUST MINUTES BEFORE the reveal was scheduled to begin, several of the rogue mercenary groups started to scuffle.

Their dingy ships, which looked like a patchwork quilt of old parts and pieces from a junkyard, fired off several rounds at each other, and the skirmish was on. Jet and his group had to maneuver out of position to avoid the fighting.

Jet kept one eye on the skirmishes and one eye on the clock. But in the back of his mind, he wondered again why the Agency and Lybra would choose to abandon a reveal. He assumed they had simply decided to focus more effort on one or possibly two reveals instead. Perhaps their missions had set Lybra back more than he'd realized. Either way, it could spell disaster for one of the other Heliographi groups. Even though it made him feel a bit selfish, he hoped it wasn't Kamber's group.

Jet glanced over at Cord, Vail, and Bo. Then back to the area where he assumed the memoir would appear. The airspace around them was filled with every manner of ship, and the cloud cover was thick and almost suffocating. The blood-soaked mist seemed to cling to the large propellers of the turbines. The churning monumental blades cut through the thick haze, pulling trailers of the puffy substance with them and leaving behind swirling eddies.

Their plan was similar to the other reveals; grab the memoir and cloak their way out of the area while the others provided cover. But as he'd learned so far, things rarely went as planned.

At three minutes past six PM, Jet braced himself.

But nothing happened.

All of the groups seemed to pause their fighting, waiting for the bright glow of the memoir to reveal itself. But there was no bright light, no commotion or hint of it to be seen.

Then, Cord's jammer rocketed off through a thick bank of clouds. Jet looked in that direction and caught a faint yellow glow through an opening in the mist. He maneuvered his jammer behind Cord's and followed after him. Thousands of other seekers soon noticed the glow and raced behind them.

The glowing light poured from the top of a tall toon, like God rays of sunlight filtering through the clouds. The golden light seemed to permeate through every opening in its metallic skin. Jet guessed the propellered toon was perhaps one hundred meters tall and sat on a massive round pole. At the base was a single entry point with stairs leading up and into the pole. Several groups had already reached the ground and were racing toward the entry, followed closely by Cord's shimmering figure.

Jet landed his jammer and hopped out, charging toward the tower base. Once inside, he took in his surroundings. There was a wide, open-rail staircase that hugged the exterior wall, circling up the cylindrical-shaped tower. It seemed to climb forever, disappearing up and out of view. Clogging the staircase were hundreds of seekers fighting and flinging each other over the railing. Jet could see that it would be impossible to get past the traffic jam of bodies. But somewhere in the mix was Cord.

Jet gripped the railing and leapt upward. By using his legs, he managed to skip several flights of stairs at a time. Soon, he was able to bypass the traffic jam and get ahead of the other seekers. When he finally reached the top, he paused to regain his bearings.

He stood on a large platform. Steel gears, which were responsible for converting the spinning blades to energy, churned away and clicked loudly. The horde of seekers was just a few flights below—he needed to hurry.

He could see the memoir now. It was suspended above the platform, about thirty meters from him, and tucked between the gears. Getting to it would be hazardous. Several seekers had managed to reach the top deck and were trying to scale the spinning gears. Some of the less cautious seekers tried to ride the gears into a better position but slipped into the cogs and disappeared.

He noticed Cord's shimmering figure from across the deck, climbing up one side. Jet sprang to one of the lower gears and clung to it. It carried him up to a larger gear, which in turn ferried him upward. He continued to leap between gears, steadily working his way toward the memoir as Cord did the same.

The group of about twenty seekers had worked as a team to reach the memoir ahead of him and Cord. They stood on a small platform near the top and held the glowing yellow tube. But instead of running, they were trying to open it, which gave Jet time to reach them. He landed on the platform, still cloaked, and brought his staff down on the rusty grate. He willed an electric pulse, strong enough to stun the entire group of seekers unconscious, but weak enough to not cause permanent injury. He stepped over them and tucked the memoir into his cloak.

Now, he had to figure out how to exit the tower. With just one entrance a hundred meters below and thousands of seekers continuing to flood into the tower, Jet realized he was trapped. Soon, there might be so many seekers inside the tower they'd all be crushed.

Jet located Cord. "What now?" he yelled.

Cord stood in the middle of a gear, riding it like a Ferris wheel as he surveyed the situation. He held his staff out, sweeping seekers off the gear who ventured too close. Cord didn't answer him, though, too busy defending himself.

Jet felt a moment of panic as he tried to think of a way out.

Where were Vail and Bo? he thought. *Had they abandoned them?*

He was about to send a thought to Vail when an explosion ripped through the side of the upper tower. A jammer shot in through the opening, rail guns blazing. It was Vail.

Jet saw an opening now and used his staff to clear the way. The staff lit up like a flaming torch and pulsed with shockwaves as he swept away seekers rushing toward him. Inside the tower, there were so many rounds from random railguns pelting the area that he was barely able to move forward. Other nearby seekers who didn't take cover were mowed down.

Jet used his staff and cloak to block the incoming fire. Before long, he was standing near Vail's jammer with Cord close behind. Vail hovered in low, using the jammer's shield to block the incoming fire. She dipped one side, and Jet hopped onto the outer hull. He held on tight to one of its small wings. With all the focus on Vail's jammer, Cord moved down the staircase, using the rails to get past the seekers. But now the seekers were turning and starting to leave the tower. Vail turned the jammer and slammed the thrusters hard. Jet braced, nearly losing his grip as they exited the hole in the side of the turbine.

They shot from the tower and right into hundreds of waiting skiffs, which immediately opened fire on Vail. She dodged easily, with Jet holding on for dear life. Vail maneuvered out and around the clutter of skiffs. The speed of the jammer could not be matched, though. Jet watched as Bo's cloaked jammer fell in behind the seekers, picking them off before they realized what was happening. Soon, another jammer fell in and joined. It was Cord.

Vail hovered in toward the base of the tower and low enough for Jet to leap and roll onto the soft forest floor. He remained cloaked as seekers' skiffs stayed on Vail's tail, firing rounds at her.

Jet raced over to his jammer, locked into his cockpit, and rocketed off in the opposite direction unnoticed.

K

Solan hunched forward in the shadows, waiting anxiously. There was a greenish glow from all the backlit overgrowth inside the large vent where she sat, bathing the area in an eerie light. Hundreds of other large vents emitted brief flashes of moonlight into the vast chamber beyond, highlighting all the activity. There were thousands of seekers milling about now, underscoring the one thing that was missing—Lybra's forces.

The chamber was filled with typical seekers dressed in standard clan or other insignia-clad garb. But the lack of Agency and Tetrahedron dominated her thoughts. Solan was surprised Lybra had simply abandoned her approach so soon. Perhaps she feared the war staffs more than Solan had realized. Or *maybe* the recent raids they'd conducted on the jammers, prisoners, and the rare-earth had been more disruptive than expected. Or maybe, Lybra simply accepted that there was little chance of collecting *all* of the remaining memoirs now. Was her new approach to focus on getting a few more memoirs and holding them as a bargaining chip?

Solan glanced back at Joshia. She stared at Solan as if she knew what she was thinking. Kamber and Tetra knelt quietly behind them, staffs clenched and anxious looks on their faces.

Solan checked the time.

It was four minutes past midnight now—just a few more minutes until the reveal. Agency presence or not, the four of them would still have their hands full. She just hoped there were no more surprises but pushed the wishful thought aside and focused. Solan nodded to the others and gave a hand gesture. Joshia, Kamber, and Tetra stood and moved out of the vent. Each hopped down and landed on a large duct beneath, then moved in opposite directions. Soon, they were all spread out across the chamber, which gave them better coverage of the reveal site. It placed Kamber out of range, which worried her a bit. A risk, but one she hoped would pay off.

The chamber grew noisier as the moment approached.

At exactly six minutes past midnight, a bright green light erupted from below Solan. It emanated through one of the lower air vents, which was barely visible through the heavy vegetation. Solan immediately dropped from her perch, sliding down pipes and conduit. Racing alongside her were hundreds of seekers falling and cartwheeling downward. Solan reached the vent first and worked her way through the air vanes in the large grill. It was a five-meter drop into the metal duct, the sound of the rushing seekers just behind her. A tidal wave of stampeding feet drowned out everything as Solan sprinted and slid along the smooth metal duct.

Solan followed the light cascading from the end of the duct, though she didn't know how far away it was. Minutes seemed to pass until she slid to a halt and stopped. Facing her was a three-way split in the duct, and the glowing greenish light seemed to be coming from all three directions.

How was that possible?

She closed her eyes, focused, and then took the duct to the right. She sprinted down it, sending her thoughts to Joshia, Tetra, and Kamber about the route she'd taken. The tubular-shaped duct sloped down, twisting and spiraling like a slide. At times she found herself on her belly as she occasionally slipped and stumbled in her haste. The duct continued to split into forks, perhaps dozens of times, and she seemed to be caught in some sort of maze. She hit a few dead ends and had to backtrack, running into other seekers on several occasions.

Eventually, a thought from Joshia landed in her mind like a ripple on a pond.

She'd found the memoir.

Solan stopped and reversed course, heading back to the surface. She could sense Joshia's presence a few ducts over and turned in that direction. Solan stumbled into an enormous ventilation room, which she assumed was an air-handling unit for the vent system. In the middle of the space was Joshia, holding the memoir in one hand and fighting off seekers with her staff. A pile of bodies lay about her, a growing mountain of seekers who had ventured too close.

But the number of seekers continued to grow at an alarming rate. Solan made her way over to Joshia, who was now backed up against the wall, and helped her fight off the seekers. She tried to think of a way out but couldn't help wondering where Kamber and Tetra were.

H

DiJinn was still confused by the lack of Agency and Tetrahedron troops.

No matter! she thought to herself. They had their work cut out regardless. These blasted seekers couldn't seem to get it through their thick skulls—*They're not getting these memoirs!* But still, they could clutter things up just by their sheer numbers.

She looked on in amusement at the circus of seekers below as she crouched high in the treetops. Her perched figure was blurry and invisible in the moonlight. The trees here were tall evergreens, thick with needles that made everything below a bit difficult to see. Ti-Leer, Sojahn, and Bofisto were all spread about the site. The two Atrum would patrol the forest floor while she and Ti-Leer covered the tree canopy above.

They held an advantage, in her opinion. Since the trees were so close together, she could easily leap amongst the branches. Even though some of the seekers were in skiffs, she felt confident that the reveal would occur below the tree canopy, making skiffs worthless. And without any Agency presence about, including their can-cans, things were lookin' *real* good.

But was it *too* good?

Something bothered her, and she couldn't place it. Her anger flared again, and she gripped the tree branch so tight that it splintered.

At eight past midnight, she prepared herself. The forest sounds quieted as if in preparation for the imminent rush of bodies. The chatter below seemed distant and faint now. She felt her palms go clammy; her skin flushed…

Time to get this show on the road! she whistled.

A blue light flared from a massive tree not far away. It glowed brighter, high up in the branches. Hundreds of seekers raced toward it from below. DiJinn hopped through the trees, spitting pine needles from her mouth and cursing as she swung between branches. But it was Ti-Leer who made it there first. DiJinn saw him grab the memoir and tuck the glowing blue tube under his cloak.

From above, skiff cannons lit up and peppered the trees. Limbs and pine needles fell, littering the forest floor below. Ti-Leer hopped between the trees, using his cloak to shield him from the railgun fire raining down from above.

DiJinn sent a thought to Sojahn and Bofisto, then she hurtled from the treetops and into the night sky, her staff glowing like fire as it ripped through several skiffs. It created multiple explosions that lit up the surrounding forest. Other skiffs banked away from the destruction as wrecked ships plummeted to the ground.

DiJinn continued to provide cover for Ti-Leer, her staff a glowing blade of destruction as it arced from skiff to skiff. But for every skiff she downed, three more replaced it. She was getting nowhere, and soon there were skiffs littering the night skies.

Then she saw two jammers break through the thicket of skiffs and light up the surrounding area. Rockets and rail guns blazed, finally scattering the seekers' skiffs. Sojahn and Bofisto hovered low to the trees. She and Ti-Leer hopped onto the jammers and clung tight. They turned and cloaked, flying low to the ground as the fighting faded away in the distance. DiJinn hated to admit it, but she'd never been so glad to see a couple of Atrum before.

M

Jet held the memoir under his arm as he radioed the others. But he kept his jammer cloaked and resisted the urge to turn around and help them. He couldn't afford to go back, that was the deal. The memoir was too valuable. However, instead of rushing back to the first belt, he stayed and waited for signs of Cord, Vail, and Bo. Soon, he counted three jammers heading his way and breathed a sigh of relief.

He maneuvered his jammer into formation as they hit cruising speed and made their way back to the first belt. Once there, the jammers landed in the Lyrinthum hangar bay, and they were greeted by several of the freed prisoners who were already organizing into a cohesive unit, thanks to Stell and her team. They immediately hooked the jammers up to a power supply and inspected the hulls for damage.

Jet hopped out and greeted Cord, Vail, and Bo in a bear hug. The three of them grinned at each other. Jet even gathered in a high-five from Bo and a playful shove from Vail.

"That was enjoyable," Cord said. "We're the first back."

"Well, we would be, right, Ledbetter?" Vail said, a familiar hint of sarcasm in her voice. "We have you and Stroud as our fearless leaders."

Cord gave her a crooked smile. "No need to thank us, of course."

"We saved you both," Bo said. "You two just launched into that tower without a second thought. I mean, what the hell?"

"We simply presumed you and Vail wouldn't want to get your hands dirty," Cord replied. "I assumed you two knew exactly what we were doing. Maybe that was giving you too much credit, though."

"Can we just appreciate the teamwork for a minute?" Jet said.

The four of them stood silently around the jammers, and Jet sensed that their victory party had taken an unexpected turn for the worse. But still, it had been enjoyable while it lasted. Bo had said more in the last few minutes than he'd said the entire time back.

"Yes, we appreciate your help, Bo and Vail," Jet said. "We couldn't have done it without you two." He tossed the memoir to Vail, who caught it and held it up to the light.

"Any ideas on how to open this thing yet, Brainiac?" she asked.

Cord crossed his arms and shook his head. "Negative. I haven't had much time to do any meaningful research. We'll catch a break for the next few days, then a long break until the last reveal. Maybe then I can do some work on it."

The four of them waited in the hangar bay, watching the crews work. They sat around in a circle and talked quietly. Jet couldn't help but smile as Cord and Vail took shots at each other while Bo watched silently, though Jet caught him chuckling on occasion. It was a flashback to their school days, and it gave him a nostalgic feeling. But his thoughts kept straying to the other Heliographi and how they were doing. He grew anxious for their return until four jammers uncloaked and hovered into the hangar bay. Solan, Joshia, Kamber, and Tetra landed and greeted them. Jet breathed a sigh of relief at seeing them, especially Kamber. He gave her a hug and Solan a handshake.

"Well?" Vail asked impatiently.

Solan held up the glowing green memoir, the metallic case shimmering in the light.

Jet smiled. "Nice work, team."

Vail handed Solan the other memoir.

"No word from the other two groups?" Cord asked.

"Nothing yet," Solan said. "But they should hold radio silence until they return. Fingers crossed they're alright. Joshia and I can wait up for them if the rest of you want to grab some sleep."

The others took their leave, but Jet and Kamber stayed behind. Jet sat in the corner of the large hangar bay and leaned up against Kamber as they watched Solan and Joshia chat quietly.

"What do you think they're talking about?" Kamber asked. She slouched a bit and leaned her head on his shoulder.

It felt good to sit with her and just talk after the stress of that day. Jet felt more connected with her now, especially after that night at Firefly Falls. They had obviously taken the next step in their relationship. At first, he'd wondered how he would feel. Would things be weird between them? Would she pull away? *Would she still like him?* But none of that had happened, and with all his nerves out of the way now, he felt he could have more serious conversations with her. And, honestly, he didn't care anymore if the other Lucem found out.

"I'm sure they have important things to discuss, strategy probably. More importantly, how are you holding up?" he asked.

Kamber yawned and blinked. "Just tired, really. I'll rest better tonight when everyone returns. I'm staying here until that happens."

"You're still concerned about the groups?"

"Of course. And I know you are too. So is Solan. She knows that something doesn't feel right. I can sense it."

"That's out of our hands, Kamber."

"Doesn't mean I'm any less concerned."

"But I really wanted to know how *you're* doing, though. This whole memoir hunt just happened right in the middle of…well, your training, I suppose."

"My training or our relationship?"

Jet paused and craned his neck to face her. "Yeah, that too, I guess."

"Primarily that," Kamber said and nudged him with her elbow. "I think you were right. Maybe we should stop seeing each other—"

Jet sat up and turned to her. "What are you talking about?"

"Wow, really?" Kamber chuckled. "I thought you were totally against this? Relax…I was just kidding."

Jet sighed and shook his head. "You're funny."

She smiled back at him and took his arm.

Jet settled back against her. "If you want the honest truth, I suppose I just gave up…and gave in. The part of me that wants to throw caution to the wind finally won. I mean, who cares about doing the smart thing. Right?"

"I feel that way all the time. I won't compromise when it comes to living my life. Don't leave anything to regret, that's what I say."

"You've certainly converted me," he nodded.

Kamber chuckled, then started to laugh. It made his heart feel light, something he needed at that moment, and hadn't even realized it.

He smiled. "What's so funny?"

"I can't wait to spend more time together. That's all I think about these days. It just seems there's always something happening. If we're not training, we're on a mission or dealing with other Lucem stuff."

"Well…I guess it's like you said. We'll *have* to make time for ourselves, somehow. I realize now how important that is."

She smiled back at him. "What are you not telling me?"

"What do you mean?"

"I can sense you're keeping something to yourself. There's no secrets between us now. What is it?"

"Is this another one of your gifts?" he joked.

She shrugged. "No. Sometimes it's pretty obvious...reading others, you know? And you don't hide your emotions very well anyway."

He held her gaze and thought about the conversation he'd recently had with Albright. He felt the desire, *the need*, to share it with her. In fact, he wanted to share everything with her. But Albright had asked him not to. If he told her, it might place her in harm's way. "Well, there is something, but I can't share it with you. I wish I could, and maybe I will at some point. I hope you understand."

"Sure. I sense that it's important. You know I'm always here if you—"

They were interrupted by several skiffs entering the hangar bay. There were seven jammers total, but two were badly damaged.

Jet and Kamber stood to their feet and hurried over. Solan and Joshia joined them.

"Shouldn't there be eight jammers?" Kamber asked as they slowed.

DiJinn hopped out of her jammer. Behind her, Ti-Leer landed his jammer and walked slowly over to them. They waited as the other skiffs settled down. Jet gave Kamber a pensive glance as they counted all the other Heliographi climbing out of their jammers. There was Sojahn, Bofisto, then Myranda, Mosstrom, and finally,

Brit. Each gathered around Solan, Joshia, Jet, and Kamber.

Mosstrom walked over to Solan, bowed low, almost in a mocking gesture, and handed Booker's cloak, ring, and staff to her.

Solan stared at the items in her hand. She gripped the cloak and wrung it as if she were about to tear it in half. She looked up at Mosstrom. "Where is his body?"

CHAPTER 32
A Blatant Betrayal

SOLAN HELD BOOKER'S cloak and staff and stared directly at Mosstrom. "Tell me, Mosstrom. Why didn't you bring back his body?" Her voice shook as she stared at him. Jet sensed that one small slip from the Atrum and Solan might rip them all apart. She was teetering on the edge.

Mosstrom glared at her, and Jet thought he caught a brief smile. It was subtle, but it was there—a quick lift at the corner of his lips. "Why, Solan, I tried. Do you doubt me?"

The other Lucem seemed to notice the sarcasm as well, and Ti-Leer launched himself at Mosstrom. The ancient Atrum sidestepped, and Ti-Leer flew head-first into a riveted bulkhead, which crumpled like paper. Ti-Leer stood, eyes crossed, and shook his head. He steadied himself and was about to leap at Mosstrom again when Bofisto lifted him off his feet. Ti-Leer kicked his stubby legs out but missed Bofisto's face. Jinn moved in behind and swept Bofisto's feet out. The huge man toppled onto his back. Ti-Leer landed on top of him, his rear-end wedged between Bofisto's chin and his neck. The other Lucem and Atrum moved in, and Jet thought he was about to witness another riot when Solan stepped forward.

She grasped Ti-Leer and flung him across the hangar bay, her eyes flaring in anger.

Joshia gripped Bofisto by the lapels of his cloak, lifted him, and shoved him against the wall. She held him there as she glanced back at Solan, along with all the other Heliographi. They waited.

Solan glared at Jinn, then took a deep breath and held out a hand, steadied it, and let out a sigh. "Mosstrom. I need to hear *exactly* what happened." Her voice was calm and measured, but Jet heard the edge of rage it still carried.

Mosstrom seemed to be sizing Solan up. Jet saw the indignation on his face as Solan stood in front of him, demanding to know what had happened. Mosstrom,

Sybold's warden and an entity who had been around perhaps longer than all the rest of them combined, seemed to be struggling with his emotions. Jet could sense the hate and disgust as if he wanted to strike out at her. Jet had gotten a sense of Mosstrom's arrogance the first time they'd met. And now, that pride was clearly noticeable by the look on his face.

For a split second, Jet thought the ancient Atrum would simply turn and walk away. Joshia tensed, and Jet wondered if she was trying to decide what to do if Mosstrom ignored Solan. But finally, he tilted his head in a mocking gesture and spoke.

"Yes, of course, Solan. The fool had the memoir and single-handedly tried to take on too many mechs." Mosstrom spoke in an annoyed tone as if explaining something to a toddler.

Solan ignored it. "Go on."

"If he'd waited for us, perhaps we might have been able to help him. I estimate that nearly all of the Agency and Tetrahedron forces were there tonight. I can only assume it was Lybra's plan all along to overwhelm our particular reveal. She must have wanted that memoir badly. There were hundreds of M-Class mech units. Lybra has full control of them now. Previously, I sensed glitches in the mech's control system. However, she's perfected the interface with a cerebral headband she wore. 'Twas the mechs that finished your Lucem off in one synchronized attack. Even with his staff, he had not a chance. Furthermore, we have no way to read Lybra's thoughts now. We cannot hold sway over her mind. Old she may be, but she is wise, all the same. She has more than enough funding to hire the finest minds. She will not make another mistake. Tonight was simply a test."

Solan looked into Mosstrom's glowing purple eyes with no hesitation. Where others might be intimidated by the elder Atrum, Solan stood defiantly as if trying to read his mind. Jet sensed her doubt about what Mosstrom was telling her. Several tense seconds passed before she turned and marched out of the hangar bay. The other Lucem followed, Ti-Leer and DiJinn giving Bofisto and Sojahn a drop-dead look on the way out.

"What now?" DiJinn asked as they entered the control suite. "Do you feel the Atrum are lying?"

Solan didn't answer at first as she held Booker's cloak and staff. She finally looked up, her eyes glowing a bit brighter. "It's my fault. I shouldn't have placed Booker in the presence of three Atrum."

"You think Mosstrom murdered Booker?" Jet asked.

"I don't know, but I sense that he wasn't being honest with me."

"Maybe the Atrum just weren't fast enough to help him?" Kamber said.

"Too slow to react, indeed!" DiJinn snapped and slammed her fist into the old, riveted hull.

"We all knew that one of our groups would be overwhelmed," Solan said. "I should have made the call for that group to retreat."

"You had a lot going on, Solan," Ti-Leer said. "Don't beat yourself up over it, lass. You've been organizing all of this."

But Solan simply leaned against Albright's table as she held Booker's effects. Jet watched her, knowing that she was once again second-guessing her decision. It was something she had struggled with ever since taking over from her father. Running the Lucem hadn't been something she wanted. Although she seemed to be getting past her indecisiveness, this event appeared to have set her back once again.

Solan took a long moment before she turned to look at the others. Jet, Kamber, Cord, Ti-Leer, and DiJinn all stood waiting.

Joshia entered the control room and walked over to stand next to Solan. She hesitated as she looked around the room, her gaze settling on the table. "I'm sorry for your loss. Let me apologize for Mosstrom's attitude."

Solan faced Joshia and held her gaze. She seemed to consider something for a brief second. "We have a week before the next reveal. I think we should keep our distance for a few days."

Joshia returned her gaze, then nodded. "I think that's a good idea."

M

Jet walked Kamber to her quarters and said goodnight. She gave him a kiss, which he leaned into and thought about sneaking into her quarters but eventually pushed the desire down.

He met Solan back in the control suite. She laid Booker's staff onto Albright's table, setting it into the void above his symbol. The staff fit perfectly in the split wooden void to the point where it almost disappeared. In the other voids were Annaka and Harriet's staff and the two Atrum who had also died recently, Hurse and Renzie.

"What are you thinking?" Jet asked.

Solan sat heavily in her own chair and crossed her arms. "We have four of the memoirs to Lybra's three. It would seem we have the upper hand, yet it doesn't feel that way. We have no idea how to open them, and we've lost five Heliographi now. I'm not sure I like that tradeoff. Not very efficient, is it?"

Jet shook his head. "Why do you think Albright isn't getting involved? I mean, this all seems pretty important, and he apparently knows a lot about what's happening right now. There must be a reason why he's staying out of it."

"He's always been like that, from what I know of him. There's a good reason for it, you can bet."

"Wouldn't your father tell you?"

"He might, if he knew anything. Which means he probably doesn't. I imagine he prefers not to know, and apparently, so does Albright. If anyone were captured, they'd eventually give up what they knew."

Jet sat down in his chair and leaned forward onto his elbows. "I don't know. It just seems like Albright should be doing more to help us."

"Hasn't he, though?" Solan said.

Jet tilted his head in thought. "I guess you're right. He did leave us the war staffs. And, he managed to bring the Lucem and the Atrum together, something he always wanted. If Albright was here, I doubt the Atrum would've joined us. I guess you could argue the same about Sybold if she was around?"

Solan nodded. "If she *was* here, this alliance wouldn't exist. There'd be too much unrest."

"I suppose Sybold is out there somewhere, lurking about."

"I'm afraid you're right. I sense that Joshia knows more about all of this. Regardless, I believe Sybold was killed recently. That's why we haven't seen her lately."

"Killed?" Jet asked, sitting up. "But how? Who did it?"

"Only Albright and Tyberius could have, and it would have taken both to accomplish that feat."

"So, you think they worked together?"

"Yes, I do." Solan lowered her gaze and held his attention. "I would say they took that risk for us. Albright would've known the importance of removing Sybold without him and Tyberius around."

Jet sat back and thought about the implications. "I wonder why Albright didn't mention this to me. I guess that means Sybold's Heliographi reset and she's starting over?"

"That may not be the case. She's extremely powerful, some of her abilities are still unknown. My father and Albright only slowed her down. I assume she was moving too quickly, and the timing wasn't right. I think they were trying to reset the table."

Jet leaned back and crossed his arms. "At least we won't have to worry about her during the next reveal. One week till then, followed by another two weeks for the final."

"There's something else I need to share." Solan stood and turned on the three-dimensional display, which flickered and closed. She hammered the wall, and it lit up again. Hovering over the table was the three-dimensional map of the Skylight System. She highlighted the ninth belt and the coordinates for the ninth reveal. Then she fast-forwarded the time and date to June twenty-fourth just after midnight, the evening of the final reveal. Solan pointed at the large chunk of debris amongst the broken ninth belt. "This is Cranium Nine, otherwise known as C9. Recognize it?"

"Yeah, DiJinn was just there to steal the rare-earth."

"That's right. It's also Lybra's stronghold."

Jet rubbed his chin, then narrowed his eyes. "It seems odd that the final memoir is hidden there. Surely Lybra knows by now. She'll have that place armed to the teeth the day of the reveal."

"True. But look at it a bit closer."

Jet leaned in, then noticed something. "It's in outer space."

"Correct," Solan said. "Just before the final reveal, the belt will be outside of the system's protective atmosphere."

"Well, that'll make things interesting!" Jet chuckled. "Why in Skylight would Albright do that?"

"Hold on, that's not all. I did some more research and found this." She punched something else into the display.

Jet leaned forward and read the article aloud. "Meteor shower expected near midnight on June twenty-fourth."

Solan held his gaze. "This *will* be a large meteor storm. Albright knew this would happen, and it appears he's timed it to coincide with the final reveal. Yet another wrench he's thrown at all the seekers."

"He really doesn't like us, it seems."

"The man enjoys a challenge, that's for certain."

"When are you planning to tell the others?"

Solan sighed. "After the next reveal. There's no sense in worrying about any of this right now. We need to stay focused on one reveal at a time."

"Should we sit this next one out?" Jet asked. "Maybe we need a break."

"I thought the same thing just earlier, especially after losing Booker. But I think the week off will help. We'll have some time to regroup."

"What if someone else dies?"

That question made Solan pause. Jet could almost read her thoughts and knew she was second-guessing her decision about Booker again.

"I'm trying to decide if we can still trust the Atrum. We *will* need them for the two remaining reveals, but we may never truly know how Booker died." Solan took a deep breath and shook her head as if moving on. "No matter what decision I make, I always think it's the wrong one. But I wonder if it even matters sometimes."

"Are you talking about fate?" Jet asked.

She nodded, her gaze focused on all the staffs laid on the table.

"Kamber talks about that sometimes," Jet said. "She believes that destiny guides us—that it doesn't matter what decisions we make because our path has already been determined. Not sure I agree with that or like the sound of it."

"I think this is one of those times. We can't sit on the sidelines. We need to be there to face Lybra head-on. That was Albright's plan, and we will follow it."

Jet lifted one of the metal tubes and held it up to the dim light in the control room. The smooth, glowing cylinder had a strange weight to it, alluring and perhaps deceptive. "I hope Cord can figure this out before Lybra does."

"All we can do now is claim as many as possible." Solan took the memoir and looked thoughtfully at it. "When we do figure out how to unlock these, I fear for the future of the human race."

"What do you mean?" Jet sat forward. Something in her tone sounded foreboding, almost frightening to him.

"I don't know," she said as her gaze lingered on the memoir. "I just get the sense that things are about to change. Once we unlock whatever secrets these memoirs hold, the world as we know it will never be the same."

M

The next day, Solan was back at it. It was evident to Jet that she didn't intend to slow down. In fact, she seemed to double down, determined to be fully prepared for their next reveal. She gathered with Linon and his other generals as they met and strategized with Stell and her team.

There was a lot of activity now. The vast, hidden inner workings of Lyrinthum seemed to be perfect for their base of operations. No one would guess that concealed in the belly of the first belt, right beneath Skylight University, a major undertaking was happening. Although there was only one hangar bay, it was large and more than adequate for their needs. Their only missing resource was food and water. But Stell had plans to tap into the belt's infrastructure for that. She had also diverted her organization's food deliveries from the third belt. Soon they would have enough supplies for an army, which is exactly what they were building. Stell's backers provided other necessities like cots, clothing, and essentials. Weapons and armor were purchased through the black market, which DiJinn arranged. Jet grew concerned that all the traffic would be noticed, but Stell was a master at subterfuge. Moving resources through her network of operatives was something she excelled at. Before long, they would have their network up and running. But would it all be ready in time for the final reveal?

Jet spent that time working alongside Solan and the troops. He also continued to train with Kamber, though he could clearly see she was able to handle herself now. Her ability in Vishmu was evident, even if her melee ability wasn't as strong. But the war staff helped even things out.

Jet also worked with Cord, trying to figure out new abilities with the staff. There were a few features he hadn't understood before. The pulse it discharged when struck to the ground also emitted an EMP, or electromagnetic pulse, which could immobilize nearby electrical equipment. Another feature that Cord referred to as the 'knockout' released a great deal of energy focused through the end of the staff. When brought to bear, it was enough to destroy just about anything it touched. However, this feature took a great deal of energy.

Jet also noticed that Cord was, once again, caught up in something else.

"What's got you bothered now?" Jet asked.

"This coordinate system is perplexing." Cord sat at his makeshift lab in an old office. The equipment barely functioned and was outdated, but Cord had managed to restore it to suit his needs.

"I don't understand," Jet said and walked over to look at the three-dimensional display.

"See. It's two-dimensional. There's no Z-axis. I mentioned that before, if you'll recall. Odd that it works out like that when we live in a three-dimensional system."

"Yeah, I remember. What's wrong with that?"

"At first, I thought Albright was just matching the paintings or his table, which is a flat surface and two-dimensional. Remember the numbers from Albright's equation—2,412,631—and Shiloe Van Saint's paintings—2,412,630? Once plotted, those gave us the nine coordinates of the memoirs, which were hidden around the system. Maybe it's nothing, but it stands out to me that all of those coordinates occur in just two quadrants."

"I'm sure you'll figure it out," Jet said and clapped him on the back.

Cord shook his head. "Perhaps. Trying to follow Albright's breadcrumbs is like running through a maze blindfolded."

Jet crossed his arms as he stared at Cord. "I've been meaning to ask you about the Atrum. Other than the Booker thing, which is still unclear, it seems to be working out well."

"Too well, in my opinion," Cord replied. "They won't change their ways, Jet. You think they will. I know you're optimistic. Just be careful you don't get lulled into letting your guard down. Once this is all over and the memoirs have been claimed, I suspect they will try to make their move."

"What do you think we should do then?"

"Take precautions…set safeguards. We need to prepare now; in case they double-cross us."

Jet took a moment to consider. "I was thinking about it just after our last reveal with Vail and Bo. Maybe, with Sybold missing, things are different?"

"How so?"

"Sybold seemed to be the worst of the Atrum. Maybe her presence was the driving force behind their behavior? What if Sybold's absence has had a positive effect on the others? It seems to me they are less aggressive. Bo is actually talking now. Vail gave me a high five. She even smiled. There was real change, I felt it. For a moment, it seemed like the days of old, you know? Joshia even seems more friendly toward us."

"I don't know that it works that way, Jet. I feel that all Heliographi have shades of good and evil, and maybe the essence in us follows that pattern."

"Solan said the same thing. But how do you know that?"

"Because I could've killed Hurse that day of the Century Eclipse, and I almost did. What I know is this; my inner essence would've allowed me to do that. I don't believe yours would, nor Solan either. It would destroy you or leave you…either one."

Jet thought about it for a moment. "That's an interesting theory. That would mean some of the Atrum aren't purely evil, then?"

"Perhaps. But they are still in a different thought pattern than us."

"I talked to Solan. She believes that Sybold was killed by Tyberius and Albright some time back. She's been missing for a while now. I still believe that as long as she's away, we have a chance to connect with the Atrum."

Cord tilted his head. "Sybold was assassinated by Albright and Tyberius? Now that is fascinating. It makes sense, actually. If I were Albright, I'd have done the same thing. Otherwise, we probably wouldn't be standing here right now. Sybold alone would overwhelm the Lucem without Albright around. Her power is unrivaled."

Jet sat quietly and considered. The conversation he'd had with Albright that day was still on his mind. Albright had tasked Jet with one mission—to 'unlock' his gift. Yet, he had asked Jet to keep it a secret. Jet desperately wanted to share that conversation with Cord, though.

"I've been wanting to ask you something, Cord. But I have to be careful how I do it."

Cord stopped working and looked at Jet as if he'd heard the concern in his voice. Cord narrowed his eyes and furrowed his brow. "Go on."

"What do you know about our…gifts?"

Cord pushed back in his chair as he looked at Jet. The inquisitive look on his face told Jet he was trying to read between the lines. "I assume you know that every Heliographi has a special ability or gift, as you say. It's not always known what that gift is, though one can often guess. For example, Shiloe is a prophet. You mentioned Kamber can see future events through her dreams. Albright obviously has the power of foresight. These gifts skip around or even go missing for long periods of time. On occasion, a new one is introduced or makes a rare appearance. I've done very little research on this, and not much is known about it otherwise. Dare I inquire why you ask?"

Despite Albright's request, Jet considered telling Cord at that moment. *To hell with it!* he thought. *I'll never figure this out on my own.*

But just as he was on the verge of speaking, Albright's words came to him.

Unlock your gift.

Alone.

Jet took a deep breath, then shook his head. "It's just…it's nothing. I was curious after talking to Kamber, that's all."

Jet stood to leave.

"Jet," Cord said. "Vail was right. You're an awful liar."

Jet looked at Cord, who he considered his best friend, someone he trusted more than anyone else. Someone who could probably solve Albright's request at that very moment.

Jet shuffled his feet. "Yeah, Cord…I know."

CHAPTER 33
The Eighth Reveal
June 10, 2286, A.D.

ΑΒ Δ   ΗΘΙΚΛ<u>Μ</u>

ΝΞΟΠΡΣ ΥΦ ΨΩ

THE DAY OF the eighth reveal dawned.
Through much deliberation, it was decided not to use their newly assembled air fleet. Linon and his crew were still working out the kinks. Jet could sense that he and his generals were anxious to get to work but had reluctantly admitted it was still too soon.

Many of the Heliographi disagreed, though, and had voiced their frustration. But Solan stood firmly behind Linon's decision. Even though it might cost them on this reveal, she preferred to wait until they were ready. Jet could sense that Solan was hoping to avoid a catastrophe. A mistake now would be a disaster and set them back. Knowing that the final reveal would occur at Lybra's stronghold meant they'd need to be at full strength. If things got too 'dicey' during that morning's reveal, Solan would pull the plug and retreat.

They met again in the control suite to discuss. This time, Solan pulled Linon, his generals, and Stell into the meeting. Jet could tell immediately that Linon was an experienced soldier and could read the battlefield. His opinion would prove to be invaluable in the future.

That day's reveal would take place on the surface of the eighth belt. It was near a portion of desert terrain and rocky outcroppings. Jet had only visited the eighth belt a few times. Once when he had toured Goliath's Gate and the other time when his skiff had been shot down. But he had never been to the desert areas, which covered a majority of the eighth belt's surface. From what he knew, the desolate landscape provided sand and rock for the system, but there was little else to see. Its diameter was large, being near the outer portions of the system, and the wind-swept surface had whipped the sand into towering dunes.

Once again, no one had any clues about what to expect. Where and how the reveal would occur was a mystery. But there seemed to be no place to hide in the desert landscape. This would be another free-for-all, similar to the first reveal, Jet assumed. But in the back of his mind was Goliath's Gate. The covert project also shared the eighth belt, albeit below the surface, and the Agency would defend access into the hull fiercely.

Jet found his group—Cord, Vail, and Bo—gathered near each other, but no one talked as they stood near their jammers. Jet examined his own jammer and gave them each a nod. Vail didn't acknowledge him, and neither did Bo.

The line of jammers left the hangar bay and cloaked as Solan led the way into a lesser-used skiff lane. The trip was silent, with Booker still on everyone's mind. It would be full force against the Agency, and this might be one of their most difficult reveals yet. Jet only hoped they could avoid any more losses and pushed down the anxious feeling in his stomach.

The eighth belt loomed large on the horizon, a massive loop that opened above them and cast its shadow across the billowing cloud cover in ominous god rays in the early morning light. The Earth stood in stark silhouette on the far horizon, along with the greenish dancing sprites of the Aurora Borealis.

An endless stream of ships of all types flooded into the area. It appeared that every seeker in the system was back for more action. The tannish color of the eighth belt's terrain shifted and danced below, mesmerizing in the blowing wind. Dunes as high as skyscrapers billowed across the barren landscape and whipped into a disorientating menagerie of dust. The gusts pushed their skiffs as they neared the belt's airspace. Jet followed Solan's jammer and maneuvered down low to an area not far from the reveal site.

When Jet stepped out of his jammer, the howling wind made it hard to talk to the others. They would have to use thoughts to communicate, which was another advantage they had. He pulled his hood and scarf tight and donned a pair of solar goggles to keep the blowing sand out of his eyes.

Solan and Joshia led the way as they climbed the sea of desert dunes. The blowing sand clouded the morning sun, soaking everything in a dark rust color. The line of Heliographi slowed as they neared the coordinates. They settled in, huddling together as they waited.

To the portside of the belt were craggy outcroppings, dark brown in color. There was no vegetation to be seen, as the wind-swept plains prevented any growth, it appeared. As far as Jet could see, there was nothing but sand and a few rocky outcroppings poking through the tan blanket.

Jet reached out to the others, listening in to their thoughts. Solan relayed last-minute details as they waited. Two of the Heliographi would stay behind, near the jammers, in case someone attained the memoir and needed quick extraction. The rest of them would spread out, when the time neared, to increase their odds of being first to the memoir. Although the coordinates were pretty specific, Jet was beginning to notice that the exact locations varied, which meant the memoir might occur anywhere in the general vicinity.

Surrounding the area were thousands of other groups and clans now. The Agency's mech units stood stonelike along one ridge, next to several hovering skiffs and large frigates. Jet only assumed that Lybra and Harok were in one of them. Jet was surprised that he'd seen no sign of General Dane. In fact, he'd not seen him on any of the reveals thus far.

As the moment neared, the Agency's forces began to advance. The Heliographi held their position and waited for Solan to give the word. Jet crouched, turning his back to the blowing sand that tore at his face. The wind whipped his cloak about as the time neared. All the Heliographi were spread out in a circle around the area everyone assumed was the reveal site.

Jet checked his watch—it was now several minutes *past* the reveal time. He was beginning to wonder what was wrong when a dark purple light flashed like lightning on the horizon. A flare like a firework shot into the sky near a rocky outcropping and lit up the cracks of the canyon. As if in response, the sandstorm grew in intensity, and the wind threatened to topple the seekers.

Jet was practically wading through the sand now, like a blizzard had suddenly descended over the entire area. It would soon engulf all of them if they stood still for too long.

The turbulent wind batted the skiffs about, and the blowing sand made flight practically impossible. Jet ran, jumped, and shoved his way through the sand as he struggled toward the outcropping of rock. Behind him, slower seekers were literally being swallowed alive in the sandstorm. When Jet hit the horizon, he guessed the outcropping to be about a kilometer away. Dark land spouts swirled past him. The massive dust devils spun up with fury, then dissipated, only to reform again. Scores of seekers were flung dozens of meters into the air. Jet looked for the other Heliographi, but the air was so thick with sand that he could barely see five meters in front of him.

Jet finally reached the outcropping of rock. Tall canyon walls greeted him, a quiet hum whistled hauntingly through the ravine, and he was granted temporary shelter from the blowing sandstorm. The low moan echoed around the chasm, ghostly whispers that disoriented him and sent chills down his spine. Undeterred, Jet followed the deep purple light as it strobed through the cracks in the walls. On his tail now were more seekers, and the light guided him. Behind were the familiar sounds of clicking mechanical parts.

Great! he thought. *M-Class mechs, and they were gaining on him.*

He continued to sprint through the maze of rock walls. The light continued to grow brighter as he approached what he assumed was the heart of the canyons. His thoughts grew frantic as noises echoed off the walls, confusing him and creating a paranoia moment. Then suddenly, he burst into a bowl-shaped void.

It looked as if a meteor had crashed down in some prehistoric era, carving out the crater. The strata showed through the rock walls, and striations of brown and rust-colored rings circled the pit in a horizontal fashion. He could hear the fighting behind him, echoing along the passages and into the crater now.

In the center of the arena-shaped canyon was the glowing metallic tube. The memoir was cradled in a rock, like some prize from a fairytale book. Its deep purple light was indigo, nearly black.

When he reached the memoir, two mechs shot past and grasped at it. Jet leapt and managed to snatch it, then immediately turned with his war staff at the ready. The spinning roundhouse of the glowing staff connected with the closest mech. It hit with such force that the mech ripped in half, its torso suspended in midair for a split second before crashing down into the sand.

Jet tucked the memoir into his cloak and planted his feet on the ground, then faced the other mech. But more mechs were flooding into the crater now. Five…ten…*twenty*. Eventually, he lost count. They surrounded him but held their ground.

A small floating skiff hovered into the space, slowly at first, then it rose above the mechs. It stopped about ten meters from Jet, and the reflective cockpit shield opened to reveal Lybra. Behind her in a separate skiff was Harok and several Recon and Tetrahedron troops.

Jet held the staff in front of him, glaring at Lybra—the one responsible for so much death and destruction. Thousands of Skylight citizens had died during the Century Eclipse, thanks to her sabotage of Chroma. *Harriet, Annaka, Booker, Professor Sylvant…Cutter!*

Jet felt his skin flush with rage, and his pulse raced as he stared at her. He gritted his teeth and felt that uncomfortable feeling rise up inside of him.

Hatred.

He almost leapt at her.

Those feelings nearly blinded him; he could barely control the rage he felt. He wanted to wrap his hands around her throat and choke the life from her—watch as the light left her soul. Just thinking about it made him feel…*satisfied.*

Then, the calming voice spoke. Was it Brindall? Albright? *Cutter?*

Jet relaxed, closed his eyes, and took a deep, steady breath.

No. This wasn't the way forward.

"I'll need that memoir, Mister Stroud," Lybra trilled. "Let's don't make a mess out of this. That would be unfortunate."

Jet held her gaze but addressed Harok. "Don't do this, Harok. Surely you're not that far gone?"

Harok ran a hand through his dark hair, feathering it back. But Jet noticed the shake in his movement. *Harok was nervous.* "The memoirs are a gift to the entire system and its citizens. They belong to all of us," Harok said, his voice a bit unsteady.

"And you actually believe Lybra will just…hand them over?"

"It's of no concern, Mister Stroud." Lybra maneuvered her skiff forward slightly and held out her hand. "Give it to me now, or you will die, just like your other friends."

Jet looked around him, considering his options. He sensed there were no Heliographi nearby, and they weren't coming either. He was alone and outnumbered. His thoughts raced now. The staff was powerful, but he wouldn't be able to fight off this many mechs and troops. Just like Harriet, Annaka, and Booker, he was looking at his own death in Lybra's gaze.

Jet opened his cloak, pulled the memoir out, and held it up as he considered. It glowed purple in the dim light, almost blinding. Even if he gave it to her, he knew she would kill him anyway.

He held it aloft for a few seconds longer. "Fine, Lybra. You win," he said. "I'll give it to you if you promise to let me go free."

"Why, of course, Mister Stroud. You have my word," she said. It was a thinly veiled lie that didn't fool anyone.

Jet knelt to one knee and held the memoir out with both hands in a ceremonious gesture…and waited.

Her skiff moved forward. He could see the glint of lust in her eyes as she held out her leathery hand. She could have sent her mechs, but her greed seemed to blind her. He *knew* she had to have it herself.

She moved closer.

Closer.

With her skiff just a few meters from him, Jet brought his staff up and channeled all his strength. Then he sprang at her skiff.

Lybra sat back, surprised by his quick movement. He brought the staff down as he landed on the nose of her skiff, just missing her head. The staff struck the inside of the cockpit, and a huge EMP erupted from the end of it. The pulse arched upward like a bolt of lightning that engulfed the entire crater. The metallic band Lybra wore around her head lit up with electricity, and she slumped forward, knocked out cold. Then, every mech unit and skiff in the area powered down.

Jet gathered his strength again and hammered his staff onto the ground. The impact vaulted him to the top of the canyon walls and out of the crater.

He cloaked as he ran along the top rim, passing other seekers below. Several were just entering the crater and confronted the Agency forces. Jet sent out a mental thought to the other Heliographi, willing Bofisto and Myranda to ready the jammers for extraction.

The sandstorm was in overdrive as he raced from the canyon. Driving winds pushed him around like a tumbleweed, and soon he was completely disoriented. The sand was so deep in some areas that he worried he might get swallowed up if he stopped moving. He took a deep breath and charged headfirst into the raging storm.

Jet sprinted, moving his feet across the top of the sand quick enough so that he didn't sink. The fluid surface felt like quicksand, soft enough in some areas to frighten him—there lay certain death if he slowed or stopped. The blowing sand choked out the morning sunlight, and occasionally he would step on an unfortunate seeker's hand or leg sticking from the dunes.

He ran aimlessly, using his thoughts to reach the other Heliographi. He kept his mind open, like a homing beacon so the others might find him. Hours seemed to pass as he ran, tirelessly moving his legs so he didn't sink and disappear.

But he knew now that he was alone; no one was coming for him. He was lost.

The landscape was bleak and desolate, a never-ending horizon that he couldn't seem to reach. He only heard the sound of the relentless wind roaring in his ears as sand peppered his cloak, trying to tear at his flesh.

In the distance, Jet saw another outcropping of rock. It loomed, dark on the horizon, a silhouette of some ancient being lying in wait. But to Jet, it was a welcome sight, and he raced toward it. His legs were growing tired and about to fold. His breath behind his cloak was labored, and his skin was soaked with sweat.

When he finally reached the outcropping, his legs gave out, and he collapsed. He crawled on his hands and knees into a small cave and breathed a sigh of relief. Minutes later, he passed out, his staff clutched in one hand and the memoir in the other.

Jet lay in a dreamlike state, his visions blurred by sand creatures that roamed beneath the dunes, waiting to swallow him whole. He passed through them, screaming and clawing at the sandy walls of his prison, a prison he couldn't seem to escape. He climbed, always falling backward in a never-ending spiral of confusion and nightmares. Buried in the sand were his friends—Cutter, Sylvant…Cord, Vail, Bo. Solan yelled at him, accusing him of her sister's death. Visions of the Skylight System collapsed around him, being sucked into a swirling whirlwind of gravity and pressure crushing him, disintegrating in on him…*erasing him from existence.*

Jet woke, sat upright, and screamed.

He sat in a cave with sweat and sand caked to his face. His hands and knuckles were cut and bloody from the sandstorm. He looked around in the dark, listening. The sound of the howling wind beyond droned steadily in the background, a white noise that chilled him to the bone.

Then, he heard Solan calling to him.

Jet stood, grasped the memoirs in one hand, and leaned on his staff. He made his way to the front of the cave and stood at the mouth in the blowing wind. Several jammers hovered just outside, and a stasis rope lowered to him.

M

It took Jet a few days to recover. The fighting and the storm had worn him out. Using his abilities, along with the staff, had drained his energy. He spent time resting and meditating in Vishmu until he had regained his strength. He thought about the nightmares and visions that had haunted him in the cave, and one thought kept returning to him…

Had he heard the voice of Brindall that night?

Or had it been Cutter?

Over those next few days, he also spent time talking with the others. Operations were coming along nicely, and it appeared they'd have an air fleet ready for the final reveal in two weeks' time. But the voice in his dreams kept calling to him…

Unlock your gift!

It continued to haunt him in the following days, constantly urging him to take action. Even when he wasn't asleep, the voice came to him. He wanted to share this with the others, especially Cord and Kamber, his two closest friends. But he was afraid he'd give too much away if he did. He was reminded again that this was meant for him alone. It was all connected somehow. He had finally made up his mind.

He had to return to the Hall of Vital Records.

The key to unlocking his gift was there—a conduit between planes that would grant him the access he needed. Only there could he achieve his goal. Now, he just needed to find the right time to do it before the final reveal.

CHAPTER 34

Voices of the Dead

AB Δ HΘIKΛ**M**
NΞOΠPΣ ΥΦ ΨΩ

NEARLY TWO WEEKS had passed after the eighth reveal, and still Jet waited for a sign.

It finally came to him late on the night before the final reveal. As he sat in his room, meditating with legs crossed on the old rug, the ghostly voice spoke to him.

He died for you…

Jet awoke from his trance, and his eyes snapped open. The jarring voice caused the hair on his arms to stand up as a cold chill descended around him. The rush of adrenaline coursing through his body told him all he needed to know.

It was time.

He gathered his cloak and staff, then checked the dark corridors of Lyrinthum. He made his way to the hangar bay and guided his jammer out and into the night sky.

He set a course for the ninth belt, cloaked his jammer, and set it to cruising speed. He didn't have long, maybe just a few hours. It was late, but he had to be back before dawn or risk others knowing what he was up to. He was taking a big risk, going back to the ninth belt. It was a foolish move; he was heading into the heart of enemy territory.

But now was the time. And now that he knew being at the Hall of Vital Records was the key to unlocking his gift, he was anxious to return. He just hoped his luck would hold out one last time.

Soon he was circling Memorial Park. The topside bunker was visible, but the museum had shut down hours ago, and there were no visitors to be seen. He landed his jammer on the wrecked hull near some debris, hopped out, and snuck toward the large domelike bunker. There were multiple ways in, but his Agency passwords were no longer valid. He found an outer vent and bent the veins, wedging between them.

Jet had to rely on his cloak. It had the ability to scramble heat and motion detectors. But there were other things in play now, things that were beyond technology and science if he wasn't careful.

He slipped deftly through the main gallery and the large causeways of the museum. The darkened hallways were dimly lit with displays, art, and sculptures. The galleries cast eerie shadows on the moonlit floors as he tiptoed along. Eventually, he found the lower portions of the Agency and the hidden areas of their headquarters. The familiar corridors greeted him as he worked toward the old Lucem wing and the Hall of Vital Records. Before long, he stood at the threshold of the hall. He paused to listen, waited, then walked inside.

The space was silent. He could still see the damage from his last scuffle with the mech units but remained cloaked. He found the meditation wall with his symbol and settled in apprehensively. He crossed his legs on the mat and tried to slow his breathing. A nervous anxiety threatened to creep in, but he subdued it. He was in the heart of the enemy base now, and he needed to be quick.

Jet let the trance of meditation take over. He struggled to relax, though. The incessant alarm in his head pushed him, making him want to hurry. He would be vulnerable during his meditation, especially here. He couldn't afford to waste a second.

But he sensed it was here. The key to his gift was nearby.

The voice.

That voice…

Yet…it wasn't the voice he was after.

It was *where* the voice was coming from, and he just needed to talk to it.

This Hall was indeed a conduit, that much he knew already. This vortex of energy, or whatever it was, seemed to provide a connection to other planes, something he couldn't get anywhere else, apparently. It was why he'd been drawn to the Hall from the beginning. Albright had wanted this, had wanted him here…had known that *only* here could Jet unlock his 'gift.'

He waited, drifting into his meditative state as he always did. His Heliographi rushing out, galloping around the cosmos, and Jet followed behind it. In that odd, out-of-body feeling, he held back as if waiting for something.

Things around him suddenly sped up, then unexpectedly slowed down to a standstill, as if time just halted, waiting for him to take notice…

…*waiting*

Then the voice spoke to him, a sudden roar that erupted inside his head. The jarring presence stood near him. As he floated there in limbo, amongst the empty space of the cosmos, in between worlds and dimensions and multiverses, between planes of existence, the presence near him grew stronger.

It was the first time Jet had paid any real attention to his surroundings. It was like a dream, one he couldn't grasp the meaning of—like waking suddenly and struggling to comprehend it. Yet here, it was so simple. All he had to do was…*listen.*

The presence demanded his attention. All of Jet's being focused on it. Still, he couldn't turn to look at it, no matter how hard he tried. The laws of physics seemed to forbid it. And if he forced the laws to bend to his will, something might break.

But he needed to see. He felt the undeniable necessity of it, something so important to him.

He had to see. Had to!

And he began to bend it, whatever *it* was.

He slowly began to turn, trying to face this 'presence.' But strange things began to happen around him. Stars and planets morphed as if they were starting to disintegrate like sand scattering in the wind. Jet felt his concern grow as he continued. Was he altering something, the universe perhaps?

But this was all just a dream, wasn't it?

He felt his concern turn to panic. His heart rate increased, and his palms grew clammy because he knew this wasn't a dream. This was real.

He continued to turn, willing his being to face the presence standing next to him. *This was what Albright had meant!* This was what he had urged Jet to find.

And what was 'this' he had found?

If Albright had asked him to find it, how could it be dangerous?

The cosmos continued to crumble as Jet continued to turn. Fire burned around him now, stars flared bright, and blackness tore at him. His inner light continued to run, faster and faster, as if fleeing from him, eager to be free from what he was doing.

Should he let it go?

Shouldn't he follow it?

He died for you!

That voice again…

What was it? Why was it so frightening, yet…

Soothing.

Jet's soul, his essence, his inner light, finally made the turn. Against all laws, seemingly against the nature of the universe and everything that held it together. For better or worse, Jet had forced his will on it. It was then that something seemed to click. Like the ominous sound of a giant cosmic gate, the lock had been twisted open; the bolt had been unlatched. Jet had a feeling he'd freed something so profound that it shook the foundations of the universe. The sound reverberated across the cosmos and beyond, rattling the fabric of time and space.

Jet turned to stare into the eyes of his old friend, who had died four years ago.

Cutter looked back into Jet's glowing eyes, a vacant expression on his face. Jet had finally unlocked his gift.

And it frightened him.

Then, a heavy blow landed on the back of his head. His vision grew dim, and he knew no more.

CHAPTER 35
Reconnaissance Party

CORD SAT IN his lab and stared at the hologram.

It pulsed, flickered, and seemed to laugh at him. Here he was, yet again, chasing down another one of Albright's riddles. When would this end? But then he thought the more appropriate question was—*how would this end?*

The layers of the riddle kept evolving, it seemed. Albright was a genius, even by Cord's standards, there was no doubt. But if there was one thing Cord swore he'd do in his life, it would be to crack Albright's code.

And now that he was looking at the coordinates, something in the way it was laid out concerned him. He'd slept on it, meditated on it, and tested multiple theories, but nothing seemed to stick.

Cord sat back in his seat and stroked his goatee. He changed his thoughts and focused on another issue that was bothering him. The Atrum.

Solan was suspicious of them, and for good reason. Jet was too optimistic, and Cord felt it was his duty to temper Jet's enthusiasm. He knew one thing; the Atrum would turn on them eventually, and that time was fast approaching. Once the final reveal was over, things would change. Jet felt the Atrum's leader, Sybold, held some influence over the other Atrum. Perhaps this was true, and her absence was having a positive influence on them. But Cord wasn't so sure. He'd seen into Vail's thoughts, and it was enough to convince him otherwise.

And what of Jet? What was he up to lately?

He thought about the question he'd asked only recently—*the Heliographi's gift*. Why was Jet suddenly so interested in that? Jet was hiding something, which wasn't like him. He usually confided in Cord. Something was up.

With all the things going on and the final reveal coming up, Cord didn't have much time to play detective. But his inner voice was urging him to find out what Jet was up to. However, he didn't plan on doing it alone.

I

Later that evening, Cord found Kamber. He had tracked her through the Clipton Forest to a place he knew she frequented called Firefly Falls. She sat on the rocky shore, gazing up at the waterfall as green and yellow fireflies buzzed overhead.

Cord watched as she sat with her knees pulled up, her eyes closed. Then she turned and looked right at him.

"What is it, Cord?"

Cord looked at her, a bit shocked and uncloaked. He walked over to her and sat down. "How did you know I was here?"

"I dreamt about it last night. I knew you'd come visit me today."

"Does that always happen?"

"The dreams? Of course. More often, lately."

"And what other dreams have you had?"

"These days…death, loss, sadness. Not very comforting, which is why I spend more time here."

"Fascinating."

"Does this involve Jet?" she asked and sat forward, hugging her knees. "I couldn't find him today. Not sure where he's at."

"Frankly, I get the sense he's up to something. I feel that we should find out what it is before he gets himself into too much trouble."

"Of course. But what should we do? Because once he sets his mind on something, he follows through."

"Believe me, I understand. Perhaps we should start by talking to him."

"Just the two of us?"

"I think so. Whatever he's up to, I feel we should keep it between us—"

"That's gonna be difficult." Vail stepped from behind a tree and stood with her hands behind her back and a devious smirk on her face.

Cord turned to face her and scowled. Then he smiled his crooked smile and tilted his head. "Clever Atrum. How did you track me?"

"It wasn't that hard, Ledbetter. You think you're so smart. You let your guard down this time. Good thing I can keep a secret."

Kamber gave Vail a long look and gritted her teeth. "I don't think so, Vail. You just tried to kill me at the Century Eclipse. Why would we let you in on anything?"

"I'm so sorry about that, Kamber," Vail said in a sarcastic tone.

"Might I enquire why you're here?" Cord asked.

"You wanted to talk to Stroud, but you can't. He already left, and I know where he went, which is why I'm here."

Cord watched Vail and met her glowing gaze. He considered searching her thoughts, probing her mind. *What challenge would she put up?* he wondered. Cord sensed that her power had grown over the years. But he knew he could still best her, and the thought of breaking down her mental defenses slowly and confidently was something he relished. But he brushed the desire away for later. "I assume you're going to make us guess where he went?"

"You already know," Vail said with a dismissive wave of her hand.

Cord didn't have to think long. Of course, Jet would go back to the Hall of Vital Records.

But on the eve of the final reveal?

He'd been hinting at it for a while, but why was he so drawn to that place in particular? Solan was going to kill Jet if she found out.

"I'm afraid this is too big now," Cord said. "We can't sweep something like this under the rug, and we certainly can't leave him there. I sense Jet will require our help. We should go fetch him, but we should tell Solan first."

"That's why I'm here," Vail said. "I'm not leaving Stroud in the hands of that Hag."

"Assuming Lybra has him," Kamber replied. "We don't know that for sure."

Vail glared at Kamber. "Yes, we do."

"I hate to admit that Vail may be correct this time," Cord said. "We must hurry."

K

Solan narrowed her eyes at Cord as DiJinn stood next to her with a suspicious look on her face. "You're positive?"

"I'm afraid Vail is right," Cord said.

Solan looked at them, her gaze finally settling on Vail. All were basically junior members in the Heliographi. She knew Cord wouldn't make something like this up and cursed under her breath. Now she was faced with a difficult decision; go after Jet first or focus on the ninth reveal. She was going to strangle Jet when she found him! *What in Skylight was he thinking?* She knew he had a penchant for being curious, but this seemed reckless, even for him. Jet must have known this would put her in a tough spot, being on the eve of the final reveal. She could only assume there was a good reason...*there'd better be a very good reason, in fact!* The combined Heliographi hadn't come all this way just to skip the last reveal. Something was warning her this might be the most important one, too.

She thought for a moment, her finger tapping the bridge of her nose.

She wasn't going to give up on either one. Somehow, she'd figure out how to go after Jet *and* compete for the ninth reveal. Once again, she would split their forces. She had a feeling deep down that if she left Jet till after the reveal, he wouldn't see the end of the day alive. How did she know this? That annoying little voice was whispering to her, and she knew she couldn't ignore it. If Jet had been captured, Lybra would hold him as bait. Of course, Lybra knew they would come for him.

"I can track Stroud. I know exactly how to find him," Vail said. She glared at Solan, arms crossed with a scowl on her face. Solan didn't like this girl, but at the moment, set her feelings aside.

"How?" Solan asked.

"I hope you don't expect us to believe you?" DiJinn said, a snarky lilt to her voice. She turned to Solan and whispered. "It's the final reveal, Sol. What if it's a trap? The Atrum may be planning something now, and Lybra won't be far away. Something's up."

Solan didn't answer as she continued to stare at Vail as if trying to read her thoughts. There was an uncomfortable silence as the five Heliographi faced each other.

"Tell me what you know, Vail. I need to hear everything."

Vail held her gaze for a moment, perhaps wondering how much she should share. She looked to Solan, then Cord, and the others. "I have a bond with Stroud."

"What?" DiJinn said, raising her voice. "How the hell is that even possible? This sounds like rubbish, Sol."

"Hold on, Jinn." Solan held up a hand. "Vail. What do you mean?"

"He has my locket. I gave it to him as a gift. He's wearing it right now, in fact."

If Vail *had* gifted the locket to Jet, then there would be a psychic bond between them. Now it all made sense. "Are you sure you can track him there?" Solan asked. "Lybra's stronghold is large."

"You know how this works," Vail said. There was a slightly indignant tone in her voice now. "The bond is strong until it's broken."

Solan considered again, glancing sidelong at DiJinn. "Okay, Vail. You and Cord will lead a reconnaissance party."

Ⱪ

An hour later, Solan gathered everyone in the control room. All the remaining Heliographi sat around the old table in their individual chairs. She stood, scooting her chair across the rusty metal floor, the noise echoing ominously around the space. She locked her gaze on Vail, then Joshia. "We have an issue. I've decided to get counsel from the group. It concerns one of our own—"

"You mean one of *your* own!" Bofisto growled, and the other Atrum nodded.

"Are we a team or not?" Kamber shot back, surprising everyone in the room. Her normally quiet and timid nature seemed to boil over. "We still need each other, and Jet is responsible for collecting at least a few of the memoirs, let us not forget. He would come to any of our aid, even you Atrum. I think you know that!"

But the Atrum remained defiant.

"Why did he run off on his own?" Bofisto bellowed.

"What's he after that's so important?" Sojahn asked. "What's he hiding? What are the Lucem hiding?"

"He's probably dead anyway," Brit said.

"Wrong. He's still alive," Vail replied. "Otherwise, I'd know. So, we're goin' after him, and that's that."

Everyone in the room grew silent. Several of the Atrum looked at her in shock, especially Brit.

Bo stood and pushed his long hair out of his eyes. "I'm going after him, too. I don't care what anyone thinks. I know he'd do the same for me."

Cord stood. "Pardon my intrusion, but you know I'm coming along."

"And I'm coming with Cord," Kamber said without hesitation.

Solan shook her head. "Kamber, this is going to be dangerous."

"I know, but Jet's my warden. I'm not leaving him there. And…I'm going…I'm going after him."

Solan looked at her, a bit shocked at Kamber's matter-of-fact attitude. She waited, thinking, then nodded. "Fine. You four will locate Jet and free him. If he has indeed been taken hostage, Lybra will try to break his will and gain knowledge about the Heliographi. We mustn't allow that. Don't forget…she knows we will send help."

"Solan, the final reveal is important to the Atrum," Joshia said. "If we send four Heliographi after Stroud, that weakens our chances."

Solan crossed her arms. "Obviously, we have coinciding challenges now. We must find a way to do both."

"This isn't like the last few reveals!" Joshia said, slamming her fist into her hand. "All of the other groups will be at full strength. We can't afford to split our forces a second time."

"You're right," Solan said. "But that also means fewer guards on Jet. As soon as he is freed, they can join us on the battlefield."

"And what if they don't get to him before that?" Joshia replied. "What if *none* of them survive to join us? Wouldn't it be better to attain the memoir first, then free Stroud?"

"They won't keep him alive that long, Joshia," Cord said. "You know that."

"Lybra will wait until the last minute," Solan said. "She'll want every bit of information she can get. I estimate we'll have until the reveal begins."

"That sounds like a gamble," Kamber said. She wrung her hands and looked a bit pale in the face.

"Lybra will wait until the reveal begins," Solan assured her, hoping she didn't sound too indifferent. She was trusting her instincts now and hoped she wasn't making another huge mistake. Deep down, she, too, felt nervous. "But *we* won't wait. That's why you four are leaving now. With Linon and Stell's teams, we'll create a distraction. Our forces will gather along the reveal site to draw the Agency's attention. We'll start the battle ahead of time."

"All of this for one puny Lucem!" Bofisto stood and looked as if he were about to lift the table and throw it.

"Enough, Bofisto." Joshia held up her hand. "Fine, Solan. We'll go along with this plan."

Solan stood there, looking around the room again. She felt her temper rise just thinking about Jet and how he'd put her, *put them all*, in such a tough spot. She forced her anger down. "You four. Gather your things and leave as soon as you're ready. At midnight tonight, we'll start the skirmish. If we time it right, we can pull some of the Agency troops with us. That'll give you a window. If you succeed, we'll need you on the battlefield. You have less than two hours to free Jet."

CHAPTER 36
War Drum

AB Δ   ΗΘΙΚΛ**M**
ΝΞΟΠΡΣ ΥΦ ΨΩ

WHEN JET AWOKE, dried blood covered the side of his face, and the back of his head throbbed like the beating of a drum.

He tried to raise his hands but couldn't. He was awake, but he couldn't move his body. He sensed there was a collar-like device around his neck and quickly realized his paralysis was because of it. His luck had finally run out, it seemed. This time, he felt that his curiosity was going to cost him.

But this particular collar must be different somehow. The one that Cord and Hurse had used in the past could only be accomplished by a Heliographi.

He took in his surroundings. The area was dark and quiet. An occasional drip echoed down long corridors, mixed with a digital blip or tone. The walls and floor were made of riveted metal and rusted. The circular chamber was perhaps five meters in diameter with a high ceiling and a metal door opposite him.

From what he could recall, he'd been inside the Hall of Vital Records, on the verge of realizing something big, something that Albright had asked him to unlock…*alone*.

Just at the moment of discovery, someone had clubbed him and taken him hostage. His thoughts were clouded, and he couldn't remember anything else right then.

He could easily free himself if not for the mental signature collar. And, if it wasn't released in the proper fashion, it might harm or even kill him. Somehow, the collar seemed to be affecting his psyche. He felt on the verge of panic as anxious thoughts infiltrated his mind, taking him to strange places. He was in some sort of waking nightmare, the area around him distorted and misaligned. The world seemed to morph and stretch as if someone had control of his vision. When he closed his eyes, it grew worse.

He sat there immobilized, and a long time seemed to pass. He couldn't tell if minutes, days, or weeks had gone by. He tried with all his will to raise his arms, but he simply couldn't get his body to respond. He was trapped, and he began to fear that this might be his final resting place—a rusty cage in some forgotten corner of the Skylight System. Worse yet, he feared for his friends, even the Atrum. He only hoped that his actions wouldn't cost the Heliographi a chance at the final reveal.

At some point, a few people entered the chamber. The rusty door groaned in displeasure as an old lady swung it open. Behind her was a man in a dark suit, his black hair feathered to one side. He had trouble placing their names. Was the man's name Havok and the lady Lyra? The lady wore a shimmering blouse, and her face and hands were shriveled and pale. She wore a metallic tiara, and her aura was dark and menacing.

"Ah, Mister Stroud," the lady said.

Then he remembered her name. It was Lybra.

He tried to speak, but he couldn't move his lips.

"It's okay, Mister Stroud. You don't need to say a word. I can do the talking. I assume you know this will be your final day. Just hours left," the lady said, barely able to control her gleeful tone. "Oh, the Heliographi are dropping quickly, and you are simply the latest, my dear. I didn't think I'd get a chance to net you this easily, but that curiosity of yours…goodness. What were you doing in that old hall, anyway?" she asked, giving him a thoughtful look. "No matter. I'll get that out of you soon. Just a few hours with this collar, and you'll be telling me everything I desire. Just sit back and relax. It'll all be over soon enough." She touched his shoulder, then gave his cheek a playful pat, her leathery skin thick and pallid.

The man in the suit remained silent. The look on his face was a mix of distaste, confusion, and…*sorrow*. Yes, it was sorrow, Jet felt sure. Perhaps his own abilities weren't so far gone that he still couldn't read thoughts.

Lybra continued to look him over, an adoring, malicious glint in her bright eyes. Then she snapped her fingertips and turned and left the chamber. The rusty door swung closed behind them with a groan and a thud.

Jet watched the light fade as they left.

What she had said to him seemed to almost fade with the light, but he was able to grasp the concept that he was being mentally broken down, and soon he would give up all the secrets he knew. He was also being used as bait. That thought worried him the most. He didn't know if he'd ever forgive himself if any of the Heliographi died because of him, because of his decision to go back to the Hall of Vital Records one last time.

Jet tried to remain calm and think through his options. Whatever the collar was doing to his mind, it was starting to work. Now his life depended on how long he could hold out. He knew as soon as he broke down and gave up everything he knew, Lybra would kill him.

He closed his eyes and began meditating. It was by far the most important meditation he had ever taken, and it might be his last.

I

Cord, Vail, Bo, and Kamber left the Lyrinthum hangar bay about twenty minutes later. Solan had been busy going through last-minute preparations with Linon and Stell. Their forces were ready, and the stolen Agency frigates were being loaded with troops. The frigates were primarily designed for transport, but they did have some cannons and other weapons. Stell and her team had modified them, and now they looked like heavy cruisers.

Cord estimated it would take fifteen minutes to arrive at the ninth belt, but Vail was leading the way. She claimed to know where Jet was by tracking the locket he wore. Though Cord had his doubts, he knew one thing; Vail would do whatever she could to save Jet. At the moment, he could trust her. After that, he wasn't certain.

The four jammers sliced silently through the intermittent cloud cover as they flew past each belt. The belts were covered in gray, misty curtains, and the deepening night was lit in bright yellow bursts of energy from far-off thunderheads. The ominous light show left Cord feeling a bit more anxious than he cared to be. He felt as if a war drum was pounding in the distance, signaling the beginning of what was to come. A lot would happen over the next several hours, and Jet's life hung in the balance. Lybra was dangerous and demented, but she was also a cunning adversary. He was playing with someone on his own level now. He smiled at that.

As they neared the ninth belt, their cloaked jammers went into stealth mode, and the vapor trails disappeared. They were now completely undetectable. Vail led them through the debris field of the ninth belt as chunks of metal zipped past them at high speeds. The four Heliographi zeroed in on the largest chunk and slowed to orbit.

Here we are, C9, Cord heard Vail whisper with her thoughts.

Vail hovered in low and used the gravity thruster to anchor her jammer to the hull of the ruined free-floating island. The gravity of C9 held them to the ground as they hopped out. The jammers remained cloaked, and Cord noted their coordinates.

"Lead the way," Cord whispered as they all cloaked and followed Vail in a single file line.

K

Solan watched the four jammers, led by Vail, leave the hangar bay. She sent a thought to them—*stay safe!* Then she turned her attention back to the frigates, Linon, and

Stell. Everything was in place and ready. The large frigates were being loaded with weapons and supplies. The troops that Linon and his generals had spent weeks training for battle were prepared. They needed every hand available for this reveal. Though some of the recruits weren't battle ready yet, they wanted in on the action and wouldn't take no for an answer.

I know, Solan, Linon had told her. *But they want in on this. And I have to say, I'd want the same thing if I were them too. This is their opportunity to fight the Tetrahedron; it's their war as much as anyone's. They have a chance to avenge their loved ones.*

And in the end, Solan couldn't say no to that. She only hoped for their safety. But she knew people would die tonight on all sides. That drumbeat was slow and steady in her head, and it was getting louder. Blood would be spilled this evening.

DiJinn stepped up next to Solan and nudged her. "You okay?"

Solan continued to look out over the men and women rushing around the hangar bay, readying themselves for battle. "Some of these people will not see tomorrow," she replied. "And there's nothing I can do to help them. Fate is moving."

"There's a lot goin' on," DiJinn agreed. "Just remember that we stand behind you."

"Even the Atrum?" Solan asked, the sarcasm evident in her tone.

"For the moment, it seems. We should be prepared for what happens after the last memoir, tho'. I get the feelin' our agreement expires tonight."

"Maybe…" Solan mused. "With Sybold missing, Jet seems to think it's having a positive effect on the others. What if he's right about that?"

DiJinn frowned at Solan, then shook her head. "Jet…" She let that thought trail off. "Sometimes I think he's the craziest of us all."

"He'll be fine," Solan said and gripped DiJinn by the shoulder. She looked at her old friend, who had always been by her side over the years. She couldn't ask for a better companion. "Thank you, Jinn. Thanks for always being there for me."

"Stop it," DiJinn said and looked away. "Don't get sentimental on me right now." But DiJinn smiled back at her.

Ti-Leer dropped in behind them and draped his arms around them both. "We 'bout ready? It's gettin' close to show time!"

They looked at him, and DiJinn brushed his arm off her shoulder, then gave him a hard elbow in the gut. Ti-Leer doubled over but let out a hearty laugh. "Let's load up!"

The Lucem and the Atrum gathered around Solan and Joshia. Solan stepped forward. "Keep your ships spread out and cloaked. We know Lybra has more jammers than us. Once we hit the ground, be prepared for plenty of M-Class mechs because she'll probably empty her hangar bays tonight. We'll start the skirmish at midnight. That's going to take a lot of our resources, but it'll buy the reconnaissance team some time. It may be the window they need. If there are other factions around tonight, and you can bet there will be, we'll want to draw them in early."

"Help get the troops on the ground and set up quickly," Joshia said. "They'll need our cover as they dig in. C9 is five kilometers long. That's a lot of ground to cover. But we have the advantage of picking our spot."

Solan pulled up a three-dimensional map and zoomed in on C9. "This area here will be our best defense, so make your way there. The hills have outcroppings for shelter. If we can gain the high ground and hold it, we'll have the best chance of making it to the reveal with as many troops as possible. The frigates will remain airborne and provide cover. Linon and Stell, you have your strategy in place. Linon. You've been through this before. You're calling the shots up there."

Linon nodded and looked at his generals. "We'll cover you…until our last ship, if that's what it takes."

"The ground is our responsibility," Joshia said and looked at each Heliographi. "We have to focus on the mechs if our troops are going to survive. That means we need to stay spread out and down in the trenches. Let the troops hold the high ground as we work from behind when we can."

"Anyone have anything to add?" Solan asked.

Ti-Leer hopped up and down. "This is the big one, lads. It's what we been waitin' for. I don't wanna see anyone runnin' for cover."

Solan didn't say anything but looked around the group and felt a split second of pride. It was something she might never see again. Together, the Atrum and Lucem had managed to battle through this and now held the majority of the memoirs. But now that the last reveal was upon them, she felt the familiar flutter of butterflies in her stomach. It was a feeling she secretly enjoyed. They would all be pushed to their limit tonight. She hoped beyond hope that Cord, Vail, Bo, and Kamber could survive their rescue attempt for Jet and rejoin them on the battlefield. They'd need every remaining Heliographi tonight if they hoped to survive, let alone, attain the final memoir.

CHAPTER 37
A State of Delirium

AB Δ ΖΗΘΙΚΛ<u>M</u>
ΝΞΟΠΡΣ ΥΦ ΨΩ

JET REMAINED IN a state of meditation.
It was his only hope to defend against whatever influence the collar was having on his mind.

He released his inner light, letting it run and recharge as if in preparation for the trial that lay ahead of him. Whether he would live or die was no longer up to him. He only knew that what he had control over at that moment was using Vishmu to fight and buy more time.

But he continued to slip. His psyche fought, his inner light battling as he watched. Like some spectator, he walked beside that light, trying to listen to it. Once again, he felt a presence near him, speaking with a familiar voice. It used a language he didn't understand, a dialect long forgotten and ancient. But it was comforting, nonetheless, and he felt encouragement as he listened.

With the help of the voice, Jet was beginning to remember things now. He had *finally* unlocked something at the Hall of Vital Records. He remembered a triumphant feeling, if not frightening. It was his 'gift,' and it had been Albright's *Plan* all along. Jet had forced the *Realization* of his gift by somehow bending the laws of physics to unlock it. Now, he simply needed *Verification* to understand what it meant.

He had *found* his gift. He could communicate with others who had passed away, others who had passed on to another realm or plane of existence.

He had *unlocked* his gift. By facing Cutter, he had unleashed something at the Hall of Vital Records. He sensed that he no longer needed to be near the Hall, or other conduit, to use his gift.

Now, he simply needed to understand his gift and perfect it, according to Albright.

But that would be the challenge. He still had no idea what all of this meant. Even after everything he'd discovered, he still wasn't certain where to begin. He only knew that he could communicate with Cutter and Brindall.

But it was more than just communication...*much more*.

It was the place where their voices originated, and he felt this was just the beginning. There would be more work to do, more prying, more discovering. Albright had meant for him to delve deeper into those realms, or planes, or whatever they were. He'd also told him that gifts sometimes skipped around, disappeared, and then resurfaced. Some were even unique.

But the thought of exploring places like that frightened him. He recalled the tortured voices down in Lyrinthum, echoes that seemed to emanate from the walls themselves. The contact he'd made with Cutter felt odd, like he was doing something wrong...*like he was breaking the laws of the known universe.*

He needed to fortify his psyche if he was to *search* those other planes or dimensions. He wondered if there was something special that Albright wanted him to find there. Jet was no detective, and he feared to look for clues in places he dared not go. Perhaps that was the real reason Brindall was here? Maybe that's why Cutter had found him? He wouldn't put it past his old friend to help him with such an unearthly task. Was Jet on a quest for clues, ones that didn't belong in this plane of existence? If that's where Albright was leading him, then he had to be prepared to follow.

Jet felt another presence near him now, and it joined the first one.

Though Cutter and Brindall were there together, he sensed they were separated by a great distance. In his delirium, Jet continued to follow the light, the essence from his Heliographi. On either side of him was the presence of Cutter and Brindall, keeping him on a narrow path like a pair of guardrails. He knew if he stepped too far out, he would fall through time and space, a lost soul, wandering for eternity.

But he walked a true line—maybe slipping and stumbling, but never falling. He was beyond tired. His soul felt cold and empty, and he was frightened by what his mind had witnessed.

He continued onward through the pain. He had to keep moving and follow the light through the darkness surrounding him. He focused on Cutter's voice and felt gratitude for his friend's help once again.

I

Cord slowed and stopped next to Vail, with Bo and Kamber waiting just behind. Inside the massive hangar bay were ranks of Tetrahedron. They stood in rows several hundred deep. On the opposite side marched thousands of gleaming mech units. Hovering above the troops were dozens of war frigates and hundreds of the deadly jammers. Cord could see that their little mission had done little. Seeing Lybra's stockpile now dwarfed their previous assumptions. They had sorely underestimated her forces, and it might cost them.

When the marching mech units neared, Vail slipped behind the crates and knelt. She shook her head and cursed under her breath. "I'm gonna kill Stroud when this is over!"

"We have to find another way around," Bo hissed. "There's too many of those bots."

"It's getting late," Kamber whispered. "The skirmish is about to begin! We need to locate Jet. Where's this tracking device you mentioned?"

"Just follow me." Vail cloaked and led the group out of the hangar bay, then up to the surface again, apparently searching for another route.

Cord trusted that she had a lock on Jet and was simply following it. They backtracked for several minutes, and he was about to say something when Vail dropped down an opening in the ground. The metal vent was barely visible in the dark night sky. Twinkling in the distance, the moon glowed ominously, and the sky carried an odd color. Purple highlights seemed to tear at the inky void as if pulling the darkness in multiple directions.

They dropped down the exhaust vent and crawled silently through the rusted duct. They followed Vail through turns and forks until finally slowing. She stopped and held up a finger, then pointed down. She pulled at a grill and dropped to the floor some ten meters below.

They were deep inside the hull now, in what appeared to be an office suite. The area was unused, with dusty desks and equipment in disarray. Cord wondered where Vail was leading them but asked no questions and followed her deeper into C9. Time was becoming a concern, though. If they spent much longer searching, Jet might not survive.

Vail suddenly stopped, and the others nearly knocked her over. She nodded to the chamber beyond. They had finally located Jet. The only problem now was the twenty or so mech units standing guard near his cage.

K

Solan led the procession of war frigates. Her jammer was cloaked, as were all the other Heliographi's jammers. They were evenly spread out around the frigates as they flew along a lesser-used skiff lane and approached the ninth belt. They'd have to navigate through the debris field, but that was the least of her worries at the moment. They were on schedule and would ensure the skirmish was on time. Once they began, there would be no turning back—they would be fully committed. She only hoped that enough ground troops would survive the battle. Otherwise, they would have no shot at the final memoir.

"Nearly there," Linon said over the intercom.

"Understood. Radio silence from here on out." Solan closed the connection and tried to relax her grip on the console. In the distance, she could see a steady stream of other crafts pouring into the ninth belt's debris field and hoped they didn't get tangled up in a skirmish before they reached C9.

Their convoy entered the debris field without incident, however. Solan breathed a sigh of relief. Now, they had to navigate through the debris. The smaller crafts didn't have much of an issue, but the larger frigates took some hits. It was nearly impossible for them to avoid all the smaller junk floating around. But the frigate's armor was heavy, and they soon broke through and hovered near the large floating chunk of belt known as C9. To Solan, it looked like a floating skull, eye sockets glaring at them in an unnerving sort of way. The ground appeared to be ash and dust. The dead vegetation and trees had been burnt to a crisp, like some hellish moonscape. Surrounding the floating island were hundreds, perhaps thousands, of ships. Even though C9 was one of the larger remaining remnants of the ninth belt, the immense number of ships ready and in position gave her pause.

And the Agency hadn't even shown their face yet.

They were in for one hell of a fight.

Solan moved into position and patrolled the area, hoping that most of the other factions would let them pass. She assumed that no one wanted to start a fight this early, and she was right. They were able to move through the area undeterred. Once they were over the higher terrain, Linon gave the order, and troops and supplies began to drop from the frigates' bays.

Solan watched but didn't land her jammer. She continued to patrol the area until all the troops had deployed. She watched them from above, rushing around to get into formation. Then she gave the order to the others, and they settled their jammers down under an outcropping.

Solan gathered the Heliographi. "Stay spread out and wait for Linon's signal. Once he opens fire, we'll have our hands full. Stay alert and remember that our mission right now is to take the low ground and keep it clear. We don't want anyone getting behind our troops and gaining the high ground."

Still cloaked, the Heliographi dispersed and took up positions around two large hills. Linon's troops were already dug in and had set up air-to-air cannons and missile batteries. Large machines were busy digging trenches in a ring around the base of the hills, making it more difficult for any army mounting a charge.

Solan settled in. She waited behind where the front line would eventually appear. She gripped her staff under her cloak and waited near a rocky outcropping. She felt a bit of anxiety hit her as she looked up at the skies above. The purple glow she'd noticed earlier on the night horizon was glowing brighter.

M

Jet had never felt so tired before.

His soul ached, and he had very little motivation left now. But he continued to walk and kept his mind busy, thinking about his friends and, most of all, Cutter. Those thoughts kept him going, pushing him forward.

There was a stinging sensation on his cheek, and he tried to brush at it but realized that his arms were still immobilized. Jet roused himself through the fog of slumber, willing himself to wake from some distant dream. There was another sting, and he finally opened his eyes.

Standing in front of him was the old lady again. Jet stared into those bright eyes with his glowing turquoise gaze. Her face close to his, her breath rancid.

"Ah…Mister Stroud. I hope you're enjoying your stay. You must be feeling better by now?"

Jet continued to hold her gaze, barely able to focus on her.

"I see you've decided to live. I was hoping we could do this the easy way. But unfortunately, I think we are out of time. I'd hoped your friends would come for you, at least. I see now they aren't as close as I assumed.

That's a pity. But you never had any real friends to begin with, did you? You must be used to this by now, being abandoned, that is. This world has been so cruel. Wouldn't it be easier to just let go?"

Lybra snapped to one of the nearby mechs, and it marched over and stopped just inches from Jet. In the tunnel beyond were several dozen more of the M-Class mech units. "I'm going to give you one last chance, young Mister Stroud. All you have to do is nod, and I will relax the collar enough for you to speak. If you do not, then this mech will break your bones until you tell me what I desire."

Lybra touched the metal tiara she wore.

Jet nodded.

She reached inside her shimmering blouse and pulled out a small holopad and pressed it to his collar. Suddenly, Jet could speak. He licked his dry, cracked lips and cleared his throat.

"Ah, there we go," Lybra said. "Now, shall we talk? I believe you have some information for me. Tell me how to unlock the memoirs. I know you are unique. Of the Heliographi, you are clandestine. You alone have the ability to unlock them. You *will* tell me!" Lybra crowed. "Speak it, and I will free you."

Jet looked at her, then at the mech unit. It stood silent, like a statue, ready for her command. Jet's mouth felt dry, and speaking was difficult. "If I knew, why would I tell you? I know you won't keep your word."

"Oh, but why wouldn't I?" she replied.

"Your word means little to me," Jet answered. "Consider what you've done."

"I know your will is strong, Mister Stroud. May I remind you that these mech units can inflict a lot of pain. Pain is a powerful motivator."

"I can deal with pain, Lybra."

"Can you, though?" She nodded to the mech unit, and it reached out and gripped Jet's arm. "Last chance, Mister Stroud, before this one begins."

Jet looked at her. Then he took a deep breath and closed his eyes, preparing himself. He would simply retreat into his mind, into Vishmu, and avoid the pain, then wait for the end. If he were to die tonight, at the hands of a mech unit, then he would be in a different plane of existence at least. He felt a pang of sadness at not seeing Kamber one last time. But perhaps he might join Cutter, and he focused on the thought as the mech unit began to bend his arm.

Suddenly, the room shook with a massive impact. It felt like an explosion from the belt's surface, and the ceiling above buckled slightly with bits of debris showering down. Some of the old equipment around them blinked and sputtered as the shockwave moved through the chamber and down the tunnel. Several of the mech units stood to attention, their armaments coming online.

Then, Jet heard fighting and yelling in the tunnel beyond. The sound of rail guns chattered around the chamber as rounds peppered the walls next to them. There was a flash of light, then an eruption that nearly blinded him. The mech unit holding his arm released him and turned to engage several cloaked figures.

Jet looked about, noticing that the dozens of other mechs were being flung into the air and against the walls.

The look on Lybra's face turned to anger. She reached into her satchel and pulled out a long, curved knife, the same knife that had been used to kill Cutter. Jet could still see the dried blood on the blade as Lybra held it in front of his face. Her eyes seemed to flash in the dim light as the fighting strobed behind her like fireworks.

"You recognize this, don't you, Mister Stroud?"

Jet held her gaze, helpless as the hatred flared up in his soul at seeing the knife. He tried with all his might to move, to grab the blade from her.

Another explosion echoed through the prison cell. Lybra stood, raised the knife, and with a wicked smile, plunged the blade down toward his chest. Jet braced himself but didn't close his eyes as he stared up into her face. The evil and malice he saw slowly turned to confusion when the knife was ripped from her hand and clattered across the rusted metal floor. Her hand thumped on his chest with a dull thud. She turned immediately, trying to figure out what had happened.

From across the prison cell, Jet could see Cord facing them, his eyes closed and both palms on the floor. Bo, Kamber, and Vail stood around him protectively, fighting off the M-Class mech units. Jet breathed a sigh of thanks—he owed Cord his life yet again.

Lybra turned and fled to a side wall. She punched in a code on a keypad, then seemed to phase through the wall and disappeared.

But Lybra had left without reengaging the collar to its full strength. Jet closed his eyes and focused what energy he had left on it. He felt his temper flare at the night's events. He'd let his guard down and been captured, placing his friends in danger. But he focused that anger onto the collar, and it began to heat up and vibrate rapidly. Then it changed color and began to separate. Jet could finally move his arms, then his legs. He stood, reached up, and ripped the collar off, flinging it to the floor.

In the corner of the chamber was his cloak, and tucked inside it was the compressed war staff. He reached for it, held it above his head, and then slammed it on the ground. The staff lit up and roared to life as if hundreds of voices were waking, ready for battle. It unfurled to full length, the metallic cuffs surging with lightning. Jet leapt into the fray alongside Cord, Vail, Bo, and Kamber.

CHAPTER 38
The Eye of the Storm

ΑΒ Δ ΗΘΙ**Κ**ΛΜ

ΝΞΟΠΡΣ ΥΦ ΨΩ

SOLAN PREPARED HERSELF for battle as the massive underbelly cannon from Linon's frigate launched two blasts into the surface of C9. The shockwave roiled the ground beneath her feet, and she steadied herself from the blast. On the hilltop above her, the troops engaged the other factions simultaneously, opening fire on their skiffs. The clock ticked midnight, and the skirmish was underway. There was no turning back now.

It didn't take long for the Agency and Tetrahedron forces to show up. Foot soldiers emerged on the horizon, and ships appeared overhead. Dozens of Agency frigates deployed soldiers, and hundreds of jammers moved into the fray. It seemed the skirmish had morphed into a full-on war. The sky lit up with explosions that peppered the clouds of steam surrounding them. Now, Solan had to maintain her forces for another hour until the reveal began. She only hoped that Cord and the reconnaissance team had made it to Jet in time.

Solan remained cloaked and unfurled her war staff, holding it in front of her as she braced for the onslaught of troops heading her way. The majority were Tetrahedron foot soldiers, mixed with some Recon troops and other mercenaries. But behind them were the deadlier M-Class mech units, which is what the Heliographi would need to focus on. Her cloaked form was undetectable by the troops but not to the mech units. They would key in on her and the Heliographi first. The mechs were programmed to assess the most dangerous units on the battlefield, and there were hundreds of them swarming her way.

Across the battlefield, the fighting began.

Solan and company were fronted on all sides. The snipers on higher ground opened fire on the troops below. The Tetrahedron crawled along the ground in armored vehicles and flying hover crafts. However, the foot soldiers struggled to cross over the trenches as heavy fire reigned down from the hilltops and frigates above. Heavy rail guns and rockets whizzed through the air as skiffs, frigates, and jammers began their air assault. All the factions were engaged now, and the traffic buzzing around the area was daunting. Fighting was in full force everywhere Solan looked, and she wondered how this would all end. With a full hour to go, she grew concerned there might not be anyone left for the reveal.

Had she miscalculated the timing? Should she have waited a bit longer?

But that had been the risk, and she'd used her best judgment. She had waited as long as she dared with Jet's life in the balance. She only hoped starting this battle early wouldn't result in too many deaths. But she could already tell that had been wishful thinking.

Around the base of the hill, the mech units were being engaged by the Heliographi now. Solan could see flashes of lightning as their war staffs arched and hammered down. But she had her hands full with several mechs charging toward her. She jumped into the air and landed in the middle of a group of them, bringing the butt of her staff to the ground with enough force to leave a small crater. An EMP shockwave erupted from her staff and scattered the mechs, knocking several offline. She felt adrenaline course through her as the sounds of battle filled the air. A smile stole across her face as she leapt forward, her staff blazing in the chaos around her.

M

Jet felt off-kilter as he, Cord, Vail, Bo, and Kamber fought off the remaining mechs. They used their staffs against the charging units as the hull of C9 continued to reverberate from the shockwaves. Jet could only assume the war for the ninth memoir had begun.

"Watch it, Stroud!" Vail screamed.

Jet turned just in time to see a mech unit targeting him with its heavy rail gun. Bo rolled in behind it and brought his staff up and into its crotch. The mech sputtered, then split open in a spark of colors before powering down to the floor in a smoldering heap of parts. One by one, the mechs were reduced to a pile of debris lying around the prison cell.

Vail turned and shoved Jet, then gave him another push that nearly toppled him. "What the hell, Stroud!"

"Hey, take it easy, Vail!" Jet said and backed away, his hands held high.

"You want to explain all of this?" Kamber shouted at him. "You nearly got yourself killed!"

Cord stepped in between Jet and the two girls and held out his hands. "You wanna give me a hand, Bo?"

But Bo looked on with a slight grin. "Nope. I'm good."

Cord turned to Jet. "I'm afraid they've got a point, Jet. I presume there's a good excuse for all of this?"

Jet looked at them each in turn. He hadn't thought he'd make it out alive, and instead, here were his friends who'd risked their own lives to save him. They deserved to know. And yet, he couldn't share that with them. He'd promised Albright that much.

He gave Cord a hug. Then he pulled Vail, Bo, and Kamber in. For a moment, no one said a word as they all stood there embracing each other, smiles amongst them and a few tears perhaps. Lucem and Atrum alike, sharing a moment of unity. But it didn't last long.

Vail pried herself free. "Well, Stroud? What's the excuse?"

Jet shook his head. "Now's not the time, people! There's a war calling our name." He leaned on his staff for support, trying to catch his breath, then he took a knee. He held a hand to his forehead, still a bit woozy from the mental signature collar. "I need a minute, then we're heading up to the battlefield."

"Not yet," Cord said. "While we're here, we might as well do some work."

"What're you talkin' about, Ledbetter?" Vail huffed.

"Solan and Joshia both asked that we join as soon as you were freed," Bo said.

"Cord. What are you thinking?" Jet asked.

"There's got to be a control center somewhere in this underbelly. If we can locate it, we might be able to disable some of those mechs' targeting systems. With the skirmish starting early, I presume there'll be minimal staff down here now."

"You've got a point," Jet said. "But we have to hurry. The longer we wait, the bigger the loss up top. Any idea where this control center would be?"

"This section of belt is roughly five kilometers long and two kilometers wide," Kamber said. "We're looking for something the size of a room. Won't that take too long?"

"I managed to steal a bit of information from one of the Tetrahedron commanders as we burst in here," Cord said. "I have a general idea of where we need to search."

"Well, what are you waiting for, Ledbetter!" Vail roared. "Lead the way!"

"Just one more thing," Cord said. He reached over to Jet and ripped Vail's locket off. Then he held it out to her. "I believe this is yours."

Vail took the locket and held it.

Jet looked at her, not sure what to say at first.

So, this was how she had tracked him? This was how she'd managed to spy on him and the Lucem?

"I'm such a moron!" Jet yelled. He wanted to bang his head against the wall. He'd inadvertently placed all his friends in harm's way in hopes of helping Vail.

"Well, it saved your life, didn't it?" Vail said. Then she dropped the locket to the ground and hammered it with the butt of her staff, shattering it to pieces.

Jet clenched his jaw, more in anger at his own stupidity. But he sighed and reached out to Vail and grasped her shoulder. "Thanks for saving me, Vail."

Cord led the group out of the cell block and up multiple levels. They moved inward toward the middle of C9 and the central most portion. The war above raged as they raced along. Jet felt a nervous anxiety in his gut with each blast or shockwave that rocked the hull. Troops were dying with every step they took—they needed to hurry.

Before long, they were working their way through damaged corridors and nearing the center. It was similar to the corridors of Lyrinthum, with most of the systems defunct and useless. The rusty bulkheads had been sheared in half or sealed off from the meteor storm long ago, and they had to stop and reroute several times. They finally rounded a corner and ran directly into a platoon of Tetrahedron troops with a few dozen mech units in tow.

К

Solan and the other Heliographi battled to maintain the higher ground.

But their forces were gradually being pushed back as the sheer number of enemy troops forced them toward the hilltops. Solan realized they were in a slow retreat now and losing ground by the minute. Nearly thirty minutes had passed, and she hadn't seen or heard from Jet and the reconnaissance team. She began to fear the worst.

But at the moment, she had her hands full with the Agency troops and mechs in front of her and couldn't worry about Jet and the others. She used her staff to parry rail gun blasts and protect the foot soldiers around her. She swept groups of Tetrahedron out of the way in bursts of energy from her battle staff. But no matter how many she mowed down, ten times that seemed to replace them.

Above, Linon's fleet of frigates and skiffs were taking a beating as well. One large frigate had been brought down, and another burned uncontrolled, its nose pointing downward. Troops and personnel were bailing out with hover packs as the huge frigate crashed into the belt's surface. The impact shook the ground like a massive earthquake, the tremor causing nearby troops to stumble. Solan used her staff to steady herself and glanced quickly around for the other Heliographi. To her left, she could see Joshia fighting alongside Bofisto. Mosstrom, Brit, and Myranda stood their ground in front of a platoon of foot soldiers. Beyond them, she could see Ti-Leer, Sojahn, and Tetra holding off a group of mech units.

The ground around Solan burned like some hellish landscape. The entire belt seemed to be on fire as the battle raged into the night. The sky was bright with the glow of battle as cannons and tracer rounds lit the dark clouds. The dirt terrain quaked, and the pitted surface grew more treacherous from all the shelling. With thirty minutes until the reveal, they were losing troops too quickly. Solan grew concerned their fleet wouldn't last much longer. Once their air cover was gone, the ground troops were doomed.

She tried to drown out the desperate feeling in her head. She didn't want to admit what she already knew—*at this rate, they wouldn't survive long enough to see the reveal.* Lybra just had to keep pouring on the pressure with her troops, and she would simply walk over everyone's corpse to the memoir without a challenge. Solan had gambled on the early skirmish, and it appeared she had miscalculated.

M

Jet, Vail, Bo, and Kamber engaged the platoon of Tetrahedron as Cord hurtled over their heads and into the middle of the mech units. His staff burned with a bright yellow-green that matched his eyes as he brought it down in the middle of the group. Yellow lightning erupted from the staff and arched upward, connecting the metallic walls and floor to the mechs, grounding them in an electric storm. They gyrated and smoked as

Vail joined him. There were about a dozen total mechs, with another dozen already lying around in smoking ruins. The platoon of troops rained rounds of rail gun fire onto them, and the Heliographi used their staffs and cloaks to shield them. There was so much firepower they could barely move. Jet found a passage in the hull and moved around behind the troops. He swept in unnoticed and attacked them from behind. Several managed to reorient on him and panicked by opening fire on their own troops, accidentally shredding them.

Soon, the fighting was over, and the last mech unit lay in a jumbled heap of wires and parts. They all leaned on their staffs and took a knee, trying to catch their breath.

"How much farther, Cord?" Jet asked.

"Come on, Ledbetter. Get us there! We may not survive the next platoon," Vail said, winded.

Jet looked into their glowing eyes, then took a deep breath. "I'm giving ten minutes, Cord. That's all we can afford. I sense that Solan needs us." Jet stood and held out a hand to Kamber, helping her to her feet.

Cord nodded, then turned and hurried down one of the steel corridors with the others following close behind. They ran, crawled, and tiptoed through the maze of destroyed corridors, occasionally turning and backtracking at dead ends. They passed several more platoons, but fortunately, there were no mech units mixed in, and they made quick work of them.

"Here we are," Cord whispered and slowed to a stop.

They peeked down into a control room from a rusted catwalk above. Jet took a knee and looked over the area. It was wide, with multiple holographic displays lining the walls. The footage showed the battlefield above, and Jet could see the Heliographi forces were struggling. Their air fleet was taking heavy fire, and a few of the main frigates lay in smoking ruin on the belt's surface. The other troops were holding their ground around two large hilltops, but the line at the foot of the hills was shrinking, and a few areas had collapsed as Tetrahedron poured through. Jet thought he could see some of the Heliographi fighting and trying to hold the line. But he estimated they would be overrun in just a few minutes.

Jet nodded to the display and tapped Vail and Cord. "We have to move. Now!"

Cord and Bo crept along one side of the control center and waited as Jet, Vail, and Kamber took the other side. Jet sent a mental thought, and the five of them hopped down and engaged the personnel sitting behind the computers. Luckily, there were hardly any troops in the control center and very little resistance. That was most likely thanks to Solan's early skirmish.

Jet hammered the equipment, focusing on it first. The computers lit up and sparked as the operators ran from the room. Before long, there was no one left in the control center, and all the equipment had been destroyed. Jet looked at the displays and saw the Agency forces were already in disarray. Their once coordinated attack was moving in different directions now. They had just managed to buy Solan a bit of time.

K

Solan held her ground, but she could see from the corner of her eye that areas of their front line were starting to buckle and break. Soon, the Tetrahedron and mech units would work their way in behind them, and they'd be trapped on all sides.

"Move back!" Solan yelled. "Retreat to the hilltops!" She sent a warning thought to the other Heliographi as she backpedaled, trying to defend herself from the heavy fire and protect the other troops around her. She overstepped bodies, both her troops and Tetrahedron, and tried not to see their faces. But it was impossible. These troops, who in reality were recently prisoners, had lived such a harsh life, and for it to end in battle like this seemed so unjust. It saddened and angered her.

The cratered surface was treacherous and uneven. Pits of burning debris smoked around her. The scene looked like something from one of her nightmares, only worse.

She was losing hope quickly as she watched her forces stumbling backward in full retreat. They were in danger of being surrounded as more Agency troops flooded around them. There seemed to be no end to their numbers. Above, heavy war frigates continued to move in, creating a net that encircled them. Large, mechanized vehicles pushed over the terrain as howitzers fired nonstop on their foot soldiers. But she also detected confusion now. The ranks of Tetrahedron seemed to be slowing down, and a few platoons were even standing around in confusion. The mech units had previously been synchronized but now moved in opposite directions. Even the frigates seemed to slow and stop as if waiting for directions. Something was happening, and Solan immediately thought of Jet. *Did he have something to do with this?* Either way, it had bought them a bit of time to retreat up the hill and a much-needed breather.

Suddenly, an explosion hit the ground near her, sending bodies flying. Solan looked up to see streaks of purple light up the night sky. Flames peppered the dark clouds beyond, puncturing through their thick mantle. At first, there were dozens, then she saw hundreds of incoming points of light. The sky's perimeter was changing over to a bright purple as the edge of the Skylight's synthetic atmosphere was thinning out. Though they wouldn't be completely in outer space, it would get much colder, and the air would be too thin to breathe in just a few minutes.

"The meteor storm!" she roared. "Mask up and take cover!"

Solan turned and sprinted up the hill and toward some of the caves near the summit. She pulled several of the nearby troops with her as the fighting ceased, at least for the moment.

M

Jet, Vail, Cord, Bo, and Kamber left the ruined control room. There would be no more coordination from that area. They raced through the corridors, searching for the quickest route to the battlefield above. Shockwaves and low booms echoed through the tunnel system, reminding Jet that people were dying at that very moment. He mentally prepared himself for battle as they sprinted. Five minutes later, a massive shockwave rocked the belt and sent them tumbling to the floor.

"What in Skylight was that?" Kamber asked, her voice unsteady.

"That sounded different. That wasn't from battle," Bo said.

"That was a meteor," Jet said. "The storm must be starting!"

They continued on as the shockwaves persisted at a greater pace. The meteors hammered the surface of C9, and Jet grew concerned for the troops above. But the timing was a godsend. From what he'd seen on the displays in the control room, their forces had been on the verge of collapsing. Now, everyone would be running for cover. Jet only hoped that when the storm ended, he and the others would be close enough to the surface to help out. If they weren't, there might not be an army left.

К

Solan breathed into her mask and crouched in a rocky outcropping as large chunks of meteors rained down. They ripped into the surface of C9, punching right through it and into the hull and the lower levels of the belt. The surface was slowly being rearranged into an unrecognizable terrain. Smoking holes littered the ground, and she prayed that nothing hit their area. At the moment, the battlefield was mostly vacant. Only the unfortunate few who hadn't found cover were being quickly pulverized by the meteor storm.

Solan and her remaining forces waited as the belt shuddered under the intensity of the storm. She witnessed a portion of the belt splinter in half, and a large section had separated and was floating off. Above, she could see smaller portions of the ninth belt taking damage as well. Meteors shattered the chunks into smaller bits, sending debris in all directions like shrapnel.

Hold tight! Solan sent the thought to the other Heliographi. C9 was passing through the atmosphere's apex now. It was as close as they'd get to outer space. The air around them grew cold, and her mask fogged up as her breath came in quick gasps. The ground surface began to heat up, and steam rose from the dirt. Solan hunkered down and placed her arm around the troops nearby, sending comforting thoughts to them. She sensed their anxiety and fear. The battle had worn them all, and the impact of the meteors had shaken everyone. She did her best to calm them with soothing vibes as they waited. Now, she had to prepare herself for the onslaught once the storm ended. The troops would look to her and the other Heliographi for strength and hope. She had to remain strong for their sake.

M

Jet and the others sat and waited near an exterior vent with the battle in a holding pattern. The percussive impacts from the meteor storm were tremendous. Concussive waves rocked the hull with greater intensity now that they were close to the surface. He could only imagine what Solan and the others were enduring right now. It was enough to shake the will of even the bravest troop, and he felt a moment of sympathy for those prisoners-turned-soldiers. It didn't seem fair that they'd been thrust into this situation.

But here they all were, nonetheless.

As soon as the belt reentered Skylight's protective atmosphere, he and the other four charged through a portal and into the fray. Almost immediately, the fighting resumed. Still cloaked, they rushed past the troops and reached the two hills in just a few minutes. They took out some of the larger vehicles as they raced. The ground surface was charred and burnt, like some extraterrestrial nightmare. The rocky moonlike surface was smoking and dusty, like the inside of a volcano.

In the distance, he could see the outline of the Heliographi fighting, the unearthly glow from their staffs arcing and exploding into the night sky. The remaining troops were being forced up the hill, like a noose that was becoming tighter by the second. Jet reached Solan and fell in next to her, his staff blocking rounds of incoming fire.

"Nice to see you could join us!" Solan yelled, her staff held in front of her. "You know I'm going to kill you when this is all over, right?"

"Get in line." Jet smirked and wiped blood and sweat from his brow. "If we make it through this, then I'll grant you the first punch."

Jet sensed that their final push was upon them now. Soon, the fate of the Heliographi, the final memoir, and perhaps, the future of the Skylight System would be determined. At least he had made it in time to be there. He had a lot to make up for and braced himself for the final push.

CHAPTER 39
The Ninth Reveal
June 24, 2286, A.D.

WITH THE METEOR storm over, and the surface around them a smoking ruin, Jet scanned the battlefield. Everywhere he looked, there were Tetrahedron and mech units swarming the scorched surface. The craters and pits were filled with fighting. It was a visual that would stick with him for a long time. The fire burning, the bombs exploding, the men and women fighting. Overhead, the sky was filled with smoke. It looked like hell on Skylight, and Jet felt the first hint of despair set in.

The Heliographi, and what was left of their army, were being forced into a smaller ring now. Further up the two hilltops, they back peddled for their lives. Above, what was left of Linon's fleet was surrounded by the Agency's air force. Occasionally, a rogue group of seekers would get caught in between the fighting but were quickly eliminated. The real fight now was down to Lybra's forces and what was left of the Heliographi army.

But Jet could see they were slowly being depleted. He knew what the others knew—when Linon's support was gone, so were the rest of them. He felt helpless, standing there on the ruined surface of C9. He and the other Heliographi had managed to hold the line for the moment, but it wouldn't matter soon. Linon was struggling. A third frigate was badly damaged and looked to be drifting toward the surface of C9. The air blazed and whizzed with gunfire and flaming ships. The ground around them quaked and shook. Everything burned like wildfire, and black smoke choked the air and blotted out the moonlight.

Jet leaned against Solan. His leg had taken a round through his calf, and blood caked his cloak. The other Heliographi battled, but it was impossible to see who was left amongst the fighting. But Jet feared the worst. He knew there would be some casualties amongst them. He wanted to find Cord, and Kamber, even Vail and Bo. But he couldn't afford to leave Solan at that moment. They were barely holding the line in their area, and if he left, it would collapse.

Linon's fleet continued to dwindle. The Agency and Lybra's forces seemed to sense the opportunity and pushed their advantage. As if gambling everything on one last attack, a flood of units suddenly poured in. Jet noticed a coordinated movement in the distance, and his heart sank. A fresh wave of M-Class mechs cruised above the battlefield. Behind them was a black armored skiff. Inside were Lybra and Harok.

The line of mechs pressed forward, shoving Tetrahedron troops out of the way. The line marched up to the Heliographi, then stopped short and paused with a resounding thud as if waiting for a command. Lybra's skiff stopped behind the line of mechs and waited. The remaining Tetrahedron stopped fighting, and the entire battlefield ground to a halt. It was an eerie silence, with only the sound of fire crackling and a few moans from injured troops.

Jet's breathing was labored as he held his staff in front of him. He stood defensively and waited to see what would happen next. Just above the line of mechs, a three-dimensional projection of Lybra shone across the battlefield.

Her voice boomed, echoing across the surface of C9. "Goodness, what have we here?" she said, her tone chipper as ever. She paused as if relishing the attention.

"I believe we have nearly all of the *brave* Heliographi, and in one spot. Isn't that fortunate?"

Jet felt the old hatred start to boil over at hearing her voice again. Lybra had been behind all of his troubles and heartache, it seemed. And once again, here she was, showing up at the tail end of a conflict to take the glory. It appeared she was here to oversee the destruction of the Heliographi now.

Was this really how it would end for him and the others?

Jet was so tired that his anger quickly faded, though. Even with all their effort, it appeared they'd failed. Lybra's forces seemed to be endless. Jet wondered if she'd had entire hangar bays filled with more troops and mechs waiting for her command. Despite their war staffs, their alliance with the Atrum, and their work with the prisoner army…none of it mattered. And now it appeared that the prisoner army would pay the price. They were all surrounded, and all Lybra had to do was snap her fingers. The mech units, the Tetrahedron, and her air fleet waited for her signal.

But Lybra continued to wait, and Jet began to wonder if she was simply gloating.

The Heliographi stood, staffs held ready. Jet looked around the battlefield and searched for the remaining Atrum and Lucem. He counted them off: next to him stood Solan, then he found Cord, Vail, and Kamber about twenty meters away. Portside of him, he could see Bo, Tetra, and Myranda. Further up the hill's summit were Ti-Leer, Sojahn, and Brit. And last, standing near the bottom, were Joshia, Bofisto, and Mosstrom.

So, what was he missing?

In the distance, a low rumble shook the ground.

Jet looked down and watched as the rocks and dirt began to vibrate around his feet. He used his staff to steady himself from falling over and looked to the horizon.

At that moment, several things happened.

In his thoughts, he heard DiJinn speaking to him.

Take cover!

At the same instant, a brilliant light erupted from the hilltop they stood on. It was a pure white blast that lit the entire area like a pulsar from deep space. The blinding light was difficult to look directly at, and Jet held his hand in front of his eyes. With all the action, he had lost track of the time, and the final reveal had surprised everyone.

Suddenly, the fighting began again, and Jet and Solan were surrounded by explosions and shouting.

Jet looked at Solan. "I'm going to find Kamber!"

But Solan was looking to the horizon as if searching the sky for something and didn't hear him.

Jet sprinted off across the smoking battlefield as the fighting raged. He felt an urgent need to find Kamber and the others now, with Jinn's warning echoing in his head. He raced over the craters and pitted landscape before finally slowing.

In the distance, he saw the arcing glow of several war staffs, rising and falling above the crowd. Behind Kamber stood Vail, their backs to each other as they fought off troops. A few meters away were Cord and Bo, battling a platoon of mech units bearing down on them. Dozens of men and women soldiers stood behind them, firing rounds into the enemy line.

Jet leapt over them and landed behind the mech units, hammering his staff into the ground. The air erupted with lightning as he upended several units with his staff. The distraction caused the mechs to turn and face him, and it was all that the other Heliographi needed. Before long, the platoon of mechs collapsed.

Jet reached out to Kamber and took her hand. She'd taken a round in her shoulder but otherwise looked okay. "Follow me, hurry!"

"What's goin' on, Stroud!" Vail hollered over the explosions. "What about the memoir? It's right there. We can reach it first."

"No, we can't! There's no time to explain," Jet replied and sprinted off toward one of the rocky outcroppings.

Jet could see the other Heliographi also moving now, pulling the prisoner troops with them. Everyone was sprinting in the opposite direction of the memoir. Soon, what was left of the Heliographi army was hiding under the outcroppings, and the memoir floated on the hill with no one racing to it.

Lybra's forces looked on in confusion. Then, as if the start of a race had kicked off, every Tetrahedron and mech unit flew toward the hill's summit.

Then the night sky lit up in fire, and several of the Agency ships burst into flames. The ground around the battlefield exploded. Jet looked to the sky and saw dozens of heavy Agency cruisers moving in. They pelted the area with rounds of exploding ammunition that ripped through Lybra's fleet and ground troops.

The Tetrahedron forces stopped and abandoned their hilltop race. Many of them scattered and left the battlefield. The mech units continued to push up the hill, though, and were obliterated by the incoming frigates. Lybra and Harok's skiff turned and rocketed off. What remained of the Agency fleet returned fire but were caught by surprise and soon retreated.

"What's happening?" Kamber asked.

"I think that's Jinn in those ships," Jet said. "But how did she manage to steal all those Agency frigates?"

Solan smirked as she hid under the outcropping. "She didn't. But General Dane did. I guess she finally convinced him."

After the area had cleared, Jet and the other Heliographi worked their way to the hilltop. The fire from Dane's cruisers covered them as they crested the summit. They all stood as Solan and Joshia walked up to the pure white light of the memoir. The two leaders looked at each other, smiled, and grasped the memoir together.

CHAPTER 40
Extinction Event

ΑΒ Δ   ΗΘΙΚΛ**Μ**
ΝΞΟΠΡΣ ΥΦ ΨΩ

THE HELIOGRAPHI, AND what was left of their army, sped along one of the skiff lanes with Dane's fleet guarding their rear flank. They flew at cruising speed and held radio silence the entire way back to the first belt.

Once they had returned to the Lyrinthum hangar bay, they assessed the damage sustained to their forces. Nearly all of the remaining ships had considerable damage. They'd lost several of their war frigates and many of their smaller skiffs, including about a dozen of the jammers. Dane had commandeered almost two

511

dozen warships, though, including four of the largest cruisers in the Agency's arsenal. He'd also managed to steal hundreds of jammers as well. On board the cruisers were thousands of recon troops and their families. Jet guessed that the majority of the recon army had chosen to follow General Dane.

Jet looked to Dane and nodded, thankful to have his expertise and the Recon army. In fact, he saw several of the troops he'd befriended on some of their previous missions together. Jet walked over and shook Dane's hand and greeted the troops. Dane looked much the same, his dark hair cut high-and-tight, his muscular frame rigid and attentive, though he hadn't shaved in a few days and looked a bit tired. He was a man of few words and didn't speak to Jet, only nodded and shook his hand.

In the back of Jet's mind, he knew what Dane's decision meant for him and his troops, though. There was no going back for these people and their families now. They would be labeled as outlaws, along with the Heliographi, and there would be bounties on them soon. They had sacrificed everything by making this decision—it was clear that their trust in Dane was unwavering.

But as Jet greeted them, he felt a sense of guilt. These troops and their families would never return to a normal life. Then again, Jet sensed that life in the Skylight System would never go back to normal, not now. This was uncharted territory for every citizen, and he feared the path they were on.

DiJinn stepped up next to General Dane.

Solan stood in front of them and grinned. "I'm glad to see you both." She shook Dane's hand. "We owe you our lives."

Dane gazed at Solan. Jet could see him assessing the situation, their surroundings, and his options. As a seasoned leader, his mind was already working things out.

"Dane, you realize you'll be court-martialed for this," Solan said.

"Yes, if they can catch me," Dane replied in a gruff voice.

"And these troops?" Solan asked. "Are they aware of the sacrifice?"

"Of course," Dane replied. "These men and women are here by their own decision. They know the potential cost."

"Well? What was the deciding factor?" Solan asked.

Dane seemed to consider and looked at DiJinn. "We no longer have a president. Harok is not who he once was. Lybra Howling has managed to deceive him. She has control over him, which makes her a de facto ruler. If you wanted a doomsday scenario, you now have it. Our civil war is just beginning."

"I also noticed that," Jet said. "Harok didn't seem like himself when they had me prisoner."

"Lybra's had him under control for some time now," Dane agreed. "The Skylight System no longer has a legitimate president, and Lybra controls the Agency. With that in mind, I have no reservations about my decision or oath. I don't serve her, and neither does the Recon army. We are sworn to protect and defend the Skylight System and its citizens, not Lybra."

Solan held his gaze. "They'll come for you, Dane, and they won't hold back. Are you prepared?"

"Always," Dane said without any hesitation.

Again, Jet was reminded why he liked this man and why he was glad to have him on their side now.

Solan gave Dane a swift clap on the shoulder. "Good, because we have some things to work out between you and Captain Linon," Solan said. "You're right, Dane. War is coming. Lybra has unlimited resources, and she'll be back for revenge after she regroups. We don't have much time."

"Were the memoirs worth it?" Dane asked.

"As of now, I'm not even sure how to unlock them," Solan said. "We don't know what secrets they hold, but to answer your question, yes. The memoirs are worth defending with our lives. Whatever secrets they hold must be important. Albright wouldn't have made everyone go to such great lengths for them otherwise."

"Lybra holds three of 'em," DiJinn said.

"But we have the other six, including the final one," Jet said. "There's some significance to that one, I think. It's different than the others."

"None of it matters if we can't open 'em," DiJinn said. "Lybra's stuck just like us. As long as they stay sealed, we should be okay."

"How secure is this base?" Dane asked.

"Secure enough. We're well hidden down here," Solan said. "At some point, we could use your expertise in shoring a few things up, though."

Solan waved to Linon, and he walked over and shook Dane's hand.

"I know of you," Linon said. "You're one of the most decorated soldiers in Skylight history. It's an honor to meet you."

Dane grunted with a nod. Then turned back to Solan. "Give me and my troops a little time to settle in and make some repairs. We need to replenish, run background checks, and tighten our belts. It's going to be a tough journey ahead for everyone."

Stell walked over and gave Dane a hug. She wore the same old knit sweater with holes in the sleeves, and her gray hair was tousled into a bun. "I can help with that, General. Our organization will get the supplies you need. Just give me your list. Our undercover agents will keep a close eye on the movements around the system. Nothing happens without our knowledge."

"Good," Dane replied with a rare smile as he greeted Stell. "We'll need supplies and necessities for these troops and their families."

"We'll take good care of the families," Stell said. "We'll get things as normal as possible around here. There'll be school and work, daily reports to hold people accountable. We'll be setting up a social network starting today."

"Skylight is in a dark hour," Solan said as she looked from Dane to Stell, then Linon. "If we are to protect our existence, we need people like you three to step up. We're counting on you." Then she turned to Jet. "You offered me the first punch."

Jet smirked. "Really?" he asked. "You're going to hold me to that?"

"No, of course not," Solan said and crossed her arms. "Unless you want to explain why you went to Lybra's stronghold...alone."

Jet considered, then shook his head. "Sorry, no can do, Boss."

DiJinn walked up to him. She looked him in the eyes and then slammed her fist into his stomach. Then she gave him a devilish grin.

Jet doubled over as the wind escaped his lungs. "Yeah...I deserve that."

M

Solan gathered the Heliographi in the control suite as Dane, Stell, and Linon continued to talk over strategies. In the control room, the others sat around the old table, bloodied and bruised. They'd all survived this round, something Jet could hardly believe. But they'd also lost a lot of troops, people who hadn't deserved to die. The prisoner army had taken the brunt of the conflict, though Jet knew they'd do it all over again. Their determination had allowed the Heliographi to attain the final memoir. He only hoped that their sacrifice was worth it.

Solan laid the final memoir on Albright's table, then looked at them all. "I need everyone, both Lucem and Atrum, to lay your staff on the table. Let this be a sign of peace between us. Tomorrow, we'll talk about how the Heliographi will continue forward."

"Do you still not trust us, Solan?" Joshia asked. "We could have turned on you at any given point over the last month. Now, after we've fought and bled together, you will ask us to lay down our arms?"

"Here," DiJinn said and laid her staff on the table. "Let me set the tone then."

Jet also laid his staff on the table, and the other Lucem followed, with Solan placing her own staff on the table last. Every Lucem's staff lay on the broken table, including Tyberius, Shiloe, and Albright. Joshia took a deep breath, stood, and laid her staff on the table. Then the other Atrum did the same.

The group of Heliographi sat there for a few quiet moments, each of them lost in thought. Jet felt Kamber take his hand and squeeze it. He smiled at her as he thought back over the last several weeks they'd shared with the Atrum. He thought about their victories, their losses…the moments with Vail and Bo and how good that had felt. He wondered how things would unfold for them now as a team. Could they learn to coexist in the long run?

The silence was broken by Ti-Leer when he let out a low, rumbling belch. "There, you see? Wasn't that easy? Now we can all play nicely until the next battle."

DiJinn shot him a look and shook her head but didn't say anything.

"Make no mistake, Solan," Joshia said, ignoring Ti-Leer. "This little reprieve won't last long. Lybra will come for us. She'll build more mechs, more jammers, hire more mercenaries."

"But we have the rare-earth," Jet said. "That should slow her down."

"Perhaps," Cord said. "But there are other rare-earth mines out there on Earth's surface. With Harok under her control now, she'll find what she needs. Our best hope is unlocking these memoirs."

"Then you'd better figure it out, Brainiac," Vail said. She stared at Cord, her arms crossed. "We bled to get these bloody scrolls, and now we're just sittin' on them? How many Heliographi died to collect these six memoirs? Did we really achieve our goal? I'm starting to wonder 'bout that!"

The other Atrum seemed to grow impatient, and they began to murmur.

"You're more than welcome to take a shot at figuring it out," Cord said calmly in his smooth drawl and gave her a crooked smile.

Brit stood and placed his hands on the table, leaned forward, and looked at Cord. "I suggest you wipe that smirk off your face, or I'll do it for you."

Bofisto stood and bared his teeth at DiJinn, the steel daggers glinting in the dim light. DiJinn stood and glared back at him. Tetra gave Kamber a defiant look. Soon everyone in the room was yelling and pointing at each other. Jet had a sudden vision of the painting called, *The Verification*, one of the three paintings used to locate the memoirs and composed by Shiloe Van Saint over a century ago. Depicted in it was a group of men and women arguing, people that Jet knew now to be the Heliographi. In fact, the painting clearly showed Albright's table at the center of the argument. It was like déjà vu, and Jet wondered if this had, in fact, been that very moment.

This is never going to work, he thought.

Solan finally slammed her fists onto the table, and the sound reverberated around the control room, the staffs rattling on the tabletop. She bowed her head, then looked up. "I suggest we call it a night and get some rest.

Tomorrow, we start a new chapter in our history…as a *team* this time. Do we have an agreement?"

Everyone remained silent. Jet glanced at Cord, who had a strange vacant expression on his face. Joshia looked at Solan, then glared at Jet as she left the room. One by one, the other Atrum followed her, leaving the Lucem alone.

DiJinn sat down and whistled in a low tone. "Well, that went as expected, eh? Seriously though, we need to figure these memoirs out, Cord."

Cord blinked as if waking from a trance. "I…I don't believe Albright wanted this to be simple. Getting the memoirs was difficult. Unlocking their secrets will be another journey."

"Yeah, but no clues? Nothing?" Jet asked.

Cord shook his head again. "I've been thinking it through since we got our first memoir. I must admit, I'm stumped on this one."

"I don't know," Jet continued. "I get the sense there's a deadline on this. We don't have much time. When Lybra comes for these memoirs, and she will, we're gonna need more than fancy staffs and jammer skiffs."

"Dane's here now," Kamber said. "That changes things. At least, it weakens her forces."

"That'll help," Jet said. "But I imagine it won't be enough. We're still severely outnumbered, even with the Atrum. This last battle was too close for comfort."

"We need more troops," Kamber said. "Can't Stell help us?"

"She can, and she will," Solan said. "She's recruiting throughout the system. But even her resources are limited. Regardless, we don't have any answers tonight. It's been a long day. Get some rest, all of you. We'll start fresh tomorrow."

Ti-Leer, DiJinn, and Solan left the room.

Kamber gave Jet a quick hug and whispered in his ear. "See you tonight," and followed the others out of the room.

But Cord remained seated, his head propped in his hands as he stared off in a trance. Jet gave him a quizzical look and sat down in his own chair.

"Cord…" Jet waved his hand in front of Cord's face. "What is it? What's wrong?"

Cord looked at Jet for a long moment, as if considering. "Mind if I inquire what the hell you were thinking?"

Jet took a deep breath. "You want to know about my trip to our old base?"

"Yes, I would."

Jet shook his head. "I wish I could tell you more about that."

"What are you up to?" Cord pressed. "I thought we agreed not to keep secrets from each other?"

"Yeah, you're right. And I feel bad about it, but I can't tell you why I went back to our base."

"Does this have something to do with your gift?"

Jet stared at him for a second. "Cord, please, don't push me on this. I don't like it any more than you. I hope you can understand that."

"You realize that your decision could have cost some Heliographi their lives tonight? We took a risk coming after you. Even the Atrum sacrificed to save you."

That made Jet bow his head. He knew what Cord was implying, and he already felt guilty about his actions. But he had done what he felt was necessary. He understood now why Albright had wanted him to visit the Hall of Vital Records—he had needed to be at that place to unlock his gift.

And what had he learned about his gift?

He could communicate with people who had passed on.

He could travel to other planes of existence.

He no longer needed to be at that 'conduit' in order to use his gift.

But there was more to it, a quest for clues that he alone was meant to find. A quest beyond this realm of existence.

BUT WHERE AND HOW WAS HE SUPPOSED TO BEGIN?

"I know, Cord," Jet finally replied. "I'm grateful. I'll make it up to everyone, I promise. But what I'm looking for is important. Please, believe me, and leave it at that, okay?"

Cord held his gaze, considering. Then he nodded. "Alright, Jet. I respect that. I don't doubt your decision. I know you wouldn't purposely put anyone in danger. Did you locate what you were looking for at least?"

Jet thought for a second. "I think I may have found some of it, which confuses me even more. I need to meditate on it and see what I can figure out."

They both sat there, silent for a moment. Jet looked at all the staffs piled on top of Albright's table.

"What about the memoirs?" Cord finally asked. "Did Solan tell you where she's hidden them?"

"She did," Jet said, holding the final memoir up to the light. The glowing white tube seemed to shine in an unnatural way. "The others are in a safe location, one that only she and Joshia know. We have six of the nine, including this final one. I suppose we owe the Atrum some thanks. They've been good on their word. Solan thought for sure something would happen tonight, that they'd turn on us. I have to admit, we may have misjudged them."

Jet expected Cord to spout off some rhetorical response, but he didn't. He continued to stare off into space as if he hadn't heard a word Jet had said.

Jet snapped his fingers. "Cord…hey. Talk to me. What's wrong? You look spooked. You just tired, or what?"

Cord turned his head slowly to look at Jet, and it made him sit back in his chair. The look on Cord's face was one he'd never witnessed from him before. His olive skin was blanched, his eyes wide, a light sheen of sweat…

Cord was afraid.

Jet stood and walked over to him, turned Cord's chair to face him, and placed his hands on his narrow shoulders. "What in Skylight is going on?"

Cord seemed to be in a trance of some sort, and Jet felt concern race through him. He snapped his fingers in front of Cord's face again.

Cord finally focused; his glowing yellow-greenish eyes met Jet's turquoise gaze. "We're dying, Jet. The Heliographi are dying off."

Jet shook his head. "What are you talking about? What does that mean?"

"I finally figured it out…just now, when the Atrum were here, arguing with us."

Jet thought about it, the visual he'd seen as they all stood around the table moments ago. "What did you figure out, Cord." Jet shook him, trying to gain his attention.

"I…I figured out the numbers…"

Jet watched Cord's attention waver again. "Come on, Cord. Stay focused on me. Tell me about the numbers!"

"2,412,630…or is it…2,412,631?" Cord said, his voice trailing off as if trying to settle some internal debate. His skin looked a bit pale, and he tugged at his hair. Cord looked around the room, as he continued to mutter to himself. "Which one is it? I…I don't know…"

What in Skylight is happening? Jet thought. He felt suddenly alarmed at Cord's languid body language, his slurred speech. "Cord. *Cord!*"

Cord stood and wavered, then looked at Jet and chuckled. "Those numbers aren't coordinates, Jet…well, they were, I suppose."

"Yeah, we already knew that. Something else?"

"Albright's so sneaky. I never even saw it," Cord muttered.

Jet stood, holding Cord upright, and waited.

"It's a countdown, Jet. It's a countdown, starting at twenty-four…divide it in half…in half…in half…"

"A countdown." Jet shook his head. "To what?"

Cord focused on Jet again and spoke without hesitation. "Extinction."

Jet thought about the numbers again, the ones they'd been chasing since his freshman year at Skylight University four years ago. Albright and Van Saint had composed different numbers *as if they hadn't agreed.* Albright's mathematical riddle produced one number, while Van Saint's paintings had a different solution. They varied by just one digit. Suddenly, Jet realized what Cord was telling him. The thought stunned him, and he sat heavily in his chair.

Cord meandered out of the control room, not bothering to shut the door.

Jet sat in his chair, deep in thought. He placed his head in his hands and lost track of time as he considered. How had they missed it? Twenty-four to twelve to six to three to one...Cord was right. The sequence was counting backward. *In halves.* He thought back to Hurse and Harriet. Then Renzie and Annaka. Then Booker, which meant...

...Tetra was next.

An Atrum, then a Lucem. *Duality...*

Albright's words came roaring back to him. *The Heliographi are tied to one another.*

The second phase of the Prism Effect had indeed set something more into motion. *The Heliographi were no longer respawning.* The second phase had been an extinction event, all set into motion by Albright, Van Saint and Hurse! Jet could hardly believe it. He felt numb all over as he sat there, bewildered.

Yet, the final numbers *were* different. One ended with a number one, and the other a zero. He recalled the equation Cord had discovered before the second phase had occurred—the quadratic formula, which sometimes provided two solutions. *Could that mean destiny was yet to be decided?*

Jet stood and looked at the table. He walked around it and found Hurse's symbol. Mirroring it was Harriet's. Then he found Renzie's symbol, and mirroring it was Annaka's. His hand brushed over the pile of staffs as he moved them to look at the symbols. When he did, Tetra's staff tumbled into place, settling perfectly into the crack in the table. The way it dropped into the slot seemed to click, as if something in his mind finally connected.

Albright, he thought.

The trickster. Always something just right in front of him…something obvious. A riddle that was…

In…

Plain…

Sight…

Could it be that simple? he wondered.

Jet took Vail's staff and dropped it into the crack above her symbol and near the bottom of the table.

The staffs were like puzzle pieces.

He moved quickly around the table, fitting all the staffs into their own cracks, and gradually, the table became whole again. At last, he stood in front of his own chair and held his staff with trembling hands. He placed it into the slot, and the table began to glow. It seemed to hum to life, and the room lit up in an eerie light that bathed the defunct equipment. He thought he could hear low, groaning voices speaking, just on the edge of perception. Thousands of ancient moans from

Heliographi past, speaking a language he didn't understand. The surface of the table quivered, warm to the touch.

"This is it!" he whispered. "This must be right."

Jet looked at the memoir in his hand, but it remained sealed.

What was he missing? This had to be the key…

The key.

Albright's Key!

Jet dove into his cloak and felt for Albright's Key, which he'd been carrying with him the entire time.

That had to be it. Albright had *literally* left behind a key.

Jet looked for the area that Cord had once referred to as the *splinter code*. If the table was a map of the Skylight System, the key had been retrieved from Revelations Plaza.

He found the area on the table near the center. It was the only piece left on the table that wasn't yet whole. He pushed the key across the ancient surface of the table, his hands shaking with anticipation. Then he slid Albright's Key into the small keyhole, and it clicked into place.

The table glowed brighter, its intensity blinding him momentarily. He looked back at the pure white light of the final memoir and watched as it literally disintegrated in front of him, falling away in bits and pieces of metallic glitter that clattered to the ground. He was left holding an old piece of parchment in one hand, and a glowing jewel of some sort tumbled onto the table.

The parchment was old, frayed, and torn at the edges as if it had been around for centuries and seen its share of battle. Scrawled on it was intricate writing in a spidery script, almost too small to read. Much of it was written in Greek and included math and charts, similar to *The Book of Vishmu*. Some of the math was projected in a three-dimensional hologram that hovered just above the parchment. Integrated into the paper was technology too—implants, tiny microchips, and interfaces, all woven intricately into the memoir and reinforced. It was such a strange hybrid, reminding Jet of the war staffs. At the corner of the page was a Roman numeral nine, which Jet assumed represented the ninth belt, where they'd found this particular memoir.

Of the numerous sketches, one caught his attention immediately. It was the *Serpent and the Prism*. The huge snake, or *Wrym*—a dragon-like creature from legend—encircled a glowing jewel, trying to crush it. The sketch next to it was a map, though there were no coordinates. Finding it in a place as vast as the Skylight System was going to be a challenge. Written at the top of the architectural drawings was a title that read *'Project David.'* It was a dark rust color—the color of dried blood. Below the title were three basic instructions:

I ~ Locate fulcrum device from map above.

II ~ Place memoir to gain control of belt's armament.

III ~ Follow code provided to initiate sequence.

Jet stood there, staring at the memoir in stunned silence, his mouth hanging open. It sounded like the memoirs were some sort of 'override key' to gain control of each individual belt. And what was this about armaments? Had the belts been designed for war?

Jet was beginning to see the whole picture now.

Whoever controlled the *memoirs* controlled the belts.

Whoever controlled the *belts* would rule the Skylight System.

The *hunt* for the memoirs was over.

The *battle* for the Skylight System was just beginning.

There was simply too much to take in. He'd have to get Cord involved as soon as possible, knowing that it was a race to decipher these memoirs now. After all, Lybra also had access to three of the memoirs, and there was no doubt she was reviewing them with her team of researchers at that very moment.

Jet turned his attention to the glowing jewel and held it up to the light. It looked to be a shattered prism, and as he looked closer, he could see it was stitched together. The jewel was about the size of his fist but cracked in several places. A bright string held the jewel together, weaving around the exterior and into the inner portions. Albright had surgically repaired the jewel in the same fashion as the war staffs. A pulsating, pure white light shone from the heart of the jewel. When he looked closer, he could see a skull in the very center.

This prism matched the one he'd seen at the Hall of Vital Records, embedded at the threshold of his own meditation chamber. Had the prism been crushed by the serpent and repaired by Albright? Was this part of his recurring dream about the Serpent and the Prism?

But there was something else.

His staff still lay on the table, and the end of it was glowing a pure white that matched the jewel. He picked the staff up and placed the spike through his palm. The metal endcap separated, and Jet instinctively took the glowing white prism and placed it in the opening. It was a perfect fit, and the endcap closed around the jewel. The staff lit up and began to whisper in a strange, perhaps ancient, language. It sounded like thousands of haunting voices were emanating from the bejeweled staff, which made the hair rise on the back of his neck. Power coursed through the ancient wood and into his body, many times greater than what he'd felt before. When he looked at the jewel, the skull inside moved and shifted in a way that brought it to life. As he watched it, he began to feel nauseous—his hands shook, and his heart rate increased. Just being near the staff now was almost more than he could handle. If he were to guess, he was holding something not from this plane of existence, but rather, plucked from another dimension. He could barely sustain the close proximity, only his Heliographi—and perhaps his *gift*—was allowing him to handle it…maybe even keeping him alive.

This must have been what Albright was referring to, at least part of it. It appeared his staff had just received a major upgrade. Jet wondered if this was now a stronger weapon, or if it was meant to guide him instead? Whatever it was, it frightened him. Was this skull—*this being*—from another dimension, one that he'd soon have to travel to? He was beginning to wonder if that was part of his gift…*part of the deal.*

A slow realization overtook him then.

He had just initiated the third phase of the Prism Effect.

Dread coursed through him. The second phase had triggered the extinction of the Heliographi.

What new event had he just set into motion?

Jet Stroud nearly dropped the staff and the memoir as shock settled in.

"What have I done?"

EPILOGUE 1
Vail's Good Deed

AB Δ ΗΘΙΚΛΜ
<u>N</u>ΞΟΠΡΣ ΥΦ ΨΩ

VAIL HID IN the corridor just outside the control suite, cloaked and silent. It wasn't long until Ledbetter walked out, seemingly in a daze. A few minutes later, he was followed by Stroud, who rushed from the control room and sped off to find Solan, she assumed. She waited a second longer, then hurried into the control room and uncloaked.

Under the table, a hidden compartment, Joshia had told her.

Solan thought she'd been clever, but that wasn't her strength, and it never had been, at least from what Vail had observed. Honesty and loyalty, those were the attributes she pushed, but both of those traits were nothing more than a weakness. The Lucem's naïve nature would cost them now. Not only had they practically handed them the memoirs, but the powerful war staffs as well. Such a gift, and the Atrum had only to pretend their cooperation.

Vail laid on her back, slid under the table, and felt for the compartment. Her hand brushed across the loose panel near the center of Albright's table. She tapped it, listening, then found the hollow spot. She slid the panel free. Five yellowed rolls of parchment tumbled to the floor, along with five colored jewels. Vail lingered, staring at the memoirs and the shining jewels, letting her glowing gaze search over them in a trance…*or was it lust?*

The colors of the different jewels and memoirs lit the space: orange, yellow, green, blue, and indigo. Lybra had the first memoir—the dark one. She also had the second and seventh memoirs, which were red and purple. Stroud had taken the white memoir to Solan. Their metal containers were gone, courtesy of Stroud. He had set the third phase of the Prism Effect into motion, just as Joshia had predicted he would.

She held all five of the memoirs and jewels, looking at them in wonder. She could only imagine Lybra's surprise now. The memoirs had been unlocked. But what information did they hold?

She let her glowing gaze linger over the yellowed parchment. The handwriting on the paper was brown, rust-colored. The color of dried blood. Albright's blood. But the bizarre diagrams and sketches meant nothing to her.

Another cursed riddle, she thought. *Ledbetter would love this!*

But they could never allow Brainiac to get his hands on all of these, just like they couldn't allow it with Lybra. *Better to split them all up,* Joshia had told her.

Vail had never doubted Stroud. He always seemed to make things happen, no matter the odds. He had a knack for working things out; it was just in his nature. His 'never say die' attitude sometimes made her want to puke; he was overly optimistic. But regardless, she admired his determination, though she would never admit it to him or anyone else.

Stroud…

She thought about him and felt a mix of emotions. It was something she wasn't familiar with, like the love one felt for a sibling or family member. Over the years, she had thought more and more about him. And when Lybra had taken Stroud hostage, Vail had felt an anger in her soul she hadn't known was there. It had shocked her. *Stroud was a Lucem for crying out loud! Why should she care?*

But she did care. A lot.

And that bothered her more than she liked.

But there it was. She cared about Stroud, and she would fight to defend him again if it came to that. Despite his annoying 'savior complex,' his 'save them all' attitude, he was like a brother to her, and she couldn't explain why.

She looked down at the memoirs. Joshia had instructed her to steal them, notify the other Atrum, and then leave Lyrinthum. Now she was second-guessing that directive, all because of Stroud.

She stood but continued to linger with the memoirs in her hands as indecision bit at her. Should she listen to Joshia and take the staffs and memoirs and flee the Lucem? But things had been going so well lately. They had defeated Lybra, though temporarily, and they held the majority of the memoirs. Maybe it was better to stay with the Lucem for the moment? They might even be able to mend their broken relationship. That *might* be a bridge too far, but perhaps small steps would do for now.

Vail waged an internal war with what to do. Her inner voice hissed at her like some ancient serpent, encouraging her to steal the staffs and the memoirs and flee. But she seemed to be able to think clearer lately, that voice not as strong as before. And at that moment, she already knew she wouldn't betray Stroud and the Lucem. She would stay…

…so she could watch over Stroud.

A noise outside the control room jolted her back to reality, and she dropped all the memoirs onto the table. Vail pulled her hood over her head and vanished just as Solan and Stroud burst into the control room.

EPILOGUE 2

An Assassin
May 17, 2262, A.D.
Twenty-Four Years Prior

ΑΒΓΔΕΖΗΘΙΚΛ**Μ**
ΝΞΟΠΡΣΤΥΦΧΨΩ

BRINDALL TRIED TO recall his conversation with Christian as he walked briskly ahead of the recon troops, scanning the corridors for traps with his glowing turquoise eyes. His tall frame and broad shoulders nearly brushed the narrow corridor walls of the cramped steel tunnel. His dark hair lay matted, and he hadn't showered in several days, mainly due to fasting that entire week. He had tried to clear his mind, *cleanse his thoughts*. He needed to be sharp. There could be no distractions today. This mission was important for several reasons. The key that Albright had created must be delivered and placed in its secret resting place near Revelations Plaza. These troops had been handpicked by Albright himself for their trustworthy nature and loyal background. They would never reveal the key's location, even under pain of death. Brindall had questioned why Christian wouldn't deliver the key himself, but he knew he was under constant surveillance now.

It was up to Brindall and this small detachment of soldiers to deliver the key.

And did the Atrum have any clue of their motive? Brindall thought they might. But Albright's Key had been developed under the most secretive of settings. Though there might be some whispering out there, he felt certain the key would remain hidden until the Century Eclipse.

The fasting Brindall had taken to that week hadn't been for this particular mission. It had been driven by his need for a clear resolution. He needed a focused mind to be certain he was making the right decision regarding Christian's request.

You must! Christian had urged him just last week, practically yelling at him, in fact.

Brindall had known Christian Albright for over seventy-five years now, even before the first phase of the Prism Effect was set into motion. But their long friendship had been strained lately, perhaps because of how little time they spent together nowadays. In the past, they had practically been inseparable. But now, Christian spent all of his time working on his math, inventions, and gadgets...*his prophecies*. Brindall rarely saw him, and when he did, Christian's conversations were focused on the Heliographi's origins and heritage. He spoke of shepherds and leading people down the right path.

Some legend of serpents and prisms.

But it was Christian's request that had caught Brindall off guard and shocked him the most. He had babbled on about some boy, an unborn child, claiming him to be their savior.

Had his longtime friend and leader, the great Christian Albright, finally gone mad?

Your symbol is the one, Christian had told him. *But you are not the harbinger, Brindall. It will be the next in line, and his time is coming. You alone must decide. Are you willing to do this to save us all?*

Brindall had thought it a joke at first. But then came the nightmares...unsettling dreams that whispered in the dead of night. Voices from the shadows, other dimensions perhaps.

Christian was asking him to make a sacrifice, which Brindall would gladly do. But he felt like he needed to understand more before he could do such a thing.

At least he deserved to know why he was being asked to sacrifice his life!

Christian was vague and always had been. And though Brindall was used to it, he sometimes wished his friend would speak in direct terms instead of riddles, as if he couldn't trust anyone. Perhaps Christian *was* the gatekeeper, and he was protecting some ancient secret?

And what of these shepherds he spoke of? *Shepherds of the human race?*

A time will come when we must fulfill a duty, a very important one. And it is this one Heliographi who can do that, Christian had told him. *You will lead him to the staff and its location.*

According to Christian, this person, *this boy*, was the Heliographi that would save them all. The next one in line who happened to share Brindall's symbol of the letter M. Apparently, it would be up to Brindall to usher him into this godforsaken world, when the time was right.

Ahead of the small group of recon soldiers, Brindall caught a flutter, then a burst of light. He stopped immediately and brought his arms up, barely managing to deflect the blow that was aimed at his forehead. Brindall swept his leg out and took the Atrum down to the rusted metal floor. He recognized the Atrum as Hanley Hurse. Though Hurse was cunning, he wasn't one of the more dangerous Atrum, in Brindall's opinion. Mosstrom or Sybold…that would've been a problem.

Brindall's cloak ripped as he rolled away from Hurse and stood facing him. The recon troops circled around behind Brindall, prepared to fight. But they were soon outnumbered by marauders, a group of pirates who frequented these lower thoroughfares. They were in treacherous territory, and Brindall's task of seeing Albright's Key safely through was at risk now.

Brindall turned his head and yelled over his shoulder. "GO!"

The recon troop holding the key, a young soldier named Dane, sprinted off, followed by two other recon soldiers. The remaining recon troops folded in tight, blocking the passage behind them as Brindall moved to grasp Hurse by the throat and held him tight.

"That's it, Hurse," he whispered. "Let these troops go, and I'll release you. I know you value your life far too much to risk it on something like this."

Hurse laughed in his ear, a deep baritone chuckle that reverberated in the narrow corridor. "You can get them down the road, Brin, but they won't make it far."

"You'll be the first to die then," Brindall whispered and compressed his grip on Hurse's throat. "Give me your word now, and I'll let you live."

Brindall knew that Hurse was cunning. *Would he stick to the deal?* Though they were enemies, there was some unspoken understanding between their groups. Brindall had to rely on that now.

"Fine," Hurse muttered. "You have my word."

The remaining recon troops sprinted off at Brindall's command. Then he released Hurse, who turned to face him along with all the marauders. They locked stares as Brindall prepared himself mentally.

Christian's words came to him—it was like a moment of clarity, like the fasting he'd just taken part in. He could have fought Hurse and likely all of the marauders as well. But this was the moment, and he was meant to fulfill it now. He closed his eyes and stepped back with his arms wide open.

Hurse removed a marauder's knife and thrust it into Brindall's midsection.

There was a moment of silence. Even the groaning of the belt's hull seemed to go quiet.

Brindall collapsed onto the cold, rusty floor, and watched his life force seep from the wound. He knew in that instant he'd made the right decision, though. He only wished he could say goodbye to Shiloe one last time. Now, it was his duty to fulfill the next part of Christian's request. But that wouldn't occur for another twenty-four years. Until then, Brindall would lie in wait, in some far-off dimension, cold and barren.

EPILOGUE 3
The Prism Effect—Phase One
May 17, 2187, A.D.
Ninety-Nine Years Prior

ΑΒΓΔΕΖΗΘΙΚΛΜ
ΝΞΟΠΡΣΤΥΦΧΨΩ

CHRISTIAN ALBRIGHT STARED into Shiloe's hazel eyes. It was the first time in their long relationship that he could remember having a disagreement with her. He stood next to her as she sat in her favorite chair, her paintbrush still covered in red blood...*his blood*. The large canvas in front of her was beginning to come to life.

Her final work, he thought. His heart ached and his eyes stung with sudden tears. He had to look away.

There was so much to consider and so many things he wanted to say to her, but their time together was growing short. The love he felt for her was beyond description and just knowing that soon he would be forced to let her go hurt his soul. He didn't know how long he'd have to wait before he would see her again— hold her and experience the color of her beautiful spirit.

The candlelight flickered, causing shadows to jump and lurch in random, tortured movements as if they, too, seemed to understand what was about to happen. Shiloe's subterranean dwelling felt like he did at that moment. Cold.

His voice echoed off the cobbled stone floor and dusty walls as he spoke softly. A wind howled through the vacant caves, a low drone that underpinned the ominous mood haunting his thoughts. "Shiloe. Are you certain?"

"The memoirs should be a gift to everyone," she said. "They should be observed and studied by all people—our contribution to the human race. Why should we deny those who seek enlightenment?"

"You know why," he replied. "The information within is dangerous. I fear they might misuse it. Is it not safer for the Heliographi to hold this knowledge?"

"Not all of it is dangerous," Shiloe reminded him.

Christian knew she wanted a clear path to the memoirs, one that was unobstructed by his riddles and safeguards. In fact, Shiloe hadn't even wanted to hide them.

"Will you not reconsider?" she asked, almost pleading. "The way you've written it will keep the dangerous secrets hidden. Those secrets can only be interpreted by certain people. Shouldn't your memoirs be celebrated, even displayed? They are lovely to behold, almost like artwork."

Albright sat down next to her and wrapped his arms around her slender waist. He brushed a stray blonde curl of hair from her forehead and stared into her eyes. "They will create more conflict than hope, I fear. You may see them as a gift, but they may also destroy."

She looked away, her paintbrush still held at mid-stroke, the tip wavering.

"Shiloe. Let's not argue about this tonight, of all nights," Christian continued. "It's our last together, at least for some time. I don't want this to be our final memory until then. I want to remember you like this, in your studio, doing what you love."

But Christian also knew that part of their disagreement centered around how all of this was to end—how her death was to occur.

Such an odd conversation to have with the one you love, he thought.

She had insisted that he leave her when it happened, afraid that he might move to protect her if he stayed. Though he didn't want to, he had finally agreed. She was the one sacrificing, yet she was still courageous enough to stay calm and think clearly. Their love had lasted through the centuries, and he would find her again, no matter what.

The plans they had laid together were not only for the good of the Lucem but for the people of this plane of existence. A danger beyond the Atrum lay in wait, and it would strike soon. Could he and Shiloe prevent this catastrophe through their work? That remained to be seen, and even he could not foresee the outcome. There was only one person who had the power to decide, and that one wouldn't be born for another seventy-five years.

Shiloe looked up at him. "I feel this is important. Please, can we compromise, at least a little?"

He held her gaze, then bowed his head. "I still haven't finished my work; it will take many years. But...I promise I will make the memoirs' location known for a brief moment. Does this help?"

She smiled at him, then hugged him, running her hands through his silver hair. "Thank you. You know that once we do this, once this is set into motion, it will be painful for future Heliographi."

"No more painful than the Day of the Nail," Christian said. "The current way of revealing a Heliographi is brutal and should be changed. There is no reason for normal people to go through that. The Prism Effect will bypass that ritual and show a Heliographi's inner light at birth. It will save much suffering for other people. We have the ability to change that right now."

"Future Heliographi will be scorned. They will become outcasts and be feared by others because of their appearance. They will suffer because of our decision tonight."

"But think of the innocent people we can help by doing this, Shiloe. You know this is the right path. We *can* start tonight. Besides, this isn't the only reason we do this. There is a higher purpose, a much greater purpose that may save the human race. I don't see that we have any other option now. This is *too* important."

Christian watched her expression as she looked down at the holes in her hands. She had faced the Day of the Nail, just like everyone else. It was a ritual, a day that every citizen in every district must go through. Thousands of innocent people, millions in fact, had faced that day when an iron nail was driven through their palms—first the left, then the right. Men, women, and children. It was all in an effort to identify a Heliographi, an *immortal being*.

Once identified, the Heliographi had been forced to fight in the Territory Wars. Shiloe had fought in those wars and witnessed so much death. He knew she didn't wish any more Heliographi to suffer, thus her reluctance. But Christian could still hear the screams and wails in those dusty caves as the nail was brutally driven through. A relentless hammering, day and night. It haunted him, seeing so many innocent people face that ritual. And it was all because of him and the other Heliographi. *But no more*, Christian thought. He could prevent that suffering, but he needed Shiloe's help to do it.

"You're right," Shiloe finally agreed. "I will have 'this' final painting ready, and it will provide your road map. And when we set this in motion, there will be no turning back. The clock starts tonight."

Yes, he thought. The clock *will* start tonight, and Sybold *will* come. He knew he had to let this happen, just as they had planned it. That was the most difficult part for him.

Yet there was something else he felt in his heart.

Guilt.

He hadn't told Shiloe about his true plan, a 'variation' to their so-called roadmap. His work, *this equation*, he would adjust ever so slightly. Shiloe didn't have to know about the key, a clue he planned to hide. There was no sense in telling her about it now, not tonight, with so much about to happen.

Just in case, he told himself.

He knelt next to her and took her hands. Her hazel-colored eyes met his piercing blue gaze, and they brimmed with tears. He reached up and caressed her cheek, brushing her tears away.

"Don't be afraid, Shiloe. You know I will be here, waiting for your return. Be brave, and know that I love you. *I will always love you.*" He leaned in and kissed her, letting his lips linger, drawing in her breath one last time. Then he stood and left her studio and didn't look back.

Albright cloaked, hurried to the end of the corridor, and stepped into a larger causeway. It was late, and the subterranean neighborhood was silent, asleep. It was mostly abandoned anyway, nearly all of the people having left Earth to live above in the Skylight System over the last year. He found a dark niche, folded into his cloak, and waited.

At five minutes till midnight, he watched as a blurry mirage glided down the narrow hallway.

Sybold had come, just as expected.

Albright had to close his eyes and focus on something else to keep his thoughts hidden. He couldn't afford to reveal his presence to Sybold. But he also needed to distract himself from leaping up and rushing to Shiloe's aid. Right now, Sybold was in Shiloe's studio. Albright's counterpart, his ancient nemesis, was there to fulfill part of the prophecy that he'd known would come to pass. The murder of Shiloe Van Saint would lead to the most important event in Heliographi history and perhaps the human race. The first phase of the Prism Effect.

And he had to sit there and let it happen.

It was the toughest thing he'd ever faced in his life. Of all the events he'd been a part of over the last three thousand years, this was the most heart-wrenching, and he could barely endure it. At that moment, his beloved Shiloe was being tortured and murdered by his greatest enemy.

A few minutes passed, and his soul seemed to be ripping in half.

Then, he knew it was over.

The Serpent had ruptured the Prism.

The Light had been Divided.

Sybold had acted as the *Murderer*, Shiloe as the *Martyr*, and Albright as the *Mastermind*.

The first phase of the prophesied Prism Effect had been set into motion, and his beloved Shiloe was now roaming the cosmos, searching for her next host. The ancient table was now shattered, splintered by the event. The shards of its sacred wood, the first tree, were ready to be forged into the powerful war staffs, which he would personally construct and hide. Of the four phases, the second would be the most difficult. What he and Shiloe had just done was something that made little sense—they were erasing Heliographi. But they had no choice now. He had seen the future. This was the only possible way to salvation. Now he could only hope and pray that he'd made the right decision for them all.

But his thoughts lingered on Shiloe. He felt something burning in his soul, a heat that seemed to boil over and threaten to erupt. It felt as if eons of anger and hatred churned within, and he wanted to scream in agony. He wanted revenge and felt the hatred threaten to seep into his heart and mind. It was the serpent's effect from Sybold's presence nearby. But he breathed deep and relaxed, letting that feeling flee. He expelled it.

Now, with the Prism Effect beginning, a century would pass. The boy who they placed all their hope in wouldn't be born for another seventy-five years. Christian's close friend, Brindall, would shepherd him in from beyond this plane of existence. For better or worse, the legend of the Serpent and the Prism would be fulfilled; they had no choice now. Christian had always known it was his responsibility to set this into motion, but the outcome was out of his control. Christian only hoped he would have everything ready in time. He had work to do, and the next three phases had to be planned out and in place *before* Brindall made his sacrifice.

When Christian Albright finally opened his eyes, their typical blue piercing color was gone. The Prism Effect had replaced it with an unearthly glowing red light.

A light that burned so bright that the corridor seemed to be on fire.

A light that seemed to drench everything in blood.

Thank you for reading The Heliographi Memoirs. I truly hope you enjoyed it. If you don't mind doing me a small favor, please consider leaving a review on Amazon or your favorite website. Reviews are critically important to a writer's work and help get the word out. Additionally, please consider heading over to the website www.theskylightseries.com and sign up for updates, information and special offers. I'd love to connect with you and talk about this series and hear your thoughts and ideas. Once again, thank you. This would not be possible without your support.

J. Wint

Reviews can be left here: